The ADDRESS

A Novel

Fiona Davis

DUTTON

DUTTON
An imprint of Penguin Random House LLC
375 Hudson Street
New York, New York 10014

First Dutton trade paperback printing, 2018

The Library of Congress has catalogued this book as follows:
Names: Davis, Fiona, 1966–, author.
Title: The address : a novel / Fiona Davis.
Description: New York, New York : Dutton, [2017]
Identifiers: LCCN 2017000682 (print) | LCCN 2017005989 (ebook) | ISBN
9781524741990 (hardback) | ISBN 9781524742010 (trade paperback) | ISBN 9781524742003
(ebook)
Subjects: | BISAC: FICTION / Historical. | FICTION / Mystery & Detective / General. |
FICTION / Literary.
Classification: LCC PS3604.A95695 A64 2017 (print) | LCC PS3604.A95695 (ebook) |
DDC 813/.6—dc23 LC record available at https://lccn.loc.gov/2017000682

Printed in the United States of America
10 9 8 7 6 5 4 3 2 1

Designed by Cassandra Garruzzo

More Praise for THE ADDRESS

"On the heels of last year's *The Dollhouse*—about life at the Barbizon Hotel—Fiona Davis is back with a compelling novel about two women, a century apart, who both find their lives forever changed by the Dakota, Manhattan's most famous apartment building." —*Town & Country*

"An unforgettable, centuries-spanning tale of life and love in the Dakota, NYC's most famous apartment house." —SouthernLiving.com

"*Maid in Manhattan* meets *The Grand Budapest Hotel*." —*InStyle*

"Davis's characters will remind readers that sometimes we have more in common with strangers than we think." —*RealSimple*

"Fiona Davis delivers her fans a richly layered historical plot that explores the stories and rumors of one of Manhattan's most prestigious residences: the Dakota. From socialites to failed careers to amazing characters never to be forgotten, this is one of 2017's most glorious NY-based tales and needs to be enjoyed before summer ends." —Brit + Co

"Davis has folded together two historical eras in this breezy historical novel that jumps between Gilded Age and Reagan-era New York City. . . . [She] overlays the two histories beautifully. . . . The book, rife with historical description and architectural detail, will appeal to design and history buffs alike." —*Publishers Weekly*

"With her nimble writing style, Davis makes pithy commentary on gender, social, and economic inequality in both eras. . . . This thought-provoking book makes you wonder what Edith Wharton would have made of these Camdens and pseudo-Camdens. Thankfully, Davis is here to tell us." —*BookPage*

"[A] richly imagined and satisfying read." —*Mystery Scene*

"An evocative and intriguing story of love, class, secrets, and pasts, *The Address* tells the tale of two very different working women who lived almost a hundred years apart and the mystery that may or may not connect them and link their fates. Set at one of the most historic and glamorous apartment buildings in Manhattan, the book is this summer's perfect beach read."

—Wendy Lawless, *New York Times* bestselling
author of *Chanel Bonfire* and *Heart of Glass*

"*The Address* transported me through the grand doors of the Dakota building and right into the hearts of its inhabitants. Rich in historic glamour and hugely enjoyable."

—Eve Chase, author of *Black Rabbit Hall*
and *The Wildling Sisters*

"A superb tale, masterfully told, with splendid detail and historical accuracy."

—Andrew Alpern, author of *The Dakota: A History
of the World's Best-Known Apartment Building*

"Fiona Davis has a genuine flair for deftly created and memorable characters and the use of historical detail to skillfully engage the readers' full attention."
—*Midwest Book Review*

Praise for THE DOLLHOUSE

"Rich both in twists and period detail, this tale of big-city ambition is impossible to put down."
—*People*

"*The Dollhouse* is a thrilling peek through a window into another world—one that readers will savor for a long time." —Associated Press

"An ode to old New York that will have you yelling for more seasons of *Mad Men*."
—*New York Post*

"Davis paints a scene of Darby's 1950s glamour for her audience that's a smart juxtaposition to Rose's modern-age New York, jumping between time periods clearly with often elegant prose. . . . Davis's descriptive words are transporting. . . . [A] poignant beach read."

—*New York Daily News*

"In her page-turning debut, Fiona Davis deftly weaves the storylines of two women living at the famed Barbizon hotel for women. . . . Davis alternates the chapters between each woman until the twists and turns of their respective storylines ultimately weave together, upping the anticipation along the way."

—*RealSimple*

"Davis layers on relationships and intrigue, while building tension through her story structure. . . . The pace quickens as the story hurtles to its surprising—but satisfying—end. Who said history had to be dull, anyway?"

—*BookPage*

"Fiona Davis's debut novel deftly blends the contemporary and midcentury storylines to form a wholly absorbing and entertaining read. . . . Period fiction mingled with twists and turns that keep the reader engrossed until the very last page."

—Bookreporter.com

"Davis's debut novel . . . is a lively one, tripping along at a sprightly clip."

—*Kirkus Reviews*

"Get ready for glitz, glamour, and a whole lot of sleuthing." —Brit + Co

"Clever and full of twists. . . . A story well told."

—*New York Journal of Books*

"Sensory and vivid. . . . A zippy plot and a refreshing focus on the lives of women many would overlook."

—*The Dallas Morning News*

"Highly readable, *The Dollhouse* conjures up 1950s New York convincingly. In particular the now-vanished world of the Barbizon Hotel for

Women, with its antiquated rules and intriguing array of female personalities and tragic fates, lives on in the pages of the novel in delectable detail. . . . This is no mere 'chick-lit,' but feminist-inspired entertainment."
—Historical Novel Society

"Fans of Suzanne Rindell's *Three-Martini Lunch* will enjoy this debut's strong sense of time and place as the author brings a legendary New York building to life and populates it with realistic characters who find themselves in unusual situations."
—*Library Journal*

"Davis delivers a fast-paced, richly imagined debut that's almost impossible to put down." —Kathleen Tessaro, author of *The Perfume Collector*

"The ghosts of the famed NYC women's hotel come to life in *The Dollhouse*. Davis expertly weaves together the stories of several women who lived in the Barbizon during its heyday in the 1950s, and the brokenhearted journalist who decides to get the 'scoop' on a decades-old tragedy that happened in the building. A fun, page-turning mystery."
—Suzanne Rindell, author of *The Other Typist*
and *Three-Martini Lunch*

"Multigenerational and steeped in history, *The Dollhouse* is a story about women—from the clicking anxiety of Katie Gibbs's secretaries to the willowy cool of Eileen Ford's models, to honey-voiced hatcheck girls and glamorous eccentrics with lapdogs named Bird. Davis celebrates the women of New York's present and past—the ones who live boldly, independently, carving out lives on their own terms."
—Elizabeth Winder, author of *Pain, Parties, Work:
Sylvia Plath in New York, Summer 1953*

"Two coming-of-age stories rolled into an ode to New York City and the young women—of past and present—who have tried to forge lives and careers there. Poetic, romantic, crushing, and soulful."
—Jules Moulin, author of *Ally Hughes Has Sex Sometimes*

Also by Fiona Davis

The Dollhouse
The Masterpiece

For Caitlin, Erin, and Lauren

CHAPTER ONE

London, June 1884

The sight of a child teetering on the window ledge of room 510 turned Sara's world upside down.

After several years toiling as a maid and working her way up the ranks, she'd been awarded the position of head housekeeper at London's Langham Hotel a month prior. One of her largest tasks was keeping the maids in line, all young girls with hardly a shred of common sense among them. When they should have been straightening the rooms, she'd more often than not find them giggling in the hallways or flirting with the boys delivering tea trays or flowers.

That morning, she'd been called into the manager's office and reprimanded for not being harsh enough on her charges.

"You're soft. We're starting to wonder if you're simply too young for the position," said Mr. Birmingham from behind his walnut desk, which, despite its elegant spindle legs, was roughly the size of a small boat.

Having recently turned thirty, Sara didn't feel young in the least, not that she'd ever acted that way. When she'd first arrived at the Langham, she'd skipped the giddy overtures of friendship from other maids her age, knowing that she had to stand out if she wanted to move up quickly. Her coolness had paid off, and her higher salary more than made up for the lack of companionship.

But for Mr. Birmingham, who found pleasure in making the younger maids cry, Sara's self-imposed isolation wasn't enough.

He directed her to take a seat, but once she had settled herself, the perspective in the room suddenly felt off, as if something in the furniture's configuration had changed since Mr. Birmingham last summoned her to this spot—or else she was so annoyed by his request for an interview during the busiest hours of the day that she'd worked herself into a kind of nervous imbalance. Sara's employer was short and had the poor luck to have a torso shaped like a chicken egg with a double yolk. She towered over the man by several inches. Yet somehow Mr. Birmingham was peering down at her from his thronelike seat. She stole a glance at the floor. The bottom five inches of his chair's legs were stained a different color than the rest. He'd had them lengthened.

When she looked back up, he puffed up like a songbird, clearly peeved that she'd noticed.

She shifted in her seat. "I'm sorry, Mr. Birmingham, I will be tougher on the girls."

"If they're difficult, give them a slap. Better yet, send them down here and I'll do it for you." He licked his lips.

Right. She imagined he'd enjoy it immensely. "Is there anything more?"

"No, Mrs. Smythe. Off you go."

She was still getting used to being called *Mrs*. Strange how a single promotion afforded not only a living wage but also a new moniker that had nothing to do with her marital status, or lack thereof. No head housekeeper could be called a *Miss*. Wasn't proper. The girls were still getting used to addressing her by her full name, and she had to be firmer with that as well. It wouldn't do for Mr.

Birmingham to overhear them calling her *Sara*. It might be the last straw on what was a very unstable haystack.

That hot June afternoon, after patrolling the halls and basement to break up any assignations, she retreated to her office on the sixth floor to double-check the laundry bills. She needed a rest from shooting dour looks at the girls; her face was tired from scowling. The one window in the room was open as wide as possible in order to catch some semblance of a breeze, but the weather refused to co-operate. All day, the air had been still and humid, making the hotel feel—and smell—a little like the greenhouses at Kew Gardens. A movement from the curtain drew her up from her desk in the hope that an afternoon thunderstorm was brewing.

To her disappointment, the sky was a hazy blue. She looked across the courtyard and there, one floor below, a flash of flesh caught her eye, a chubby arm with fingers that grasped the edge of the sill. Then another arm flailed out and did the same, followed by a head covered in golden curls. The girl sported a velvet bow on the back of her head at a skewed angle. Sara's breath caught in her chest. Surely a minder would appear at any moment and guide the child back into the room.

With some effort, the child eased her chest up onto the window-sill and stayed motionless for a second, surveying the ground below, arms dangling downward. Sara willed the child away from danger. If she called out, there was a chance she would frighten the child into pitching farther forward. But still no one came. To her horror, a foot swung up and over the sill—three limbs in all. The child was climbing up, possibly drawn to the cooler air and away from the stifling room.

There was no time to waste. Sara sprang out of her office and down the corridor, one hand clutching the heavy chatelaine of keys that dangled from her waist. She lifted her skirts far higher than was decent and dashed down the stairs, her eyes riveted on the few feet in front of her so she wouldn't lose her footing on the slippery marble. At the fifth floor a couple of guests stepped off the lift and she swooped by them, muttering a quick apology, without losing a beat. Then a turn left and what seemed like an eternal race to the door of room 510. No banging, it might startle the child, and at this point it didn't matter if she was barging in on anyone. Even if doing so was against hotel policy.

The key turned smoothly in the lock and she opened the door. The girl, wearing a peach-colored dress, now stood upright on the sill facing out, one hand clutching the casing. She had to be around three years old. What was she doing alone?

Walter, one of the porters, and Mabel, the floor's chambermaid, appeared by Sara's side, breathing heavily. They must have sprinted after her, knowing something was terribly wrong.

Sara put out her arms to stop Mabel and Walter from moving any farther into the room. "Shh. We don't want to send her off balance."

"Where's her minder?" whispered Mabel. "Is anyone in the bedchamber?"

"I don't know." Sara took a step into the room, walking as if the floor might give out at any point. The plush rugs softened her footfall.

As she grew closer, she realized the child was singing to herself. A lullaby about being on a treetop.

The child turned her head and stared at Sara. Her rosy lips parted and her eyes grew round.

Sara held out one hand, palm up, and began humming the same tune softly. In response, the child laughed, but then, with the changeability of her age, her eyes suddenly filled with tears.

"Mama!" the girl demanded, then shook her head. Sara didn't

dare move any farther, and her muscles tensed with the effort of doing nothing, staying frozen. A breeze blew in and ruffled the girl's curls, pushing her slightly off balance. If she fell backward, into the room, Sara might be able to reach her in time to break her fall.

But instead, the little girl overcorrected, and her hand began slipping off the window frame. Such tiny fingernails, tiny fingers.

Sara lunged forward. Her hand grazed the voluminous skirt of the child's dress, and she gripped as much of the material as she could, yanking hard. The girl, shrieking, flew off the ledge, inside, to safety. They hit the ground together in an awkward tangle of limbs and petticoats, the girl practically sitting on Sara's lap.

The girl twisted around and looked at Sara, blinking in astonishment. Sara was sure she'd cry out, but instead the girl resumed her babbling song while reaching up with one hand to stroke Sara's chin.

"Well done, just in time," said Walter as he and Mabel gathered on either side of her.

"Do you think she hurt herself?" asked Sara.

"No, not a whit. You broke the fall. Are you all right?" Mabel scooped up the child while Sara let Walter help her to her feet. She was straightening her skirts and rubbing her hip, which no doubt would sport a large bruise by tomorrow, when a tall, thin woman appeared in the doorway.

"What on earth is going on in here?" the woman demanded, clutching the hand of a little girl a few years older than the one held by Mabel.

The name popped into Sara's head from the guest book: the Hon. Mrs. Theodore Camden. Traveling with three children, a husband, and a small coterie of servants. Mr. Birmingham had instructed Sara that all of the Camdens' needs be anticipated, as the wife was the daughter of a baron.

Sara stepped forward. "The child was standing in the window and we brought her inside."

"More like saved her life," said Walter. "Mrs. Smythe here leaped in and dragged her back inside in just the nick of time."

The child, as if realizing the heightened emotions of the grown-ups around her, began to wail. The woman dashed forward and scooped her out of Mabel's arms, holding the girl close. When her cries subsided, Mrs. Camden looked up, as if seeing them all for the first time.

"I thank you for your assistance, but where is her nanny?"

As if on cue, a plain-looking girl stepped into the room.

"Ma'am?" she inquired, her face scrunched up in confusion.

"Miss Morgan, where have you been? Lula almost fell to her death due to your absence."

"I'm sorry?" The girl gazed around at everyone in the room. "I popped out for only a minute, to drop off a postcard at the front desk. I thought Mr. Camden was here." Her voice trailed off and she looked about, as if trying to summon him out of thin air.

"You were supposed to be here minding the children."

The child buried her head in her mother's shoulder, weeping again.

"Where is Luther?" Mrs. Camden rushed into the adjoining room and they all followed. Another child—a boy who seemed to be around the same age as Lula—lay on the enormous bed, fast asleep, his curls damp around his head.

Sara, standing beside Mrs. Camden, could practically feel the woman's fear and relief emanating from her body, like aftershocks of an earthquake. The nanny took Lula from her arms and set about calming the girl down, avoiding her employer's eyes.

How awful if something had happened. Two little children left alone with a wide-open window; the thought was unimaginable.

Sara turned to Mrs. Camden. The woman's profile was precise, her coloring fair other than thick black lashes that framed hazel eyes. Sara had encountered innumerable members of the peerage at the Langham, and they all shared a common way of moving in the world, a confidence that their every desire would be met. It was rare to see one in crisis.

She sensed Walter and Mabel hovering behind them and became protective of the woman's dignity. "Is there anything else we can do, Mrs. Camden?" asked Sara.

"No, that is all." The woman's face softened. "Thank you for saving her."

"Of course, ma'am." Sara nodded to Walter and Mabel and led the way out of the room. Once the door was closed behind them, Sara exhaled with relief.

"That was a close call." Walter rubbed his forehead with the back of his hand.

"You were spectacular, Sara. I mean, Mrs. Smythe," said Mabel.

Sara wanted more than anything to crumple onto the floor, but she couldn't allow her staff to see that.

"That's more than enough excitement for one day. Back to work. And, Mabel, please remember to address me properly."

"Of course, Mrs. Smythe."

Sara turned away and strode down the hallway, grateful her quaking knees were hidden under multiple layers of petticoats and skirts.

The rest of the day, whenever Sara's mind returned to the events in room 510, her heart thumped wildly in her rib cage. What if she hadn't grabbed the child in time? What if she'd had to peer over the edge and see the lifeless body splayed on the hard ground of the courtyard below? Sleep tonight, in the damp heat of her Bayswater bedsit, would be impossible.

But there was enough to keep her busy until then. She finished updating the ledgers and was about to head out to inspect the turn-down of the guests' rooms when a man rapped on her office door. She knew it was a man from its hard, hollow sound. Maids' knuckles were barely audible, already apologizing for disturbing her, but the men, whether Mr. Birmingham or the janitor, had no such qualms.

She stood and opened the door, expecting Mr. Birmingham to have made a special trip upstairs to upbraid her for causing a scene with the guests. Instead, a stranger's face peered down at her. As if he sensed her discomfort, he stepped back a pace. "Mrs. Smythe?"

"Yes. May I help you, sir?" He was clearly a hotel guest, dressed in a fitted, bespoke suit with a Broadway silk hat tucked under one arm.

"I apologize for intruding." He wiped his brow with an enormous hand. "How do you manage up here, with this insufferable heat?"

"It's a rare occurrence, luckily."

"I believe you saved my daughter Lula today. I wanted to thank you in person. My name is Mr. Theodore Camden." His accent was American, his voice a warm tenor.

Sara gestured to a chair opposite her desk, offering him a seat. He moved with an unexpected grace, given his large build. Nothing about him was handsome, by standard measures. His head was small in contrast to his broad shoulders, his eyes close-set to an irregular nose. But when put all together, he was magnetic. She sat, looked down, and closed the ledger in order to stop herself from staring.

"I'm glad she's safe. She is all right, isn't she?" The image of the wailing girl came to mind.

"Yes. We offered her a slice of Battenberg cake and she's completely forgotten the incident." He chuckled before a brief look of pain crossed his face. "I don't know what would have happened if you hadn't gotten there in time. The twins, Lula and Luther, are constantly getting into trouble."

"Best not to think of it."

Sara was unsure how to proceed. She'd never had a hotel guest in her small office, and he was so tall he took up much of the space.

"How did you know what was happening?" Mr. Camden leaned back in his chair, his hat in his lap. He didn't seem to realize how indecorous it was to be sitting together like this, even if the door was open, so nothing could be construed as irregular. It was almost as if he enjoyed it, while most guests wouldn't dream of mingling with the staff.

"I can see your hotel room from my window. I stood to get some air and saw her climb up."

"The girl was supposed to be watching the twins while Mrs. Camden was out. Needless to say, she was fired immediately."

"Well, luckily all turned out well." Other than for the nanny, of course.

"What is the ratio of staff to guests here?"

Such an odd question. "We have three hundred rooms and a staff of approximately four hundred."

"How long have you been head housekeeper?"

"This is my first month." He hadn't come up here just to say thank you, she was sure. Something else was driving his line of inquiry. She squared her shoulders and leaned slightly forward, as if into a wind, curious to figure him out. "But I've been working here in some capacity for the past eleven years."

"You know the place well."

"I do."

"Mr. Birmingham says you're highly efficient."

Mr. Camden had inquired after her. "That's kind of him to say."

"It's a grand building, the Langham. Beautifully built."

"Yes." Americans were very strange indeed. He didn't seem to be in any rush to get back to his family. What if Mr. Birmingham had sent him up here as some kind of a test? "I'm happy to be employed here."

"This hotel featured the first hydraulic lifts in England. Did you know that?"

Perhaps he was the type of man who collected facts and loved to show off how much he knew. She nodded politely.

Mr. Camden smiled. "I'm going on and on, sorry about that. I simply want to figure out a way to thank you."

"There is no need. The hotel staff does everything it can for its guests."

"You did more than that. I hope you didn't injure yourself in the process."

"Not at all."

One of the laundry girls popped her head into the room and then jumped back, startled when she caught sight of Mr. Camden.

"Sorry, Mrs. Smythe. I'll come back later."

"That's fine, Edwina."

"Edwina, my mother's name." Mr. Camden swiveled around and gave the girl a smile. His face beamed with delight. "Edwina, may we trouble you for some tea?"

He was here to stay. But what for, she couldn't guess. Edwina turned to Sara. Her eyes held the same faint alarm Sara's must have, but Sara checked herself. "Yes, please, Edwina."

The girl shuffled off and Mr. Camden turned back to Sara. "If I'm not keeping you from anything, of course."

"Not at all. But there is no need for further mention of the incident. All's well, as they say."

"May I ask about your background?"

"I'm not sure if that's necessary, Mr. Camden."

He blushed. She hadn't meant to embarrass him, just wanted to redirect the conversation. But how easily he'd gone all pink, like a schoolboy. Caught off guard, he tilted his head and stammered. "In a professional capacity, of course. I'm quite interested in how a big place like this keeps running along day after day, crisis after crisis."

"I assure you we seldom have crises like the one today. Most of the time it's a well-oiled machine." One of Mr. Birmingham's favorite expressions. She'd never liked it, as it turned the flesh-and-blood staff into cogs in an engine, but she was uncertain how to keep the conversation with Mr. Camden flowing.

"Of course not. What would you say is the biggest problem the staff encounters?"

She considered the question. "We are a first-class hotel, Mr. Camden. We make sure that every guest's whim is answered. Sometimes that can be a juggling act, as the turnover is quite high."

"Do many of the guests bring their own servants?"

"Of course. But they still need rooms cleaned and freshened. Ladies' maids and butlers have their own roles to play, separate from the hotel's amenities."

"Before this, did you work in service?"

"I did not; however, my mother was housekeeper to an earl. Before this I was a dressmaker's apprentice."

"Yet you still ended up in service?"

She should never have offered so much of her own history. But something about the man's manner made her speak more than was proper. And now she'd stumbled into uncomfortable territory.

The tea arrived and Sara welcomed the interruption. Enough with Mr. Camden's incessant questions. She would turn the tables, regain the upper hand. As she poured the tea, she inquired after his work. Americans seemed to enjoy chattering on at great length about their accomplishments.

He rose to the occasion. "I'm assisting the construction of an apartment house in New York City."

"You're an architect?"

He beamed. "Yes. I work for the great Henry Hardenbergh."

Sara shook her head. "I'm afraid I'm not acquainted with his name."

"He's taking New York City by storm. He's designed a place where the best families can live with elegance and privacy, sharing amenities like laundry and housekeeping. Why, we're even keeping a tailor and baker on staff. As you can see, I'm fascinated with the inner workings of places like the Langham. Who keeps it humming, and how."

That explained everything. Her shoulders dropped and she offered a warm smile, relieved that Mr. Birmingham wasn't behind the interrogation. "It sounds like a large project."

"The Dakota, it's called, and it will change the way the upper class of the city live. At the moment, the elite of New York reside in brownstones, equivalent to your terrace houses, with one family per abode. The idea of sharing common space and amenities with others, as the French do, is considered gauche."

"And why is that?"

"It's too similar to a working-class tenement, where dozens of families live together in poverty and squalor."

He continued on about the new building, barely stopping for breath, and she drank down her tea quickly, grateful for the liquid on her parched throat. Finally, he pulled out his watch. "I must go. We leave very soon, heading back to New York. I say, you wouldn't want to work at the Dakota, would you?"

Her cup clattered against the saucer. She'd looked up when he'd spoken and missed the center.

He laughed. "I see I caught you unawares. We're in need of a head housekeeper, and you are obviously well qualified. New York City is an exciting place, I promise. I could mention your name to Mr. Douglas, the building's agent."

His words came tumbling out, as if he'd only just thought of the idea. Perhaps he had. Typical American boldness. It was a ridiculous suggestion, going to another country when she had a perfectly good job here, even if Mr. Birmingham was never pleased.

"I'm quite happy where I am, Mr. Camden. But thank you for the offer."

"I'm serious." His voice and visage grew animated as he worked through the details. "I'm going to send you a formal letter when I get back, as well as fare to come over. The opening is set for the end of October. Consider the idea. It's the least I could do, after what you did for my family today. Will you consider it?"

She shook her head. He was caught up in the moment, an impulsive American like many others she'd encountered at the Langham. Too loud, too close, no sense of propriety.

"No, Mr. Camden. But thank you. Please let me know if there's anything else you need during your stay. Good day."

After he'd left, she shut the door behind him and went to the window. The one to room 510 was firmly shut, curtains drawn. Good.

She'd had more than enough excitement for one day.

CHAPTER TWO

Fishbourne, August 1884

"I really don't know why you bothered to come; I'm perfectly fine."
Sara's mother pulled the wool blanket around herself with trembling hands, and Sara stifled the impulse to jump up and arrange it around the woman's sloping shoulders. Doing so would only cause further aggravation.

She took a sip from her sherry glass. "I come this time every year. Remember? My holiday from the hotel."

"Of course I remember; I'm not losing my faculties, Sara." Her blue eyes settled on her daughter, lips turned down in a perpetual frown. "I just don't see what the point is. You might as well stay in London and work your fingers to the bone, since that's what you enjoy doing. I have every mind to speak to his lordship about this."

They were gathered around the fire at the cottage in Fishbourne, where her mother had settled years ago after leaving her position at the estate of the Earl of Chichester, forty miles to the east. Even during the long evenings of August, the house stayed as chilly as a November morning, as if the walls, like her mother, repelled any warmth from the outside.

Sara attempted to guide her back to the present day. "You no longer work for his lordship, remember? It's been thirty years." The number was an easy one to remember.

Her mother shook her head. "No, I don't think so." Her words seemed far away, as if she were speaking down a long tunnel.

"Now I'm head housekeeper at the Langham, just as you were at Stanmer House."

"Why you'd want to take after your mother when I gave you every chance of bettering yourself is beyond me." She waved a hand. "Pour me more sherry."

Even before her mind grew soft, her mother had commanded Sara and her charwoman, who was paid with a good portion of Sara's wages, without a "please" or "thank you." Perhaps she lived a different life in her imagination, one where his lordship made her his countess after getting her with child, instead of the reality, where she toiled day in and day out until her shaking made even holding a teacup untenable.

After refilling the glass, Sara held it to her mother's lips, then sat on the settee and picked up a ragged petticoat that needed mending. She could feel her mother's eyes on her fingers as she deftly fixed the rip at the seam.

"Your stitches are better than mine."

A compliment. Sara kept her eyes down, knowing that she could easily ruin the moment. "Thank you, Mum."

"I still don't know why you left Mrs. Ainsworth to go to London. Your hands could have made a fortune."

"It wasn't a good fit."

"You tossed over an opportunity, if you ask me. Mrs. Ainsworth's husband died three months ago, did I tell you that? Got run over by a carriage."

Probably driven by one of the women who'd apprenticed with his wife. Sara would have run him over herself, given the chance.

"London suits me. The Langham is a first-class hotel. As big as Stanmer House, but so many more people come through every day."

"But are they the right sort of people?"

"They ought to be, if they can afford fifteen shillings a night for a room." They had this conversation every year, and Sara couldn't help but defend her decision.

"You work in a hotel. Fancy or not, it's no place for a good girl. Money's no sign of good breeding."

"Nor is good breeding an indication of morality."

Her mother gave a sharp intake of breath. Sara looked up, an apology on the edge of her lips, but her mother spoke quickly. "You don't know a thing about it."

"Of course, Mum." To change the subject, she blurted out the next thing that came to mind. "I've been given a new opportunity." She'd put off mentioning the letter she'd received from Mr. Camden since arriving at her mother's, knowing it might increase her contempt. But now she had something to prove.

"Eh? What's that?"

"To work as a head housekeeper at a grand apartment house in New York City."

There. She'd said it.

Her mother's face curdled. "In the States?"

"Yes. You see, the child of a guest almost fell out a window, and I happened to see her and save her and the father was so appreciative, he offered me this position."

Her mother remained silent for a moment. Sara tied a knot in the thread and folded up the petticoat, smoothing the dingy material on her lap. She would give it a good wash tomorrow.

She had to admit that she'd been shocked to receive the letter formally asking her to come abroad and a ticket for second-class passage on a ship from Liverpool, as well as a check to cover her expenses. Mr. Camden had asked her to consider the offer and, if she decided not to take it, to send the monies and ticket back. She found the fact that he'd trusted her to do so quite unusual, as their acquaintance had been so brief.

"The child fell out of the window?"

"Almost. But I got there just in time. To be honest, I'm not sure what I should do."

"If you go to America, I will never see you again." The delivery was a statement of fact, the only sign of worry a slight waver in the last word.

"The passage takes only a week. I can come back to visit."

"How soon do they want you there?"

"The apartment house is due to be finished by the end of October, and they'd want me to arrive a month before to get everything in order."

"You can't seem to stay with one thing, can you? Always taking risks and changing your mind."

"Mother, I've been working at the Langham for eleven years. I would think my constancy is not in question. It's more money, much more. Which means we can afford to buy you a new petticoat and have Avril to take care of you, not choose one over the other."

"Avril's a silly nit. And what do I need money for? I'm soon to die."

"You're not soon to die."

"That's not what Dr. Torrington says."

"He told me you're doing beautifully."

Her mother turned her head away and shut her eyes, and the subject was closed.

Later that evening, after her mother had been helped to bed and Sara could hear her snores through the walls, she went to the bookcase and took down the tin box from the highest shelf. She did this every visit, had checked it every year since she'd first noticed it as a girl of ten. Inside were four letters from Lord Chichester to her mum, all businesslike in manner, arranging for Sara's expenses and care, as long as they promised to stay away.

Sara had shown her mother the letters and been met with vitriol, as if her mother had been waiting for the moment of truth. She raged about being forced out by the countess, banished with an ungrateful child to care for. From then on, every misstep Sara made had been an excuse to berate her as the cause of her mother's downfall. Never mind the Earl of Chichester's part in the matter.

Her mother had loved running Stanmer House. Her militaristic need for order made her good at her job, and Sara was certain she'd worshipped Lord Chichester with the devotion of a lapdog. In return, she'd been dismissed. How awful it would have been for her to relinquish the set of household keys, an emblem of her power over nearly every other servant, from where they had hung on her ever-expanding waist.

Her mother had retreated, and expected her daughter to do better. But in spite of her mother's determination, Sara had failed as an apprentice and become a lowly maid. Her mother had never forgiven her nor asked why the sudden change occurred. Not that Sara would ever tell her.

Still, how horrible it must have been for her mother to be forced out of a familiar role and setting. Hidden away, after years of servitude. Sara bristled against the injustice, as her own position at the Langham was similarly precarious, dependent on the tyrannical whims of Mr. Birmingham, no matter how competent her administration. Her short meeting with Mr. Camden, while curious, had reminded her that she was, in fact, good at her job.

When she'd first been promoted, the challenge of balancing the many duties of head housekeeper had exhilarated her. She maneuvered her troops like a general at war, ensuring the precision and consistency of service that had made the Langham one of the top hotels in London. But it was never enough for Mr. Birmingham, and the job had recently begun to fray her nerves. She ran herself ragged all day, before flopping into bed exhausted but unable to sleep because of the many details to be dealt with first thing in the morning: cajole the irritable head laundress into putting less bleach in the sheets, determine which maid had stolen a tortoiseshell comb from room 322.

She put the letters away and wandered out the back of the cottage. The thick stems of the fleur-de-lis lay across the pathway like fallen sentries. The orange evening sky lit the water in the pond with a flame of color, as if both water and air were burning. She was thirty years old. Too old to change, to go to a completely different continent and start over.

Yet, what she'd read about America in the papers intrigued her. No worrying about using the proper titles. Everyone was called a Mrs., Mr., or Miss. The American guests she'd met, like Mr. Camden, tended to be far less demanding than the English ones.

As it stood, she could stay at the Langham for another thirty years, then retire to this cottage and take up where her mother had left off. Tea by the fire, sherry by the fire, before beginning all over again the next day.

Or she could try something new.

CHAPTER THREE

New York City, September 1985

Bailey sank into a stiff, mid-century chair in the waiting room of the offices of Crespo & O'Reilly, happy to be out of the stifling New York City heat. She took a tissue out of her handbag and dabbed at her cheeks and forehead. The unfortunate perm that Tristan O'Reilly had insisted she have six months ago had begun to grow out, but after the boiling subway ride, she probably looked like a disheveled poodle. Not the look she was going for when she started out this morning. Tristan, who cared only for beautiful things, wasn't going to be pleased.

"He'll see you now." The receptionist wasn't familiar. But then again, Tristan went through them every three months, so he was right on schedule.

Three months she'd been away. It felt more like three years. An itchiness spread up her spine to her neck and she took a deep breath.

The receptionist stood. "This way, please."

Bailey followed obediently, passing her old office. The woman behind the desk glanced up and gave Bailey a startled smile before snapping her head back to the fabric samples in front of her. Wanda, of all people. Wanda, who couldn't tell the difference between shantung and dupioni. Bailey could outshine her with a client any day.

She was shown into the corner office.

"There you are, my girl."

Tristan rose and did some kind of balletic shuffle on his way to embrace Bailey. He'd trained with American Ballet Theatre before joining interior design superstar Diego Crespo as an assistant, then worked his way up to boyfriend and business partner. Diego spent most of his time in East Hampton these days, while Tristan helmed the organization. They'd brought on Bailey right out of Parsons School of Design, and Tristan had been her main confidant and party partner until everything had tipped over the edge.

She sank into his hug. "Tristan, I missed you so much."

"I bet you did, baby. How are you doing?" He held her at arm's length and she blinked under his penetrating stare.

"I'm hanging in there." A second wave of sweat, from nerves, not humidity, broke over her.

"Your hair . . ." He didn't bother finishing the sentence.

"I know, it's a mess."

Tristan gestured to the chair and sat on the corner of his desk. He wasn't a handsome man, at least not as handsome as the swarthy Diego, but he knew enough to dress his lithe body with the perfect colors and cut. Today he wore an azure linen blazer that set off the blue of his eyes. His blond hair, while thinning, was pomaded into place like a schoolboy's. Impeccably put together, as always.

"Tell me, how was Silver Hill?"

Bailey shrugged. "It was rehab. Lots of talking, lots of people bitching about their sad lives."

"You're feeling better?"

"Much better."

She didn't mention how most of the time she was dying for a

drink, and that once five o'clock hit, she made herself hole up in the East Village studio apartment of her roommate from Silver Hill, where she was temporarily crashing until the girl got sprung. Bailey would pull down the Murphy bed and lie with a pillow over her head to block out the sirens and shouting, hoping it would do the same for her cravings.

"Did you see any celebrities? I heard that Liza Minnelli checked herself in. Did you meet her?"

Bailey hadn't drunk the Kool-Aid of the counselors there, all that touchy-feely stuff, but the stories she'd heard had been brutal and she respected the idea that it was all anonymous. That some dirt ought not to be dished. Of course, there was no explaining that to Tristan, who lived on gossip.

"No, didn't see her." She leaned forward. "But I wanted to thank you and Diego. For everything. I know you guys probably saved my life."

Tristan waved at her and walked to the chair behind his desk. He paused a moment, dramatically, before sitting down and squaring his shoulders. "It was the right thing to do. You're just going to have to watch yourself going forward. Only two glasses of champagne at Palladium, then I'm cutting you off."

"No, Tristan. No more champagne." She hoped he was joking. "I can't drink anymore. Or do anything else."

"Of course you can't."

She was eager to get that part of the conversation over with, the one that shamed her to the core. "How is business?"

"Excellent. We just got the town house on East Seventy-Seventh Street, the one that Rebecca Meyer bought in the spring." He didn't wait for her to respond. "The renovation started a couple of weeks ago and she's insisting on importing all the antiques from Morocco and London, if you can believe it. And get this: Last week, Lilly-

Beth Latwick flew me by helicopter to her place in East Hampton because her maid had rearranged the throw pillows on the sectional, and she couldn't remember which way they should go." He snapped his fingers. "Chopper, baby."

"Wow. That's insane."

"We also landed the Sanfords' beach house. Massive place, all Zen aesthetic and ferns. I have Wanda on that one. I figure she can't go wrong when everything will be shades of white. White carpet, white sofas."

"You better stay on top of her. If anyone could choose clashing shades of eggshell, it would be her."

"Good point." He smiled, offering a view of gleaming teeth, like a row of Chiclets.

"In fact, that was why I wanted to stop by today."

The teeth disappeared.

"I know I blew out of here in a spectacular fashion, but I'd like to make it up to you and Diego. For everything you've done for me these past few months. I could work with Wanda, act as a go-between with the Sanfords. You know her people skills leave a lot to be desired."

Tristan sighed. "I know, darling. We would love to have you back."

Thank God. One problem solved.

"But the news got around fast. Of course, how could it not? You were screaming at Mrs. Ashfield-Simmons in the middle of the Oak Room, telling her that her daughter's apartment was a nightmare. 'A blend of medieval bullshit and white trash,' I believe you said."

Bailey cringed. She didn't remember any of it. She knew, of course, that she'd made a fool of herself and the company. "I'll call her and apologize. I'll write a letter to her daughter, too. I'll make it all good."

"It's already been taken care of. The important thing is you're okay."

"I'm sober now, so I'll probably be twice as productive. I promise you'll get a real bang for your buck." God, she sounded like a used car salesman. "I'll obviously take a pay cut. I understand that would have to be a precondition."

If he didn't take her back, she didn't know where she'd turn. No other interior design firm would touch her now. Not to mention that she only had another week left to crash in the East Village before her Silver Hill roommate returned to claim it. Before Bailey's epic breakdown, she'd shacked up with a boyfriend named Rocco, who, now that she had better clarity of mind, she could see was really a drug dealer, not a Basquiat-esque artist. So that option was out, as was slinking home so her father could point out that he had been right all along, that she should never have come to New York in the first place.

"Look, Tristan. I messed up. But you know I can run rings around anyone else here, when it comes to interacting with the clients, with the contractors, you name it. My eye is the best, you've said that yourself so many times. Even when I was strung out, I was great. Let me have one more chance."

Tristan peered sideways at her through slitted eyelids. Not good. "Listen, Bailey. You put us through hell. We covered for you this past year. You have no idea how much we covered for you, because we love you and because, yes, you were good. You were the best, and you could have done amazing things here. We all party, we all have a good time, but you took it too far."

The harshness of his words stung.

"Okay. Wow." She looked down at the floor, hating the lucidity of sobriety more than ever. "I didn't realize how bad it was."

"'Bad' is an understatement. I love you, but I'm dropping you."

Dropping her. Like she was contagious. "You're being really harsh about this. If you don't mind me saying it, you're being an asshole." She said it with a slight smile on her face, in the same way they used to banter back and forth.

Bad idea.

"You disappointed me then, and you're disappointing me now. Do you actually have the nerve to waltz in here and practically demand to be hired back?" Tristan twitched his shoulders before tugging on the cuff of each sleeve, a familiar tic that meant the meeting was over. "I love you, and I always will, and that's why we paid for you to go to Silver Hill, which, by the way, is fucking expensive. So don't expect any more from us, okay? You wouldn't fit in here anymore."

She sat for a moment, too stunned to move.

"I'm sorry, Bailey. But we're done here. You're done here."

❧

Bailey stood outside on the sweltering sidewalk, trying not to think about how good a chardonnay would taste right now. The touch of the glass on her lips, the intense acidity followed by the velvet sensation that all was right in the world. Back when she drank, she could live in the moment. High on weed or on coke, the past and the future ceased to exist. While ensconced in the lush, landscaped grounds of Silver Hill, she was able to see that way of thinking wasn't helpful, and she had talked about her past openly, more than she had with anyone. But here in the city, no one cared.

If she turned right and headed down the side street, she was sure to come upon one of the dozen Irish pubs that lined the blocks of Midtown. Places where office workers could escape from the monotony of their lives.

The room where they'd had group at Silver Hill was covered in mottos from the program. "One day at a time" and "No matter where you go, there you are."

Well, here she was: a drippy, pathetic mess, desperate for a drink in a dive bar.

She checked her watch. There was no time for liquid distractions. She was due to meet Melinda at Cafe Luxembourg in the West Seventies in a half hour. That was truly her last chance. The train would be a steamy cauldron of humanity this time of day, the windows slanted open, like the heat of the tunnels wasn't just as unbearable as the fiery furnace of the subway car. She couldn't face it. Instead, she headed north on foot, cutting into Central Park at Seventh Avenue.

Before her mother's death, Bailey and her parents would venture into the city a couple times a year from their house in New Jersey, usually to see a Broadway musical where dancers executed fast, furious combinations that took Bailey's breath away while her father, Jack, squirmed in the too-small seat next to her. But Bailey and her mother always buzzed with excitement the morning before, choosing their dresses with care, as if they might get "discovered" during their big day out. Once in Manhattan, her mother would point out her old haunts, like the building where she attended some posh secretarial school for three months before getting married, and the Horn & Hardart Automat where she and Jack met.

During one excursion, having arrived two hours before curtain, Bailey had suggested they visit the boat pond in the park. She'd brought along a magazine with a photo of a gondola passing under an arched bridge, and thrust it between the front seats of their Volkswagen Beetle. "It's so pretty."

"No one goes in the park," Jack warned. "It's full of gang members, all dust and graffiti because the city ran out of money to take care of it. It's a ruin, like the rest of Manhattan."

Her mother studied the magazine. "What if we walk along Central Park West? We could stop by the Dakota and drop in on your relatives."

"For God's sake, Peggy. No one drops in like that in the city. And they're not my relatives, remember?" The conversation came to a halt as Jack slammed on the brakes, narrowly missing a bicycle messenger. They'd eaten soggy fries and overcooked burgers in a diner to kill the time instead.

Bailey didn't see the city as a ruin. She saw important people going to important places. She'd wanted to be one of them.

For a while, she had been. But now her fall from grace was complete.

As Bailey got deeper into the park and away from the grid of streets, the air became noticeably cooler. A light wind blew in from the west—thunderstorms were predicted for the afternoon—and the rhythmic whispering of the leaves helped slow the beat of her heart and her desire for a drink. She took a deep breath.

The park was a mess still, that was true. But a private group had taken over the maintenance, and the place was getting spruced up. The trash situation seemed better than ever, no more overflowing bins with rats leaping out of them. Progress.

An ugly chain-link fence lined the north side of the Seventy-Second Street park entrance. Bailey was breathing hard from the walk and the heat and she stopped for a moment, clawing the metal with her fingers and pressing her face into the diamond pattern like a child. The area, recently dubbed Strawberry Fields in John Lennon's memory, was due to open to the public next month. Five years since he'd been gunned down. Every one of her generation remembered where they were when they found out, as if it had just happened yesterday.

A shout from one of the workers brought her out of her thoughts. A couple of the guys at the base of the excavator stared down at something in the dirt, then called to what seemed to be a supervisor, who ambled over, coffee cup in his hand. The supervisor motioned for the excavator driver to cut his engine and wiped his forehead with a red bandanna. They all stood in a circle, necks craned downward, as if in prayer.

Bailey moved on. The Dakota loomed large as she waited for the light to change. The sides were gray, coated with a century of soot, but it still stood out from its neighbors. No subtle art deco motifs here, this was pure decadence. Gables, windows of all shapes and sizes. A filthy, aging dowager of a building. Bailey counted up four stories and located Melinda's apartment.

When she was a child, Bailey and her parents had visited Melinda, her twin brother Manvel, and their mother once a year, usually around the holidays. The twins' mother, Sophia, was a throwback to the old days, encrusted with jewels, even at breakfast, her manner cold and officious. The early family gatherings had always been awkward affairs, the tension between Bailey's dad and her "aunt" palpable, the economic divide an enormous chasm. Once, Melinda had insisted Bailey stay for an overnight visit. They'd raided the kitchen in the still hours of the early morning, cramming Lucky Charms into their mouths straight from the box while Melinda whispered the gory details of the murder of her great-grandfather, the architect Theodore Camden, in that very apartment. They crept into the dark library and Melinda pointed to the far corner, near the window.

"He was killed by some woman who used to work in the building," Melinda whispered. "She stabbed him, and he bled to death on this very spot. Begging for mercy. She was crazy, they say. Cut off his finger and kept it as a souvenir. Look closer, you can see the blood."

Bailey leaned forward, squinting, to make out a dark pattern on the floor. Melinda suddenly tweaked her on either side of her waist, making her jump and scream, and they ran back to the safety of Melinda's canopied bed, crying and laughing at the same time.

The girls had gotten closer once Bailey moved to the city for college, the two of them gradually increasing the dosage and frequency of banned substances in their systems. Manvel, meanwhile, graduated from Yale and headed to the Deep South to do a dissertation on self-taught artists, only returning a few times, including when Sophia died seven years ago.

Melinda had a brashness that Bailey envied, and together they measured their lives by the number of parties attended. But every so often, usually as Bailey's body expelled the toxins ingested the night before through cold sweats and vomit, she recognized that her mother, had she still been alive, would have been dismayed and worried. Peggy would have taken Bailey aside and given her a thoughtful lecture on her extended absence from their New Jersey home and the sallow, unhealthy tone of her skin. She would have held her accountable. Jack wasn't up to the task. He'd retreated into his shell as soon as they put Bailey's mother in the ground.

In rehab, the counselors had asked her lots of questions about her mother's death, suggesting that Bailey "process" it. She'd fought back, insisting that being left alone at eighteen had toughened her up. There was no need to process anything. The facts were the facts: drunk driver plus Garden State Parkway equaled Bailey packing up her things and starting freshman year at Parsons with hardly a peep from her dad. She'd kept busy with classes and socializing and exploring every dark crack of the city, until Tristan hired her and pulled her into the fabulous world of Crespo & O'Reilly.

Cafe Luxembourg was practically empty this time of day, the waiters standing in pairs chatting in order to fill the empty hours between the lunch and dinner crowds. Melinda wasn't there yet, so Bailey took a booth seat where she had a good view of the door. It wasn't long until Melinda swept in, wearing a jumpsuit with enormous shoulder pads, her blond hair in perfect swirls down her back, as if she walked in a bubble that protected her from the humidity that plagued the common man. She threw the Barneys bags she was carrying on the floor and held out her arms.

"Cousin!"

Melinda. Her last hope.

CHAPTER FOUR

London, September 1884

M r. Birmingham gave a low growl when Sara gave her notice. "Think you'll find something better over there, do you?" he asked.

She didn't answer, and instead made suggestions for a trouble-free transition and offered to interview her successor. The staff threw a small party on her last day, but it had a desultory air. She packed up her bedsit and that was that. On to a new continent.

During the eight-day journey from Liverpool to New York City, Sara spent as much time up on the ship deck as possible, to avoid the stench of seasickness from her cabinmates below. To her surprise, the incessant rolling of the ship didn't bother her at all, and she found the week off to be something of a delight. She read in peace in one of the deck chairs, with no schedule and no Mr. Birmingham to tell her what to do or when to do it. It was all she could do not to stow away on board and enjoy another week instead of disembarking.

From her favorite spot on deck, she could see over to the first-class passengers, barricaded by a gate, as they wandered the decks in their gowns and were fussed over by the waitstaff. Some of the sharply dressed servers made their rounds with goblets of lemonade on gleaming silver trays. Others brought sugar cookies still fragrant from the oven that made Sara's mouth water. But she didn't mind the meals in the second-class dining room, and every morning carried a weak broth and tea to the women in her cabin who were unable to move from their beds. A moan was the most she could hope for in response to her bright greeting.

On the last day of the voyage, a gray drizzle fell as the ship made its way into New York Harbor. The city was made up of a mishmash of buildings crowded together like a mouth with too many teeth. She imagined the ones on the edge of the waterfront being pushed into the sea as more and more popped up to fill any crevices. One dark church spire erupted from the rooftops, and she overheard another passenger say it was Trinity Church. She'd be sure to visit, thinking it might be a calm place where she could gather her thoughts during an afternoon off.

The passengers in steerage had to wait until they reached Castle Garden to be processed, but with her second-class ticket, Sara was provided the dignity of an onboard inspection and interview. The confusion on the docks made her anxious once she stepped off the ship. The smell of rotting fish and fried oysters overwhelmed, and everyone seemed to be shouting at the top of their lungs. Newspaper boys, street urchins, and vendors called out in abrasive accents, the vowels all wrong and flat. Everyone seemed to know where they were going and were intent on getting there in the fastest way possible, stepping into the middle of the street even though a wagon was bearing down, and narrowly missing being hit. London was a pastoral village compared to this.

Through the riot of noise, she heard her name. A driver in a fine black carriage stood up, yelling above the din. She waved back and let him help her climb inside, admiring the burgundy velvet interior.

She eyed the driver through the rear window to ensure her trunk was securely fastened to the rear, and then settled in. They drove through town and kept on going, until vacant land and fields outnumbered the buildings.

She knocked on the roof to get his attention. He twisted his thick torso around to see her. "Yes, ma'am?"

"Are we going to the Dakota? The new apartment house?"

"We are indeed."

"But it appears we've left the city."

"This is all New York City, ma'am. You can see the markers for the streets."

Indeed, even if the streets were no longer paved with granite, they remained regularly spaced apart. "But there's nothing here."

Around her was treeless farmland and cattle grazing in muddy fields. It was as if the landscape had been flattened by an enormous gust of wind and only now was coming back to life with tired shanties and sad barns. This was New York?

They carried on. Outside, a pretty young girl walked down the street, followed by a gang of boys who tossed pebbles at her. The girl whirled around and ran at them and they scattered into the street. When Sara was younger, her face had garnered more attention than she would have liked, but now her features were less of a liability. No one mistook her for an innocent maid, and her aquiline nose and raised eyebrow worked in her favor as a tool to stare down unruly sorts, whether a shifty janitor or a haughty guest.

New York wasn't going to frighten her.

Yet as the carriage swayed up the wide avenue with an empty park on one side and a wasteland on the other, her heart sank. In London, you could wander the squares and see loveliness; you just had to know where to look. Nothing was lovely here.

She shifted to the other side of the carriage and stuck her head out the window. An enormous building, the color of butter, seemed to have been plopped down on the flat landscape by a giant, like something you'd find in a German fairy tale. She counted nine stories with windows that a man could stand in and not reach the top pane, and a complicated gabled roof lacking any consistent pattern.

"Is that it?"

"Sure is. They've been working on it for years." The driver turned his head and shouted back at her. "Built by a fool named Clark."

"Why is Clark a fool?"

"It's a monstrosity in the middle of nowhere. No good families would dream of living here, I tell you. Can only imagine what sort will end up inside. Lucky devil died before he could see it finished."

She'd pictured a handsome building like the Langham smack in the middle of the city, surrounded by shops and parks, where broughams with well-matched pairs of horses pulled up to discharge their passengers. But this place was dismal, the streets still unpaved. She should have asked more questions about the owners, the location. If the driver were correct, the clientele would be ignorant of the niceties. Fine linens. Good manners. A certain distance from the staff that made the role of housekeeper manageable.

The man pulled into an arch cut through the middle of the building. When she stepped out, the ground seemed to shift underneath her. She'd been told by one of the ship's porters that it might take a few days for her sea legs to let her be.

A wiry old man approached, speaking out of the side of his mouth. "Are you Mrs. Smythe?"

She nodded.

"Been expecting you. I'm Fitzroy, the head porter. Why don't you wait inside while I arrange for your belongings?" He gestured to the right, where a steep set of stairs led to a small reception room. Two large windows let in ample light, and the walls were covered in handsome wood paneling that matched the built-in desk and countertop. A switchboard took up most of the back wall.

The porter joined her, rubbing his hands together. The side of his face drooped, as if it was falling off his skull, but his eyes, including the one that turned down at the edge, were a warm brown. He pointed at the switchboard.

"Got all the latest gadgets here, you'll find. We have private wires going to the fire station, the stables, the telegraph messenger office, and the florist. Four thousand electric lights, even."

"Very modern."

"How was your journey? You came from abroad?"

"Yes, England."

"Right. The building agent, Mr. Douglas, said to show you around."

He led her into the courtyard, currently in use by the craftsmen, and they wove around toolboxes and sawhorses supporting large pieces of wood. She looked up once and the dizziness returned. The courtyard felt too small for the massive building around it, like the walls were about to cave in.

Mr. Fitzroy touched her lightly on the elbow to steady her. He pointed up. "That's where you'll be, on the top floor. Lovely view. Once the elevators are working, you won't have to trudge up the stairs. First of their kind in a residential building in New York City, I'll have you know."

"We had several lifts in the London hotel where I worked previously."

His enthusiasm remained undamped. "I'll show you ours tomorrow, if you like. An amazing piece of machinery. Runs on water, all hydraulics."

He must be balmy, a lift run by water. But she was too tired to inquire further.

Exhaustion swept over her. This Bavarian behemoth, out in the middle of nowhere, was to be her home. She should have stayed in London. Instead of continuing on with her comfortable, if predictable, life, she would have to figure everything out anew: the confusing geography of the building and the city, not to mention the foreign customs of America. The people who agreed to live in such a place must be desperate, unable to afford lodging in the city proper, and she'd seen desperate sorts before she'd started working at the Langham. Demanding, petty, and changeable. At least in her previous positions, the guests would check out at some point, head off to other destinations. The Dakota residents would be here to stay.

"For now, I'd like to get settled and rest, Mr. Fitzroy."

They entered a door set in the far left corner of the courtyard that led into a dark foyer. A wide set of marble stairs wrapped around the lift, and the railings of the stairs were carved with ornate designs that gave the impression of serpents twisting their way down and around. Nothing warm and inviting like the Langham's cream walls and brass finishes. Her room, down a claustrophobic hall at the very top of the building, had a small bed, desk, and chair. Simple and plain, as suited a domestic servant. But her attention was immediately drawn to the window.

In her London bedsit, she'd had no view, other than roofs and a blank sky. But here, at the very top of the tallest building for miles around, she could see farms and streets and even a wide river beyond.

"On a good day, you can see the Orange Mountains of New Jersey," offered Fitzroy.

She thought of the harbor at Fishbourne, and her heart settled ever so slightly at the idea of having a view of water. Pathetic, that she should need to cling to something. But it helped.

"If you'd like a cup of tea or a bite before bed, come down to the kitchen in the basement. There's no one else about; you can help yourself. I'll be heading home in an hour or so, but I'll lock the front gate so you'll be safe."

"No one else is here?"

"You're the first of the resident staff to arrive."

Her throat constricted at the thought of being alone.

Fitzroy shrugged his shoulders. "There's a lamp on the desk for you to see your way after dark. I can stay late if you're nervous."

It was a kind offer. "Not at all. I will be fine."

After he left, Sara remained at the window, watching the gray sky turn to black. It occurred to her that she was trapped, locked inside. What if there was a fire, or if she had to get out in an emergency? A terrible unease crept over her, uncertain whether she was safer locked inside this tomb or in the vast nothingness outside. Panic fluttered in her chest and threatened to take over her senses. She didn't dare wind her way through the labyrinthine hallways down to the basement, not now, so she ignored her rumbling stomach, changed into her bedclothes, and laid on the bed until exhaustion took over, sending her into a deep, drugged sleep.

CHAPTER FIVE

New York City, September 1884

A distant hammering startled Sara awake. She put on her nicest day dress, a dark hunter green with thin black stripes, and swept her hair up into a severe bun at the back of her neck before heading down the stairs. She wound her way down, landing by landing, the noise growing louder. As she stepped into the courtyard, she was greeted with a cacophony of sounds: men shouting, hammers and saws being wielded with great ferocity. Fitzroy appeared at her side and guided her back into the building through a different door and down a maze of narrow hallways with very high ceilings. The proportions seemed all wrong, but maybe that was the American way.

He opened the door to the dining room and pointed inside. "Help yourself to some coffee and eggs or whatnot. It's meager pickings at the moment. Oh, and Mr. Camden asked that you come to see him after."

"Where is he?"

"You'll find him in apartment number 43 on the fourth floor. Take the stairs on the northeast corner of the courtyard to get there."

The dining room rivaled her mother's description of the grand one at the earl's manor house. From the inlaid marble floor to the carved oak ceiling, no detail had been spared, including the enormous fireplace of Scottish brownstone. The room contained several recurring motifs: The bronze bas-relief covering the walls was decorated with ears of corn, arrowheads, and Indian faces, a play on the name of the building, she assumed. She gulped down her coffee but passed on the watery eggs. Hopefully, the cook would put more effort into the job once the tenants arrived.

The door to number 43 was partially ajar. She opened it and looked about. Beside her was a fireplace, unusual for a foyer, and away from that led another long, dark hallway. To her left was a grand library, where bookshelves flanked floor-to-ceiling windows. A Juliet balcony overlooked the park beyond, and a pocket door connected it to the adjoining room. The craftsmanship astounded her. Even the Langham, the most luxurious hotel in London, lacked this sort of detailing.

"Mr. Camden?" Her voice echoed off the walls.

"Right in here."

She hadn't seen him, tucked out of view on the side of the library.

Mr. Camden leaned over a draftsman's desk, a pencil in one hand. He looked up at her and smiled. He was the only person she knew here, and the familiarity, though scant, lessened the panic that had gripped her ever since the Dakota had emerged into view.

"How was your trip, Mrs. Smythe?" The room was smaller than the adjoining parlor, but the eastern exposure granted it a lot of light. He put down his pencil and gestured to the two armchairs arranged on either side of the window.

"My trip was fine, thank you."

"I'm glad to hear it."

He ran his hand over his chin. He didn't have a beard, which was disconcerting at first, as most men wore thick, shaggy whiskers. His smooth skin made it difficult to gauge his age. Midthirties, she suspected.

She cringed with embarrassment. The silence had gone on uncomfortably long as she'd studied his face. "The work inside the building is quite beautiful."

He shrugged off the compliment. "*Overwrought* is the expression that comes to mind. But I suppose I had better get used to it, as this will be my new home."

"You'll be living here?" She hadn't meant to sound shocked, but she imagined he would prefer to live in the more established part of the city.

"In this very apartment. Mrs. Camden had her misgivings, but I told her the wilds of the West Side were soon to be tamed. The rest of the furniture as well as my family arrive in a couple of months, once the building is up and running. It's no Langham Hotel, but I'll manage."

"I'm sure your family will enjoy it very much, and it will be a delight to meet your children under less strenuous circumstances. I trust they are all well?"

"Indeed."

Enough with the niceties. She had much to learn before the building opened for business. "How many apartments have been rented?"

"All of them. Fitzroy will give you a proper tour of the building, but I can show you on the plans." He stood and led her to a table pushed against one wall, and leafed through several white linen sheets until he found what he was looking for. "This is the fourth floor. We're here."

The apartment was enormous, with several bedchambers, anterooms with fireplaces, pantries, servants' quarters, and an expansive parlor.

Sara examined the layout of the entire floor. "Every apartment seems to be a completely different configuration from the others."

"Initially, Mr. Hardenbergh assigned six apartments to a floor, all roughly the same size. But after the owner, Mr. Clark, passed away a couple of years ago, the building agent took over, and he unfortunately allowed tenants to have a say in the number of rooms they preferred. I can't tell you how many nights I spent piecing them together like an enormous jigsaw puzzle, but we've finally done it. We're slightly behind schedule, and I have Mr. Douglas breathing down my neck, but that's where you come in."

Before he could continue, a man's voice echoed down the hall.

"Back here, Mr. Douglas." Mr. Camden gave Sara a smile. "Your boss has arrived."

She wished Mr. Camden were her boss, and one look at the man entering the room didn't change her opinion. He had a lumbering body and blue-black hair. He took off his hat when he saw Sara, and she couldn't help notice the dark stain of hair dye around the inside of the rim.

"Mr. Douglas, I'm pleased to introduce Mrs. Smythe; she arrived from England yesterday."

Mr. Douglas eyed her much like a horse dealer might evaluate a disappointing mare.

"Right, then, Mrs. Smythe. We don't have much time left to us, and things are a mess, as you see. We'll have to make the adjustments quickly."

"I'm happy to do whatever needs to be done," said Sara. "It would help, of course, to know how many maids have been hired and how soon we can get them here." From the minute she'd awoken, her mind had already swum with the best way to direct a crew of girls to do a deep clean of the place, ridding it of sawdust and polishing the mahogany to a shine.

"Right, well, we have a minor problem there."

She steadied her gaze and placed one hand on the table. "A problem?" If he'd changed his mind, she'd have nowhere to go. Would he or Mr. Camden pay for her fare home? Would the Langham take her back?

"Now, don't go all pale on me. It's not as bad as that." Mr. Douglas was breathing hard, like he'd run the entire way. He had ruddy cheeks and his lips were unexpectedly cherubic, like a baby's. "The man we hired to manage the building is unable to join us. His mother is ill, and he's off to St. Louis to care for her. So I'd like you to be lady managerette. With your qualifications from the Langham in London, we figure it'll be a good fit."

"Instead of resident housekeeper?"

"Exactly. It will come with an increase in salary and you'll be in charge of not only the housekeeper and maids, but the entire staff."

"I've never worked as a lady managerette before." She'd never even heard the term. It sounded ridiculous, overly feminine and precious.

"No matter. The very fact you were brought in from abroad, from some fancy hotel will impress the tenants. I can't get anyone else on this short notice, and Mr. Camden spoke highly of you."

"What does it entail, this job?"

He looked at the ceiling and rattled off a list. "As I said, you'll oversee the entire staff, be in charge of general operations. Make sure everyone from the porter to the chambermaids are doing their jobs, that they get paid on time, that the invoices and such are taken care of. Keep the place humming. The second floor is to be rented to the out-of-town guests of residents, so that sort of arrangement will certainly be familiar to you. You'll also screen prospective tenants and ensure the move-in process is seamless."

"Looks like you've got a promotion already, Mrs. Smythe." Mr.

Camden began folding up the plans. "Not bad for the first hour on the job."

She managed a weak smile. The managers at the Langham came and went every few years, never able to please the owners or the guests, blamed for any mishap. And they were always men. "How many apartments are there in the building?"

"Sixty-five, ranging from four to twenty rooms," answered Mr. Camden.

"How many will be on staff, once it's up and running?"

Mr. Douglas took a moment to answer, configuring the number in his head, apparently. "One hundred and fifty."

She recoiled. "I'd be in charge of one hundred and fifty people? What would they all do?"

"Let's see, this is a good test for me." Mr. Douglas chuckled, as if it were all a silly joke. "Elevator staff, doormen, janitors, porters, watchmen, resident laundress with staff, gentlemen's tailor, two painters, cabinetmaker, electrician, plumber, dining room staff. I think that's everyone. Practically a city within a city, no?"

"Don't forget the carpenter and glazier," added Mr. Camden.

The two men discussed the schedule for installing the finishing touches on the Otis elevators for a few minutes, until Mr. Douglas turned on his heel and exited down the hall, puffing like a train.

Mr. Camden went to the wall and rang a button. "Well, that's exciting news, isn't it?"

She was frozen on the spot, unsure of how to answer. She was to be responsible for the entire staff and the well-being of hundreds of tenants.

"Fitzroy will be here in a moment and can show you to your office. I think you'll prefer it to the garret you had at your previous employer's. I designed the interior myself."

For a moment, she ached for the small office at the top of the hotel, where she had showed up every day knowing exactly what was expected of her. "I'm not sure I'm right for this position."

"Then you'll be on the first steamer back."

She blanched, and he laughed. "Don't be ridiculous, give it a whirl. Douglas is in a pickle. You'll do it, right?" Before she could reply, Fitzroy appeared.

"Sir?"

"Take Mrs. Smythe to the front office. And, Mrs. Smythe, first order of things is to find a new resident housekeeper. Off you go."

Dutifully, she followed Fitzroy back down the stairs. He moved nimbly for his age. "I'll have to bring you through the basement, as they're causing a ruckus in the courtyard."

She nodded, unable to speak. Her throat had tightened and she wanted a cup of tea desperately.

They descended to the lowest level of the building. Even though they were underground, the place was bright with natural light.

"How are there windows underground?" she asked.

"There's a waterless moat around the building. But that's not the only source. If you look up"—he pointed at the ceiling—"you can see the skylights set in the courtyard fountains."

Fitzroy carried on with the tour, pointing out the water pipes that powered the lifts, she wasn't sure exactly how, and dozens of small rooms. "Here's where the tailor will go, and here will be a storage room for the tenants' trunks. A ramp on the west side of the building allows for deliveries to be made directly to the basement."

They took an elevator up one flight and Fitzroy unlocked the door to an office off the reception room, flinging it open.

Mr. Camden was correct. No expense had been spared. On the mahogany walls were handsome wood bookshelves, beside which sat a matching desk. The tableau was more suited to an old schooner, the place where the captain of a ship plotted the navigation.

Piled on top of the desk were stacks of papers and unopened envelopes. Several had fallen to the floor.

"What's all this?"

"Bills, requests from tenants, that sort of thing. The manager was supposed to have been here a week ago, so we're a little behind."

Fitzroy picked up the envelopes from the floor and laid them carefully on one of the shorter piles. "Did Mr. Camden mention the staff meeting?"

"No. No, he did not."

"Right, then." He checked his timepiece. "The entire staff will be arriving shortly and meeting in the dining room in one hour to receive their orders."

"Mr. Douglas's way of leading the charge?"

"Mr. Douglas?" Fitzroy looked at her askance. "No, Mrs. Smythe. You'll be heading the meeting. You're leading the charge."

The next thirty minutes were spent rifling through the piles of papers, sorting them out by invoices, resident requests, vendor notices, and the like. It didn't speak much to the organization of the place that Mr. Douglas had assigned her these duties without telling her exactly what was expected of her. She doubted he even knew. Everyone was starting from scratch with this apartment-house-that-ran-like-a-hotel nonsense. As far as she could tell, her job as lady managerette was to keep the Dakota Apartment House afloat. How that broke down into responsibilities was beyond her, and was probably beyond Mr. Douglas as well, who was busy with his own deadlines and duties.

She knew how to manage housemaids, nothing more than that. All right, perhaps more than that, as Mr. Birmingham at the Langham had presented her with additional responsibilities over the years.

Particularly those he disliked, like hiring and firing staff and dealing with the more finicky guests.

She'd fought her way up to housekeeper there, so why should she
not jump on this opportunity as well?

Because she might fail, horribly, and have to return to Fishbourne
with her tail between her legs, as her mother expected.

A girl with strawberry-blond hair peered in from the doorway.
"Mrs. Smythe?"

Sara nodded. "May I help you?"

The girl walked in, followed by a thin, reedy woman. They
couldn't have been more different from each other. The younger one
was soft and round with a smattering of pale freckles that dotted
her nose and cheeks. Her expression was curious and eager, like that
of a girl who'd just walked into a bakery full of pastries. The older
one's mouth turned down at the sides, and her plain gray frock had
the unfortunate effect of turning her skin tone rather ashen.

"I'm Daisy Cavanaugh, your assistant," said the girl. "This is Mrs.
Haines, who is also your assistant."

Sara rose. "It is quite a pleasure to meet you both. Please, sit." She
gestured to the two chairs. "I'm afraid I have yet to find the staff list.
Can you tell me a little about yourselves and what your jobs entail?"

Maybe that would give her some clue about her own.

Daisy leaned forward in her chair. "I was told that I'm to do whatever I can to assist you. I assume my first order of business is to lo-
cate the staff list."

She liked the girl already.

"Previously"—Daisy cocked her head—"I worked at the Cosmo-
politan Hotel, assisting the manager."

"This is an entirely different animal." Mrs. Haines's mouth barely
moved when she spoke, as if she had problems with her teeth. "I
worked at the Hubert Home Club for the past three years, and I as-

sure you, managing an apartment house is quite a lot more work. My duties will include checking in guests and calling up to the owners to grant them permission to visit, as I did there. A gate-keeper, if you will, to keep out the riffraff. The switchboard shall be my domain."

"Will you both be residing here at the Dakota?"

Mrs. Haines nodded. "We are moving in today, on the ninth floor."

"Yes, our rooms are right around the corner from each other," offered Daisy, looking pleased.

Mrs. Haines didn't bother to mask her disappointment at the arrangement. The two women were unlikely to become bosom friends, but with luck they'd learn to work together.

The front bell rang and Mrs. Haines sprung up. "I'd like to get started, if that's all right with you."

Sara dismissed them, but Daisy turned back in the doorway. "Mrs. Smythe, is it true you came from London?"

"Yes, yes, I did."

"That's a long way."

"Indeed."

"I hate to speak out of turn, but Mrs. Haines told me she'd thought she would get your job when it came open. You might have your hands full with that one."

Sara would not tolerate gossip.

"I'm certain Mrs. Haines and I will manage just fine," she said. "I treat every member of my staff with respect and expect the same treatment in return. Which means that, in the future, Daisy, you need only inform me of matters that pertain directly to you or your duties."

"Of course, ma'am." Daisy bit her lip.

Sara did not regret chiding the girl; it was important to establish boundaries from the first. Still, she did not want Daisy to think her cruel or cold. It would be nice to have a friend in this peculiar place.

"Speaking of duties, I'm drowning in all of these papers." Sara held up a thick stack of bills in each hand and offered Daisy a wry smile. "I'd surely love your help running through them. Do you mind pitching in?"

Daisy's face brightened. "Of course not, Mrs. Smythe. Can I get you a cup of tea before we dive to the bottom?"

"That would be lovely, and fetch one for yourself as well."

They made great progress in a short period of time. While Daisy focused on the invoices and began entering them in the ledger, Sara looked over the staff list the girl had found, miraculously, under the desk. In the few minutes before the tolling of the hour, they heard the employees shuffling in through the reception area.

"We should go." Sara took a deep breath.

She led the way into the dining room, which was packed with men and women of all ages and sizes, from the mischievous-looking messenger boys to the resident laundress, easily recognizable by her chapped, red hands. Everyone stood, careful not to touch the walls or the silk-covered dining room chairs. She was glad they were meeting in this room, which held an awe-inspiring grandeur. Here she had some sway. Or so she hoped.

Mr. Camden loped in, nodding his head and weaving his way through the crowd. Sara noticed Daisy give a quick intake of breath. The man had a rough elegance about him, an unlikely combination.

"Thank you all for assembling," he said. "I am Mr. Camden, part of the architectural team here. As a future tenant, I've also been put in charge of getting the place up and running, along with Mrs. Smythe, the resident managerette." He gestured in her direction. "We are here to provide our tenants with the sense that they're not living in an apartment house but instead in a mansion of their own, with everything they could possibly want at their very fingertips. My boss, Mr. Henry Hardenbergh, has created one of the most modern buildings in New York City. We open on October twenty-seventh. That's very little time, and we will require your utmost attention and assistance.

"I'd like to turn the meeting over to Mrs. Smythe. Mrs. Smythe hails from London, where she worked at the grand Langham Hotel."

The abrupt introduction threw her. Sweat beaded beneath her chemise and she was glad for the many layers that hid the signs of her terror. She should have been one of the women staring back at her now, expectant, wary, hoping to please.

She took a deep breath and surveyed the room, lifting up one eyebrow and lowering her chin just a bit, exactly as her mother used to do when passing a group of gossiping women in the village. She spotted Fitzroy, holding his cap in his hands, the one recognizable face.

"I am delighted to meet you and look forward to getting to know each and every one of you. As Mr. Camden has said, we are taking ownership of a flagship building, one that will be talked about by the citizens of New York City for years to come. It is under our control, each and every one of us, to make this a building that is admired and whose tenants are envied. The structure may be made of stone and wood, but you will be its heart. We must all do our jobs with pride, and work together.

"I'd like the heads of each department to see Miss Cavanaugh and make an appointment to meet with me in the next two days. From there, we will be able to devise a working schedule and goals and approach opening day with confidence."

She turned to Mr. Camden. There really wasn't much else to say.

He threw her a quick smile. "Well done," he murmured under his breath. "Not only do you save little girls, you are a force to be reckoned with. I knew my instincts were good when it came to you."

Then he was gone, leaving her enveloped in a crush of voices and questions.

CHAPTER SIX

New York City, September 1985

B ailey had risen only halfway from the booth before Melinda wrapped her in her skinny arms, her jangly necklace digging into Bailey's neck.

"I missed you so much," she said, "and I've been thinking about you nonstop, you naughty girl." The words were flip, but the embrace was genuine and fierce.

They finally untangled and Melinda sat in her seat, swishing her long hair back from each shoulder and tightening the scrunchie at the very top of her head, where a section of hair fanned out like a whale spout. The zipper on her jumpsuit revealed a plump cushion of tanned cleavage. "I should have visited you, I'm so sorry about that. You know I wanted to."

"Please, I didn't want any visitors. I had to work on myself." More twelve-step jargon. Funny how sometimes that was the only way to explain it.

"I'm so glad you did. I heard that Tristan took care of the cost, is that right?"

"He did." She couldn't help but cringe, thinking of their conversation this morning.

"First things first. Tell me about Silver Hill. Meet anyone famous?"

"Liza was there. Lovely woman but, of course, I can't say anything about it."

That did the trick. Melinda looked both awed and chastised.

She'd have to remember that the next time someone asked.

The waiter poured water for the table and Bailey gulped down half her glass.

"It breaks my heart, what you went through." Melinda's eyes welled with tears. "I should have been there for you the way you've been for me. Remember when you pulled me out of the Roxy right before the cops swooped in?"

"Right. The Roxy. One of our many close calls."

The waiter came by and handed them a couple of menus. Melinda didn't bother to glance at it, kept her gaze rooted on Bailey. "Did you make any friends in rehab?"

"No. Not my type. Bunch of addicts and drunks."

Melinda's big blue eyes grew even bigger. "Don't make fun. I know it must've been hard."

Getting sympathy from Melinda made Bailey squirm. "The worst thing is not remembering much about my apparent night of infamy."

Melinda let out a guffaw. "You were a trip, I have to say."

"You were there?"

Bailey couldn't remember much from that evening. She knew she'd had a few glasses of champagne and done some coke in one of the guest rooms at the Plaza. It was a big night out to celebrate Tristan's birthday. They were to hit the Oak Room for martinis and then eventually end up clubbing at the Limelight, a former church from the 1800s where high-society families like the Astors and the Vanderbilts used to pray.

"Uh-huh. We ran into you guys in the Oak Room. Tony and I said hello and you were out of your mind already."

A faint recollection of Bailey mimicking Tony's English accent emerged through her hazy memory. She hadn't liked Melinda's latest boyfriend. He was one of those guys who always knew someone who knew someone, and liked to impress with how connected he was.

Bailey grimaced. "I was a bitch that night. Why did I insult Tristan's top client?"

"Because she deserved it! You were completely right about the daughter's apartment. That family never had any class."

"She wanted her living room to have a rotating floor, for God's sake."

"I was at a party there a few weeks ago. Awful. You can't buy taste."

The waiter appeared. "Can I get you something to drink?"

Bailey ordered an iced tea, and Melinda paused for a moment before ordering the same.

"You don't have to avoid alcohol on my account," offered Bailey. "Feel free."

"In that case, I'll have a vodka on the rocks. I'm hitting Area later with Tony, so I'll start slowly."

"You and Tony are still good?" They'd been dating for a year now.

"You bet. I think marriage is in the cards. How do you feel about a new cousin-in-law?"

"If he makes you happy, I'm all for it. I'll even babysit when you guys start adding to the family tree."

Melinda giggled. "I guess I'll have to produce at least one little rug rat for the sake of the Camden legacy. It's not like Manvel is going to breed anytime soon. He's way too in love with his creepy country artists."

Bailey brushed some imaginary crumbs off the table. "Maybe he'll find a nice girl in Alabama to settle down with."

"I wouldn't stop him, in any case," said Melinda with a wink. "It isn't as though I'll be bumped down the line of inheritance if poor Manvel produces an heir. We each get an equal share, the day we turn thirty. Which is only a month away. Yee-haw, cuz!"

Melinda could play the family card all she liked, but she and Bailey weren't actually related. Not by blood, anyway. Melinda and Manvel were real Camdens, heirs to the Camden money, co-owners of the Dakota apartment. While Bailey was extraneous. A fake Camden, whose grandfather was granted the family name but not the birthright, when he was taken in as a baby. "It's not like we're really cousins, *cuz.*"

"Don't be ridiculous. Our grandparents were raised together, as if they were siblings. That makes us cousins, in my mind." Melinda took a sip of her drink. "Cheers to that."

Bailey's senses were overwhelmed by the glass in Melinda's hands. The clinking of the ice cubes, pink lipstick on the rim the color of cake frosting. Her own iced tea proved a bitter disappointment.

"So what now for you?" Melinda asked. "Back to Crespo & O'Reilly?"

"No. They won't have me back. Tristan made it clear that because of what I did, I'm a liability."

"Fuck them. You deserve better, after all the work and connections you made for them. Where are you staying?"

"At the apartment of my roommate from Silver Hill, down on Avenue A."

Melinda blinked a couple of times. "Is that the best neighborhood for someone fresh out of rehab to stay? Is your roommate a junkie?"

"Ex-junkie. Nice enough girl, just got herself in over her head. I make a point of staying in once it gets dark. Luckily, my fear of needles keeps me from falling down the rabbit hole of smack." Melinda's look of disdain was too much to bear. "How about you? How's the Dakota?"

"Ugh. It's falling apart. But now that the trust fund is coming due, I'm having it all redone. Tony and I are staying in the Hamptons, and I drive in every couple of weeks to check on things."

"Who's doing the work?"

A sheepish look passed over her face. "Tristan. He has some girl called Wanda in charge. I can't stand her." Melinda let out a squawk that startled a passing waiter. "I know! You can take over. I trust you more than him any day, and you can stay there and keep an eye on things. It's perfect. And it'll get you out of Alphabet City."

"But it's under renovation."

"You can hole up in the maid's room. It'll be great and you can oversee the work and I'll pay you." She paused. "As soon as the trust fund comes due."

A paycheck. A place to stay. Melinda's offer would solve a number of Bailey's short-term problems. Even if it came with a heavy dose of drama.

"You turn thirty in October, right?"

"You betcha. At which point I'll pay you in full and you'll be able to start your own business. Fuck Tristan."

Bailey had so far squandered all of her chances, and here was Melinda coming to the rescue. She reached over and hugged her across the table, breathing in the scent of Fracas perfume. This wasn't exactly how Bailey had figured her post-rehab life would play out. But maybe Melinda was right.

Maybe this was just the fresh start she was looking for.

Bailey smiled at the doorman as they entered the Dakota—if she was going to be working here, she would need the staff on her side—but he didn't respond. During her visits with her parents, she remembered the man stationed outside chattering away with them, handing out lollipops from a basket just inside the porter's office. But then again, so much had changed.

Across the street, a gaggle of tourists aimed their cameras toward the Dakota. They hadn't done that before Lennon's murder, when the building was grand and mysterious but not marred by tragedy. Or at least a world-famous tragedy, she amended, recalling the murder of Melinda's great-grandfather in the very apartment she'd be staying in.

"God, I hate this neighborhood," Melinda said as they crossed the courtyard. Bailey wanted to stop, take a look up, and relish all the cornices, finials, and gargoyles. It was like walking through a time portal and ending up in 1800s Europe, but Melinda moved at a fast clip.

"Why? What's wrong with the neighborhood?"

"It's a wasteland. All crappy little bodegas and run-down brownstones. Walking down Amsterdam Avenue is like trudging through a pigsty. Last week, when I came out of the deli, a guy standing outside spit right in front of me. Gross."

"That is gross."

"I'd rather live on the Upper East Side. I absolutely hate having to say I live in the Dakota. Never mind the buses of tourists gaping into the windows."

"You could move."

"I figure I'll sit it out for another few years, then sell. At least that's what Fred advises. He says it'll be worth a mint by then."

"Fred's still going strong?" Fred, the family's advisor on all things financial and legal, had steered the trust for the past twenty years, after taking over from his father and grandfather.

"Still telling me what to do, just like he told my mother what to do. Old fart." They exited the courtyard into the northeast corner foyer and waited for the elevator.

Bailey walked over to the stairway and ran her hand over the elaborately carved banister. "Gorgeous."

"I guess so. Everything's so heavy in here, it's like a mausoleum."

"But there's so much history."

"Whatever." Suddenly, Melinda let out a string of curses. "Quick, follow me."

Bailey looked outside into the courtyard to see a man with shaggy blond hair approaching. "Who's that?"

"The super. He's a total jerk. We've got to hide."

Melinda pulled her down the hallway and around a corner, out of sight from the foyer. They heard the man enter and then start up the stairs. Once his footsteps faded away, Melinda exhaled.

"Why do you have to hide from the super?"

"He's an ass. Hates me. I have no idea why. I give him a big tip every Christmas, but I think he wants more money, now that I'm renovating. You know how it is in New York. Everyone has their hand out."

Not a good sign. Getting the super on your side was crucial to working in the city. Without his support, the job would fall apart. The super could revoke access to freight elevators, harass the workers over minor infractions, and make life generally miserable for everyone involved.

The door to the apartment was unlocked. From the foyer, Bailey could see directly into the library, which had been stripped of all furniture, the barrenness emphasizing the enormous windows that looked right out on the park.

"Hello? Anyone home?" Melinda called out.

The response was a thundering bang from down the hall.

"Jesus."

Wanda's head popped out from the living room. "Melinda? I didn't know you'd be coming by today."

"Surprise! I've brought your colleague. Or former colleague, I should say."

Wanda stepped toward them. She was a ghost of a woman, with pale, flaxen hair and yellowish skin, and an unfortunate preference for neon colors that only served to enhance her pallor. She seemed to wilt perceptibly as she grew closer. Poor spineless Wanda. Tristan had probably been making her life impossible ever since Bailey left.

"Wanda, I'm afraid I have some bad news."

Wanda seemed near tears already. "Yes?"

"I'm letting you go. Tell Tristan the job is now in the hands of Bailey Camden, and she'll be taking over from here."

"I'm fired?"

"Yes. It's time for a change of direction, and Tristan's an ass for not giving Bailey a second chance, after all she did for him."

"You want me to tell him that?"

"Yes. Now off you go."

"But what about the workers?"

"They can stay on doing what they're doing. Their contract is with me, not Crespo & O'Reilly. Now scat."

Wanda gave a little shake of her head and skittered past them. Bailey couldn't help but feel sorry for the woman. She was in way above her head when it came to dealing with the strong personalities of the New York upper class.

"Ouch." Bailey waited until Wanda had closed the door behind her to speak. "That was harsh."

"Whatever. She's a peon. Now I can show you the masterpiece that I plan on building. You're going to love it."

They walked down the hallway, and Bailey looked into the living room, where the initial boom had come from. Two workers were up on ladders, prying a five-foot-long cornice from the top of the doorway that led to the library. It came loose and crashed to the ground.

"What are they doing? That's original. Why are they letting it drop?" The floor was already littered with shards of wood. "Be careful, don't let it break."

The men looked over at Melinda.

"Carry on." Melinda beckoned Bailey with her index finger, the nail of which was lacquered in fuchsia polish. "Come with me. I'll show you your new digs."

They turned right into the corridor that led to the kitchen. Bailey remembered there being several small rooms off of it, perfect for hiding when they were little. A bathroom, a pantry, a laundry room, she wasn't sure which was which. Melinda opened the last door on the right.

The room possessed none of the grandeur of the apartment's public spaces. In fact, it reminded her of her dorm at Silver Hill in its plainness and size, no bigger than a hundred square feet, with a small cot shoved against one wall. Maybe it would be a good thing to have some kind of continuity, to keep her baser desires in check. Still, it was depressing.

"You can stay here and oversee them so they don't fuck up any more than they have."

"Right. What exactly are you doing to the place?"

"That's the fun stuff. Let's sit down in the kitchen and I'll show you."

A binder lay on the kitchen table. Bailey recognized it as a client book from Crespo & O'Reilly. Wanda had forgotten to retrieve it in her haste to escape Melinda's wrath.

They sat at the table and Melinda leafed through it. "It's all cosmetic, we're not moving walls or anything like that."

"What's the look you're going for?"

"This place is dingy and dark and depressing. All that old wood is a bore, and Tony agrees that it could use a serious face-lift."

The hair on the back of Bailey's neck stood on end. "Face-lift?"

"Yes. We want it to be more of a Palm Beach feel, you know what I mean?"

"Pastels?"

"More than that. I want people to walk in and feel like they're entering a beachfront Roman villa. Here." She opened the binder. "We're stripping out everything and then redoing it. I want lots of trompe l'oeil, so we'll paint the columns as if they were marble, like with pink and gray veining. Tony's friend has a company that does that kind of thing and it's glorious. In the gallery, we'll use this cool sponge technique on the walls. I think it should be ochre but Tony wants more orangey. We'll decide once you get us swatches."

Bailey swallowed. The thought of painting over the fine wood and taking off all the molding made her sick. "Huh."

"I know, you're speechless, right?" She turned to the back of the binder, where furniture spec sheets had been inserted into clear plastic sleeves. "You can still get a designer discount at the showrooms, right?"

"Sure." Bailey flipped through. Gilt dining room chairs, armchairs covered in a leopard print, a Lucite coffee table. She didn't even know where to begin. In Malibu this might work, but there was something unseemly about doing this in the Dakota.

She closed the binder. "Are you sure? There's so much history in this apartment. Your family, Theodore Camden's legacy. It feels kind of drastic."

"I am so tired of hearing about Theodore Camden, blah, blah, blah. That was a hundred years ago. He's dead. Times change. Everyone in the building is doing this kind of thing." Melinda snorted. "Well, not everyone. There's some old fuddy-duddies who won't change a thing. But we have celebrities, musicians, artists, actors. It's all shag carpets and white walls and stainless steel. You of all people should know that."

Bailey did the calculations in her head. She had enough money in her bank account to cover basic living expenses, and if she could stay here during the renovation and end up with a big fat check, she'd be in good shape. It would give her time to catch her breath and figure out her next move. Maybe she'd have enough to start her own design firm.

Maybe Melinda was right. The apartment had a sad, old-person smell to it, a mix of laundry soap and stale rosewater.

"I'll take care of your renovation, and we'll celebrate the end of the job and your trust fund money coming in at the same time I launch Bailey Camden Designs." She held out her hand.

Melinda shook it and yelped with joy. "I'm your first official client. Remember me when you're a big star."

"I will do my best."

CHAPTER SEVEN

New York City, September 1884

Two days later, Sara hadn't slept more than a few hours a night. Whenever she tried, the list of what was still needed to be accomplished ran through her head, like a runaway train that refused to stop to let passengers off. Luckily, she was able to take the Langham's operations and apply most of it to the Dakota, drafting staff work schedules and committing to memory significant details, like Mrs. Knoblauch had not one but two butlers coming with her, and the Putnams loved to entertain and would be having their grand piano delivered within the week.

She'd arranged for regular coal and wood deliveries to begin the last week in October, and even made a point to visit the boarding stables a few streets away and introduce herself to the head groom. Hallways were swept and runners laid down, muffling the echo of footsteps and making the building feel less like an institution and more like a home. Or so she hoped.

She had seen very little of Mr. Douglas, which suited her, as his anxiety only increased her own. The few times she'd bumped into Mr. Camden, they'd exchanged basic pleasantries and she'd tried to appear calm and in control, to tamp down the unease lodged in her throat. Daisy had been a delight to work with, Mrs. Haines not as much, but that wasn't surprising. Sara had no doubt that Mrs. Haines would make an excellent gatekeeper for the residents, ensuring the unwashed masses didn't get through to their castle in the sky.

After a quick lunch in the staff room off the downstairs kitchen, Sara headed back to her office, where a stout woman stood in the reception area, an ermine wrap around her shoulders and an air of impatience coming off her like steam.

"May I help you?" Sara inquired.

"I certainly hope you may. I've been standing here for minutes, and no one has attended to me."

"I do apologize." Mrs. Haines, who should have been at her desk, was nowhere to be seen. Sara stepped closer. "I'm Mrs. Smythe, the managerette. What can I do for you?"

The woman sniffed. "I'm here to meet Mr. Hardenbergh. We have an appointment to view my apartment."

"Of course. May I ask your name?"

"Mrs. Horace Putnam."

Apartment 63. Mr. Putnam, an attorney, and his wife. They'd taken one of the larger apartments in the building, encompassing fifteen rooms including a parlor with twin fireplaces and Baccarat chandeliers.

"How lovely to meet you. I will be happy to escort you. Please come this way."

Sara's attempts at small talk were rebuffed as they crossed the courtyard. The door to number 63 was cracked open and Mr. Camden's voice, more passionate than usual, carried into the hallway.

"I am doing everything I can, Mr. Hardenbergh. You can't go back on your commitment."

A deeper voice responded. "I have made no promises. We must wait and see how things turn out. Don't try to force my hand, Theo."

Sara called out Mr. Camden's name in a loud voice, alerting him to their presence, as they entered. Mr. Camden stood in the foyer next to a tall, balding man. The waxed tips of his handlebar mustache curled up like parentheses.

"Why, Mrs. Putnam!" Mr. Hardenbergh stepped forward. "I'm eager to show you about. Please follow me."

Mrs. Putnam disappeared into the dining room with Mr. Hardenbergh. Sara glanced over at Mr. Camden.

"She's one of our toughest critics," whispered Mr. Camden. "Wants nothing to do with the place. Her husband is the one who's keen to move uptown."

"And that's Mr. Hardenbergh, I assume?"

Mr. Camden nodded as Mr. Hardenbergh's voice rang out from the other room. "We need you, Camden. And bring your woman as well."

Your woman. Lovely.

A long gallery ran the length of the apartment, and seemed to go on forever. Sara glanced into the rooms on either side as she made her way down. The library connected to a drawing room twice the size, and to the right was a wainscoted dining room, where Mrs. Putnam stood examining the corner china cabinets. "I don't like this wood. Too dark. Strip it down and replace it with something else."

"For the china cabinet?" asked Mr. Camden.

"No, the whole room."

Mr. Camden brought his hand to his forehead. "But this is the finest mahogany and oak."

"The Rutherfords imported some kind of tiger maple. I want that." She turned to Sara. "You're in charge of the moving, is that right?"

Sara nodded. "Yes, ma'am."

"I don't think my dining room table will fit. And I'm not getting a new one."

"I will determine the measurements with your housekeeper, Mrs. Putnam, and report back. If not, we can have a carpenter make adjustments."

"The doorknobs are sterling silver, is that right?"

Mr. Camden forced a smile. "Exactly as you directed."

"Excellent. I want more plaster molding on the walls and ceiling, covered in gold leaf. The room is rather dingy."

Dingy was the last word that came to mind. Mr. Camden stuttered but couldn't seem able to come up with a response, whether from shock or anger at the insult.

Mr. Hardenbergh fiddled with his mustache. "That will be no trouble at all." Sara didn't miss the pointed look at Mr. Camden as he spoke.

Sara spoke up. "I can see why you'd want to liven up the room. What if we ordered a set of Limoges jade dinnerware for the cabinets? The color would be lovely and bright."

The woman looked up as if seeing Sara for the first time. "Limoges. Right. That might work."

Mr. Camden's shoulders dropped an inch.

"And do the plaster as well. Gold leaf."

Mr. Hardenbergh offered to escort Mrs. Putnam back to her carriage. After they'd gone, Mr. Camden ran a hand through his hair. "This is the third time she's come in and demanded drastic changes. I have no time to redo this room. We're behind schedule as it is."

"Leave it for a week or so," advised Sara. "My guess is she'll have a new idea by then that may be less painful."

"Or more."

They laughed.

"Thank you for trying to reason with her," he said.

"Well, it's not like the building is subtle to begin with." She glanced away, hoping he wasn't offended.

"It's far from subtle. I see it as a last gasp in an age of excess. Maybe if I overdo it completely, as is all the rage, we will as a society move on more quickly to another way of design."

"There's much to look at. I especially like the gargoyles out front."

A smile crept over his face. "Now you are teasing me, I can tell. Save it for Mr. Hardenbergh. I promise I won't take it personally if you find it distasteful."

"*Distasteful* is too harsh a word. If you did indeed design this, it appears as if you enjoyed yourself. I see a sense of humor throughout. Is that your contribution?"

Mr. Camden shook his head. "You've found me out. I keep waiting for Hardenbergh to come down on me for taking it too far. Corncobs and Indians, for goodness' sake. Do you mind if I show you something?"

She really should be getting back to her desk, but she couldn't resist his enthusiasm.

They walked back down to his apartment. Mr. Camden laid his drawings out on the table in the library, blocking the glare with his own shadow. "Blasted sun. Here's my favorite contribution."

Mr. Camden was so close to her, she could feel his breath on her neck. She pressed her arms to her sides, embarrassed by the intimacy, as he pointed to a drawing of the low fence that encircled the building. The cast-iron visage of a man with a long, fluffy beard and mustache emerged from each post, with a couple of dragons coiled around the horizontal railings at either side. "Is he supposed to be Father Christmas?"

Mr. Camden's lip curled up on one side, as if he were trying not to laugh. "It's a sea god entwined with sea urchins."

She couldn't help teasing. "Sea gods and sea urchins, of course. That was my second guess."

"Just wait until the city gets a sight of what we've done up here. Hardenbergh's reputation will be solidified."

"And yours?"

"I've only just begun. Hardenbergh has promised to help me start up my own firm if the Dakota does well."

"Won't you be in competition with each other?"

"Not at all. He'll continue on with his grand apartment houses and hotels. I want something else entirely. I'm like the canary in the coal mine. If my vision takes off, he'll have a stake in it. If not, he won't have risked any damage to his reputation."

A gust of wind made the drawings flutter. Mr. Camden placed a paperweight on the edge to keep them still.

"It's awfully bright in here." Sara pointed to the window. "You really need some draperies. That would help with the wind as well."

"I hadn't thought of that. I'll see if the tailor can put something together."

Sara had seen the tailor's room in the basement, which so far was empty of everything other than a sewing machine.

"I'm afraid he's not set up yet. I can make you something, if you like. It won't be grand, but at least it will keep out the light."

He looked up. "Could you?"

"I apprenticed as a seamstress, before going to London."

"That's right, you had mentioned it. But then you ended up working in a hotel?"

"Yes." She quickly changed the subject. "I could have them for you within the week, once I have the fabric."

A lopsided grin crossed his face. "Say, have you been into town yet?"

"No, there's been no time."

"You need to see the sights. Tomorrow morning, then. At the same time, I can check in at the office and we can purchase some fabric for the drapes. Thank you for offering to make them—as long as you're sure it won't take you away from your duties."

"Of course not. I assume you'd like them to be Limoges green?" She couldn't help but tease, and was rewarded when he laughed out loud. She liked his laugh.

"I knew I made the right decision to ship you overseas, Mrs. Smythe."

Sara slipped out into the hallway before he could notice the blush spreading across her cheeks.

CHAPTER EIGHT

New York City, September 1884

Sara had been asleep only a few hours when the sound of heavy footsteps woke her up. A man's footsteps. They stopped, and for a moment she thought she'd imagined it. A storm had rocketed through earlier in the evening, bringing with it lightning and fierce, rolling thunder, like the dynamite used to break through the granite boulders along the avenues. But this sound wasn't thunder. She strained to listen, but now all was still. Unnaturally so.

Someone was outside, in the hallway.

She put her ear against the door but heard only the blood drumming in her ears. She grabbed a poker from the fireplace and yanked the door open.

A man.

He wasn't one of the staff, she was fairly certain of that. In the dim light, he appeared to be in his late twenties, with a dark beard and mustache.

Her voice quavered. "Who are you? What are you doing here?"

He looked away, behind her. "I work here, a builder. Sorry, ma'am. Got lost, is all."

"No one is meant to be here after hours."

From around the corner, Mrs. Haines appeared, pulling her wrapper around her and carrying a lamp. "He came out of Daisy's room."

The man tensed.

Sara's insides crumpled with fear. Her breathing was shallow, cutting off the possibility of speech.

"How many are you, then?" The man had a rough voice, thick with menace.

Mrs. Haines glanced over at Sara, her face white with fear.

Sara held the fireplace poker firmly in her hand, pointed midway between the floor and horizontal. At the ready. "There are eight of us on this floor."

The man eyed the poker, then Sara. "Eight? Where are the other five, then?"

"You best be gone."

"Is that right?"

His sneering tone reminded her of Mr. Ainsworth, from when she apprenticed as a seamstress. Someone who enjoyed wielding power. As well as Mr. Birmingham, with his filthy looks at the young Langham maids. The Dakota was now her domain, her responsibility, and the thought of this man strutting about like a peacock, as if he owned the place, infuriated her.

An electrical energy surged through Sara. Without thinking, she heaved the poker up over her head and let out a scream that echoed down the hallway, hurting her own ears. The dramatic transformation, from quivering lady in distress to screeching madwoman, worked. In a flash the man was gone, sprinting down the hall and turning the corner. The poker fell to the floor with a clatter, leaving a white scar in the newly varnished floor.

Mrs. Haines and Sara scrambled around the corner. Daisy's door was cracked open and at first it seemed the room was empty. Until the girl emerged from behind the bed, crying.

A wave of memories flooded over Sara. Of smiling at the seamstress's husband, who was so kind at first. Of him moving past her and brushing his hand over the small of her back, a gesture that was difficult to parse as to its exact meaning. Of such pride in her work, in what she could accomplish at the sewing machine, and how wonderful it was to hear compliments from him, as his wife was so dour and cold. She'd been a young, eager girl, like Daisy.

"Daisy, are you all right?"

Daisy took a moment to answer, as her big eyes filled with tears. "Yes, Mrs. Smythe. I was in my room and he entered, and . . ." She trailed off.

Sara grabbed Mrs. Haines and Daisy and herded them into her own room, then locked the door behind her. Together, she and Mrs. Haines lifted the desk and placed it in front of the door. She grabbed a handkerchief and sat next to Daisy on the bed. "Here, take this."

"He said he was lost, but then he pushed his way inside." Daisy's voice wavered with fear.

"There now, we're safe." Sara looked up at Mrs. Haines, whose face was pale in the lamplight. "We'll stay together until the morning. He can't get out through the gate, as Fitzroy locked it behind him, so he'll be discovered when they all arrive."

She went to the window, hoping that she might see Mr. Camden and call for help, but all was dark in the courtyard below. "I'll discuss this with Mr. Camden first thing and make sure it doesn't happen again." Hopefully, Mr. Camden slept with his doors locked.

"I'll feel better when the other residents arrive," said Daisy.

"No matter what, you ought to lock your door and never open it to an unfamiliar voice." Mrs. Haines's tone was chiding.

And unacceptable. "The poor girl has been through enough," said

Sara. "Let's leave her be." She didn't know how to ask the question that dogged her. "How long was he in your room?"

"Only a minute or so. I fought back the best I could."

"You were very heroic."

Mrs. Haines took a seat in the upright chair against the wall. "They shouldn't leave us trapped in here with no protection," said Mrs. Haines. "We all could have been killed. We still could be."

She was right, but Sara didn't respond. Daisy lay on Sara's bed, her head in her lap.

"Poor girl." Sara stroked her hair. "We're here now."

Sara and Mrs. Haines stayed up, listening to the soft sleeping breath of Daisy, craning their ears for the sounds of footsteps, until the dawn broke.

At the clanging of the front gate, Sara and Mrs. Haines gently woke Daisy. Sara led the way downstairs, where Fitzroy manned the entryway as the workmen traipsed into the courtyard, joking and yelling at each other.

"There's a man here, on the loose," Sara said. Fitzroy's eyes squinted with concern as she recounted last night's episode.

Fitzroy immediately closed and locked up the gate. He shouted for the foreman to take a head count and then asked the women to wait in the reception room while they did a search. Mr. Camden was called for and his tone remained soothing as he questioned a teary Daisy, patting her shoulder when he was finished. The protective gesture almost caused Sara to burst into tears herself. If only she'd had someone who'd seen fit to do the same after her own encounter with Mr. Ainsworth.

Fitzroy blew through the door, huffing. "A window on one of the eastern apartments on the first floor is broken from the inside. He got out that way. I swear, though, Mrs. Haines and I accounted for all the workers at the end of the day yesterday."

Mrs. Haines nodded but remained silent.

"I assure you we will not let this happen again," Mr. Camden said to Daisy. "Fitzroy, get that window repaired this morning and we will require a watchman here at night. No point in waiting for the official opening."

"I'll add them to the payroll," offered Sara.

"I'm very sorry, sir," said Fitzroy.

"You should be." Mr. Camden glared at him. "The press and the rest of the city are waiting to see the Dakota fail. A scandal like this would have ruined us before a tenant steps foot inside."

"Right, sir." The man looked every one of his sixty-odd years.

"Mrs. Smythe, let's speak in your office." Mr. Camden dismissed the others.

She followed him inside, shutting the door behind her.

He paced the small room. "Again, my apologies for the intrusion. It pains me to think I was here the entire time but wasn't able to come to your aid."

"We are fine, and I have no doubt Fitzroy won't let it happen again."

"As a father, the thought of a strange man roaming the halls and breaking into Daisy's room is abhorrent."

His protective nature toward his family touched her, but a small sizzle of jealousy flared underneath. She liked the idea that they were friends, and having his family around would no doubt change that once they arrived.

What an awful, selfish thought. She vowed to be more generous.

He placed his hands on his hips and lowered his chin. "I'm afraid I must ask a delicate question."

"Yes?"

"Does Daisy need a doctor?"

Sara breathed deeply. "I don't believe so. The girl insisted that he'd only been in her room for a minute. I believe she was unharmed."

Mr. Camden looked away, embarrassed. "I am glad of that. In any case, if you do think there's any need for further help, I hope you won't hesitate to reach out to me."

"Of course not."

She wondered if he still remembered his offer to go into town for curtain fabric. She'd been looking forward to seeing more of the city. Even now, the odor of the dank pigsties wafting in from outside reminded her how far out in the hinterlands she was.

Mr. Camden stood to go but paused at the door. "And let's not forget—"

"Yes?"

"The housemaids will be arriving this week. Are you prepared to get them settled?"

"Of course. I've already assigned them rooms and plan on conducting an orientation."

"Excellent. And for the trip into town, shall we meet at the front gate at ten o'clock?"

He'd remembered. She smiled, then tamped it down. It was a trip to town, after all, nothing to be so excited about. A similar excitement had very nearly ruined her years ago, while in Mrs. Ainsworth's employ, and she had remained wary of the ulterior intentions of men ever since. Yet in the intervening decade and a half, she'd proved uncanny at detecting the cur among gentlemen, and Mr. Camden seemed to fall into the latter category. "Very good, sir."

To Sara's delight, Mr. Camden arranged for an open landau for the journey, which meant she could view the city without obstruction. Her gaze swiveled around left and right as he pointed out various mansions along Fifth Avenue below the park.

He ordered the carriage to stop at Fifty-Second Street. "Behold the masterpiece that made Richard Morris Hunt the most sought-after architect in New York."

Sara gasped out loud. "Is this a house for one family?"

"Not just any family. The Rutherfords. Mr. Stafford Rutherford and his wife, Mrs. Alma Rutherford."

The pale limestone, littered with a multitude of gables, balconies, and finials, seemed to shimmer in the sunlight, rendering it like a mirage compared to the earthen-colored buildings nearby. The structure resembled a doll's house that had been grossly inflated, as if at any moment it might burst through the severe iron gate that surrounded it. It belonged on a mountaintop in Europe, not a crowded city street.

The design was so ostentatious she almost laughed out loud. "I'm not sure where I'm supposed to look," said Sara finally.

"There are four thousand millionaires in the city, every one of them trying to top the other. I call the current movement European wedding cake."

"I have to agree. It's awfully loud."

He smiled down at her. "Like the Dakota, no?"

"The Dakota is rather busy as well, I must admit. But it's a showpiece, and I assume that's what the tenants want. If they can't live in one of the Fifth Avenue mansions, why not take up in a building even bigger and fancier?"

"What kind of house would you like to live in, Mrs. Smythe?"

No one had asked her anything of that nature before. Flustered, she couldn't answer right off. Indeed, she had never imagined living somewhere other than the London bedsit or her Dakota garret. Her place of residence had been secondary to her place of work, always.

"I like my current lodgings perfectly well."

"That's not what I asked."

"What would you design if you could do anything, and not have to answer to Mr. Hardenbergh or the Mrs. Putnams of the world?"

"You're dodging the question." He gestured for the driver to go forward.

"Very well, then. I suppose a cottage in the country, with a small garden. That would suffice."

"Not at all. I won't have it. If you had all the money in the world and could build anything you wanted, here on Fifth Avenue, what would it look like?"

"To think that this is what you do all day, come up with designs. I admit, I haven't the faintest idea. Certainly not a Richard Morris Hunt mansion. I'd get lost on my way to breakfast."

He let out a guffaw that pleased her.

"I will draw you a house, how's that? Once all the chaos has calmed down and the Dakota is moving along smoothly, I'll draw you something. Even if it's a thatched-roof cottage that reminds you of home."

She looked away. Home. As soon as she received her first paycheck, Sara would send half of it back to the cottage at Fishbourne, with a short, cheery note assuring her mother that all was well. Hopefully, that would alleviate the guilt at having moved so far away, but she knew better than to expect a letter of thanks or a return letter at all. Not from Mum.

By the time the carriage made it to Grand Street, Mr. Camden had pointed out the many ways the city had changed during the past several decades, from the weathered wood shacks that dated back a hundred years, to Federal-era brick dwellings, and finally the chocolate brownstones that now dominated the side streets. They passed the Academy of Music, where members of New York's high society gathered for a taste of culture, and a rustic Gothic Revival church on Twentieth Street where they prayed.

Mr. Camden was the only man in the fabric shop other than the store owner, but he didn't seem to mind. Together, he and Sara examined silks and damasks, but he dismissed both as too heavy and unwieldy. "I know Mrs. Camden will want to hang something like this once she arrives, but for now I simply need something to block out the harsh rays and still let in light."

"How about this?" Sara pointed to a tea-colored sheer.

"That will do nicely." He gestured to the shopkeeper, who came running over.

"When do you expect your family to arrive?" she asked as the fabric was wrapped in brown paper and string.

"Sometime after opening day." He gestured back to the shelves stacked with a rainbow of fine material. "Now you must pick out something for your own windows."

"No, indeed. My windows have shutters and they'll do fine." She ran her finger over a spare piece of black ribbon that lay on the counter.

"Here you are doing me an enormous favor, and I must return it. How about this?" He pointed to an exquisite, finely woven white lace.

"Oh no, sir. I couldn't."

"I insist."

She couldn't help but imagine how they would look in her windows, waving in the breeze when she woke each day.

She bit her cheek to stop from breaking out into a beaming smile and thanked him profusely as he put her back in the carriage bound for the Dakota.

Mr. Camden shook his head. "No need to thank me. I'm still making it up to you for saving my daughter's life. Now I owe you a second debt for putting off Daisy's attacker. I figure you're a good one to have in my corner, and I'll do whatever it takes to keep you there."

How different Mr. Camden was from the other men she'd encountered at work. He needed no assurance that he was powerful, the way Mr. Birmingham at the Langham had, no tests of loyalty. He seemed to simply enjoy her industriousness, as well as her company.

His words stayed with her the entire journey home.

CHAPTER NINE

New York City, September 1985

Once the workers left, Bailey spent an hour examining the apartment and the architectural drawings of the renovation. True, it was mainly cosmetic, but most of Melinda's ideas consisted of either stripping off the original details or covering over them, remaking the place into something else entirely. While change was well and good, there was no way around the basic configuration of the place: skinny hallways, huge expanses of great rooms, a nest of smaller ones clustered around the kitchen. The bones of the place screamed "tradition," not "Barbie beach house." But it was Melinda's money.

Usually, Bailey was able to keep her mouth shut when a client wanted something that she found to be outrageous and in bad taste. Obviously, the truth had begun squeaking out over the past few years, fueled by her drinking, culminating in her massive verbal slap-down of Mrs. Ashfield-Simmons and her half-wit daughter. But for some reason, the idea of giving the family's Dakota apartment a major face-lift really irked her. Bailey's own grandfather, Christopher Camden, had spent his childhood in these same rooms, after being taken in as the ward of Theodore Camden, the celebrated architect, and his aristocrat wife, Minnie. Bailey had never really known her grandfather—he'd died when she was a baby—but she felt a curious sort of pride in the Dakota apartment because of his history here. It wasn't a sense of ownership exactly; she understood her place too well for that.

But it was something.

Bailey's father never said much at all about Grandpa Christopher. Bailey got the impression that he was a crusty sort when her dad was growing up, not what you'd call a warm or involved parent. A man from a different era, with a different way of thinking, who left home at the age of fifteen, joined the navy, and ended up fixing cars in New Jersey.

On the way to each pilgrimage to visit Sophia and the twins, Bailey's mother would question her father about what exactly happened back then, only to be met with a couple of shrugs at best. The fact that Grandpa Christopher had completely cut ties with the Camdens was absurd, according to Peggy. Surely, there must have been some kind of mistake or misunderstanding.

But maybe Bailey's grandfather wasn't interested in living the same way his foster parents did. Maybe he thought the rest of the family were terrible snobs or something. If so, Bailey's sentimental attachment to the Dakota was sadly misplaced. Perhaps the Camdens were so mean to Christopher, an outsider, when he was a kid that he would have loved to see the place trashed.

Like Bailey, Peggy had been enamored of the building. She would enter the Dakota courtyard wearing big sunglasses as if she were a movie star, even on the cloudiest day. But Bailey knew they were mainly for hiding her sidelong glances into the dizzying array of dark windows that surrounded them, hoping to catch a glimpse of one of the famous inhabitants. How excited Peggy would have been to learn that Bailey was not only working, but living, in the building.

A cold sweat made Bailey shiver. Even though it had been years since the accident, the thought that her mother's physical being no longer existed—or no, it did exist and, even worse, was buried in South Jersey's sandy soil—still gutted her.

Bailey made the long journey down to the East Village, collected her two suitcases, and unpacked back at the Dakota. It took all of three minutes. Luckily, she'd stashed most of her belongings in her dad's basement in New Jersey before moving into the ex-boyfriend's cramped apartment, which had probably kept them from being pawned off during her stint at Silver Hill. Not that she needed much at the moment.

Her stomach grumbled. *HALT.* God, she had been conditioned. It was more like brainwashing than substance abuse counseling: Avoid being hungry, angry, lonely, or tired if you want to stay sober. Well, she was all four, when it came right down to it. She stood in line at a pizza place on Columbus and then wolfed down a couple of slices back in the apartment's library, where a ratty folding table had been set up to review plans. She really should find an AA meeting nearby, but it was getting dark and she didn't feel like wandering around without having a better idea of the neighborhood, which streets to steer clear of, which were safe. Tomorrow, for sure.

A scratching noise up in the ceiling caught her attention. Mice, most likely. What a field day the critters must have in this building, with its thick, horsehair-stuffed walls and three feet of mud between each story. Plenty of room to make nests from which to make forays into the residents' kitchens and feast on crumbs. The thought was weirdly comforting.

The mirror on the opposite wall reflected her image back to her. At thirty, after a decade of hard living, the skin around Bailey's eyes had lost the baby smoothness of her teenage years. But lately her face had begun to fill out, as the hollowness of addiction disappeared. Without alcohol and drugs, she'd started eating again, hence the two slices of pizza.

She'd always thought her hair and eyes to be unremarkable, brown on brown, her mouth too large. As a young girl, people often asked her if she was about to cry when she was just lost in space, thinking about something, minding her own business. Her mother had liked to say she had a "kind" face. Whatever that meant.

Bailey pushed her hair behind her ears. God, that perm. Never again.

She sat back and looked about her, her gaze settling on the spot where Theodore Camden had been murdered. Poor man, struck down in his own home. She hoped his ghost wouldn't come back and haunt her for the destruction of his property.

Bailey walked back to the kitchen, tossed the pizza box into the trash, and reluctantly stepped into her tiny room. In the darkness, it was no longer cozy or reminiscent of Silver Hill. It was the servant's apartment, where the kitchen maid, or whoever, had made a tiny life by serving other people, and then probably died after she was no longer of use, with no pension, no security.

That would not be Bailey's fate. She had her wits about her now, her mind no longer clouded with toxic substances. The cot creaked beneath her as she lay flat on her back, exhausted. After being abandoned in her teens without any guidance at all, she had been shown a world of pleasure and fun by Melinda, and it had been a wild ride. But no more. Bailey had veered toward a dangerous precipice the past few years, and now she had an opportunity to straighten herself out.

The jarring sound of the doorbell woke her the next morning. Bailey opened her eyes. A soft, gray light came through the window of the room. Her watch said it was seven o'clock, too early for the workers to be here. She pulled on her jeans and threw a sweater over her T-shirt.

"Hold on, I'm coming."

The ringing became incessant. For God's sake.

She unlocked the door and swung it open. An elderly black man stood before her, wearing suit pants, a crisp white shirt, and purple bow tie. Deep creases lined his forehead and cheeks, and the pouches of skin below his eyes drooped, lending him a sleepy air. Yet his carriage was that of a far younger man: tall, upright, and broad shouldered.

He didn't look happy.

"Can I help you?"

"I hope you can. I live right below you and water is streaming down from the ceiling of my bathroom."

Bailey rushed to the bathroom in the master bedroom. The workers had yanked out the grand claw-footed bathtub the day before, in order to replace it with some monstrous hot tub.

A dripping noise came from the floor.

"The pipes must've broken," said Bailey. "I'll call my guys right now and get them here to fix it."

"You bet you will."

Bailey sighed.

What had she gotten herself into?

⚜

The plumber agreed to come right over after Bailey phoned him. She reluctantly trooped back down the stairs to tell the other tenant, and realized that she didn't even know his name.

He answered her knock, his mouth set in a firm line. Bailey had dealt with angry residents in adjacent apartments during other renovations. It was standard practice in New York City to piss off at least two out of four during a renovation.

"Hi, me again."

He raised his gray eyebrows.

"The plumber will be here in an hour and he'll figure out what's wrong. I've turned off the water, so at least the worst is over."

"You think so?"

"Yes. I do. Is it all right if I take a look at your bathroom? That way I'll be able to figure out which tradespeople to call to put it back in order."

"You may."

He opened the door and let her in. The apartment was one of the smaller ones, but with the high ceilings it really didn't matter. Especially as almost every inch of wall space was covered in framed paintings from multiple eras, a joyful abstract pop art inches away from a stern, nineteenth-century portrait. The Victorian sofa and chairs were loaded with mismatched throws, while rugs of all sizes and colors zigzagged along the floorboards. The effect was dizzying, like being inside a spinning kaleidoscope.

"I'm afraid I didn't get your name?" She held out her hand.

His grip was soft, his fingers long and delicate. "I'm Kenneth Worley."

"Bailey Camden. I'm the interior designer slash owner's rep for Melinda Camden. Pleased to meet you, although I'm sorry it's under these circumstances."

"As am I."

The ceiling of his bathroom looked like a wet diaper, with enormous bubbles of plaster threatening to burst through at any moment. Water stains marred the wallpaper, a gorgeous pattern of wild roses, and obviously antique.

"God, this wallpaper is ruined. I'm so sorry."

"Yes. It was put up in the roaring twenties. I'm guessing I won't find its replacement." Although his voice stayed even, she detected a faint sense of panic behind the words. He blinked a couple of times. Was he on the verge of tears?

"No, sir. You won't. But I will find something as similar as I can. Or I'll draw it on the walls myself."

She was half joking, but he seemed to take her seriously, giving her a nod of his head. "I take it you know Melinda well?"

"I do. We're related. Very distantly." That was the best way to put it, probably.

He surveyed the room, as if memorizing it, then turned to her. "I need a cup of coffee. Would you like one?"

Bailey nodded and followed Kenneth into the kitchen, uncertain where she stood with this man.

From what she could tell, the layout consisted of a small bedroom, a living room, and the kitchen tucked back on the other side of the dining room. All the period details remained intact, the cherry floors and fireplace gleaming as if they were encased in ice. Along the top of the kitchen cabinets, he'd arranged a dozen colorful cookie jars.

"Your home is lovely," she said. "It's obvious you've taken good care of it."

"Unlike Melinda upstairs, who's dismantling the place, from what I hear each day."

"She's not dismantling. Well, maybe she is. But it's part of a new look."

Kenneth poured her a cup of coffee and one for himself. "Sugar or cream?"

"Neither. I think I'll be needing it black today."

"You will. Look, I know I sound like an old grump, but Melinda's no different from the rest of the new generation, or most of them, anyway. No respect for the history of the place."

"I have to say I agree."

"You're just a young girl; what do you know about history?"

"I know that they called this the Dakota because it was so far away from the rest of New York at the time."

"And you would be wrong." A sly smile appeared on his face.

"That's not true?"

"Not at all. The owner, Edward Clark, was enamored of the American West and hoped to name everything on the West Side, including the avenues, after territories and states. Luckily, he was overruled, so instead of the ghastly moniker Idaho Place, we have West End Avenue. The story you refer to was mentioned in passing during a press tour on the building's fiftieth anniversary, as mere speculation, and took on a life of its own."

His eloquence and knowledge delighted her. "I stand corrected. But I do know that Melinda's great-grandfather helped design and build this place. I keep wondering what he'd think of her redecorating plans." She took a sip of coffee—it was strong and delicious. "How long have you lived here?"

"I came to work here back in the late thirties."

"You worked here?"

"As a butler. Right before the war. After that, they began letting in the artistic types. Lauren Bacall, Leonard Bernstein, Rosemary Clooney. It was a fun place to work, even if the snooty old guard were unhappy with all of us throwing parties, having a gay old time. Literally."

"It must've been wonderful."

He shrugged. "I wouldn't go that far. I may own this apartment, but that doesn't mean I belong. Oh, three or four of the old housekeepers and nannies were tucked away in studios on the ninth floor after their shelf lives expired. But I lucked out. My dear boss, Oscar—of course everyone knew we were shagging but no one spoke of it—left me this place in his will. All gloriously mine, so I could die in peace, other than Sophia Camden's disdain whenever we passed in the courtyard. And the fact that my bathroom is now wrecked."

Bailey could only imagine the outrage Melinda's mother and some of the other longtime residents had directed Kenneth's way at the very idea of a servant turning shareholder. Taking over an entire apartment, as if he were their equal.

"I promise you I'll make it look as good as new. Or as old." She got a smile out of him at that. The coffee was taking over her brain, making her feel a nice buzz. Honestly, waking up to a strong cup of coffee was a better drug than any of the others she'd dropped over the past decade. "You must have seen so many changes during your stay here."

"More than you know. This place used to have a tenants' dining room, down on the main floor, though the food got less interesting after the war, and they eventually closed it down. By then the tailor had moved out, as had the laundry and maid service. No one valued what a special place this was. In the sixties, I remember, before it became a co-op, you could rent a seventeen-room apartment with six bathrooms and eight working fireplaces for six hundred and fifty bucks a month."

Bailey found her mouth watering at the idea.

A half hour later, the plumber—a stocky guy with a thick Polish accent—arrived. He prodded the ceiling and shook his head. "This'll take a couple days."

Kenneth sighed. "I shall wash up in the maid's bathroom until then."

Bailey put a hand on his arm. "Thank you for being so understanding. Once it's fixed, I'll have my contractor stop by and we'll discuss the plaster and wallpaper."

"I trust you to find a replacement wallpaper, if you like."

"Would you? I'd be happy to do so." Bailey knew exactly which vendor in the D&D Building, the wholesale resource for every designer in the city, would have a similar pattern.

"In the meantime, I want to see Melinda's apartment, so I can get a sense of how much history you're destroying."

Upstairs, Kenneth ran his fingers over the woodwork like a lover as Bailey led him through each room. "The craftsmanship still blows my mind."

"Melinda wants a clean look, which means tearing all this down. I have to admit, it kills me to have to do it."

"You know you can save it."

He had her full attention. "How?"

"You can put it in storage in the basement. They have the original elevators down there, lots of crown molding and fireplace mantels. You name it. Then, in thirty years when the pendulum swings back to appreciating a traditional look, the new owners will be able to replace what was lost."

"I'm so happy to hear that. It makes me feel less like a tyrant with a wrecking ball. I'll talk to the super and arrange that."

"Yes, you'll want to talk to Renzo. He's part of the Dakota mafia as well. His father was super here for practically his entire life, until he passed away."

"I haven't met Renzo officially yet. Melinda seems to want to avoid him."

"He can be a bit testy. You should make sure to bring your game face."

"Why's that?"

Kenneth shrugged. "We've had a spate of unfortunate, and by 'unfortunate' I mean *hideous*, renovations of late, and he's wary of outsiders."

She was doomed. "I'll treat him with kid gloves."

They were interrupted by a knock on the door.

She recognized the super from the quick peek she got of him out in the courtyard with Melinda. Renzo had arrived.

He looked Bailey up and down, which was a thoroughly unpleasant experience. He wasn't looking at her like a man checks out a woman but as if she were some alien from Pluto.

"I hear you've damaged the riser." He looked to be in his late thirties. His strong Italian name didn't match his gray eyes and fair hair, which hung just above his shoulders. The hippie look was long gone, but he seemed to have missed the news.

Bailey held out her hand. "Good morning, we haven't been introduced. I'm Bailey Camden."

He held up a dust-covered hand, palm out. She withdrew hers. "I was in Kenneth's apartment ripping down the ceiling."

"Aren't you the sweetest." Kenneth swooped behind Bailey. "Bailey and I were just discussing the fabulous wallpaper she's going to put up to replace the damaged one."

"The one in your apartment was from the 1920s. Not sure how you're going to find an equivalent."

What an ass. Here she'd solidified what she hoped was a little bit of goodwill from an unfortunate situation, and the super was stirring things up again.

"I'll make sure Kenneth is taken care of, that the bathroom is fully restored. I've already assured him of that." She couldn't help herself. "You seem to be more upset than he is, at the moment."

"I am, if this is the way your contractors plan on carrying out the renovation. The 'cosmetic' renovation."

"Right. I'm new to this project, so bear with me as I play catch-up, but I believe they filed an amendment with the Department of Buildings last week. The leak might have happened whether or not there was construction going on. The building is over one hundred years old, after all."

He cocked his head. "Where's Wanda?"

"My firm has taken over. I'm the new owner's rep."

"Does the building management know?"

"Since I just took over yesterday, no. But I'll phone them today and give them all my information."

Kenneth touched Renzo lightly on the arm. "She's a good egg, Renzo. Don't be so hard on her. Look, show her the storage rooms so she can save some of the loot from the reno. She's on our side, you'll see."

"Fine. I'll be in my office in an hour." Renzo studied Bailey again. "Tell your contractors to salvage anything they can."

Bailey took the elevator down to the basement at the appointed time. The lowest level of the Dakota was bright, with well-lit hallways and a fresh coat of paint on the walls. The area directly under the courtyard was mostly open space, other than an office built off to one side that had a large glass window. She knocked on the door.

"Come in."

The room overflowed with newspapers, green industrial filing cabinets, and cardboard boxes, but Renzo sat at a grand desk, an antique from the looks of it, made of ebony and elm. The harsh fluorescent lighting accentuated its incongruity, like a sapphire in a puka necklace. On the wall opposite was an oak cabinet, the doors wide open, displaying tools of every size and shape, small and large drawers, cubbyholes and shelves. A masterpiece of design and utility, everything in its place. This was a man who prized his wrenches.

She'd win him over with flattery. "That's a beautiful desk."

He shrugged. "A lucky hand-me-down from a former tenant."

"And what a cabinet. Did you design it?"

"My father did."

"Stunning. Do you do woodwork as well?"

"I used to, but there's no time these days." He looked annoyed. She'd overplayed it.

Bailey made a mental note to ask Melinda for a hundred dollars to hand him when she saw him next, as a way of greasing the wheel. The cost of doing business in Manhattan. Until then, she'd have to tread carefully.

"You were going to show me the storage unit for the apartment?"

He rose and grabbed a huge key chain from his desk. "Follow me."

They turned down a passageway with doors on either side, every five feet or so, like a prison. Renzo stopped in front of the one marked 45 and found the key. He unlocked and pushed it open. Inside, a bare lightbulb hung from the ceiling. He pulled the chain.

The space was empty, except for a stack of dusty tiles piled up in one corner.

Bailey shook her head. "I won't be able to store everything in here. It won't all fit. Melinda's taking down the mantels, the molding. Everything."

"Why?"

She was unprepared for the question. "Because her taste sucks."

"And yours doesn't?"

She hadn't realized how close they were standing. He smelled like wood chips and grease. Not a bad combination, surprisingly. She'd market it as ManSmell, The Cologne. The thought made her smile.

Renzo rubbed his eyebrow with the inside of his wrist. The veins on his forearms were thick, a faint purple blue. "It's not funny, what's going on. A new shareholder on the fifth floor tossed out everything before I could stop them."

"I heard you were able to keep the original elevators. I'd love to see them."

"Three of them were taken in by tenants. One's become a sitting alcove, another tenant combined two to make a bar."

"That's thinking outside the box. And the fourth?"

"Gone. It disappeared."

"How can an elevator disappear?"

"Not sure. During my father's reign. My guess is one of the contractors realized its value and stole it. But no one was held responsible."

A loud noise rumbled through the basement, like an earthquake. Bailey looked up in alarm.

"Just the subway. Although sometimes I do hear screaming at night."

He was trying to scare her.

Bailey shrugged. "I assume a place like this has lots of ghosts, so much tragedy inside these walls."

"We don't discuss that. Not with outsiders."

"I'm not exactly an outsider. My grandfather was raised here; he was Theodore Camden's ward. There's another tragedy for you. Another murder. Almost like the building's cursed."

"You have no idea what you're talking about."

He looked like he was about to lock her in the storage room and leave her there. She'd told Kenneth she'd handle the guy with kid gloves. Even if he didn't really deserve it. Talk about prickly.

"Sorry. I didn't mean to overreach." She stepped out of the small space. "Is there somewhere else you'd like us to put everything?"

He led her to another locked door. She'd become disoriented, and was no longer sure which side of the building they were on. The room was all interior, no windows at all. He flicked on the light switch and she caught her breath. It was a catacomb for the glorious detritus of the Dakota: four claw-footed tubs, dentil molding, mantels, baseboards, dozens of massive mahogany pocket doors. Her eye traveled over piece after piece, some in fine condition, others nicked and scratched. An old chandelier sat on top of a beat-up grand piano, and a trio of trunks were piled up in the far corner.

"This is so sad. Like the Land of the Forgotten Toys."

"At least we know things are safe here." He pointed to the trunks. "You can have your guys move those into the alcove to make more room. But you'll need to supervise your workers both coming and going. I don't want to find anything missing."

"I'll make sure everything goes smoothly."

"Like earlier at Kenneth's?"

She'd had enough of his smugness. "You know as well as I do that when renovations happen in New York City, things break. I've offered to make it right, and, to be honest, I'm not sure what else you expect me to do. I can't change my client's tastes. This is my job, this is how I make money."

His lips parted, as if he was about to say something. But instead, he slid the key to the room off the key ring and placed it in Bailey's palm.

"Give this back to me when you're through."

He turned and walked away, leaving her unsure if they'd reached a détente or if she'd simply harangued him into submission.

CHAPTER TEN

New York City, September 1884

Sara awoke early the day after the trek into town and headed downstairs to the tailor's room. The Singer sewing machine was one of the latest models, with ample room for cloth on the walnut cabinet and a smooth, shiny shuttle. She placed her feet on the treadle, gave the shuttle a whirl, and the machine clattered into action. The years away from a sewing machine had taken their toll, and at first the work took longer than usual. She couldn't help but worry that Mrs. Camden, with her fine upbringing, might make fun of the curtains when she eventually saw them. Laugh with her husband at the sight of such simple window dressings.

Eventually, the fabric slid under her fingers with ease. Once finished, she folded the material into a large square before working on her own. On the last hem, the thread bunched up, creating a small bird's nest on the underside of the fabric. As she concentrated on rethreading the machine, a shiver of memory ran through her. Rose-colored silk, smooth under her touch. Mr. Ainsworth, standing behind her, placing a large hand on her shoulder. How the strength of him was palpable, and how her heart had beat faster at his praise.

He'd taken his hand away quickly, but then came more touches, more familiar, lingering ones that she squirmed under.

"Mrs. Smythe."

She jumped, pricking her finger. Luckily, the fabric remained un-stained. Mrs. Haines stood in the doorway, her thick eyebrows giving the unfortunate effect of a perpetual scowl.

"Yes?"

"Mr. Camden asked for you. He's in his apartment."

"Thank you." She stood and gathered up her work. "I've made him some curtains to keep out the sunlight. He's probably eager to receive them." Why was she explaining? Mrs. Haines was not her employer.

"Right, ma'am."

Always the cipher, that one. Between Daisy's chattiness and Mrs. Haines's reticence, at least her charges balanced each other.

To her disappointment, Mr. Douglas was with Mr. Camden when she entered the library, the finished curtains in her hand.

"Ah, good. Mrs. Smythe." Mr. Camden looked at the cloth in her arms, confused.

"Your curtains."

"Right, yes. Leave them over there on the windowsill."

"Of course." She put them down on a chair to the side of the window. If he opened it, the dust from the roadway might dirty the cloth. But he didn't seem to care about the curtains. In fact, all of the familiarity of the previous day was gone from his demeanor. He barely looked up at her as he and Mr. Douglas ran through a list of items with her to be taken care of before opening day.

A vague frustration settled over her, but she shrugged it off quickly. Her job involved keeping the tenants happy, and Mr. Cam-den was a tenant. Not a friend. Best to remember that and not over-step her official duties.

When she finally finished up her work for the day, she retreated to her tiny room, where the setting sun cast a reddish glow. She hung her lace curtains and marveled at how they prettied up the place, made it sweeter and cozier.

Daisy knocked and peered in. "You in for the night?"

"I believe I am."

"Curtains! How lovely." Daisy walked to the window and ran her hand along the delicate folds. "Where did you get them?"

"I made them."

"You're quite handy, then."

"I've sewn a frock or two in my day." She wished she'd had enough fabric to make two sets, as Daisy, such a young girl, ought to have something nice to look at.

Daisy draped the material around her head. "When I'm married, I'm going to hang gold velvet draperies in my windows, the better to show off my scarlet Worth dress."

"What a lovely tableau. But you'll need to find yourself a very rich husband in that case."

"I plan on it." Her blue eyes twinkled. "Did you hear that Mrs. Stuyvesant Fish had elephants in the ballroom at her fancy-dress party? Guests fed them peanuts as they waltzed by."

"I didn't realize elephants could waltz."

Daisy giggled. "No, silly. The guests did the waltzing."

"Such excess." Sara crinkled her nose.

"But such fun."

"I hope you'll be able to stay focused on the building, with opening day coming along."

Daisy nodded. "Of course."

She didn't want to be too hard on the girl, not after the trauma of the man in the night. But Daisy was a dreamer. She'd managed similar types at the Langham, especially among the pretty girls. "Good night, Daisy."

The sun disappeared over the horizon and drew Sara back to her window. Part of her envied Daisy's hopefulness. The girl had a grand plan, and wasn't that why Sara had come to New York City in the first place?

Sara's grand plan involved running the Dakota according to the expectations of her employers, and while her gray bombazine silk was a far cry from a gown of seed pearls and antique lace, it would certainly do.

One mustn't get carried away.

"Quickly, unlock the back gate." Sara shoved the key into Fitzroy's hand. "There's a line of moving wagons on Seventy-Third Street waiting to get in."

Fitzroy squinted down at the metal key in his hand, as if unfamiliar with the whole concept. "But it's only seven in the morning. No one's supposed to be here for another hour."

"Let them in, we can't keep them waiting."

She'd risen earlier than usual, knowing that a smooth opening day was crucial to the future reputation of the Dakota. If chaos ensued, the building and its management would be written off. Already, there had been snide remarks in the press about the class of citizen who had signed up, that they were of a lesser sort than established society, wondering why anyone would choose to live in the hinterlands amidst squatters' sagging homes.

Fitzroy skittered off. They were a sad pair, she had to admit. She knew nothing about this job, and was learning on the fly, while poor Fitzroy was far too old for the demands of his position. His hip had given him trouble lately, and his lopsided face was sure to disturb the ladies. Now this. Her meticulously scheduled agenda for the day was already in ruins.

Sixty-five families had rented out apartments, and of those, thirty were to move in today, while the others would file in over the course of the next week. She'd enjoyed having the full staff around during the past few weeks, the maids doing a final cleaning and the electricians fiddling with wires. Even the tailor, elderly and rather deaf in one ear, turned out to be a fine man, assuring her in a loud voice that she could use his sewing machine in the off hours whenever she liked.

The order that had been barely established was about to be turned on its head. She'd seen Mr. Camden only in passing recently, as they both rushed from one corner of the building to another, but his demeanor remained serious. As if their jaunt downtown had never happened.

A few minutes before eleven, Sara retreated to her office to catch her breath, as she'd been inundated with questions and concerns from the tenants' staff for the past four hours. Although the servants' rooms in the apartments were enormous by any other standard, she'd had to shut down squabbling about which maid got which room in apartment number 36, and barely prevented the new resident housekeeper, Mrs. Quinn, from giving the butler in apartment 32 a tongue-lashing when he complained about some invisible grime in the parlor. She was used to juggling two levels of help at the Langham: the guests' maids and valets, who generally expected to be treated as royalty, and the hotel's staff, who put up with their airs but talked about them behind their backs. She could allow no animosity like that here. No one would be checking out, hopefully, and the hierarchy had to be carefully maintained.

Daisy rushed in, breathless. Tendrils of blond hair fell along her white neck. Beautiful, but not acceptable.

"Fix your hair, Daisy."

The girl caught her breath and then shoved her hair back into place. "The residents are here, Mrs. Smythe."

Dread washed over her. "But they're two hours early." The plan had been to get the tenants' staff and rooms settled before allowing the actual tenants entry. She'd imagined greeting them as they swished down the halls, opening their front doors and exclaiming aloud at their gleaming new homes in perfect condition.

Daisy shoved a piece of paper toward her. "There was an error on the letter that went out. It says eleven o'clock, not one o'clock."

"Daisy, you typed this for me."

The girl stuffed her hands into the pockets of her dress. "I'm sorry, I didn't realize I'd hit the same key twice."

A critical error, but still. "At least you got the date right."

Two hours. She had to stall them, keep them occupied. Otherwise they'd chime in with opinions about what should go where and which way to arrange the dining room table, and the day would never end. Or they'd decide the place was uninhabitable and move out before they'd even arrived.

"What's this I hear about the residents coming early?" Mr. Camden stood in the doorway, fuming.

"There was a miscommunication," said Sara. "We'll take care of them."

"We spoke about this, Mrs. Smythe. How important it is that they enter a well-run, elegant apartment building. From what I can tell, it's a madhouse on every floor."

She'd be sent back to London on the next ship if she didn't fix this fast. Mr. Camden was absolutely glowering at her.

She turned to Daisy and spoke with clipped vowels. "Get the cook and tell her to put out some champagne in the dining room. I'm going to the courtyard to round them up. I'll take care of this." The last sentence she directed at Mr. Camden. "If you would come with me, I would appreciate your assistance."

Thankfully, he did as he was told, although she could see him clenching and unclenching his fists as they stepped outdoors.

Indeed, a line of broughams encircled the two fountains; and after the footmen helped off the ladies, Fitzroy moved the vehicles out and brought in another round of carriages. The residents were milling about, unsure of where to go.

"Why isn't my personal staff here to greet me?" demanded a stout lady in a black beaver cape.

Sara stood on the stone base of the southern fountain. Using her natural height to her advantage, she called for everyone's attention.

"I am Mrs. Smythe, the managerette here at the Dakota, and I would like to welcome you to this magnificent building. Please join me in the dining room for a champagne toast to your new home, followed by a tour of the highlights of the Dakota by Mr. Camden, one of the architects of this stately, modern apartment house."

As she'd figured, the word *champagne* perked them up. She led the way into the south entrance and was relieved to see that the cook had done as asked, and set up a marvelous array of delicate glass coupes and champagne nesting in ice buckets.

While the bottles were uncorked and poured, Sara eyed the room, Daisy at her side.

Daisy leaned into her, disappointed. "They're not the upper crust of society. The papers were all saying that no one of Mrs. Astor's set would be caught dead living here."

True enough, the tenants' names were unlikely to overlap with Mrs. Astor's list of acceptable society members. Certainly not Mr. and Mrs. Gustav Schirmer, of the music publishing company, or

Mr. and Mrs. Solon Vlasto, who were moving downtown, not uptown, from Ninety-Second Street.

"I've seen enough of high society at the hotel in London. Believe me, you don't want to have to deal with that set."

"But they're the ones with the power in the city; it's in the newspapers every day. Everyone here is so ordinary. Dry goods and woolen merchants, that sort."

"As they're paying three thousand dollars a year for a ten-room apartment, I would think that's far from ordinary. Perhaps you'd be happier working as a maid for Mrs. Astor?"

Daisy didn't answer.

Mr. Camden appeared, checking his timepiece. "How long do you think you can prevent them from storming their new apartments?"

Sara lifted her chin. "Follow me, please." She sidled up to one of the new residents, Mr. Camden trailing in her wake.

"Mr. Schirmer, how are plans going for the printing plant?"

Mr. Schirmer smiled, quite pleased. "Very well, Mrs. Smythe. Thank you for asking. We hope to have it running in the next year or two."

"Of course you must know Mr. and Mrs. Steinway." She turned to the right and drew them into the group. "We are so lucky to have true music aficionados among the residents."

Mrs. Steinway threw her fur over one shoulder. "We will create our own private village here beside the park, shan't we, Mrs. Schirmer?"

"What a lovely way to refer to the Dakota." Sara offered up a subtle smile, one that suggested agreement without being overly familiar. "I was just saying to Mr. Camden here that the uptown rural landscape is much better for one's health."

Mr. Schirmer spoke up. "I consider this to be my ode to Magellan, heading into the northern frontier, weapon at my side."

"What exactly is your weapon, dear?" asked his wife.

"Why, you, of course."

Mr. Camden chuckled, playing along beautifully. The atmosphere tinkled with laughter and heady conversation.

"I daresay I like this idea of having cocktails before luncheon," Mrs. Steinway said to Mr. Camden. "Will that be a regular occurrence?"

"If that will please you, Mrs. Steinway, of course." The traces of Mr. Camden's irritation with Sara disappeared as he made a subtle bow.

A man with a thick mustache stepped over. "I say, as members of the F.F.D.s, this is a bang-up way to begin our communal living experiment."

While the group gaped at the impolite intrusion, Sara spoke up. "Mr. Tatum, what a lovely thought. The First Families of the Dakota, no?"

"On the nose!"

Never mind that he'd been using the term in his correspondence with Sara, where he'd inquired weekly about the size and number of water closets in his apartment.

"Commodore, we're honored to have you on board."

The group closed in on itself, and Mr. Camden guided Sara away.

"'Commodore'?" Mr. Camden murmured.

"Mr. Tatum is the head of the New York Yacht Club. I've been reading the society columns religiously since I arrived."

"Clever girl."

Once the last drop of the champagne had been downed, Mr. Camden led the group on a tour of the public rooms on the ground floor, the basement level with its amenities, and then up to the roof garden, where the clear day offered a view twenty miles in all directions.

Finally, the group splintered off to their own apartments, the ladies walking with a slight sway to their step and the men whistling under their breath.

The Dakota was officially open.

CHAPTER ELEVEN

New York City, October 1884

The wind threatened to blow her away, but Sara stood firm on top of the roof of the Dakota, holding on to the metal railing. Opening day had been a success, thanks to the champagne toast. In fact, the alcohol had lubricated more than the throats of the tenants; it had eased the transformation of the building from one that was under construction to one that was up and running, teeming with life. She'd finished up the day by meeting with all of the tenants' staff, making sure they understood where their duties ended and the building's began—and so far she'd seen no bruised egos—before climbing up to the very top of the building to get some air.

The roof garden looked out over Central Park, with its picturesque castle and lake in the distance. Although the sun had set, the glow of gas lamps lit up the pathways that carved through the trees.

"Mrs. Smythe!"

Mr. Camden sauntered toward her. He carried the afternoon edition of the newspaper in his hand and drew up beside her, his eyes twinkling with excitement. He unraveled the paper, not easy with the breeze, and read aloud.

*"Probably not one stranger out of fifty who ride over the ele-
vated roads or on either of the rivers does not ask the name of
the stately building which stands west of Central Park."*

A corner of the paper blew loose from his grasp and she reached
out and held it taut while he continued on.

*"The name of the building is the Dakota Apartment House,
and it is the largest, most substantial, and most conveniently
arranged apartment house of the sort in this country. An astonishing geographic and architectural landmark, the Dakota will
undoubtedly be known as 'The Address' of New York's West
Side."*

"How wonderful. You must be pleased."

"I gave the reporter a private tour last week, but he was tight-
lipped the whole time. I couldn't tell if he was impressed or horrified. But here, look at the headline."

She glanced down and followed his finger, which tapered to a
curved, elegant tip. *"'One of the Most Perfect Apartment Houses in the
World.'* That's brilliant."

"Mr. Douglas will have a waiting list for years to come."

Mr. Camden's boyish excitement made her laugh. "You've done it,"
she said.

"We've done it." He closed up the paper and tucked it under his
arm. "I don't know how I would have managed earlier today; it
would have been an angry stampede of F.F.D.s without your quick
thinking." He looked down at her. "Sorry to disturb your stroll on
the rooftop, but I was walking across the park and saw you."

To think that he was able to recognize her from so far off. A
breeze played with her skirts and she patted them down.

"Shall we sit out of the way of the wind for a moment?" he inquired.

A bench beside the enormous gabled roof protected them from the elements. Sara tucked the loose strands of her hair back into place. "What shall you do next, now that this project is finished up?"

He leaned back and stretched out his legs. "Hardenbergh has me already assigned to a new building, all the way downtown. But in another couple of months, I'll be starting up my own firm, thanks to this newspaper article and Hardenbergh's backing."

"I'm sure it will be a great success. You'll probably be quite happy to have Mrs. Camden and your children back in town."

"Of course."

Silence fell between them. She struggled to fill the space. "Where did you study architecture, Mr. Camden?"

"I was on a scholarship at the Hasbrouck Institute in Jersey City, where I first met Hardenbergh. When he got an early commission from Rutgers and asked me to work for him, I jumped at the chance."

She admired the way he'd forged his own path. Part of her had hoped that by coming to New York City, to America, she would do the same, but she lacked his brash confidence. Her mother had done her a disservice, constantly reminding her of her blood connection to nobility, while at the same time cursing her bastardy. She didn't know where she belonged.

But it had made her good at her job. She could tell people what to do and sound authoritative, even if underneath it all was a fear of being discovered, found out, a fraud. In some ways, her natural reticence, her refusal to get too close or to let someone know who she truly was, had decreased since she'd arrived in the States. Being thrown into the lion's den of the Dakota, among strangers who didn't know or care what her parentage was, had toughened her up a touch. America seemed to be a more open, forgiving place.

She didn't want to go back into her shell.

He stared hard at her. A warmth spread up her chest and neck.

The blanket of evening, a cerulean blue, was creeping across the sky from east to west. She looked up. "Funny how I thought I'd be pressed in on all sides in New York, yet here I am surrounded by vast views and an even vaster sky."

"Makes the people down below seem like ants." Mr. Camden pointed to a man who wobbled along the pathway below them. "Ants on bicycles."

"I imagine it's difficult with six legs."

"Have you ever ridden a bicycle?"

Sara nodded. "I grew up in a small village on the southern coast of England. My mother bought me a used one to run errands and make deliveries." She didn't mention the times the boys threw rocks at her as she pedaled furiously by, calling her and her mother unmentionable names.

"We should go for a ride in the park sometime. Will you join me?" Before she could answer, he jumped in. "When is your day off?"

"Not until Saturday afternoon."

"Very well, Saturday afternoon. I will supply the bicycles and you wear your best riding outfit."

"Shall I bring a crop?" she asked with a grin.

"Two, as I'll need one myself."

As they entered the doorway back into the building, he held his hand out to assist her in stepping over the small curb.

Before he let go, she thought he gave her hand a quick squeeze. But when she looked at him, he avoided her gaze. She must have imagined it.

Or wished he'd done so.

On Saturday morning, Mr. Camden left a note for Sara to meet him at the Mall in the park at one o'clock. The city's elite paraded along the promenade in their carriages between four and five each afternoon, and she would be sure to excuse herself long before the crowds assembled to gawk at the sight. Although it was fine for men and women to stroll together without causing raised eyebrows, it would be unseemly to be seen with a married man during the grand promenade.

She'd craved his company the past few days, the way he looked at her and the way he listened to her when she spoke. Not in an intimate way, she told herself, as that wouldn't be proper. But he was a kind person and she hadn't had many friends.

He stood beside two safety bicycles that leaned upon a wooden bench. One of them had a wicker basket strapped onto the front handlebars.

"Are you ready for an enjoyable day in nature, Mrs. Smythe?"

"Indeed I am." The past few days of moving in the last of the new tenants had left her exhausted, and a change of scenery would do her good. For being the first of November, the air was uncommonly warm, the equivalent of a London summer day. She gathered her skirts and mounted the bicycle. At first, she was unsteady, but the frame was sturdy and the tires thick. As long as she kept her focus on the black-clad figure of Mr. Camden on the bicycle in front of her, she found it easy to stay upright.

Leaves from the elms planted along either side of the roadway fluttered to the ground. She crunched through the sumptuous palate of reds and golds, feeling a bit like Moses cutting through the Red Sea. Mr. Camden glided down a pathway that led to a fountain, where they dismounted before walking to a small rise of grass overlooking the lake.

He pulled a blanket out of the wicker basket, which Sara laid out carefully on the ground, followed by a fresh loaf of bread, salmon mousse, and apricot tartlets.

"Quite a feast, Mr. Camden."

"I had the chef prepare it specially. We can't have our star employee going hungry."

Disconcerted by his effusiveness, she busied herself unwrapping a block of Stilton cheese.

"Isn't this grand." He gestured to the passersby. "A mix of society, neither high nor low, and everyone meeting in the heart of this great city to enjoy a lovely autumn day."

"It's a beautiful park, but I have to say I like the gardens of Hyde Park better."

He pretended to be offended, his hand on his heart. "Why put up with those stodgy English gardeners when you have the wilds of America here? Streams tumbling down rocks, paths that go every which way. Besides, here a simple boy from Buffalo can become whatever he wants, including an architect. Not so easy over the pond."

"Could Fitzroy work his way up to become a man of your station? I rather doubt it."

"I doubt Fitzroy could find his shoes in the morning if his wife didn't put them on his feet herself."

She laughed. "You're being unkind. He's a delightful man."

"He is. But I'm talking about opportunity. That's what we have, you must admit it."

"You have it, perhaps."

"Do you not think you could move up in the world?"

His lack of awareness astounded her. Of course a woman could not move up in the world. Not the way he had. "It's easy for you to think so, but there are very clear delineations. Here as well as in England."

"What would you do if you'd been born a duke's daughter, then?"

Caught off guard, she almost spilled her lemonade.

He sat up. "I've hit a chord, it appears."

She shouldn't say anything, keep quiet as she'd done for years and years. But his inquisitive look told her she wouldn't be able to divert his attention. Not that she wanted to. She had to admit, part of her wanted to impress this man.

But would admitting that she was a bastard impress him? She took a deep breath.

"My father was the Earl of Chichester."

Now it was his turn to sputter. "Yet I found you working in a hotel. A grand hotel, indeed, but one where an earl's daughter ought to be paying for a room, not cleaning it."

"My mother was his housekeeper, if you must know. He would never recognize me as his daughter."

He grew quiet. "You deserve better than that."

The unexpected kindness brought a lump to her throat. "Certain lines must not be crossed."

He reached into the picnic basket and drew out a small sketch pad and a fountain pen. "I promised you I'd draw your dream cottage, and I come armed and ready. If you like, you may describe a castle fit for an earl's daughter, and it will be yours. On paper, at least."

"You really don't have to do that." She ducked her head to hide her obvious pleasure.

"I insist."

He began by asking her simple questions, how many rooms she required, what type of stone she preferred.

When she offered up the idea of an iron bench for reading under a trellis covered with wisteria, he'd smiled. "Grand idea. I knew there was something about you, the minute I saw you up in that dreadful office with a tiny window. You didn't look like you belonged. And that look you give."

"Which one is that?"

"When you need someone to do something they don't want to do. Don't deny it. I've seen you give it to Daisy a dozen times. One eyebrow goes up."

She laughed. He had figured out her secret weapon.

He continued on as he drew. "Speaking of moving up in the world, here's an example for you: What about our esteemed builder, the late Mr. Clark? He built himself up from nothing, and ended up owning half of the Singer sewing company and our beloved Dakota."

"Like the sewing machine in the basement?"

"The very one."

"I'm quite fond of Singer sewing machines. To no longer be a slave to the needle is a magnificent thing. However." She hesitated but continued on when Mr. Camden indicated his encouragement. "We both know Mr. Clark wasn't accepted by high society. Like London's peerage, in New York you are either on the list or not."

"In a hundred years, Mrs. Astor's list will be mocked. These demarcations are no longer important. Eventually, the entire lot will have intermarried themselves into oblivion."

The forcefulness of his words shocked her.

He leaned up on one elbow. "May I ask you a rather personal question?"

"What might that be?"

"What became of Mr. Smythe?"

"He never existed. It's for work purposes only. The tradition of lines and lines of housekeepers, probably going back to the Middle Ages in England, is to be a *Mrs.* The irony being that if a housekeeper did marry, she'd be out of a job."

"Better off to remain unmoored to another person. Look at Mrs. Camden. She is a member of the land-rich, cash-poor aristocracy, and where does that get her? With an obnoxious American as a husband who refuses to play the silly games. You have so much ahead of you, having taken the leap to come to this country. I hope you'll take advantage of it."

His confidence in her future thrilled her. What could she become, if she really tried?

"May I ask how you became involved in architecture, Mr. Camden?"

"You certainly may." He continued drawing as he spoke. "My stepfather, a brute who worked in a grain mill, never liked my artistic leanings. He liked to say I might as well have been doing needlepoint. I drew everything. Flowers, faces, whatever was in front of me. One late Saturday afternoon my friends and I, troublemakers all of us, snuck into a mansion that was being built outside of town. It was an empty shell; the framing had been completed but little else. Inside, I found a set of plans, and while the other boys ran around playing chase, I studied the drawings like they were a treasure map. Which they were. I was entranced, and took them with me when we left."

"Did you get caught?"

"Of course. My stepfather dragged me back to apologize, and the foreman insisted I work as a site rat for a month to atone."

"Sounds awful."

"Oh no. I was in heaven. Picking up nails, bringing the workers water, watching as the one-dimensional design came to life in three dimensions. Extraordinary."

He blotted the drawing before handing it over to her.

The delicate pen strokes captured a handsome cottage with three gabled windows above a trellis dripping with wisteria. A wooden door with a solid knocker was offset by a large window carved with diagonal muntins and a smaller round window on the other side. The asymmetry lent the building an unexpected jauntiness. She asked him to sign it, and he did so with a flourish before rolling it up for the ride home.

On the way back to the Dakota, Sara's bike hit a large hole. She stayed upright, but her front wheel began to wobble. She disembarked near the statue of Daniel Webster and examined the tire.

"Something wrong?" Mr. Camden asked.

"Looks like this needs to be tightened." She pointed to the hub of the wheel.

He leaned his bike against the statue and knelt down to examine hers. She wished he didn't have a hat on, as she'd have liked to see what the top of his head looked like, how the hair whorled this way or that.

He looked up suddenly, his eyes wide. Her own expression had been unguarded. She gave him a quick smile and looked away, unable to meet his gaze.

He stood, one hand on her bike's seat, and spoke quietly. "I'll have one of the staff take it to be repaired. Thank you for a remarkable afternoon, Mrs. Smythe."

The vibration of his voice practically undid her. He was so close, and it was as if the sound traveled through her skin and muscles and into her bones.

She loosened her grip on the bike handles. "Off I go, then. I must check in and make sure there have been no fires that need putting out."

"Wait, you must take this." He dug into the picnic basket and handed over the rolled drawing.

The act felt overly intimate and improper, as if he were handing her a lacy chemise in the middle of a city street. She took the paper and hid it behind her back, embarrassed. "Thank you, Mr. Camden."

She ran off without waiting for his reply.

"There you are. Sit and tell me the day's gossip."

Sara took her usual place in Mr. Camden's library. Even though it was only two weeks since the opening, the Dakota ran as smoothly as if it had been occupied for two years: Boys brought coal up to the apartments, past maids carrying buckets and mops, while downstairs, residents ascended into their broughams with the help of the porters. Fortunately, the new residents were far from the demanding upper-crust guests the Langham catered to, apart from the irritable Mrs. Horace Putnam. The men were debonair and kind and the women, while discerning in their tastes, exuded an unexpected warmth.

Not that her job was easy. While the deliverymen were obsequious enough, the clerks of the companies they worked for balked when Sara registered even the most minor complaint. Yesterday, she'd showed up in person at the offices of the kindling supply company after sending multiple letters complaining of damp bundles. The clerk refused to believe she was in charge, insisting that she instead send the "true manager." She'd fired the company on the spot and directed Daisy to find a suitable replacement.

Each day at four in the afternoon, when Mr. Camden returned from his office, they shared tea and ran through the day's events. What a relief it was to speak with a man and not have to prove herself. He encouraged a friendly banter, as if she were his equal.

"I'm afraid Mrs. Putnam's son wore his skates in the parlor. The floors will need to be redone."

Mr. Camden froze, cup half-raised to his mouth. "He did what?"

She smiled. "I'm joking. Sorry, couldn't help it. She has insisted we polish the silver inlay of her floors twice a week, however."

Mr. Camden burst out laughing and barely got the teacup back on its saucer without spilling. "That image will haunt me for days, thank you very much."

"No, no gossip to tell today, I'm afraid. I hope that doesn't disappoint you."

"Not at all. Between the good notices in the papers and the current residents' satisfaction, I've been told we have a waiting list pages long for residence here at our private village." He idly lifted an invitation from the table beside him. "That's a shame."

"What's that?"

"The Rutherfords are having one of their mad masquerade balls on Friday. Mrs. Camden would have loved to have gone."

Sara forced a smile. His wife and children were due the following week. The apartment had been furnished with their overstuffed armchairs and delicate French tea tables, and was just waiting for the rest of the family to arrive. She'd so enjoyed Mr. Camden's company these past few weeks, but their relations would have to become more formal once Mrs. Camden arrived from London. It was only right.

For the first time, she reconsidered her mother's relationship with the Earl of Chichester. Sara had never been able to imagine how her mother had fallen into the man's hands, made herself so vulnerable. But perhaps they'd been united by the common goal of running a large manor, leading to shared confidences and a mutual respect that wasn't bound by class. The loss must have been insurmountable, if that was the case. Her mother's livelihood, and her love.

"Mrs. Smythe?"

She looked over. Had he said something? "I'm sorry?" Her face flamed with embarrassment.

"I said you should go with me."

"To where?"

"The Rutherford ball."

"No, of course not." He was mad. A glorified servant did not attend balls.

He sat back and ran his finger over the thick card stock. "Too bad, as I'd love to show you the interior work. And they're known for their soirees. Last year they held a costume ball for twelve hundred people, and even the discerning Mrs. Astor showed up."

"What was her costume?"

"Good question. I'll have to find out. You always stump me, you know that, don't you?"

"In any case, there's no reason you shouldn't go unescorted."

"I don't want to go for any other reason than to prove to you the level of inanity the world has attained."

That again. She hoped he wouldn't go off on another tear. "I can read about it in the newspapers every day; there's no need to go to a ball."

"I suppose you're right." He sighed. "In any case, I'd forgotten we'd also have to find you proper clothes."

Sara looked down in her lap. This morning, knowing she'd be performing an inspection of the basement rooms, she'd worn her gray day dress, her shabbiest outfit, and shame flooded over her. There was no use pretending to be Mr. Camden's equal, exchanging witticisms and teasing him, when really she was no better than a scullery maid in appearance and social ranking.

Yet the man ought to be put in his place. "I'll have you know that I own a lovely ball gown."

He slapped his knee. "Of course, I forget that you're the daughter of nobility. How awful of me to assume otherwise. Then it's settled, we must." He didn't give her an opportunity to answer. "It's a masked ball. I will introduce you as my second cousin from England. We will enter, I'll give you a quick tour, and then we'll leave. It's the perfect opportunity. Perhaps the only one."

True. Other than being hired as their housekeeper, Sara would never set foot in a house like that in her life.

"Please go with me. Sara."

The use of her Christian name stopped her cold. What on earth was she thinking?

"I couldn't."

"One night, for ten minutes. We'll leave in separate carriages, then I'll join you nearby." His face grew serious. "I think we both know this time next week our friendship will be swallowed up by society's dictates. Shall we enjoy it now, while we have it?"

He held her gaze. "No one will know, I promise."

Had her mother heard the same words, at some point?

No. Sara was wrong to romanticize her mother's relationship with his lordship. That wasn't the case at all. The man was known as a beast throughout the county, one who whipped the boys who poached on his land. Her mother had been tricked, seduced against her will. The offer from Mr. Camden was nothing like that. He was American, for a start, and believed that all people, regardless of standing, deserved a chance. He'd seen something in her back in London and given her the greatest opportunity of her life. And now he was asking her to the ball, but not as Prince Charming. As a co-witness to the madness of the elite. This was the class of people the residents of the Dakota wished to be like, in their heart of hearts. By attending, she'd gain a deeper understanding of the resentments, frustrations, and aspirations of the very people for whom she worked.

Ten minutes out of her life. Ten minutes of being on Mr. Camden's arm.

Only ten minutes.

CHAPTER TWELVE

New York City, September 1985

"Where the fuck is everyone?"

Melinda tore through the apartment like a well-coiffed whirlwind, dropping her Birkin bag with a *thud* on the floor.

Bailey had been in the kitchen, furiously trying to reach the contractor on the phone, with no luck, when she heard the front door slam and knew exactly who it was. Now, as they faced off down the long gallery, Melinda reminded Bailey of a bull in a bullfight, about to charge. A bull wearing Candie's high heels.

"So, where are the workers?"

Bailey's footsteps echoed through the empty apartment. "I'm trying to reach Steve to find out. I don't remember him saying anything about taking the day off; they know we're on a tight schedule."

"You bet we are."

"I have to ask, did you pay their bill, for the next installment?"

Melinda rolled her eyes. "I think so."

She had her answer. "My guess is they've been pulled away on another job."

"Why is that?"

"Because they're due the next installment on their payment, and they haven't gotten it yet."

"Jesus Christ. Steve knows I'm good for it. I told him my situation."

"I'm sure you did. But they don't only work for you. If another job comes along, they jump if they aren't happy."

Melinda's shoulders dropped a few inches. Progress. Bailey kept talking. "I'll try calling them today, see if I can entice them back. But right now the only thing we know for sure will work is a big fat check."

"Fucking Fred won't give me anything early. I've tried already, trust me."

"Then maybe it's a good idea to wait until you have the money in hand to continue." Bailey hated saying this. It meant she'd be at loose ends, and broke, for an extra month. Unlike Melinda's idea of broke, hers actually meant it.

"I'll ask Tony. He'll front me the cash."

"How soon can you get it?"

"I'll go by his office today. Tonight we're hitting the Limelight, so he'll be in a good mood later even if he's cranky when I ask for the money."

The Limelight. Bailey's jaw tightened and her heart raced. Like Pavlov's dog, she only needed to hear one word. The many nights they'd spent dancing and drinking and doing coke until dawn had imprinted themselves on her.

She'd hit an AA meeting at a small church on Sixty-Ninth Street a few nights ago. The place had been packed and the coffee strong. She listened to the stories and nodded encouragement, but felt like a fraud, like an actor in a movie about recovery. Playing the role of the penitent sinner. Until one woman brought her to tears with her story about waking up in an apartment in the Bronx, beaten and sore, not remembering how she'd ended up there. The bruise around her eye had faded to a shadow, but her words and anguish were still raw. So many nights, especially during the last year, Bailey hadn't been sure how she'd gotten herself home. She'd dodged a bullet. Maybe a whole cartridge of bullets.

As she'd turned to leave, she spotted Renzo standing in the very back. He disappeared in a flash, but she was sure it was him. It made her feel defenseless and small, knowing that he had stared at the back of her head the past hour. Knowing that he knew.

A couple of days later, when she'd been showing Kenneth the wallpaper choices for his bathroom, Renzo stopped by to inspect the work the plumber was doing. She tried to shape her expression into a smile that meant *Your secret's safe with me*, but he had barely made eye contact. Maybe none of the other tenants knew he had a problem, and he wanted to keep it that way. That was fine with her. Still, he could have been nicer.

Melinda picked up her Birkin and brushed imaginary dust from her denim culottes. "You should come with us tonight, Bails. It'll be like old times."

"Are you kidding? I just got back from rehab. The Limelight is the last place I need to be."

"Fine, then come to dinner with us beforehand at the Odeon. You don't need to drink and it'll be better than sitting in this tomb. You look so pale; have you had any fun since you've been back?"

"I don't have the funds for fun right now."

"It's on me and Tony tonight. Okay? Our treat."

If Bailey had another slice of pizza for dinner, she'd lose her mind. The thought of a real meal, with cloth napkins and waiters, seemed like an exotic expedition. She could use the change of scenery.

"What time?"

"Nine o'clock."

So late. "I'm not sure. There's no way I can go back to partying like I used to."

Melinda punched her playfully on the arm. "I know. I don't mean to push you. I just want to get you back in my life. I've missed you."

"You have me. I'm not going anywhere. Unlike your contractor."

"And I'm so happy about that, and I want you to join us. Okay?"

Bailey agreed, touched by Melinda's insistence.

Her choice of clothing for the evening was limited. She had some indigo jeans and a pair of high heels, but the only "nice" item for going out to dinner was a sequined top that tied around her neck and exposed much of her shoulders. She found it wedged into a corner of her suitcase, underneath the sensible T-shirts she'd brought with her to rehab. It was risqué for the Dakota, but not for Odeon.

Of course Renzo was in the porter's office as she passed through the porte cochere. She looked like she was heading out for a good time, and it put a lump of guilt in her belly.

He waved at her from the window, and she waved back without smiling. What business was it of his where she was going or what she looked like? Who was he to judge? The man was the super of a building in New York City, not a potential client or friend. The need to please him pissed her off, and the feeling didn't go away until she was in a subway car hurtling downtown.

Tony stood and pulled out a chair for her as Bailey entered the restaurant. The room was loud and crowded, and a couple of men's heads turned as she walked by. It was nice to know she wasn't all washed up. The liquor bottles behind the bar glittered like jewels as Prince sang about raspberry berets from the speakers.

She ached for a drink. If she wanted to stay in New York, she'd have to learn to manage temptation, and tonight was her first real test. Her hand fluttered to her throat—it was all she could do not to claw at it—as she ordered a seltzer with lime, before thanking Tony for letting her be a third wheel.

"Not at all. We missed you terribly."

His accent was so posh, the fact that most of what he said was gossip and self-congratulation tended to be forgotten by his listeners. Including Melinda, who doted on the man. The few times Bailey had asked Tony what exactly he did for a living, he'd brushed her off with tales of dashing around Ibiza with his university chums. He had an air of wealth, which meant the other details didn't matter.

Although, to be fair, Tony *had* stuck by Melinda and was basically supporting her lavish lifestyle these days, at least until the trust fund kicked in. A good boyfriend to have. He had widely spaced eyes, sparse eyelashes, and a jet-black, gelled mane that shot out of his hairline like the edge of a well-manicured lawn. He'd gone to either Oxford or Cambridge, and Bailey knew better than to ask again and risk his derision for failing to remember the correct answer.

Tony ordered another round of drinks. Bailey got the steak frites and dove into the bread basket as soon as it arrived.

"Take it easy, tiger," said Melinda. "It's like you haven't eaten in days."

She put the piece of bread back on her plate and took a sip of seltzer. The place was buzzing with coke-fueled energy. Being here sober wasn't much fun. Too loud, impossible to talk.

Tony said something and she leaned forward. "What did you say?"

"You're looking awfully good these days. Rehab agrees with you." He looked her up and down and she squirmed.

"He means you've got a figure, doll." Melinda pointed to Bailey's breasts. "Filled out." She turned to Tony. "I blossomed before Bailey, even though she's a year older than me."

Bailey put her elbows on the table, eager to stop Tony from checking her out further. As if this could get any more uncomfortable.

"Remember the holiday visit when you tried on one of my bras and we stuffed it with socks?" Melinda threw back her head and laughed, exposing her neck. "My mother took one look and practically spit up her tea."

Certain memories were made to be quashed, and that was one of them. The pressure of the bra around her chest had been unfamiliar and tight but made her feel grown up, and she'd draped one of Melinda's soft cashmere sweaters over it. She thought she stepped into the room full of adults looking like one herself, but her father had turned beet red and her mother had gasped before insisting she change right away.

"I do remember."

"We were silly kids." Melinda linked arms with Tony. "In fact, Tony and I were just discussing the possibility of having kids of our own the other day, weren't we?"

Tony patted her arm. "Right."

Thank God the subject had changed.

Melinda put her face right next to Tony's. "Can you imagine how cute our baby would be?" She kissed him on the cheek before wiping off the waxy smudge with her finger. "Or babies. You know, twins run in my family. They'd be the perfect mix of my brains and your good looks."

Bailey almost choked on her seltzer, and she could have sworn Tony grimaced.

"Your brains?" he inquired.

Melinda leaned over the table and spoke in a mock whisper. "Tony never passed his exams at university, but don't tell anyone that. He doesn't like to talk about it."

Tony bristled. "Only one exam, my dear. I'd like to see how you would have fared. Not well, is my guess. In any case, my family is known for its brilliant men. My cousin, in fact, is going to win a Nobel Prize for science sometime in the near future, I am quite sure of that, so you might want to rethink your judgmental attitude."

"Sorry, Tony." Melinda batted her eyelids at him. He sniffed and seemed to calm down.

Bailey took another piece of bread. "What's your cousin done that's so amazing?"

"He's invented a way to match DNA to the person it belongs to."

"I don't understand. Of course DNA belongs to the person it came from."

"It'll be used in criminal cases. Like if someone leaves a drop of blood or hair at a crime scene, they can tell exactly who did it. So, say they get a suspect in custody, they do this test and know for certain that they've got the right bloke."

"Gross. Can we not talk about hair and blood right now?" Melinda made a gagging sound.

Bailey ignored her. "He certainly deserves the Nobel for that; it almost sounds like magic more than science. Did he go to Cambridge as well?"

Tony gave a quick shake of his head, annoyed. She'd got it wrong. "Oxford. Our family always matriculates at Oxford."

"Right. Sorry."

The food arrived, her steak glistening with juice, but she barely had a few bites before Tony insisted they leave. Bailey didn't want to go clubbing; she preferred to stay there and finish her dinner, but sitting alone at the table would be humiliating. She grabbed a few more fries before following them out the door and into a cab.

They pulled up to the former church, where a line of impatient partygoers wrapped around the block. Bailey had every intention of continuing on uptown, but Melinda yanked her out of the taxi. From there, it was as if a magnetic force took over, pulling her past the bouncers and over the gaping maw of the threshold. She vowed to spend only ten minutes or so at the club, as a test of her willpower, until Tony and Melinda were distracted by new friends and new drugs. She checked her watch. She'd be home before midnight and would wake up early, in time to attend the eight thirty AA meeting.

The theme for the night was "Bare as You Dare." Long, skinny limbs erupted every so often from the mash of bodies on the packed dance floor. The lights flashed to the beat of a Tom Tom Club song, and at times the dancers seemed like they made up one organism, a pleasure-seeking, pulsating beast.

Once inside, Tony and Melinda had peeled off to the right. They were probably in search of more coke, which usually could be found in one of the tiny rooms downstairs, the private areas where club goers could writhe around one another or drop acid or do whatever else they'd regret in the morning.

She climbed the stairs for a better view and leaned over the balcony, scanning the crowd. No familiar faces. Four months ago, she would have been treated like royalty from the minute she passed the bouncer. As part of Tristan's entourage, doors opened and people sucked up.

"Well, if it isn't the backstabbing bitch Bailey."

Speak of the devil. Tristan.

And not only Tristan but Wanda and a couple of assistants from the firm, who hovered in the background, trying to look bored and cool.

"What are you talking about?" She knew it was better to go on the offensive with him but couldn't think of any other response.

He glowered at her. "You took over Melinda's job, did you? How's that going? Everyone knows your cousin can't pay up. And how do they know that? I told them myself."

That explained the missing crew. Tony's money would solve that problem, but for now she had to deal with Tristan.

He'd given her so much, had taken her in and trained her, made her feel smart and talented. She'd once been a lowly assistant, but he'd noticed that she always made the extra effort by staying late and doing whatever it took when an emergency cropped up.

"Look, Tristan. I'm sorry for that. Really. Melinda's throwing me a bone here. Like you said, she can't even afford it yet. Why would you even want to be bothered with that?"

"You're doing me a favor, is that how you justify it?"

"No, I don't mean that."

Wanda thrust her long neck forward. "She totally scooped it out from under you, Tristan. I was there."

Tristan sniffed. "I got you to rehab, and this is what I get in return?"

He was right. Whatever defenses she had left crumbled. "You've done so much for me, Tristan, I'm sorry. I should have come to you first, but it all happened so fast. I was desperate. I didn't have any money, a job, a place to stay. Melinda offered all three. At least temporarily."

He cocked his head, mollified for the moment. "You can have your cousin's apartment. But it's the last job you'll ever do. I won't have you poaching my business. Remember, I can ruin you in this town."

They left Bailey shaking, one hand on the balcony and the other over her heart, which beat as if she'd inhaled an eight ball.

Tristan had the power to shut her out of her career completely. Why hadn't she seen that? In rehab, her counselors had advised her to make a plan for when she got out, and she'd considered moving somewhere else, like Los Angeles or San Francisco, to make a fresh start. But that was hard to do when you had no money, no contacts.

She should call someone from AA. Or her roommate from Silver Hill. Confess that right now all she wanted was a shot of tequila. Something searing and quick to take the pain away and the edge off. But the idea of standing on a street corner, putting quarters into a pay phone and waking up a girl she barely even knew, was pathetic. Desperate. She wasn't that. Not yet.

One drink. That's all she'd have. Then she'd walk out of here and never come back.

Her purse held only a few subway tokens and a five-dollar bill. She went through all of the side pockets and almost cried with joy when she spotted a twenty. Her emergency fund.

The tequila was as good as she'd expected it to be. No, better. Hot fire. She would leave after saying good-bye to Melinda and Tony, warning them that Tristan was pissed. She found them in what used to be the undercroft of the church, now decked out with funky couches and low lighting. A line of coke was laid out on the table in front of them, a bottle of champagne in a bucket on the floor.

"Bailey, where have you been? Sit here, give me a kiss."

Melinda was sloppy, happy, and a mess.

Bailey sat beside her. "Tristan's on the warpath. He's mad that you hired me. Really mad."

"Screw him. I'll take care of you. Don't worry about a thing." She poured Bailey a glass of champagne, spilling some on her lap but not noticing.

"No, I'm not having any more."

Tony leaned forward, a curled-up dollar bill in his hand. "You've already partaken?"

"Just one."

Melinda let out a cackle. "Go on, have a glass of champagne."

The warm feeling from the shot was beginning to dissipate. She could sneak out the back way and catch a cab, go home thinking about the steak she never got to finish. Or she could stay in this one room, deep in the bowels of a building where generations of New Yorkers had found absolution from their sins, and make herself feel good for the next hour or two. Feed that particular appetite.

It wasn't even a toss-up.

Chapter Thirteen

New York City, November 1884

As promised, the carriage stood waiting on Seventy-Second Street in front of the Dakota at precisely eleven o'clock. Once inside, Sara removed her long cape, glad that the evening was quite temperate, and smoothed her dress. She'd spent the past three nights hard at work at the tailor's sewing machine, narrowing the silhouette and adjusting the sleeves to bring it up to date, and while it wasn't perfect, it would do. Her hands were clammy in her gloves.

At Fifty-Ninth Street, the carriage stopped abruptly. The door opened and Mr. Camden appeared, lit from behind by the lamplights.

"Are you ready to see the worst of society?" He took a seat next to her and handed over a delicate mask decorated with peacock feathers, the blues and greens iridescent. His was painted an antique gold.

Even in evening dress, he looked like he'd just come from a fight. With that crooked nose, there was no getting around the fact that he wasn't at all like the upper class. But the delicious discord between his fine clothes and his rugged build took her breath away.

"Are you sure this is a good idea?" She clutched the ties of her mask tightly. "It wouldn't do for you to be seen with a member of the staff of the Dakota. They'll have my hide. And yours."

"I've informed them that my second cousin, Imogen Cuthberg, will be joining me. We'll flit around the edges before making a run for the door. No one will notice, I promise."

"'Imogen Cuthberg'? Is that the best you can do?"

He gave her a mock pout. "I'll have you know I do have a second cousin named Imogen Cuthberg, and she's a delightful soul." He paused, thinking. "Her teeth are quite crooked and she's not the quickest wit, but delightful nonetheless."

"I can only imagine what you see in me, in that case." The darkness made her bold.

"Lovely teeth and a rapier-sharp wit, if you must know."

Thankfully, he couldn't see the pink glow that stole up her neck to the top of her head.

The carriage finally lurched to a halt in front of the Rutherfords' mansion. Sara took a deep breath and descended. Now that she was wearing a proper gown, all of her mother's admonishments regarding posture and deportment kicked in, and she glided along the sidewalk to the enormous front door encased by white marble columns.

Inside, they found themselves in a crush of guests. Mr. Camden had said the invitation list numbered over a thousand, and for that she was thankful, as it encouraged anonymity. Everyone was trying to squeeze into the great hall, and Sara let herself be swept along, with Mr. Camden's hand on her elbow providing reassurance. He maneuvered them into a corner of an enormous ballroom where they could gape without being trodden upon.

If this night weren't already a dream, the great hall was designed to be just that. Its recessed fountain alcoves and climbing stone vines turned the world inside out. The weight of the rusticated walls added to the soaring illusion of the trompe l'oeil sky that covered the vaulted ceiling.

"Your dress is lovely." Mr. Camden took a few steps back, his lips parted. No mirror was needed to know that she filled out the gown nicely—his face showed his delight. "It matches the flowers." He pointed to the vase of blush roses that blocked them from view, only one of hundreds of similar arrangements in hues from ivory to crimson. The current craze for indoor greenery was evident as well, with enormous palms and ferns clustered around the marble columns.

"It's like a jungle." She was proud and bashful and eager to deflect his attention.

"A jungle with wainscoting stripped from a château in France."

"I believe their fireplace rivals ours," Sara noted.

Mr. Camden studied it. "Carlisle stone and carved oak. Looks about twenty feet wide. The one in the Dakota dining room is a slight fifteen feet wide. I do apologize for that, Miss Cuthberg."

"As you should."

He might as well have shouted out her true name for all the attention, or lack thereof, they garnered. Mr. Camden purloined a couple of champagne glasses from a passing tray and handed one to her.

"Come, let's explore." He took her down a hallway that led away from the crowds, the tails of his dress coat fluttering behind him.

"How many servants does it take to keep a place like this running?" she asked. The champagne bubbled in her nose and she coughed.

"A little under forty, from what I've heard." He opened a door and raised his eyebrows. "Here we go."

They stood inside a library, the grandest Sara had ever seen. Bookshelves lined every wall, three levels in all, ringed by narrow balconies. The fireplace of bloodred marble reminded her of a piece of raw steak, streaked with fat. She drew closer, drawn to the figures carved along the mantel: a row of a dozen fat babies, all grabbing at one another in anger or churlishness.

"What on earth?"

Mr. Camden drew closer and sighed. "I know, awful, isn't it?"

"I would have thought cherubs would be better suited for such a grand space." She gestured up at the coffered ceiling. "Not these devilish creatures."

"Now do you understand my frustration? To have so much money, to waste it on such garishness." He turned to her. "That's why I want to get away from Hardenbergh, start my own firm and begin changing the world. One building at a time. No more European flourishes. Straight lines soaring into the sky."

"You're talking about remaking the entire city, aren't you?"

"Maybe I am. Someone must."

Sara studied the stained-glass windows and porcelain vases. "How do you know what's truly valuable, when everything is valuable?"

He laughed. "Precisely." His mask covered his expression, but his eyes danced with pleasure.

Sara froze as a deep voice from the hallway drew closer. "Someone's coming. What shall we do?"

Mr. Camden took her hand and pulled her into an alcove off the main room, out of sight.

She resisted at first, but it was no use. They were trapped.

Mr. Camden put his mouth close to her ear. "We'll stay here, quiet, for a moment. They've probably come for a smoke and will leave soon enough."

Sara squeezed as far back as she could. Shelves lined the alcove, but instead of leather-bound books, they contained artifacts of all sorts. Ancient manuscripts sat alongside gleaming swords, and grotesque figurines from some foreign land leered back at them. Terrified she'd knock something over, Sara stood as still as possible.

The squeak of leather, followed by the smell of cigar smoke, indicated that Mr. Camden was correct. The men's voices rose.

"They're running rampant." The speaker had a grumbly wheeze. "Why, Mrs. Rutherford was almost leveled by one on Fifth Avenue the other day. Our carriage driver had to give the kid a good beating. No sense, those street children."

"I wish we could put them on a boat and send them off somewhere," answered another. "They make New York City a dangerous place."

"Such generous souls," muttered Mr. Camden, so quietly Sara could barely hear him. He picked up a knife that lay on a shelf about hip level. The long, single-edged blade ended in a pointed tip, and the hilt was decorated with gold and silver that had been hammered and patterned into swirls. "I'm sure the child would've loved to get his hands on one of these, show them what's what. I know I would have. Pompous fools."

"We shouldn't touch anything." She mouthed it more than said it.

A woman's high voice broke through the men's murmurs like shattering glass. "Mr. Rutherford, you can't stay hiding in here. It just won't do."

Mr. Camden set the knife back down and Sara huddled closer.

"My dear Mrs. Rutherford, I should have known you'd find us."

After more grumbling, the men shuffled out, leaving behind the fetid odor of cigar smoke.

They were no longer playing at mocking the rich, they were hiding out in Mr. Rutherford's private library, eavesdropping, fingering his treasures. Mr. Camden had access to high society through his wife, but Sara was an absolute impostor. She'd been stupid to come. "They're gone."

Mr. Camden didn't move. "Wait a moment, give them time to disperse." He drew his hand up and lightly touched Sara's cheek.

She held her breath, riveted by the steely look in his eyes.

"You're lovely."

The gesture's power was as physical as if he'd crushed her in his embrace. Even though she lacked the wealth or standing of the other guests, Mr. Camden didn't care. His own humble background meant that he understood Sara more than anyone else ever had. He saw her not as a servant or supervisor, but as a woman.

He touched his finger to her lips. "We must go back to the Dakota. Now."

By the time they returned home, it was after one in the morning, the building quiet as a cathedral. Theo insisted Sara join him for a glass of sherry. In his parlor, she let the cape fall from her shoulders and placed it on a nearby chair while he poured their drinks. She'd never wear such a delicious dress again. So many temptations, all for such a short time. When the sun rose, she'd be back at work taking care of everyone else's complaints. But the night was her own.

He returned and placed a glass in her hand, and they settled on the settee. "May I call you Sara?"

She nodded. "You may."

"And will you call me Theo?"

"Of course. In private."

He sighed. "We're a couple of misfits, I know. The only reason a lowly architect is allowed to a ball is because his wife has standing, while you are the daughter of an earl and yet you must sneak in under an assumed name."

"If you remember, neither of us is interested in that sort of life. Only to laugh."

"But it bothers me, the thought of you toiling away in this prison, managing the likes of Mrs. Haines and Fitzroy. You deserve so much better."

She laughed. "You call this a prison?"

"A magnificent prison."

"We all have our own magnificent prisons, even the queen, I'd venture."

"Now you're getting all philosophical on me." He sipped his sherry. "Do you know who you reminded me of tonight?"

She shook her head.

"Cinderella. At the ball, anonymous and beautiful."

"If so, I seem to have left with both slippers and without my prince." The intimacy was too much to bear. She set down her glass and rose to her feet. "Please, I must be going. I don't want to keep you up any later than necessary."

He stood and handed her the mask. "Will you keep this, as a remembrance?"

"I'd like that." She smoothed the feathers. "Thank you, Theo."

He moved closer.

Unexpected memories, horrible ones, filled her head. Of Mr. Ainsworth's tongue, his hands on her, blood.

She braced herself, uncertain of what to do next. Theo stayed still as well, waiting, watching her.

"Tell me."

"I can't." The darkness, the misery of what she'd done, almost made her weep.

She turned toward the fire, staring, watching the flames.

"Was it something I did?" Anguish in his voice.

"No. Of course not."

"I hope you understand what a friend you've been to me, how much I've enjoyed having you near. I don't mean to make you uncomfortable, and I apologize if I have. By being too close."

"It's not that. Not that at all." If only she could explain.

"Then, what?"

She began speaking, uncertain at first what she'd reveal. "When I was young, I was sent to an apprenticeship for sewing. Mrs. Ainsworth was a horrible sort, and she'd keep us working late into the evening, when your eyes strained from the effort of properly stitching by candlelight. But where she was mean, her husband was jolly, sweet. He'd slip us butterscotch candies and praise our work. I didn't realize that he was preying on the other girls. One by one, he'd get them alone. At the time, though, I thought his attention meant I was special."

"You were a young girl. Innocent."

"Mrs. Ainsworth was working on a gown for a countess." Sara plucked at the fabric of her skirt. "This gown. When it was almost finished, she had me try it on, to check the length. He came in when I was wearing it." She didn't mention the look Mr. Ainsworth had given her, one of pleasure and longing. How she'd been pleased by her power. She didn't tell Theo how the other girls had warned her about Mr. Ainsworth's attentions that afternoon, and told her of the sick things he'd forced them to do. The bloom of her schoolgirl flirtation had rotted away, replaced by embarrassment and disgust. And rage.

"Late that night, she asked me to finish the trim and Mr. Ainsworth snuck in behind me. I didn't hear him."

Theo shook his head.

"He leaned over me, one hand on the table, and whispered awful things while pressing against my back. For a moment I froze, but then I did something horrible." She took a deep breath, remembering the cold feel of steel under her fingers. "I picked up the scissors and stabbed his hand. Right through to the tabletop."

"Then what happened?" Theo turned her to face him, but she couldn't meet his eyes. She breathed in his scent of oranges and smoke.

"I ran upstairs, still holding the gown, packed up my things, and ran off to London. Took a job as a maid in a horrible place, a seedy inn, and worked my way up."

"Goodness, Sara. What you've been through. What you've done." He lifted her chin and stared down at her. "I understand completely, though. I would have done the same to my stepfather."

"You would?"

"One year, for my mother's birthday, I had made a book of sketches for her. Drawings of castles and manor houses, one of her in a fancy dress, similar to the one you're wearing now, even though she'd never owned such a gown in her life. She lingered over each page, running her fingers over the lines like they were Braille. But it enraged my stepfather. He insisted that she toss the sketchbook in the fire. He knew doing so would kill her spirit, and mine. The triumph in his eyes as she placed it onto the flames made me wish I had a gun. I would have shot him in the face." He rubbed his eyes, as if trying to erase the memory. "I'm sorry."

"What for?" She wanted him to keep talking, to extend the agony of being so close as long as possible.

"I can't seem to stay away from you. If something ridiculous happens with one of the tenants or the construction workers, you are the person I want to share it with, right off. I worry I've overstepped, and I have tried at times to pull back."

"I understand. You were doing the proper thing."

"I'd never want you to think of me like Mr. Ainsworth, but, Sara . . . I don't want to do the proper thing anymore."

She, not he, initiated the kiss. The silk gown slipped from her shoulders like rose petals in the heat of summer, and with it went her troubled memories of Mr. Ainsworth. Then Theo took her, carefully and gently, in front of the fire.

Sara let herself go, lost herself in the shadows of the Dakota, within the thick walls that shut out all sounds and fears.

"Mrs. Camden is here!"

Daisy flew into Sara's office, her cheeks a rosy red. Sara hadn't gotten any sleep the previous night, slinking back to her room from Theo's, peacock mask in hand, as dawn broke. Maybe she'd misheard. "I'm sorry?"

"Mr. Camden's wife and children arrived; they're heading up to their apartment now, and Mrs. Camden said she had to see you right away."

"But she's not due until next Thursday, isn't she?" The question was a silly one, and didn't alter the fact that the woman was in the Dakota already, but Sara needed to buy time to absorb this new information.

"I know, but she's here now. The children are adorable, all dressed alike. I'm going to do just the same when I have children."

"I'll be there right away. In the meantime, call the maids for that floor to unpack their belongings."

The unexpected strident note in her voice drew Daisy up short. "Yes, ma'am."

After the girl had closed the door behind her, Sara rose and went to the window. What did she hope to see? Theo striding across the courtyard, ready to take her in his arms and tell her he loved her? Of course not. It had been a momentary dream, when they'd both escaped into another world, fueled by the ostentatious beauty of the people and surroundings at the ball. Now it was over.

She wished she could hide up in her room and sleep. Sleep until years had passed and Theo no longer lived here and she could go about her duties without hoping she'd run into him around every corner.

Theo's apartment was a bustle of activity, porters heaving in trunks, and the maids scrambling around like a flock of white-capped geese. She hesitated in the foyer, one hand on the brass fireplace, listening. A woman's voice, with a melodic English inflection, rose above the rest.

"Now, Emily, I'm sure your doll is here somewhere. You must be patient and she'll turn up eventually."

Sara moved forward. In the parlor stood the woman Sara recognized from the day at the Langham. Her hair was perfectly coiffed on her head in blond waves, and she wore a navy plaid traveling dress. The woman was beautiful, Sara had to admit. Her fairness of skin and hair would have washed her out completely except for her enormous green-gold eyes and those lashes, so black they looked like they came from someone else entirely. No doubt, Theo had been captivated the first time he'd laid eyes on her. She was an artist's dream.

She stood very upright in the middle of the room, speaking to a girl Sara recognized as the older daughter from the day at the Langham. The girl's hair was a thick brunette, much like Theo's.

"Mrs. Camden." Sara's voice gave an unexpected squeak. She cleared her throat. "I am Mrs. Smythe, the managerette."

"Right. We met in London."

"Yes."

Mrs. Camden stepped forward, holding out a gloved hand. "You saved my daughter Lula that day, and I was never able to thank you properly. Luckily, Mr. Camden insisted you come all the way to America with us, so I am finally able to do so."

Sara paused. She'd forgotten the pliability of an English accent. With a slight change in the tone of voice, it was easy to make a statement an accusation, or have it drip with sarcasm. Her first week at the Dakota, Sara had realized that Americans didn't understand the subtext behind her voice. She had to spell out exactly what she needed, as well as the urgency, and couldn't depend upon a phrase like "I do hope you'll find it in you to show up on time for work" to do the trick.

There was an underlying message beneath Mrs. Camden's statement. A warning. Or was she imagining things?

"No thanks are necessary."

"In any event, we're having some difficulty getting settled. The beds in the children's room need to be moved around; I don't like the placement."

"Of course."

"Minnie."

Theo strode into the room but stopped when he spotted Sara. For a moment the two remained frozen, their eyes fused on each other, before the young girl rushed to him. "Papa!"

Theo knelt down and took her in his arms. "My darling Emily, what an unexpected delight." He looked up at his wife. "You arrived early."

"We certainly did. The seas were in our favor." She gestured to Sara. "I was just giving Mrs. Smythe her instructions. That's all for now, Mrs. Smythe."

"Of course." She burned with shame.

"Wait."

Theo's voice stopped her in her tracks. "Mrs. Smythe, thank you for your assistance."

She refused to meet his gaze. "You're welcome."

"But my doll!" Emily grabbed her father's sleeve. "She's gone and Mummy won't do anything about it."

"Enough." A weariness in Mrs. Camden's voice reminded Sara of her first day in New York City, and she felt a small pang of sympathy. "The maids are busy unpacking, but I'm certain Mrs. Smythe might help you."

The pang dissipated.

"Mrs. Smythe has other duties I'm sure she must take care of," said Theo.

For a moment, Sara was tongue-tied, until the girl gave her a shy smile. "Would you, please?" she asked.

"Of course."

As Sara led the girl from the parlor, she overheard Mrs. Camden speaking to Theo. "I thought our apartment would be much farther along. The bedchambers are in a terrible state."

"I've been working, Minnie."

The woman didn't answer him. She imagined them in an embrace, Theo kissing his wife. The taste of his lips and mouth were still on her own.

Sara and Emily searched for the doll for only a couple of minutes before Sara discovered it wedged between a dresser and the wall. They were soon joined by the twins, Lula and Luther. Lula, the girl Sara had saved that day that now seemed so long ago, marched over to Sara and yanked on her skirt before running back to her brother with a sly smile. A spirited child, Sara decided. Too bold by far, which explained her near disaster in London. The boy had pretty blond curls, like his sister, but hung back, uncertain.

Having found the doll for Emily, Sara left, closing the apartment's front door behind her with a solid *click*. She vowed to steer clear of the entire family from now on.

"Sara."

Theo was waiting in the corridor. "I'm so sorry, we didn't have even a minute together. I wanted to apologize."

She looked up at him. "No need to apologize. It's better this way."

"But last night—"

"Let's not talk about it." The wail of a child rose from behind the door. Another crisis. "You must go back to your family."

Instead of waiting for the elevator, Sara took the stairs, careful to make sure her footsteps echoed evenly up the stairwell, even though she wanted more than anything to run willy-nilly away from the man she'd been running toward for the past month.

That evening, she wished she could eat her supper alone in the staff dining hall, but Daisy and Mrs. Haines waved her over to their table, where they sat with a young woman who had a vacant stare and chestnut hair.

"This is Miss Honeycutt, the nanny for the Camdens," said Daisy by way of introduction.

Sara gave the girl a curt nod. "Please let me know if the family needs anything as they settle in."

"Of course. So far, all seems to be calm. Though you never know what's going to spring up." Her features, though pleasant, were scrunched close together in the frame of her face.

"Have you worked for the family for very long?" asked Mrs. Haines, skewering a piece of potato with her fork.

"I took over in the summer, after they let the previous nanny go."

"The children seem delightful." Daisy propped her elbow on the table and fiddled with a loose curl.

"They're a handful." Miss Honeycutt gave a sweet smile. "I'll tell you, it'll be a reprieve to have Mr. Camden around more, to provide a fatherly sense of discipline to them."

"He's quite busy with his work."

Sara hadn't meant to bring attention to herself. Mrs. Haines cocked her head, curious.

"I mean, even though the Dakota is up and running, he's off to work on the next project for Mr. Hardenbergh. I'd advise you to keep a close eye on the girl Lula. She has more temerity than most girls of her age."

The nanny nodded. "I agree. Quite the sprite."

"What's Mrs. Camden like?" asked Daisy.

Sara knew she should stop her from prying, but she wanted to hear the answer. She sipped her tea in an effort to help the mutton haricot go down easier. The cook would need a good talking-to, as the servants' dinners were in stark contrast to the delicacies from the picnic. Sara added that to her list of tomorrow's duties.

Miss Honeycutt waved her fork about, thrilled to have an audience. "She's quiet, often takes to bed with some illness or another. Too bad, as she has the most beautiful dresses. I don't know if she'll be able to manage up here in the wilderness. I hear it takes forever just to get into town."

"The city is gradually moving north." Sara couldn't help herself. "There are some grand mansions on Fifth Avenue in the Fifties, and they say they may build along the park as well. We happen to be the first."

"Can't happen soon enough for me," said Daisy. "Did you hear about the masquerade ball at the Rutherfords' last night?"

"No, what about it?" Miss Honeycutt practically jumped out of her seat. Daisy had met her match when it came to dreaming.

"It's in the afternoon paper. They had over a thousand guests, but someone stole some kind of treasure."

Mrs. Haines sniffed. "Treasure? What treasure?"

Daisy looked about and lowered her voice, eager to share the intrigue. "This morning they discovered a valuable knife was missing from Mr. Rutherford's library. Worth thousands of dollars. From Tibet, it was."

The image of the gold- and silver-plated handle popped into Sara's head. She'd stood less than a foot away from it. What if Theo thought she'd taken it?

She cleared her plate and sent a porter with a sealed note to Theo, asking him to meet her on the roof at eight o'clock.

As she paced and waited for him, the silliness of her actions became clear. She'd been desperate for a chance to speak with him and had used the knife as an excuse. She was about to run back downstairs when he appeared.

He looked around and then stumbled over to her, pulling her into his arms. This is what she'd wanted, more than anything. To be held by him one last time.

"My dear, I am so sorry we didn't get any time to speak. I was about to come to you when I received your note." He pulled her to a corner where the chimney rose up, and leaned her against the brick. His hand stroked her face down to her chin, which he held with his index finger and thumb. "This is what I like. This is what I want."

He kissed her then, long and sweet, peppered with small strokes of his tongue that made her insides turn over.

After a moment, she leaned her head on his shoulder. The cool air whipped her face, but she didn't want to go back down.

"Did you hear that something went missing from the Rutherford library last night?"

Theo threw his head back and laughed. "Was that you? Do I need to search you for contraband?"

"It was right where we were standing."

"Probably one of the servants. In any case, I wouldn't have taken a knife."

"Really? And what would you have absconded with?"

"One of those fantastic books from the Middle Ages. I'd have something to entertain me, at the very least, until the police found me out."

She'd never spoken so easily, so openly with another person, and she ached at having to let it all go. But there was no way to continue on, with his family so close at hand. He was married. He had three lovely children. She would not jeopardize their happiness.

"We're lucky we weren't caught together, Theo." Her voice was firmer than she'd believed possible. "We have to move on with our lives. You have Mrs. Camden and your children here now. We can't do this anymore."

He sighed and rubbed his hands together. The wind picked up, lifting up the lapels of his jacket. "I am sorry, Sara. You are the world to me. You've been such a help in every way. I want you to know I've fallen in love with you."

"Enough." She remembered the way her mother had hardened her heart. Now it was her time. Even though this was much harder. They were in love and would be working in close proximity. "We won't speak of this again. Good-bye, Theo."

She grabbed her skirts, which seemed to have a mind of their own, flapping around Theo's legs, and walked away.

CHAPTER FOURTEEN

New York City, December 1884

If only Sara had had more resolve. In the month since their meeting on the roof, while Sara didn't allow Theo to kiss her or do anything else untoward, his looks, and the way he lightly touched her arm when they passed each other in the hallways, were enough to fuel her dreams at night. She was convinced his intentions weren't to make her feel guilty but simply to show her he was thinking of her, too. That the one night they'd had together was something they both cherished.

Of course, she couldn't deny that there were times when she looked out the window of her office and saw him in the courtyard, speaking to one of the other tenants, and decided it was most certainly time to check on whether or not the new porter was correctly outfitted. A few times a week, Theo would stop by and sit across from her for five minutes or so to inquire about the tenants, and her answers were even and low, knowing Daisy and Mrs. Haines could hear every word.

Standing now at her office window, Sara watched as the Camden family left to go to a holiday party, the children in matching velvet outfits and Mrs. Camden in a pale-blue silk dress with ecru lace.

Sara, in contrast, looked frumpy and old, a dowdy spinster. She'd tossed her rose silk dress and peacock mask into her trunk the day after the ball, out of view. Never to be worn again.

After the Camdens' carriage disappeared through the archway, Sara put on her boiled-wool cloak for a trip downtown. She had to buy Christmas ornaments for the enormous fir that Fitzroy had propped up in a corner of the dining room. They needed wreaths and all such nonsense, although her mood couldn't have been gloomier.

"Do you mind if I come along?" Daisy's voice drew Sara out of her dark reverie. "I have the afternoon off and promised my mother I'd visit. She's not been well."

The last thing she wanted was Daisy's incessant prattle, but she could see no way of making an excuse. "Of course. If you're ready now."

Together they walked to the elevated train stop on Ninth Avenue. Sara's legs felt heavy, like logs instead of flesh and bone, and her body ached with every step. Flakes of snow fell limply down from the clouds, as if even the weather couldn't be bothered today, coating the piles of rocks in the empty lots with a veil of white.

The train entered the station just as they ascended to the platform. "Where are you off to?" asked Daisy as they secured two seats near the front.

"I planned to shop at Stewart's on Broadway."

"Lucky me. We can get off at the same stop, as it's on the way to my family's place."

Sara winced as the train chugged forward. She was still getting used to taking the El. The convenience was an asset, but she never liked the feeling of being suspended high above the city in a narrow car, pulled by what seemed like a too-small locomotive. A major gust of wind would be enough to knock the entire thing off its tracks.

Daisy, on the other hand, took great delight in staring outside and pointing at the various people and buildings they passed.

"Do you see your family every week on your day off?" Sara asked as they paused at Forty-Second Street.

Daisy brightened, eager to share. "I do. There are ten of us children, and mother always makes stew. I wouldn't miss it for the world. We do a lovely Christmas as well. You should come."

The invitation was wildly inappropriate but sweet. "You're a kind girl, but I'll have enough on my hands, running the building that day. I believe we have seven parties being held."

"Did you see Mr. and Mrs. Camden and the family today? Mrs. Camden is something of a sourpuss, I must say. Although Mr. Camden is a kind man."

Sara hated how pleased the description of Mrs. Camden made her. "Daisy, you must not speak of the tenants in that way. You're too familiar, by far." She didn't want to think of the Camdens. Or of the sad Christmas she'd be having. A day at her desk, followed by dinner with the staff. No different from holidays at the Langham, but this year was harder.

She loosened her cloak. The car was stifling, the aisles filled with bodies as the train got farther downtown. "Were you born in Ireland, Daisy?"

"No, born here. I'm an American. The freckles always give me away, though. Wish I could scrub them right off my face."

The train shuddered to a halt, and for a moment Sara thought she might be sick.

"You all right?" Daisy cocked her head.

"This swaying makes me feel ill."

"I thought you said you never got sick once on the crossing from England."

Daisy seemed to remember the strangest things. "That I didn't.

But I could always get out and get some air. I wasn't trapped like a kipper in a tin."

Why had she said that? The image made her almost retch. Which was odd, as she'd ridden the El many times before and never been bothered.

"You look quite awful, Mrs. Smythe."

"No, no. I'm fine."

She did the calculation in her head.

She was late. But it couldn't be possible. Maybe she had her dates wrong. If only she could take a look at a calendar.

They reached their stop. Daisy bounced down the stairway, and Sara took deep breaths as she descended behind her. It couldn't be.

A red-haired boy screamed out Daisy's name before they reached the street. His voice was not one of excitement, but panic.

"Daisy, come quick." He flew to his sister's side. "Mother's ill."

Daisy grabbed Sara's arm. Her face had turned as ashen as the sky.

"Daisy, do you want me to come with you?" Sara couldn't leave the girl; it wouldn't be right.

"Please, Mrs. Smythe. Would you?"

They headed east, to a rough neighborhood where the residents of the Dakota would never venture. Daisy pointed to a tenement building across the street, made of redbrick, distinguished from its neighbors only by the color of the cornice at the very top. A black fire escape zigged down the front like a game of tic-tac-toe.

Inside, an uneven wooden stairway led to a fourth-floor landing with two doors. Daisy opened the one on the street side of the building, and Sara followed. They stood in a kitchen with a dirty sink, full of dishes, and an old stove. A teapot patterned with buttercups was the one thing of beauty in what could only be called a hovel. A table for two beside the stove seemed laughably small, considering the number of children gathered in the parlor just beyond. Raw, uneven floorboards ran lengthwise to two windows, where curtains embroidered with matching buttercups hung. Sara felt an immediate kinship to Daisy's mother, who had tried to make the best of it.

Daisy spoke briefly with a boy of around fourteen with black hair and blue eyes, his mouth set in a grim line, before disappearing into a dark room off the parlor. Sara looked around at the rest of the brood scattered about the room. They seemed to range from two to eight and, despite the squalor, appeared clean and well fed.

There were no words Sara could say to these children that would help, so she stayed quiet and sat in a wobbly cane chair in the corner. They remained mute, the younger ones sniffling every so often. Daisy walked out of the bedroom accompanied by a doctor with an unkempt beard and rheumy eyes. He barely acknowledged the group assembled and stomped to the door, letting himself out.

"How is she?" asked one of the younger boys.

Daisy didn't answer. Sara followed Daisy into the darkened room.

"The doctor said it was her lungs." Daisy pointed to the figure on the bed, covered over by a quilt. "She's gone."

Sara drew in a sharp breath. She hadn't expected this, wasn't sure what she should do or say. "I'm so sorry. Is your father about?"

Daisy shook her head. "He left a few years ago. No one knows where he ran off to. Mother kept us going with her sewing, and my wages help, of course." Sara recognized shock behind poor Daisy's matter-of-factness. All those siblings to take care of.

"Will you be able to keep the flat, to keep the children here?"

Daisy glanced about, as if seeing the room for the first time. "I don't know how we'll pay for it. My mother wanted me to be part of a better life, and that's what I've done. But I can't afford it."

The regret and pain in her voice moved Sara. "My mother did the same thing. Sent me away so I could rise up above my station. Your journey's just beginning. Your mother must've been very proud of you."

The boy with the black hair entered the room. "She dead, then?"

Daisy didn't respond. The answer was obvious.

"We won't be able to manage, not without her wages," the boy said.

Discussing such pedestrian matters over the body of their mother might have seemed inappropriate, but Sara knew the very survival of the family was at stake.

Daisy straightened the quilt on the bed as if she were tucking in a child. "We'll manage. Always have."

"I'll get another job."

Daisy shook her head. "You're a lowly stable boy, Seamus. What else are you going to do? Be valet to a gentleman? Nothing you find will match Mum's sewing."

"Then you can stay home and sew. How about that for an idea?" He jutted out his chin.

"Makes more sense for you to do that instead."

"I don't do women's work. Don't be daft." His words had a sharp edge to them, as if he'd funneled his grief into fury. "I won't stay home. It's not right. I'm the man."

Sara hated seeing them at each other like this. "There must be a way to manage."

Seamus pointed a finger at her. "Who's this, then?"

"She's in charge of me, my supervisor," said Daisy. "Leave her be."

He left in a frenzy of curses. Tears rolled down Daisy's cheeks, her gaze never leaving her mother's body on the bed. "Seamus was her favorite. He'll settle down after a while."

Such hardship. "I'll speak with Mr. Douglas, see if we can arrange your schedule so you can come downtown twice a week instead of once. Perhaps we can add to your responsibilities, and raise your wage."

Daisy looked up at her, her mouth beginning to wobble. "Would you do that for me?"

"Of course."

Sara left Daisy and her brothers and sisters to mourn, after telling Daisy to take the time she needed to make arrangements. Back on the street, in the midst of the noise and grime, her words to the girl sounded silly, trite. There were no guarantees. It struck her that the staff of the Dakota had become their own kind of family over the past couple of months, including Sara in the role of wise older sister and Daisy as the brash young thing, in part because of the far-flung locale but also because there were no longtimers who rued "the way things used to be." They'd all jumped on board the train at the same time. And, while at the Langham she'd have stayed removed from the staff's personal lives, Daisy's well-being truly mattered to her.

Sara would try to help. It was the least she could do.

Sara looked up from the payroll numbers she'd been staring at for the past five minutes. Mr. Douglas showed up every Tuesday like clockwork to go over the books, taking her place behind the desk and making her wait as he double-checked the figures, the only sound in the room the thin whistle of his breathing. She had to be prepared, but this morning the interruptions seemed endless. The porters had tracked pine needles everywhere while wrestling the denuded Christmas trees out of the tenants' apartments, Mr. Bates on the seventh floor had lodged an official complaint about the barber's political rants, and Mrs. Westcott had insisted the chef serve a Washington pie for tea, even if it wasn't on the day's menu.

Sara's stomach was still queasy and the Washington pie discussion hadn't helped matters, even after she'd taken an extra swig from the bottle of Dr. Walker's Vinegar Bitters. The prettiness of the sea-blue glass belied the nasty taste of the liquid, but Mrs. Haines, who'd recommended it after inquiring after Sara's health a week ago, had sworn the elixir would settle her indigestion. Sara took a dose every day, eager for anything to reduce the nausea.

Since that awful moment on the El, Sara had steered her thoughts away from the possibility that she was with child. The weather had turned brutal; everyone on staff was catching some kind of bug or other. That had to be the reason for her illness, her recent weakness.

"Here are the day's receipts for your signature, Mrs. Smythe." Daisy dropped them on her desk and stood waiting in silence as Sara signed each one.

Mr. Douglas had denied Sara's request for Daisy's pay raise, and only given her one extra day off a month, much to Sara's chagrin. She felt terrible about having raised the girl's hopes and had tolerated her sulkiness in the three weeks since her mother had passed. Yet so far the worst hadn't happened, and the family were all still ensconced in the tenement apartment on the East Side.

When Sara handed the receipts back, she noticed Daisy was carrying a bucket with a cloth draped over the top.

"Daisy, what's that?"

But before Daisy could answer, the rancid odor of fish hit Sara's nostrils. Without warning, the toast Sara had eaten for breakfast threatened to come up, and she gestured for Daisy to shut the door fast. The girl was quick on her feet, and with a mix of relief and horror, Sara vomited into the wastepaper basket by her desk. She lowered herself to the floor, her back against the cabinets.

"God, oh God." The only words that would come out of her mouth. She was ruined, completely ruined.

Daisy was by her side, handing her a handkerchief. "What's wrong?"

"It's the bucket of fish. Put it outside."

Daisy did as she was told, closing the door softly before kneeling down beside Sara. "Fitzroy asked me to bring it down to the cook. I'm sorry."

"No, it's not your fault."

"Are you ill?"

"No. Well, I don't know."

Daisy hesitated before responding. "Don't worry, you'll be all right. I've seen it before."

Sara looked up in panic. Daisy knew.

"I won't tell. My mother had the same symptoms with every child." She gave a solemn nod. "Your secret's safe with me. You were so good to me when my mother died, I want to help you."

Daisy's eyes were wide, encouraging. Although just a girl, she'd seen so much of babies being born, and of death. Sara's life so far had been void of any close relationships, save Theo, and for a minute she envied the girl her worldly knowledge. Would it be wrong to open up to her? "You're a child, Daisy, you don't need to be burdened with the knowledge of my terrible deed."

"It's Mr. Camden, isn't it?"

Sara put the handkerchief to her lips, trying to keep her stare blank.

"I noticed the way he looks at you. He loves you." They'd spent so much time together, of course the girl knew. Sara had been stupid to think she could keep it hidden.

"He's married."

"But now you're carrying his baby." Daisy sighed.

The girl was caught up in the romance of it. "He can't ever know." Sara clutched Daisy's wrist. "You can't tell him."

"Of course I won't." Her words rang true and released in Sara a flood of unspoken fears.

"I don't know what to do. I can't have a child. I'll lose everything."

"I know someone who can help. Downtown, there's a woman who knows what to do."

Sara had heard of such things, of course. She also knew they were terribly dangerous and didn't always work. But her job was on the line; she would be fired if she got too far along.

"How would it work?"

Daisy patted her hand. "I'll ask about her and let you know."

"I'm not sure if it's the right thing to do."

"Of course it is. What other choice do you have?"

The door of the office flew open and Mrs. Haines's sour face glared down at them. "What are you doing on the floor?"

"I had dropped a pen, and Daisy was helping me find it," said Sara. They got up, and for a moment Sara thought she might swoon. She planted herself in her chair. "Can I help you?"

"I have more applications for apartments. They keep coming in, even if there is no room." She placed the envelopes on the desk. "You look peaked. Is there anything I can do?"

"No, thank you, Mrs. Haines."

Once Mrs. Haines had left, Daisy put her fingers to her lips. "Not a soul, I promise."

"Do you think Mrs. Haines heard what we were talking about?"

"Not unless she pressed her ear against the door, and I doubt she'd stoop that low."

The woman was always sneaking around, appearing right when Sara least expected her. She had a stealthiness to her so that even her skirts didn't swish when she walked.

Daisy was true to her word, but on the day Sara was scheduled to go downtown and take care of matters, a newspaper article described in great detail a recent crackdown on abortionists throughout the city. Doctors and their patients were being arrested in raids, and the punishments were severe, as a lesson to anyone who tried something similar.

She told Daisy they couldn't risk it, not until the raids stopped.

For now, she would have to live with the consequences.

CHAPTER FIFTEEN

New York City, September 1985

Bailey opened one eye. She was in her bed, in her room at the Dakota. That was the good news. The bad was that her head felt like it contained several large rocks, in addition to her skull, and her mouth was as dry as Death Valley.

Her last memory of the evening was Tristan sticking his head into the room where Melinda and Tony and a couple of other hangers-on were hiding out, and shaking his head. He didn't say anything, just gave Bailey the look of a parent who is very, very disappointed.

She hadn't lasted a week out of rehab before diving back into the joyride of Manhattan nightlife. Melinda was the first person she'd like to blame, but she knew from the treatment center that the fault lay only with herself. She'd dressed up, gone out with people she knew would drink and do drugs, and figured that she'd be strong enough to say no. Unbelievably stupid.

She opened both eyes and followed the dust motes as they drifted above her. The apartment was a dirty construction site, there was nowhere comfortable to sit and recover, and she was stuck here all weekend. She'd gotten a message on the answering machine saying the workers would be back on Monday, so there was solace in that. Tony had made arrangements to cover the cost for the month.

Desperation sucked. Her intentions had been grand, but she was still back in the same gutter. No rich, snobby boyfriend to bail her out. No one at all. The silence of the apartment weighed on her like a malevolent ghost, judging her for every transgression.

Bailey wedged her way into the maid's room shower, which was more like a half bathtub wedged in a corner. Wet and bedraggled, she trudged to a local diner and had some scrambled eggs, toast, and coffee. By the second cup, the rocks in her head had diminished in size, and her thoughts came clearer. As did the shame.

But now what? She'd overslept and missed the early AA meeting, but a glance at the crumpled brochure in her purse showed another one at noon. In the meantime, she needed a distraction from her self-loathing.

Instead of taking the elevator back up to the apartment, she hit the down button and descended into the storage area of the Dakota. The place was cool and quiet, and she doubted Renzo worked on weekends. He was probably off with a girlfriend or working on a project outdoors with other like-minded guys who preferred building a shed to engaging in conversation. He wasn't her type at all. She preferred the skinny artists with a penchant for declaring love at first sight. Tortured boy-men who were only too happy at first to reassure Bailey that she was beautiful, that she was worth adoring. After a few months, every last one of them inevitably drifted away. She'd been a parasite, leeching their love and validation. No wonder she was alone.

Bailey turned on the light and looked around the storeroom, eager to heave large things about and use up some of her pissed-off energy. The three trunks in the corner would be a good place to start. The top one wasn't too heavy and she let it *thump* to the floor. Curious, she opened the latch.

On the very top was an old-fashioned gown in a navy plaid. The lace around the collar had yellowed, but the strong smell of mothballs indicated that the worst of the intruders had been kept away. Bailey lifted it and held it up against her. The hem reached her ankles, but the waist of the dress was ridiculously small. She put it aside and kept digging. A pair of high-topped leather shoes in black that would be trendy today. Four corsets and a couple pairs of drawers had turned a dingy tea color from their original white, but were still intact. She dug deeper, looking for anything that showed which apartment the trunk belonged to.

She shut it and as the dust blew off the top, she spied the initials M.C.C. engraved in gold. But no other labels or identifying tags.

The second trunk was labeled T.J.C.

Now that was something. Theodore Camden, it must be. And Theodore Camden's wife had been named Minnie. What were the chances that some other residents had the exact same initials?

If these items, many of which were in good condition, were worth some money, Melinda might be able to sell them and perhaps pay Bailey a commission. The trunks had obviously been sitting down here, untouched, for decades. Renzo would probably be glad of the chance to clear them out.

The T.J.C. trunk was, disappointingly, locked. She'd have to find a key or figure out how to break into it. The last trunk, the one on the very bottom of the pile, wasn't made of the same top-grain black leather. This one was brown and worn. The initials carved on the top in black, not gold, read S.J.S.

The latch was locked but she was able to snap it open with a twist of her wrist. Inside were the same period of dresses, but shabbier. All hues of brown and gray, and some of the materials were so itchy they made Bailey's skin crawl just looking at them. Near the bottom of the trunk, she found a silk evening gown in a dusky rose, and within its folds was a mask made of peacock feathers, of all things.

She pulled out a sailor suit made for a baby. It was the old kind, more like a dress, and the little blue tie had hardly faded at all from its original navy. And a couple of silk scarves, in different shades of blue. If they hadn't smelled so musty, Bailey would have been tempted to make off with them.

Tucked in one corner was a delicate glass bottle the color of the sea, with a label on the outside that read DR. WALKER'S VINEGAR BITTERS. She put it aside. It was far from valuable, and she would smile whenever she saw it on her windowsill.

Underneath everything was a traveling booklet for a Sara Jane Smythe, from Fishbourne, England. The date she came to New York was stamped on her booklet: September, 1884. As Bailey leafed through it—there were no other markings—a photograph came loose.

A woman with thick, dark hair and a wry smile stood in front of two girls and a boy, holding in her arms a baby wearing the exact sailor suit from the trunk. The baby's head had moved during the photo, as had one of the girls', so they were blurry and ghostlike. She could make out what looked like a sailboat behind them.

A typical late-nineteenth-century photo. No sense of laughter or animation. But she liked this better than the false, toothy smiles that slid out of Polaroid instant cameras, because to Bailey they offered a truer sense of the subjects, not their flashy masks.

The door to the storage room slammed shut, the sound reverberating around the cement walls like a gunshot. Bailey leaped to her feet, still holding the photo. She stood, frozen in place, wondering what had just happened.

"Hello?"

No answer. Kenneth had given her a rundown of the Dakota's ghosts over tea as the wallpaper hanger took measurements in the bathroom. One was a creepy little girl, bouncing a red ball, who was considered a bad omen, a harbinger of death. An electrician working in the basement in the 1930s had seen a phantom wearing a frock coat, winged collar, and glasses. Rumor had it he was Edward Clark, the man who built the Dakota but died before he could see it completed.

Bailey didn't believe in ghosts or Kenneth's tales of ghostly wanderers. The door couldn't have slammed shut on its own, just like that. Someone had to have walked by it and done so, not knowing she was inside.

She tucked the photo into her back pocket and walked over to reopen the door, but as she reached for the knob, she heard footsteps coming closer. Whoever had shut it was returning.

The door handle turned. She backed away, uncertain.

"What the hell?"

Renzo stood in the doorway. He stared at her for a moment before bursting out laughing. "You look like you're ready for a fight."

Without thinking, she'd put up her dukes, like an idiot. Kenneth's ghost stories had gotten her worked up. She dropped her hands to her sides, standing stiffly. "You scared me. The door slammed shut."

"Huh. That's weird. Sorry, didn't mean to frighten you."

Bailey shoved her hands into the pockets of her jeans. "It was just loud."

"What are you doing in the basement?"

"Clearing a space for the workers, seeing what you have down here."

He didn't seem angry at her nosing about. "Find anything interesting?"

She pointed to the trunks. "I think the two black ones belonged to Theodore Camden and his wife. The one marked s.j.s. belonged to a woman named Sara Jane Smythe, who came here in 1884. That one even has her official papers in it, an immigration booklet."

Renzo wore faded Levi's that fell low on his waist, and a maroon T-shirt. He ran his hand through his hair. "Right. Sara Smythe. That was the year the Dakota opened."

"Have you heard of her?"

"Sure, I've heard of her. She lived here for about a year."

"Then what happened?"

"You don't know?"

Bailey shook her head.

"Follow me."

Renzo led her down the hall to his office, where he rummaged around on a high bookshelf and took down an ancient photo album, the kind with black paper and tiny triangles for tucking the corners of the photos into. It was covered with a fine layer of dust, and he took a rag out of his back pocket and wiped it down before opening it up.

"This is a book of clippings about the Dakota from the time it was built, passed down from super to super."

He started to flip through it, but Bailey stopped him. "Do you mind? I'd love to see the whole thing."

"Suit yourself." He moved out of the way and let her go through it, page by page.

The first page held a yellowed article from the *Daily Graphic.* Bailey read out loud. "'*A Description of One of the Most Perfect Apartment Houses in the World.*' You can't do better than that, can you?"

"I guess not."

She sat down in a chair and scanned through it. The Dakota had made quite a splash when it first opened. How strange to think that the rooms had been filled with people wearing petticoats and top hats, the sound of horses' hooves clopping in the courtyard. Someone had actually worn that corset and pair of shoes from the trunk. They weren't just artifacts in a museum.

Later in the book were cutouts from magazines. One showed off the bedroom of Rudolf Nureyev, decorated in a riot of textures and patterns, including an Elizabethan canopy bed.

"Not one for subtlety." Renzo stood behind her now, his hand resting on the back of her chair.

She hurried through the rest of the scrapbook, mainly 1960s shots of apartments with minimal, contemporary furniture.

"Not to your taste?" Renzo asked.

"No. Maybe in an East Side high-rise, but not here." She shut the book.

"But you didn't see the part about Theodore Camden."

He took the book from her lap and laid it back on the desk. A delicate scrap of paper had fallen behind one of the photos, and he unfolded it with care.

The newspaper headline, dated March 4, 1886, read: MURDERESS FOUND GUILTY.

> *Mrs. Sara J. Smythe, former lady managerette of the Dakota Apartment House, was found guilty in the November 13th stabbing death of architect Mr. Theodore Camden. Mrs. Smythe had suffered from delusions in the past, but Mr. Camden had nonetheless taken pity on her, and his act of kindness was answered with violence and mayhem. Mr. Camden is survived by his wife and three children. According to Judge Wilton, "This undoubtedly proves that rehabilitation of the insane is a pointless enterprise."*

"She was the one who killed Melinda's great-grandfather, then."

"That's the legend. Which explains why her belongings were packed up and sent to the basement."

She pulled the photo out of her back pocket. "This was in the trunk, too."

Renzo examined it closely. He turned it over, where the words *S. Smythe and the Camden children, 1885,* were written in a loopy cursive.

Bailey gasped. "The murderer standing with the children. That's ghoulish. Does the scrapbook have anything more about the crime? Like why she killed him?"

"I'm afraid not."

"Now I'm dying to know more. I'll have to ask Melinda if her mother ever talked about it."

"Right after you've fixed Kenneth's apartment back to the way it was."

She glared at him. "Of course I'm going to do that."

He cocked his head. "That's weird."

"What."

"Do that again."

"I have no idea what you're talking about."

"Look at me like you just did."

She did so, like he was an idiot.

"Don't move." He held up the photo next to her face. "You have the same eyebrow thing going on."

"Are you telling me I look like a murderer?"

"No, seriously." He tugged on her arm and brought her over to a small mirror that hung on the back of the door. "Check it out."

Bailey repeated the gesture into the mirror, as Renzo held up the photo.

Obviously, a great percentage of people could do the same trick.

Her father had worn the same expression whenever he was unimpressed or skeptical.

But it was the way the woman stood, the line of her neck, the set of her mouth. Bailey's parents had a photo album with a photo that was an exact match, except that it was taken in this century, not the last. Her father holding a newborn Bailey in his arms, with the same half smile.

Bailey looked like her father, everyone said so. And they both looked like Sara Smythe. The murderess.

Renzo blinked. "The resemblance is uncanny. Even to me, and I don't know you at all."

The scrutiny unnerved her. She felt stripped bare, just as she was doing to Melinda's apartment, all of the usual crutches and comforts peeled away. The dank basement seemed like it was closing in on her, the draftiness making her shiver.

"Well, I'm not sure I see it. I better be getting back upstairs."

"I didn't mean to upset you."

"I'm not upset." The words came out harsher than she'd intended; her headache threatened to come raging back. "Rough night last night. I'm exhausted. See you around."

"Sure. Take it easy."

She couldn't get out of there fast enough.

The day's *New York Post* had been left near the elevator door, and Bailey picked it up and leafed through it while she waited. Her horoscope said something about "reconnecting with family," and she supposed she'd done so, working for Melinda and living in her apartment. Check that off.

But then she saw the list of famous people born on that day. Sonny Rollins was fifty-five.

Her dad loved the fact that he shared the jazz great's birthday. Today was Jack's birthday, and she had almost missed it entirely.

Upstairs, she called home. So many nines, the rotary phone took forever to spin back to its place. Bailey hadn't talked to him since she'd gone into rehab, and hadn't told him about it either. No need to worry him.

He picked up on the second ring.

"Dad. It's me."

"Hello there."

"I called to say 'happy birthday.' Do you have any fun plans?" Better to not give him time to ask her about what she was up to. Keep the focus on him.

"Haven't heard from you in quite a while. What's going on up there in New York?"

No luck. "Right. It's been crazy. I'm decorating Melinda's apartment now, in the Dakota."

"Is that so?"

"Yes."

Silence.

"What's on your social calendar today? Going out with Scotty?" His oldest friend and employee, who annoyed her father to no end, but she was certain he secretly enjoyed it.

"Nope. Scotty's married now. He's got his own thing going on."

"I see."

She waited, hoping he'd change the subject to the latest plumbing disaster at the house that he'd fixed without having to call a plumber, using bubble gum and tape. Or how he'd finally stopped the screen door from banging shut. The summer before she died, her mother had admitted that every so often she'd intentionally break things around the house so her father had something to do on weekends. He was never one to sit and read a book. Or chat.

The silence stretched on. "Hey, Dad. I have an idea. Why don't I come on down on the train and we'll go out to the Lobster Shanty?"

"No, you don't have to do that. I'm perfectly happy."

The thought of him alone on his birthday was too much for her to bear. No matter how little they had in common these days. "I'll be on the next train. You'll pick me up?"

"All right. If that's what you want." His voice offered no hint of pleasure. But then, hers probably didn't either.

She threw some clothes into an overnight bag and navigated the subway to the train, which then sat at the Newark station for more than forty-five minutes. By the time she disembarked at Point Pleasant Station, the sun was fading in the sky and her stomach growled with hunger.

Her father, Jack, was leaning against the hood of his ancient Volkswagen bug. She'd hated that car through high school, a jalopy that constantly broke down. He gave her an awkward hug. "Thought you'd got lost."

The last time they'd seen each other was in the spring, when she was bursting with news of her many clients through Tristan. She'd walked around their house, pointing out small changes he could make to bump up the decor, knowing he wouldn't do a thing but desperately wanting to impress.

Jack couldn't care less about Moorish tiles or Laura Ashley linens. He ran an auto repair shop, for goodness' sake, as his father had. He must have seen through her posturing as she dropped names of fashion and art world icons, then laughed at his ignorance. Her stomach curdled with shame and she wished she hadn't offered to visit. They were so different from each other.

"Since you're so late, I figured we'd just pick up a sub."

Did he want her to insist on the restaurant, or was he just too hungry to wait for a table, like her?

"Sure. Sounds like a good plan."

They drove along the main road, and she tried not to stare too hard at the spot where one of her classmates sophomore year had launched his car into a tree, killing himself and his passenger. Her first taste of the capriciousness of life. Jack's hands gripped the wheel a little tighter until they were past, probably thinking of another car accident and her mother's last moments. One that they would not discuss, not even on the anniversary of her death. She checked her watch. Twelve years ago today, at five o'clock in the afternoon, Peggy had been driving back from the mall, where she'd bought some last-minute gift for Jack, and had never come home.

Twelve years ago, at this very moment, Bailey had been sulking in her room because they wouldn't let her skip the birthday dinner to go out with her friends.

How badly she still wanted to try to reverse time, to change the outcome. Because this outcome was unacceptable.

Jack turned down their street, at the corner of which stood Bob's Beetle Shop. No one in the family was named Bob, but her grandfather had liked the alliteration, apparently. Or he didn't want people to know who really owned it. It must've been a shock, growing up in a luxurious city apartment and winding up fixing cars in a New Jersey beach town.

"How's business?"

"Same as always."

"The shop looks good. Did you paint it?"

"Nope. Same as last time you saw it."

This was going to be a titillating evening, she could tell.

He pulled up to their house, two stories clad with cedar shakes sporting powder-blue shutters on the upper-story windows, the color chosen by her mother. Squat summer beach houses with low-maintenance yards of round, white stones peppered the neighborhood. Old ladies down from Newark for the summer would sit and yell from their screened-in porches if the kids got too noisy in the after-dinner hours. No sidewalks lined their roads; instead, the asphalt crumbled into the sandy shoulder and the roots of stunted pine trees.

The stairs creaked as she headed up to her room. The upstairs hallway was lined with family photos and framed artwork from her high school days. She paused a moment, examining each one with a fresh perspective, looking for signs of Sara Smythe in their faces. At the very end, near the top of the stairs, was a sketch she'd seen a million times in passing but never really studied. Not one of her own. A pen drawing of a pretty cottage, like the kind you'd find in a fairy tale, with some kind of vine growing along the side. Even though the drawing was small, the details drew her in.

In the corner was scrawled *Theo. Camden.*

She lifted it off its hook and held it up to the light, examining every inch. Her grandfather must have taken it with him when he left, one memento to remember his family by. The leaves of the vine were exquisite, each leaf outlined and shaded in. Along the trunk, she noticed an irregularity and turned the drawing sideways.

For Sara.

The words were clearly scrawled inside the trunk, but only readable from an angle.

Theodore Camden had drawn this for Sara Smythe.

Bailey settled in at the kitchen table, her mind whirling with questions. Jack offered up local town gossip between bites of an overstuffed sub. She filled him in on the Dakota job, and together they muddled through another meal, painfully aware of the lack of her mother, who'd acted as the connective tissue between the two of them.

"Do you have cake mix? I'll make you a cake," she offered.

"No need. I bought a pack of Snickers bars. You can put a candle in it if you like."

"Really?"

"No. I don't have any candles. Just kidding."

She went to the pantry and pulled out two Snickers bars. "Do you want me to sing to you? Because you know I will."

He laughed as he unwrapped the candy. "Only if you want to encourage the feral cats that live behind the D'Agostinos' house."

When they used to go out in the family car, Jack would turn up the radio as loud as it could go to drown out Bailey's voice, and she'd hit the wrong notes on purpose, egging him on as her mother screeched for him to turn it down.

His teasing softened her anxiety, lowered her guard. "You know, Dad, I'm sorry I haven't been around."

"You're doing your own thing these days, as you should." He shrugged.

"Actually, I've been digging around some of the old family trunks in the Dakota, ones that belonged to Melinda's great-grandparents, Theodore and Minnie Camden. They're the ones who raised Granddad, right?"

"I guess you could call it that. Theodore Camden died when he was a baby, so your grandfather was really raised by the wife."

"Right. When did Minnie die?"

Jack considered the question as he chewed on his birthday candy bar. "When my dad was fifteen or so. He'd been raised as if he were one of her children, but when she died, he found out he got nothing. All of the inheritance went to the other three kids. Hit him hard."

Before finding the trunk, Bailey hadn't thought much of her family tree. They'd been ghosts, not important in her life or her future. But touching the items in the trunks had changed all that. Not to mention seeing that photo. "Then he joined the navy?"

"Nope. He joined the merchant marine."

"What's the difference?"

"During peacetime they work on ships that carry goods. Only in wartime are they called out to transport troops and equipment."

"Huh. How did he end up in New Jersey?"

"He met my mother while at port in New York and they settled down here, where she'd grown up."

"Then he opened up the auto shop."

"That's right. Why all the questions?"

She chose her words carefully. "I found this weird photograph in one of the trunks. It's really old, but the woman looks like me."

"Who is she?"

"Name was Sara Smythe. She worked in the Dakota, for a time. In the photo, she's holding Granddad, and the other kids of Theodore Camden's are standing next to her."

"And she looks like you?"

"Yeah. The super of the building pointed it out. He's right. Looks like you, too."

He sat back and rubbed his belly with one hand, an amused grin on his face. Which made his right eyebrow stand up.

"Even more intriguing, she's the one who killed Theodore Camden. And get this, before dinner, I noticed that sketch of the cottage at the top of the stairs. It's signed by Theo Camden and in the drawing he's written *For Sara*, kind of like Hirschfeld does his *Nina*s."

"Who?"

"He's this artist who draws Broadway stars and in every one . . ." She waved her hand. "Never mind. What if Sara Smythe killed him in a fit of passion because they'd been having some mad affair?"

He shook his head. "You've been reading too many romance novels. Christopher was a ward of the family, not a member of it."

"How do we know? Did he know anything about his birth family?"

"Never mentioned it."

She wished he were alive now so she could ask him all the questions that were burning inside her. "Because if Theodore had an affair, and had Granddad Christopher, who had you, who then had me, it means I'm related to Theodore Camden."

Jack considered her for a moment. "You'd like that, would you?" His tone had turned cold.

She'd pushed too far. "I guess. I don't know."

He stared at his hands, studying the dirty fingernails and the cracked skin as if they belonged to someone else. "Your mother loved the few months she lived in New York City, and to be perfectly honest, I wasn't sure that she'd be happy returning home, settling down. When she learned about the connection to the Camdens, she insisted we get back in touch. I think she imagined we'd be welcomed like long-lost relatives, invited over for cocktails and dinner parties. Little did she know."

"Granddad hadn't stayed in touch at all?"

"Nope. He felt rejected, orphaned twice over after Mrs. Camden's death. Can't say I blame him. The others, the ones we called our 'cousins,' had an easy life. While he was left to scrimp by." He crumpled the Snickers wrapper in his hand, then took her wrapper and did the same before getting up and walking over to the garbage. "I'm not like them, and I'm proud of that. No need to be fancy."

Meaning Bailey was. She twisted in her seat but couldn't see his face.

He continued on. "Your mother wanted to be part of their family, to be accepted. She did this because she wanted better things for you. I guess that all worked out."

"I guess so."

Two thoughts struck her at the same time: That she hadn't thought of drinking in more than three hours, a record to date. And that she really wanted a beer.

Christopher, her grandfather, had carried a chip on his shoulder all his life because he'd been brought up to believe he was an equal when really he was not. Jack had inherited that same chip.

To be perfectly honest, she had as well. She wanted desperately to be related to a killer, because then there was a chance she was really a Camden.

In which case, the circumstances that shamed her, growing up in a run-down neighborhood in a sad shore town, would not apply.

"Look, Dad. I've been having some trouble lately. Not now, not anymore. But earlier this year. That's why I haven't reached out."

"What kind of trouble?"

"With drinking. That kind."

"Your grandfather was a nasty drunk. Hope you don't mean that kind." His eyes were guarded.

A family history of alcoholism. She'd been told that was likely in rehab. It must've been bad if Jack had never mentioned it before. He obviously didn't want to revisit the issue now.

"It's no big deal. Everything's fine."

"I'm sure you have a lot on your plate." He eyed the oven clock. "I have an early start tomorrow. What time do you want to get dropped off at the train?"

His dismissal landed hard, like a blow to her gut. She turned the conversation back to the auto shop and busied herself with the dishes. Her father was disappointed by her lack of fortitude, and her first response was to do something, anything, to assuage his discomfort. To smooth down her own rough edges in order to keep the peace.

In any event, he wasn't interested in the story of her addiction. Or he knew what was coming and didn't want to hear it without her mom by his side to soften the blow. Jack wasn't that type of parent, never had been. Not interested in the hard stuff. Why should he be, since she'd not taken much interest in his life at all these past many years? She'd tackled the big world and figured he'd stay as he was, inaccessible and immovable as a figure in a snow globe.

She dried her hands with a dishrag. "Don't worry about tomorrow morning, Dad. I'll call a cab. I'm going to head upstairs now, dig around for some winter stuff to bring back to the city."

"All right, then. Thanks for the birthday treat."

"A sub and a Snickers. I'll do better next year, I promise." She crept up the stairs and rummaged around as he locked up the house. She could hear his heavy footfalls as he went from room to room, checking windows, closing latches, when the worst had already happened.

In the upstairs hallway, she lifted the drawing off its hook, wrapped it in a sweater, and stashed it in her bag. Jack wouldn't even miss it, if he'd ever even noticed it in the first place.

Bailey retreated to her room and closed the door. Jack paused for a moment when he finally came up, but her soft "Hello" was answered by the *click* of his own bedroom door closing.

CHAPTER SIXTEEN

New York City, January 1885

Something wasn't right. The week prior, Sara had headed to the
Westlakes' apartment on the third floor only to find herself lost
on the other side of the building, saved by Mr. O'Connor, one of the
elevator operators, who pointed her in the right direction. The blun-
der had left her shaken. She knew the corridors of the Dakota better
than anyone, save Theo and Fitzroy.

Sara's stomach problems had only gotten worse, and she'd been
unable to eat more than a few bites each meal, leaving her weak. The
weakness made her even less inclined to eat, and around and around
she went, a downward spiral of malaise. If she called for the doctor,
she'd have to tell the truth about her condition, which would take
her away from the Dakota and Theo and everything she'd worked
so hard for. Her fragility compounded her confusion.

To make matters worse, two days ago, Mrs. Camden had reported
an emerald necklace missing from her jewelry box. Mr. Douglas had
insisted that Sara grill the staff, but she had to quit halfway through
questioning the maids because she couldn't seem to find the right
words. The silly woman had probably mislaid it in any case. Surely,
it would turn up on its own.

This morning she'd barely been able to rise from her bed and had had to steady herself as she splashed water on her face. She'd staggered into her office and remained there the rest of the day, unsure where the time had gone and petrified she would not be able to get back to her room. At four o'clock, Daisy popped her head into the office.

"You look rather green." She closed the door.

"I'm not at my best," admitted Sara. "Did your mother ever get confused when she was with child?"

Daisy shrugged. "Sure. With Mickey, I remember, she would ask the same question over and over."

"What question was that?"

"'What did I ever do to deserve such ungrateful children?'"

Sara laughed in spite of herself. She couldn't imagine her own mother ever teasing like that. "You were lucky; she sounds like she was a charming lady."

"Yes." A flicker of sadness crossed the girl's features.

Someone knocked on the door. "Come in."

Daisy opened the door to reveal Mr. Douglas.

Sara stood. "Mr. Douglas, how may I help you?"

"I'm here to see the books, of course. It's Tuesday." He placed his hat and coat on the rack near the door and lumbered over.

She'd completely forgotten. "Right." She yanked the ledger out of the top shelf of the bookcase, opening it up to the correct page.

"Don't bother. I can do that myself. Daisy, fetch me a cup of coffee."

Once Daisy had left, Mr. Douglas lowered himself into the chair behind the desk with a groan. Sara sat opposite him, hands in her lap, in case he had any questions. After ten minutes of turning pages, the only sound the scratch of his pen, he peered over his spectacles at her. "This is a frightful mess, Mrs. Smythe."

She'd never been chastised by Mr. Douglas before. "I'm sorry, Mr. Douglas. Next week it'll be much better, I promise."

He leaned back in his chair. "I've adjusted the figures. Really, Mrs. Smythe. I'm surprised." He scanned the top of the desk with irritation, looking for something. "Do you have blotting paper?"

"Of course. Lower drawer on the left."

She heard the drawer slide open, followed by a wheezy exhalation from Mr. Douglas.

He looked up at her. "Mrs. Smythe."

"Yes, sir?"

"You found Mrs. Camden's necklace?"

She shook her head. Partly as an answer and partly in an attempt to clear the fuzziness in her mind. His words sounded like they came through water. Or maybe she'd misheard.

Instead of pulling out a sheet of blotting paper, a string of brilliant colors hung from his outstretched fingers like a waterfall.

The necklace. The craftsmanship was breathtaking: three tiers of pearls connected to a front piece with four large emeralds embedded in gold.

Daisy appeared with a cup of coffee, which she almost dropped when she saw the jewelry.

Sara's mouth was dry, her limbs heavy.

Mr. Douglas rose to his feet. "It appears that we've found the missing necklace. In Mrs. Smythe's desk, of all places."

Sara shook her head. What was wrong with her? She could barely get out the words to speak. Mr. Douglas and Daisy were both looking at her as if she had two heads, waiting for her to say something. She imagined her other self, the one that she knew so well, who would take charge and get to the bottom of the mystery and at the very least not stand here mute like an idiot. But she could not form the words.

"Is something wrong with her?" said Mr. Douglas.

Sara stared over at Daisy, begging her to keep quiet, not say a word.

Then she fell to the floor, giving in to the blackness with the abandon of a drowsy child.

Chapter Seventeen

New York City, January 1885

When Sara came to, she was in the staff sitting room in the basement, lying on a hard settee. The room was furnished with castoffs from the new residents, including unmatched, scratched-up chairs and a couple of wobbly tea tables. Sometimes the maids gathered here for a game of whist in the evenings, but mostly the room sat unused, as there was simply too much to do and by the end of the day the workers were too exhausted to bother with socializing.

Mr. Douglas sat in a chair opposite her, his round form squeezed in between the arms. She wondered if he'd be able to rise without taking the piece with him. A small giggle escaped from her lips.

"I see you're recovering," said Mr. Douglas.

"Sir, yes." She sat upright, fighting a wave of dizziness. To lie horizontal and not have to speak or be spoken to, that was all she wanted right now.

"Do you remember what's happened?"

The necklace. Of course. It had been found in her desk.

"I'm so sorry, Mr. Douglas, I don't know what's wrong." Her eyelids began drooping. "I haven't been feeling well, but that's the first time I've seen that necklace, I'm certain. How did I get down here?"

He rubbed his chin with the edge of his nubby index finger. "A couple of the porters carried you down. Thank God there were no tenants coming or going. This is a terrible situation we're in. Do you need to see a doctor?"

What if the doctor guessed her condition? "No, I'm fine. That's not necessary. The necklace. I'm sure there's an explanation. There must be. Please, I must speak with Mr. Camden."

"He's not available at the moment." He breathed out a deep sigh, and his acrid breath made her nose crinkle. "As you can understand, Mrs. Smythe, we cannot have an occurrence such as this at the Dakota. We will need to make a full investigation, and I suggest that you go with the police and answer their questions fully."

"The police?"

Mr. Douglas stood and opened the door. Two men in uniform came forward and lifted her up by her arms.

She craned her neck, searching for Mr. Douglas. "Where are they taking me?"

"Simply answer their questions and you'll be back here in no time. Go quietly." He looked at the men. "Take her up the ramp and out to Seventy-Third Street. Not the main gates."

The general haze that had wrapped around her thoughts the past week lifted, and for a few seconds her thinking rang clear. She was being arrested for stealing, taken away. "Please, I must speak with Mr. Camden before I go."

Mr. Douglas patted her arm as he would a child's. "For now, go along with these men. It's all a misunderstanding, most likely. The main thing is we have the jewelry and I doubt Mrs. Camden is interested in making a fuss. But we do have to get to the bottom of all this. Don't you agree? I'm sure you want that as much as I do." He shook his head and spoke to the policemen. "Of course, I knew we were taking a chance with putting a woman in charge, as sometimes pretty baubles can be too difficult to resist."

She shook her head. Had she taken it? If only she could sleep for a few hours, the answer would come to her, she was sure of that. It would all be cleared up, just as Mr. Douglas said it would.

"I'll need my cloak and hat." Sara managed to get out the words and addressed the smaller of the two policemen, who barely even had a beard, he seemed so young.

The man looked at his partner, who nodded.

Daisy was waiting at the top of the ramp. "Here you go, Mrs. Smythe." As she handed the cloak and hat over, she gave Sara a reassuring touch of her fingers. "What can I do?"

"No speaking," said the older policeman.

"At the very least can I tell her where I'm going?" asked Sara.

The man nodded. "To the police court on Sixty-Fifth."

"Tell Mr. Camden that, ask for him. He'll be able to help."

"Of course he will. I'll tell him right off."

Sara had passed the police court a dozen or so times. It resembled a fortress, with thick gray stones and a chunky parapet across the roofline. The policemen escorted her there by foot but refused to answer any of her questions about what was going to happen to her. To them, she was a thief, and an addled one at that. She stumbled once or twice on the way and swore she heard the older man mumble "drunkard" under his breath.

Inside the courtroom, dozens of people milled about, some shouting, others slumped on benches. Sara was taken into a back room and placed on a wooden chair outside a door marked JUDGE'S CHAMBERS. After ten minutes of waiting, the door swung open and she was brought forth into a gloomy room filled with books and papers. The judge looked on her kindly over his spectacles. He shooed away the policemen.

"Now tell me what's happened, Mrs. Smythe."

She was about to plead her case, to attempt to explain the preposterous circumstances she'd found herself in, but before she could get a word out, Mr. Douglas and a man carrying a medical bag entered. Her heart began to pound. How had they gotten a doctor here so quickly? If she was subjected to an exam, would he know that she was pregnant? She hadn't even begun to show yet; her belly didn't look much different than it had before.

"Judge Harrington, I'm Mr. Douglas, the agent for the Dakota."

"I see. Next time, please do me the courtesy of knocking." He leaned forward and looked at Sara. "Where are you from, my dear?"

"Fishbourne, England, sir. I arrived in the country last fall."

"Fishbourne! I visited the village a number of times, summering in Portsmouth last year. Delightful place. You work at the Dakota Apartment House?"

"As resident managerette, yes."

"How long have you worked there?"

"I began the day I arrived." No. That wasn't the right answer.

The judge frowned.

"Thank you, Mrs. Smythe." He took off his spectacles and lowered the timbre of his voice. "Tell me what's happened, Mr. Douglas. You must have a good reason to request a private appearance."

Mr. Douglas cleared his throat. "Your Honor, Mrs. Smythe has been acting strangely the past few weeks. She's been found wandering the hallways, seemingly confused. There have been complaints. Then today we found a valuable necklace belonging to a tenant in her desk drawer."

"Mrs. Smythe, did you take the jewels?"

She shook her head. "No, sir." Her voice caught in her throat, and tears burned her eyes. "I've had a difficult time of it lately. I've been ill. But I swear I didn't take them. I assure you. Someone else did and placed them in my desk."

"Why don't you conduct your exam, Dr. Wilde." The judge waved a hand in her direction. The evidence was against her; she'd lost her early momentum.

"Have you been drinking, Mrs. Smythe?" asked the doctor.

"No. I haven't."

"Have you been taking any laudanum or such drugs?"

"No. Of course not."

"Yet Mr. Douglas says you passed out while being questioned at the Dakota, and that you appeared disoriented."

"I was, but I think that's just because I've been unwell."

Mr. Douglas interrupted. "Look, Your Honor, it's important that this not make the papers. The building just opened and we can't have current or prospective tenants knowing that there was a thief in our midst. The Clark family and I request that this be taken care of swiftly and quietly."

"What do you propose, Mr. Douglas? Being that you seem ready to take over my job for me."

She saw her chance. "Ask Mr. Camden to vouch for me. He'll say that I didn't steal the jewels, that someone else did and made it look like it was me."

"How would he know that?" The judge looked at her from under his bushy eyebrows.

"He knows I wouldn't do such a thing. We are friends, you see."

Mr. Douglas shook his head. "She's deluded, clearly. Mr. Camden is a tenant of the Dakota. He lives there with his wife and family. As a matter of fact, it was the wife's jewelry that went missing."

She had no hope. No hope at all.

Mr. Douglas shot Sara a hard look. "Nothing the girl says explains who took the property, if she didn't. But we don't want to
send her to jail."

"You don't?"

"No, sir. As I mentioned before, that would attract unnecessary
attention."

"Then where would you like me to send her?"

"Somewhere she can get help, for whatever is causing her confusion."

Perhaps she'd misjudged Mr. Douglas. Indeed, he laid a hand on
her shoulder, like a father might. She certainly needed to find out
what was wrong with her, if it was the baby causing her befuddle-
ment or something else. If she could avoid going to jail, she could
straighten herself out, get well, and then figure out what exactly
had happened. Without meaning to, she began to weep.

"She is certainly fragile," offered the doctor.

"So you agree that she should be sent off?"

"I do, Your Honor."

The judge sighed. "Very well. She can leave for the island this afternoon. They will determine if she can be rehabilitated."

Rehabilitated?

Mr. Douglas gestured to the doctor, who pulled out a piece of
paper from his bag and placed it on the judge's desk. The judge
glanced at it for only a second before signing it at the bottom.

"To the island, then, Mrs. Smythe. And may God help you."

"What island?"

The policeman practically shoved her up into the wagon, ignor-
ing her question.

"I have a right to know. Where am I being sent?"

After the judge had made his pronouncement, Sara was shuttled out a side door and into a transport where a worn-looking woman sat shivering in the corner, wrapped in a dingy gray blanket. The policeman shut the door, and Sara tried to ask the woman if she knew anything about where they were headed, but she looked back at her blankly. Another girl, wearing garish face paint over a blackened eye, lay against the backboard, mouth open, asleep.

The wagon stopped three times, and each time a new mixture of women climbed on board. Two were seriously confused and babbled to themselves. Several had terrible coughs that made Sara worry about her health, but at least it did seem that they were all going to a hospital of some sort.

Finally, the wagon stopped. Outside, the East River ran fast and cold, fierce waves dodged every which way with the turn of the tide. Across the river, a half dozen enormous buildings emerged through the sleet, spaced out in wide intervals on a thin strip of land.

If she got on this island, how would she get off? Panic built up in her throat, but there was nowhere to run, no means of escape. The women—they now numbered about a dozen or so—lumbered onto a boat that strained wildly in its moorings like a chained, rabid dog. On the other side of the dock, twenty men were being herded onto a separate ferry. A disheveled drunk called them all whores before being clocked by a guard's baton.

She stared out the grimy window as the boat chugged away from the city. Several stocky officers and two nurses met them on the other side. A list of names was called out. Sara's was not among them.

"I'm sorry, but what is this? Where are we?" she asked the woman holding the list.

"This is the Charity Hospital. If I didn't call your name, stay put."

She sat back as the boat headed off to the next stop, another pier several hundred yards north of the first one. A large sign indicated it was a workhouse for petty criminals and the like. Again, her name wasn't called.

Sara looked at the four companions who were left with her. Two of them were the babblers.

Finally, near the northern tip of the island, Sara and the other women disembarked. "Out you go. Move along."

Several orderlies herded them toward a five-story octagonal building of white stone with two wings flanking it at right angles. A windowed cupola on top of the octagon stuck out like an insect's eye. "What is this?" Sara spoke softly, almost to herself. The woman walking next to her took her hand.

"Do you not know where you've been put away?"

Sara looked at her. The woman was young, with kind brown eyes. She didn't wear a hat, and snowflakes dotted the waves of her hair. "A private hospital?"

"No. We're going to Blackwell's Island Insane Asylum."

A madhouse.

They thought she was insane.

"But I'm not mad."

"Nor am I," said the woman.

"Shut up, you two. No talking." A nurse the size of a bear banged the girl hard on the shoulder, causing her to stumble.

They were brought inside the octagon and placed on hard benches that lined the walls. Sara stared about her, trying desperately to get her bearings, to make sense of where she was. A wide staircase rose from the ground floor, twisting upward, and she could see doors off each landing. The place was cold, and most of the nurses wore several layers over their uniforms of brown-and-white-striped dresses and white aprons, making them appear much bigger than normal, and quite threatening. One by one, the new patients were brought into a room. When Sara's name was called, she stumbled in and sat at a desk opposite a man who introduced himself as Dr. Fields. He asked her the same questions as the judge, her name, where she was from.

"Do you know why you are here?" He took off his glasses. His eyes were bloodshot, with puffy half-moons underneath.

She must make them see their diagnosis was wrong.

"I was told I needed to go to a hospital, and I think if you'll check, you'll see that I've been ill and my memory's not been very reliable, and because of that I fell into a bit of trouble. But I don't belong here. I need to rest and get my strength back, and once I'm well, I'll be able to explain what happened, I'm sure of it."

She was rambling on too long. The bored look in his eyes told her he'd heard this before and was immune to her distress.

"Stand up on the scale and we'll take your measurements." The nurse called out her weight and height and then grabbed her by the arm. "That'll do. You can go now."

"But can I please ask a question?"

The doctor sighed. "Yes, Mrs. Smythe."

"How long do I have to be here?"

"Indefinitely. Until you are well."

"But I am well. Don't I appear well to you? Is there anything at all in my conduct or appearance that seems mad?"

"Illnesses of the mind are notoriously difficult to cure, I'm afraid. You'll be here until we deem that you are no longer a threat to society. Or yourself. Good day."

She returned to her bench and avoided the inquiring gazes of the women still to be called. The cold made her teeth chatter and outside a blizzard blew up full force, the sound of the wind muting the mutterings of the other women.

Her mother had been considered mad. They'd been walking back from church once when a group of boys caught up to them. One leaped forward, possibly on a dare from the others, and called her the madwoman of Fishbourne. Sara had prayed that her mother would ignore them, walk forward. The cottage was in sight; they were close to home. But instead, her mother had turned and screamed at the boys until spittle came out of her mouth, her face turning red. They'd taken off, scared witless, at which point her mother had turned to her and smiled. "That takes care of that, then," she said.

As a madwoman might.

A bell rang and a long line of patients made their way down the spiral staircase. Sara and the other new arrivals stared up at them, taking in every detail. The women didn't speak, just marched with vacant stares until they reached the door of what had to be the dining room. Then they raced off like children, disappearing out of sight. Sara and the others were told to follow.

In contrast to the detailed beauty of the octagon, the dining room was stark, with no decoration or molding. She found an empty spot at a table where a tin plate and spoon with a piece of bread and a cup of weak tea sat. The bread was stale, the butter rancid, the tea cold. But she forced it all down, knowing that she'd regret missing the meal and her strength had to be kept up. The nurses stood around, bored, and the chatter of the patients almost sounded normal, as if it were mealtime at a boarding school for girls.

"Bath time for the new girls," announced a nurse with an inordinately large head. Sara heard one of the other nurses call her Nurse Garelick.

Sara followed the queue upstairs to the very top floor and into a large room filled with several sinks and three tubs. Her hopes for a hot bath were dashed when she saw the girl at the head of the line, a small thing whose freckles reminded her of Daisy, stripped of her clothes by the nurses. Crying, she was forced into a tub and cold water was poured over her head, followed by a harsh scrubbing with a sponge. When Sara's turn came, she took a deep breath as the cascade of freezing water poured over her, into her ears and eyes and down her back. She'd gotten used to taking an unheated bath in England on the warmer summer nights, but this was different, and she cried out in shock. The hard scrub would have almost been a salve to the cold if it hadn't seemed like they were intent on taking off a layer of skin.

Sore and shivering, she got out of the tub and dried herself, before being offered a nubby underskirt and a calico dress. The stains on both indicated they'd been worn by previous inmates. On the back of the dress, in black letters, read LUNATIC ASYLUM, B.I., II. 6.

The dormitory was located down the hall from the washroom. Sara walked to one of the large windows and stared out into the cold, wintry night. Somewhere out there was the Dakota, and Theo. By now, Daisy had to have reached him, and maybe he was already tracking her down.

"Into bed, there's no mooning out the window here."

Nurse Garelick's massive hand gripped the back of Sara's neck. She squirmed as the woman shoved her down onto one of the beds, which creaked under her weight.

Sara's eyes welled up with tears. "You have no right to treat us like this; it's inhumane."

The woman leaned over her. "No one cares what you think or what you say. I'll be keeping a close eye on you. Best to keep your mouth shut from now on. Understand?"

Sara nodded.

"Now, go to sleep."

The bed was covered by an oilskin and a sheet, with a rough wool blanket on top. She shivered with cold and fear, and when the lights went out, she turned and cried into the pillow. How had she fallen so far?

Her sobs subsided and for a while she had a fitful sleep, until the loud bang of the door pulled her awake. A nurse entered and walked the length of the room, every so often smacking her truncheon on the metal footboard of a bed. Not to get them up, just as a way to keep them from sleep. This occurred four times in the night, so that there was no way to get any real rest. The snores and grunts of the other inmates didn't help matters.

After the third check, Sara heard a soft crying in the bed next to hers. She turned her head to see a woman with long, gray hair and a face filled with wrinkles. One of the women from the wagon.

"There, there, you'll be all right," whispered Sara.

At the sound of her voice the woman's cries increased in volume and several of the other inmates shouted out for her to stop.

Sara quietly slipped out of her bed, wrapping the scratchy blanket around her, and knelt down by the woman. She took her cold hand in her own and rubbed it. The woman's cries softened back to low moans, and Sara sang softly to her, as she would a child. Soon, her neighbor's breathing lengthened.

Only when she was certain the woman was asleep did Sara slip back into her own bed.

CHAPTER EIGHTEEN

New York City, September 1985

"Here's what I'm thinking we should do."

Melinda opened up a glossy architecture and design magazine. She'd shown up on Sunday night on her way back from the Hamptons, grinning from ear to ear, and plunked down at the kitchen table, where Bailey was heating up a can of chili.

"The house where I went to a pool party this weekend had a bamboo divider between the dining room and living room. Like this."

She pointed to a photo of a minimalist space with a low planter running down the middle, from which eight or ten bamboo poles ran up to the ceiling. Some crisscrossed, others were exactly vertical. It resembled some kind of POW jail cell in the jungles of Vietnam.

"It's very striking." The best Bailey could do.

"I know, right? According to Tony, Oriental is coming back with a vengeance. I thought we could tear out the wall between the library and the parlor and put something like this there."

"But the fireplace is in the middle of it."

"Well, we'll do it on either side."

"Let's take a look." Bailey stood up and held her breath the entire way, hoping her instincts were correct.

They were.

"Shoot. Check this out." She knocked on the walls to either side of the fireplace. "You see how the wall sticks out about three feet on either side?"

"Yeah." Melinda drew out the syllable, her eyes wary.

"Well, that's all the flues from the other fireplaces. You can't break through there. Which means you'll only get a foot or so of bamboo at the very far right-hand corner, and another foot next to the wall to the living room."

"What if we got rid of the door and put all bamboo between the flue and the left-hand wall? That's like five feet of bamboo."

"Do you think that would look right, on only one side? The symmetry might be off."

Melinda wasn't so easily dissuaded. "Well, check with Steve. See how much it will be and we'll go from there."

"Of course. I'll let you know what I hear back tomorrow."

They wandered back into the kitchen. "You were pretty messed up on Friday night. You doing okay?"

Bailey went to the stove and stirred the chili before turning off the heat. Her face probably burned the same color as the flame. "I'm fine. Need to stop that from happening again."

"I guess I shouldn't have invited you out."

"No, it's not your fault. I need to get tougher with myself." She turned back. "Did I make another huge scene?"

Melinda shook her head of blond curls. "Not at all. We hung out down in that room the whole time; you were perfectly well behaved. If rather fucked up. I tried to tell you to stop."

Had she, really? Bailey couldn't remember that. Melinda was the type of person who drew power from others' frailty, and Bailey was vulnerable. Had been for a couple of years now.

But thoughts like that were ungenerous and unkind. Look how much Melinda had done for her just this past week.

Time for a change of topic. "Hey, what do you know about how your great-grandfather died?"

"Not much. Just what you know. He was stabbed in the library with a knife. Like a game of Clue is how it always sounded to me. Don't you think?"

"It does. But what about my grandfather? Did your mother say anything about who he was or how he ended up a ward of the family?"

"Not that I remember. They did that all the time back then. You had orphans and they got raised by someone else. It was the right thing to do. Otherwise, he'd have been dumped in some orphanage and then where would you be?"

If her grandfather had been raised in an orphanage, there was a good chance she'd be right where she was anyway: broke, an addict, a loser.

"What do you know about the woman who killed him?"

"You're quite the history buff. Where's all this coming from?"

Bailey explained her expedition to the basement and the discovery of the trunks. She didn't mention Renzo's part in her investigation, since that would probably make Melinda shut right down. She also didn't bring up the sketch. Not yet. It had been passed down on Bailey's side of the family, and for now, she wanted to keep it to herself.

"I found an article about the killing as well, from the 1880s. It said that the woman who did it had worked at the Dakota. That she was insane or something. Also, there's this photo. Hold on a sec."

She plucked it off the windowsill in her room, where she'd perched it next to the bottle of Dr. Walker's Vinegar Bitters, and handed it over to Melinda.

"Who are these people?"

"If you turn it over, it says that the woman is Sara Smythe, the lady who killed Theodore Camden, standing with Theodore's son and two daughters. The boy is your grandfather, Luther. I'm pretty sure this is the ward, my grandfather, in the woman's arms."

"Huh. This was in the trunk?" Melinda looked up at her. And it wasn't her normal "I'm so pretty and want to make sure you're looking at me" glance. She was studying Sara's face, her eyes flicking from feature to feature. She'd noticed the resemblance, just as Renzo had.

Bailey pointed to the photo. "This seems crazy, but don't you think I look like her?"

Melinda placed the photo on the table. "Not really. She's harsh-looking, and you're such a sweetie."

"Black-and-white photography, along with corsets, will do that to a girl." Bailey took a deep breath. "This may be a long shot, but what if Sara Smythe was Christopher's mother? I'd love to find out why Theodore Camden and his family took in the kid of someone who then killed him."

"Who knows." Melinda chewed on the inside of her mouth. "Sounds like a bunch of looney-toons."

"Maybe Theodore Camden was the father of the kid." There. She'd said it. "That it was a crime of passion, not madness."

Melinda shook her head. "Ugh. Now I'm just confused."

Her resistance only increased Bailey's fervor. "Sara Smythe looks like me. A lot. I know you see it, too. That's not all. See the outfit the baby is wearing? It was in Sara's trunk. Not Theodore or his wife's. Sara's."

"So they raised this woman's child because she wasn't married. Seems really generous of them. But it doesn't mean Theodore Camden was the father." Melinda put her hand over Bailey's. "Does this make you miss your mother?"

The non sequitur threw Bailey for a moment. But then it clicked. If Bailey was the great-grandchild of Theodore Camden, then she was also a threat. By sharing the family legacy, she might also deserve a share in the family trust.

She refused to be deterred. "I do miss her. But seriously, what if Christopher was the love child of Sara Smythe and Theodore Camden?"

Melinda yawned, obviously bored with the subject. "It's not *General Hospital*. The lady was a freak, a sociopath. No way do you want that hanging over your head."

"Like I'm not enough of a nut already?"

"You've had a tough time, but I think right now it's important for you to move forward, not back. All that happened a long time ago. Let it lie. My mom and dad were horribly embarrassed about the notoriety of the murder. No one wants to talk about that."

No one but Bailey. If only she had the courage to show Melinda the drawing.

No, not yet. The evidence was still flimsy at best.

Melinda snapped her fingers. "In any event, I totally forgot something really important I wanted to tell you."

"Yes?"

"Koi pond."

Bailey offered a polite smile, hoping Melinda would eventually speak in a whole sentence. "What about it?"

She clapped her hands together like a little child. "We're going to put one in the living room! How cool will that be?"

"So cool." Bailey sighed.

There would be no more talk of Sara Smythe.

Sunday evenings were usually quiet in New York, as families retrenched for the coming week, and the streets were fairly empty, except for a group of guys slouching outside the bodega on Seventy-First Street. Even though Bailey knew it was smarter to cross the street than get too close, tonight she couldn't be bothered, and she took their nasty words in stride, staring straight ahead, shoulders hunched. Like she deserved it.

Bailey practically ran up the steps to the AA meeting at the church on Sixty-Ninth Street, avoiding any eye contact with the people standing outside, smoking and chatting, and took a seat near the back. Everyone seemed to know one another and she was content to listen to their snatches of conversation rather than join in. The room was warm and close and smelled like smoke and burned coffee, but that didn't bother her. She took a deep breath and joined in the serenity prayer.

When the time came for people to share concerns of the week, Bailey lifted her hand. The chairperson, a woman of about sixty with bright red hair, nodded in her direction. Bailey spoke without making any eye contact, her gaze directed at the front wall.

"I was recently in rehab but I went out and drank on Friday night. I put myself in a situation where I knew I might drink and do coke, with friends who I knew would drink and do coke." She shook her head. "Stupid, I know. But I guess, in a way, it was good. It showed me just how precarious I am in recovery. It's not a joke, a passing phase. If I drink, I can't stop."

Her throat strained from the effort of keeping the tears at bay. "I'm not in a good situation at the moment, and I'm not sure how I'm going to manage. But it's helpful to come here and hear your stories and I thank you for that."

"Keep coming back." The phrase echoed around the room once she'd finished, and the man sitting next to her offered her a tissue.

She took a deep breath. The best thing about meetings was that you could vomit up all your thoughts and feelings and crap, but you didn't get advice in return. Just acceptance. That's what she needed right now.

At the end, Bailey tried to sneak out but got caught in the bottleneck near the door. The redheaded woman touched her on the arm and pressed a pamphlet for newcomers in her hand. Bailey thanked her and folded it in half, embarrassed by the attention.

"Hey."

She turned to see Renzo right behind her.

"Oh, hi."

When she'd first arrived, she'd glanced around the room to see if he'd come, and been relieved that he hadn't. She knew she wanted to share but didn't think she could do it with him in the room. Hopefully, he'd arrived late and missed her pathetic whining.

"I appreciated your share."

No such luck.

"I guess I have a lot to learn."

"Don't we all."

Great. Now the guy knew what a fuck-up she was. He was probably one of those book thumpers, sponsoring people right and left, an all-knowing guru of all things sober.

"When did you go to rehab?"

She laughed. "Got out a week ago. Nice, right?" The words came out harsher than she meant them to, and she could have sworn he flinched. She sounded coarse, like a New Orleans tramp in some Tennessee Williams play.

"Took me about a day to start back up again, so don't beat yourself up."

She looked up at him. His expression was soft but guarded, and his eyes didn't quite meet hers. He didn't seem like a self-righteous counselor type. He was as nervous as she was.

"You were in rehab?"

"Not exactly. I went to Alaska. I figured, out in the wilderness I'd get dry."

"What happened?"

"Turns out Alaska is full of bars and lushes. Not much else to do there."

"You lasted a day? I'm impressed."

She'd forgotten what a relief it was in rehab to laugh at the absurdity of it all. Renzo shrugged and hooked a thumb toward the door. "Wanna grab a hot dog on the way back?"

"Okay."

This time, as they strolled by the bodega, the guys outside yelled out to Renzo by name.

"Yo, Renzo, you got a girl now? Nice goin'."

"Mind your own business, Mortimer, and go home and take care of your own woman."

The man cracked up, shaking his head. "Yeah, right. Mr. Renzo, she's a fine one."

"'Mortimer'?" Bailey waited until they were out of earshot. "Is that really his name?"

"We used to play together in Central Park. As we got older, we'd steal beers from that bodega and go drink there instead of play."

Outside Gray's Papaya, a sign read: RECESSION SPECIAL, $1.95 FOR TWO FRANKS AND A MEDIUM DRINK.

Bailey pointed to it. "Aren't we out of the recession?"

"I think they just can't be bothered to change the sign."

"I like that. Everything else changes so fast. Especially in New York."

"Not Gray's Papaya." He ordered the hot dogs and handed one to Bailey. While he paid, she pumped mustard in a long, thin line out of an enormous plastic tub.

Delicious. The hot dog snapped when she bit into it, and the piquancy of the mustard made her smile.

"You look happy."

"This is amazing. I guess I'm a cheap date." She regretted the words as soon as she said them. This wasn't a date. "You live in the Dakota?"

"I do. My family's been there for years. My grandfather was a porter, my dad became super, then me."

"Where's your apartment?"

"I'm on the first floor, west side. Facing the courtyard."

"So you can keep an eye on the neighbors."

"That's a good way of looking at it. Some sunlight would be nice, but it's not a bad address to have."

"Was it fun, growing up in the Dakota?"

"Sure. Even though it's a lot of wealthy folks, it's different from what you find on Park Avenue. Lots of singers, actors, producers. People who are loaded, sure, but also have an artistic bent. I don't know how long that'll last, though. The city's changing fast. And there are tenants, like Melinda, who just don't care."

She really should stick up for her cousin, but she couldn't help herself. "Now she wants a koi pond in her living room."

"I can see why you needed a meeting tonight."

A lump built up in her throat again. Did she have the courage to tell him what was really bothering her? The quiet hum of the street noise and the darkness enveloped her, made her feel safe. As did walking beside Renzo. "And yesterday was the anniversary of my mother's death."

Renzo stopped. He didn't attempt to make any comforting movements or noises, just stood still. "What happened?"

She took a deep breath, close to bursting into tears. "Twelve years ago. I was eighteen. She was on her way home to celebrate my dad's birthday. Car crash." Talking about the subject, which was taboo at home, was difficult. Saying the words out loud made it real. She didn't want it to be real.

"I'm so sorry."

"I guess it's better I'm eating hot dogs instead of hitting a bar for a drink, which was my first impulse this afternoon."

"My mom died, too, but when I was little. I didn't really ever know her."

For a few seconds Bailey stared, unabashed, into Renzo's face. Words were inadequate, and unnecessary.

Renzo broke the silence. "How did you manage, after she passed away?"

"I went off to Parsons, studied, partied, pulled away from my dad, as he did the same to me. It's taken me this long to realize there's only so much running you can do. It's weird, but seeing that photo helped." She confided in him about the drawing, with its secret inscription, and Renzo's eyes grew large.

"That's an interesting turn of events."

"I know. Somehow imagining I'm a descendant of the love child of Theodore Camden and Sara Smythe makes me feel a little better."

"Like you belong to someone."

"Yes. Exactly like that. Then Melinda and I would be true cousins, not fake ones."

"You sure you want that?"

"Yes, and not just because it might come with a share of the Camden trust fund. I want to feel like I'm part of a legacy, that it's not just me spinning alone in the world. Then again, who knows what happened in the past? Maybe it's better it stays that way."

"If it were up to me, I'd put my money on it. Just on that eyebrow thing."

He touched her gently on the temple and she flushed with self-consciousness. She took a couple of steps back, the moment broken. "How did you end up back here after Alaska?"

"I never imagined I'd come back to New York. But when my dad passed away, it seemed like a good thing to do, until I figured out my life."

She wasn't the only one hiding out at the Dakota and licking wounds. "And did you figure out your life?"

"I guess. I love the building. Not all the tenants, but some of them. Sure, every so often I get treated like I'm an idiot who only knows how to unclog a toilet, but it's an honor to live there."

"That's lovely."

He blushed under the lamplight. "Not something I tell most people. Don't want them to think I'm a puddle of mush."

"'Puddle of mush'? Anyone who uses that phrase is, indeed, a puddle of mush."

"You know what I mean."

"In fact, I do."

The building soared above them, and they both paused and studied its grand facade.

"She's a beauty."

Even without looking at him, Bailey could hear the smile in his voice.

CHAPTER NINETEEN

New York City, January 1885

Breakfast the next morning was a chunk of stale bread along with some tepid brown liquid that one of the other inmates referred to as cocoa. Sara downed the brew in one gulp and gnawed on the crust until it became soft enough to swallow.

Today she'd explain that she was not one of the dribbling ladies or maniacs, that they'd made a mistake. In fact, she'd awakened this morning feeling better than she had in several weeks. The headache and lethargy had dropped away. Her clearheadedness had come too late to save her from the trip in the tub of misery, as a nurse had referred to the ferryboat this morning.

After breakfast, they were again made to sit on the benches in the octagonal room. No movement, no speaking. Sara took the time to study the interactions of the nurses—there were five that day—and the doctor. Four of the nurses were stolid, nasty sorts, but the youngest one hadn't yet turned bitter. Her interactions with the inmates were calmer and more patient. Sara heard her referred to as Nurse Alden. Dr. Fields preferred Nurse Alden, and seemed to go out of his way to speak with her instead of the others.

Many of the other patients were foreign and had little or no mastery of the language. Sara was certain the majority of these were also of sound mind but hadn't been given the chance to plead their cases in their mother tongues. Of the others, the ones who spoke English, a few babbled to themselves endlessly, at the risk of being on the other side of a striking hand, and some were nasty, stealing bread from others' plates or grabbing themselves inappropriately. Sara avoided eye contact with them, pulling into herself when they passed, trying to be invisible.

A bell rang and the group was herded outside into the January morning, where hundreds of other women huddled against the building or valiantly walked the grounds. Sara marched to the water's edge and stared across the gunmetal waves of the East River at Manhattan. In the cold, clear air, she found what she was looking for immediately.

The Dakota.

The three triangles that made up the east roofline pointed into the bitter sky like beacons. She wondered if Theo had gone up onto the promenade to see if he could find her. He must be mad with worry. No doubt as soon as he figured out where she'd been sent, he'd get her released. It was only a matter of time.

"No point staring at the city. Will only make you sad."

A woman with olive skin and black hair stood close by, arms wrapped around her chest for warmth. She looked to be around forty years old, with creases like kitten whiskers across her cheeks and a streak of gray in her hair.

"I'm Natalia." Her foreign accent made the word sound delicious. Or maybe Sara was just hungry.

"I'm Sara. Sara Smythe."

"You got here yesterday, right?"

"I did." Sara looked back at the asylum.

"Don't worry, no one's in sight. They hate going out in the cold, so this is one of the few times we get for freedom."

They began walking together along the pathway.

"How long have you been here?" Sara asked, fearing the answer.

"Five years, I think. *Non lo so*, time gets lost here."

The blood drained from Sara's head. She wouldn't make it another week, never mind five years. "Why were you sent here?"

"I stole some jam from my employer, a rich *signora* on Twentieth Street. I worked as her kitchen maid. My kids were sick; I could sell it for their medicine. She searched me and found it, and when I told her what I thought of her stingy ways, she had me committed."

"How could she do that? You seem perfectly normal to me."

"I see that in you as well. How are you here?"

"I'm not sure, to be honest. I'd been feeling off the past month or so." A hand went to her belly, a reflex. "I work for a large apartment house, and when a necklace went missing, they insisted I'd taken it. But I have no memory of it. How can that be?"

"You seem *sano di mente* to me. Very good, very smart."

Natalia's bright comment lifted her spirits. "I feel that way as well. I'm going to explain that to the doctor today."

Natalia stopped. "Best not to. They don't like the idea that they are wrong."

"But I can't stay here another minute."

"Take care." Natalia blew into her cupped hands, the spectral steam escaping through her fingers. "If you make a fuss, they put you in the Retreat or the Lodge. You don't want that."

"What happens there?"

"They're the wards where they put the worst, most violent patients. You're in danger if you end up there."

"I won't be violent. That's the whole point. I'll be civil and logical. I'll show them that I'm sound of mind."

Natalia didn't respond. Another bell rang. "We go inside."

As they retreated back inside, a thought occurred to Sara. "What happened to your children?"

"I don't know."

"Do they know that you're here?"

"Probably no. I didn't even know where they were taking me."

"Nor did I." If she had known, could she have done anything to change the mystifying turn of events? If she'd kicked and screamed, she would have ended up in jail. Poor Natalia, having to leave her children to fend for themselves. She struggled for something kind to say. "You speak quite good English."

"I listened carefully, picked it up fast when I came from Italy."

They stood in a line behind the other inmates funneling back inside the octagon. Like hens going back to the henhouse. "It's wrong, what they've done. To you and to me. An injustice."

Natalia laughed. "Do you think we band together, fight back? No good."

"We must do something."

"Others have tried."

"How?"

Natalia made a motion with her arms. "Swim across, to escape. Drowned."

Sara looked back at the frigid expanse. Even in summer, powerful currents roiled the brackish water, as if giant sea serpents thrashed just below the surface.

They were getting nearer to the door, and Sara was reluctant to enter. It was such a comfort to speak with someone, someone who understood. Ahead of them, a young girl with matted hair and a sweet face garbled out a song.

"An idiot. We have many," said Natalia. The girl's song faded out into a hum. "But at least she doesn't know where she is. I am jealous, sometimes."

Lunch was a chunk of rancid beef, eaten with the hands due to the lack of a knife or fork, one boiled potato, a bowl of soup, and another piece of bread. Sara was so hungry by then and chilled from the cold walk that she ate and drank as much as she could, trying not to look at the greenish tinge of the bread crust. The strength in her appetite gave her hope for her general health, as the past couple of weeks she'd been unable to eat much and figured that had contributed to her mental lapses.

The work assignments that were handed out at the end of the meal offered a chance to move around and get the blood flowing again. Sara was assigned to scrub the octagon's stairways with a half dozen others. Nurses handed over buckets and brushes, and the women spread out, each taking a landing and a stair. Although the water made her fingers cold, the joints in her shoulders and knees welcomed the activity. She looked up at the skylight high above her. Theo would have appreciated the grand Ionic columns that lined the balconies.

"Keep on scrubbing."

A nurse glared at her from the balcony above. Sara went back to her work, and even though her staircase was finished in thirty minutes, she noticed the other women stayed at it, going over what they had scrubbed before, so she did the same. It wouldn't do to attract attention by announcing that the job was done. As she was working on the lower steps, a couple of nurses walked by.

"Superintendent Dent is due in an hour. Dr. Fields said to lock up the noisy ones until he's gone."

"They'll miss supper."

"No matter. There'll be another meal tomorrow." At this she laughed. It was Nurse Garelick, and she caught Sara staring.

"What are you looking at?" She stepped over and placed a dirty boot on the step Sara had been working on. "Clean that up, will ya?"

The other nurse guffawed and they walked away. Superintendent Dent. Sara would pick her moment and approach him, tell her story. Even though she was no longer wearing black silk, and her hair was braided down her back like a schoolgirl's, she still had the accent and the countenance of a good English girl. She'd stop him in his tracks, raise one eyebrow, and ask for a private moment. It had always worked before, and she knew it was best to do so now, as a fresh arrival.

With renewed energy, she scrubbed off the dirty footprint and when the next bell rang, she followed the other girls, dumped the dirty water outside, and stacked her mop and bucket on the landing. They walked out into one of the wings and entered a long room with tall, barred windows along one side. Severe-looking yellow benches ran along each wall. Most of the women rushed for the seats opposite the windows, and only later did Sara realize why.

They were to sit for hours at a time. If yesterday's wait to be seen by the doctor had been excruciating, it was a mere blip in a day compared to the afternoon's torture. Sara took up a bench under one of the windows, a cold wind blowing on her neck and down her back. The women who sat across from her looked out the windows, their eyes lifted to the light like churchgoers to the cross, while she had only their worn faces to watch.

If a woman shifted in her seat, the nurses—all sitting around a table in the middle of the room—would yell for stillness. No one spoke, but a couple of inmates dozed off while remaining upright.

After an hour, Sara did indeed wonder if she was mad. She wanted to stomp out of there, yell at the top of her lungs. Her eyes played tricks on her; the light in the room changed from gold to green to blue. When she closed her eyes, the colors still shimmered behind her eyelids. If she wasn't careful, she'd lose her mind here anyway, and it would be no different than if she'd been mad in the first place.

The door opened and a man in a black suit, with white whiskers, walked in. The nurses all rose.

"Superintendent Dent, welcome," said Nurse Garelick.

"Ladies, thank you." He put a hand in one pocket and with the other fingered his timepiece, as if he were worried it might be grabbed off of him at any moment.

"How do you do?" The superintendent walked the full circle of the room, hardly pausing to hear an answer. Not that he got one. Few women dared speak, other than to say "Fine" and "Thank you, sir."

As he headed along her row, Sara braced herself. She had to say something. Now.

She opened her mouth to speak, but Nurse Garelick cut in. "Superintendent Dent, I hate to cut your visit short, but Dr. Fields was hoping to get five minutes of your time, if you please."

"Of course. Lead the way."

Nurse Garelick shot Sara a nasty look as she turned. The woman knew exactly what she'd been planning. Like she'd read Sara's mind. She might have won this round, but Sara would outwit her. She had to.

More sitting. With the dregs of the supper settling badly in her stomach, Sara took a seat between Natalia and the woman with the long gray hair who'd cried in the night. Sara tried to make eye contact with her, to make a connection even if it was by blinking, but the older woman only stared down at her feet.

"So cold."

It was only a murmur, but in the silence of the room it sounded like a scream. Sara made a soft shushing noise. The nurses were just outside the door, jabbering on about a new dress shop that was opening up somewhere in Manhattan, which might as well have been Russia, it seemed so far away. Oh, for the luxury of speaking of dress shops, something she'd taken for granted before being thrown into this dungeon of filth and misery. How she wished she'd not been too caught up with the pettiness of daily life to appreciate such freedom.

"Cold. My feet. So cold."

Sara leaned close. "I know, we'll be done sitting soon and we can go to bed. But no more speaking."

The woman looked up at her with trusting eyes.

"It's all right. What's your name?" Sara whispered.

"Marianne."

The woman must have been lovely once, the bone structure of her face sharp under paper-thin flesh.

"It's a beautiful name, Marianne." Sara took the woman's hand in her own and rubbed it.

"No. No. Cold." Her teeth chattered in between the words.

"No talking," said Natalia from the other side of Sara. "You'll get us all in trouble."

Sara kept ahold of Marianne's hand. "She can't help it."

Without warning, Marianne leaped up from the bench.

She whirled around and began hopping, her hands crossed tightly over her body. Her mouth opened wide and a guttural yowl erupted. Over and over, she screeched out her anguish, the sound echoing around the vast room.

The nurses charged in, Nurse Garelick leading the way. "What's going on?"

Marianne ran to the far side of the room, still hopping and howling.

"She's cold," offered Sara.

"Don't say a word." Natalia, speaking under her breath.

But it was too late for that. Nurse Garelick turned on Sara. "Quiet."

Unused to taking commands, Sara stiffened. "She's simply cold. Is there any way she can get another covering, a blanket? Please, you can see how thin she is. The cold goes right through her."

Marianne was busy evading the grasp of the other two nurses, running around the table with them trailing her. Nurse Garelick stuck out her arm, which was the size of a tree branch, and grabbed her by the throat.

"You about finished there, dearie?"

Marianne nodded, but when Nurse Garelick loosened her grip, she screamed louder than Sara would have imagined possible. The sound came from her very core, embodying all of the hunger, cold, and hopelessness of the place. Many of the inmates shrank from the sound, but Sara stood. "You must help her."

Nurse Garelick laughed and shoved Sara back down with her free hand. She turned to Marianne, studying her like a wicked child would an injured butterfly. "I hear this one used to be a dancer, back in the day."

Marianne's arms dropped to her sides.

"That got your attention, did it? I think you should dance for us, then, since you're incapable of sitting still like the rest of the patients."

Marianne shook her head.

"Dance. Or don't eat for three days."

Sara flinched, ready to spring to the woman's aid, to try and distract the nurses, but Natalia grabbed her arm. "Don't do it. Stay put."

"Dance. Now."

Marianne hopped like a robin, wary and watchful.

"That's not dancing. No dancing, no food."

Tentatively at first, the woman began moving her feet in dainty steps, then her hands fluttered and she hummed a tune under her breath.

"That's right, keep on." Nurse Garelick stared hard, licking her lips.

Marianne's movements became stronger, her arms wide out, then up above her head, her legs extended in long, clean lines. For a moment, Sara forgot where she was. The bare room might as well have been a London stage, and Marianne a debut ballerina in a skirt of layered gauze. Her hair whirled about her as she spun on one leg, the other wrapping around and back out, the momentum turning her around and around. She finished and gave a low bow, her aged body still limber, the steps fixed in her memory.

For a moment, no one stirred, mesmerized. Nurse Garelick indicated for the other nurses to sit and took a seat herself at the center table. No doubt the dance had transported them away from the mundane tasks at hand, to a place where beauty and kindness were still possible.

But when Sara got a glimpse of Nurse Garelick's profile, her heart sank. A vein throbbed on her forehead, her eyes shone with a shrewish ferocity. The unexpected grace of Marianne had enraged her further.

"You'll keep dancing until I say you can't."

Marianne did so, but less committed to the steps this time, her eyes never leaving Nurse Garelick's face. After ten minutes, she had become a ghost of her former self, all energy sapped by the unexpected exertion. After twenty, she fell to her knees.

The bell rang, but Nurse Garelick put up her hands and everyone stayed seated. "More dancing. Jump around like you were doing before. You're pathetic. A weakling. A sad, old lady."

The other nurses joined in, teasing and laughing at the woman. Tears slid down Marianne's face; her mouth was slack with exhaustion.

"Get up, you old bitch. Get up."

Sara silently willed for the woman to do so. They had to be ex-
cused soon, and then she'd take her upstairs to bed and tuck her in.
Show her some kindness.

Marianne was on her hands and knees, trying to get a foot under
her to stand, when Nurse Garelick strode over and shoved her with
her boot so hard she collapsed on the stone floor.

"Enough!"

Sara raced to her side, not caring what happened. If only all of the
other women would do the same, they could overpower the nurses,
take over a boat, and ferry themselves to safety and sanity.

"You're the maniacs, how could you do this to a poor old woman?"
She held Marianne in her arms and looked up.

Nurse Garelick's expression, which she expected to be full of hate,
was not. Her eyes shone, her cheeks burned red. She was happy. The
thought of having another person to torture was a pleasure in her
sick mind. Physical pleasure. The thought turned Sara's stomach.

Her baby. The world slowed down for a second as she saw Nurse
Garelick's black boot draw back, but she didn't have enough time to
protect herself. The impact landed on the exposed side of her torso,
hard, her body sliding a few inches across the floor. Her breath left
her lungs in a rush and she groaned, releasing the woman and wrapping her arms around her own belly. The next kick struck her hip
bone, reverberating through her pelvis.

A deep-throated cackle was the last thing Sara heard as Nurse
Garelick's boot connected with her temple.

CHAPTER TWENTY

New York City, January 1885

Sara stared out of the window into another bleak dawn. She'd been locked up for five days now, and other than resting on the cot, allowing her sore ribs to heal, she spent hours standing at the window. During the day, she could hear the shouts of the nurses rounding up the inmates after their walk, but other than that, no human noises reached her ears. Her meager ration of food was shoved through an opening in the bottom of the door. For the first two days, the silence was a respite from the commotion of the place, but now she was desperate for a human touch, a smile, something that acknowledged her presence in the world. By the third day, she'd looked around to try to find something with which to kill herself, but the bed had no metal springs, nothing sharp. She considered smashing her head against the bare walls.

The door to her room opened and she jumped at the sound, her ears unused to the squeaking of the hinges.

"Mrs. Smythe, you're out."

"I'm out?" A burst of joy collected in her throat. Had Theo finally come?

An unfamiliar nurse smiled. A missing front tooth gave her grin a menacing air. "Not out like that. You're back on the main ward. Back to hall six."

Of course. How stupid to think she would be released.

But being with the other women was a consolation. Natalia pulled her over to sit with her at breakfast and insisted Sara eat her own piece of bread. "We must build you back up. You look like a ghost."

Sara dutifully nibbled at the hard crust. "What happened to Marianne?"

Natalia shook her head. "They took her away. I hoped maybe you were together."

"She won't last long."

"Enough about her. You must fatten up. No more jumping in to help. That is only punished around here."

"I know. I realize that now." As she said the words, part of her humanity eroded away.

Natalia patted her shoulder. "Don't blame yourself. This place is broken, bad. Stay alive. That's all you have to do."

Eat, sleep, and breathe. If only it were that simple.

"The good news is we haven't seen Nurse Garelick since. We think she was sent somewhere else."

After the first hour of sitting, her panic began to rise like a fast-moving fever. She wanted to run like Marianne had, to dance, to move.

She had to figure out how to manage this if she was going to survive. She'd read about monks in Asia who sat for hours and days at a time without moving. They'd lower their breathing until it was almost like they weren't alive, and somehow reach a transcendent state. How odd to think that they did it voluntarily, as a way of life.

Maybe if she had something to focus upon. She considered her girlhood, the hours she'd traipsed the long paths that wound through meadows and wandered barefoot in the sand along the ocean.

She settled on her mother's vegetable garden and, in her mind, explored it inch by inch. The golden ring of marigolds that kept the caterpillars away. The gangly stalks of Brussels sprouts, the squat cabbages all in a row. At one point, she picked up the heavy fragrance of the lilac bushes that stood along the far fence. The time flew by instead of crawling.

Soon, instead of dreading the hours of sitting, she looked forward to the daily session as a way to escape the dreariness of the asylum. To replace the weak winter light that seeped in the barred windows with the image of a sun-drenched bed of pansies.

After three weeks, Natalia linked arms as they stood at the end of a session. "I looked at you and you seemed so peaceful. Like you were off somewhere else."

"I was, in a sense." Sara filled her in and, after the next time, Natalia described her own ruminations—of her mother's vegetable garden in Tuscany. "We left when I was five, so I didn't think I'd remember much, but it all came back. Even the taste of a fresh tomato."

On their walk together, each would take a turn sharing where they'd traveled during the day's session. They described in great detail their favorite dresses, songs, and books, and as the weather improved, Sara's outlook did as well.

As long as she spent the time looking backward and didn't think too far ahead, the panic in her throat remained a flutter instead of a roar.

By the end of June, the ice and snow was a distant memory, as were her days at the Dakota and the hope that Theo might come to her rescue. To her astonishment, the baby had survived Nurse Garelick's onslaught and was active, especially at night. A few days earlier, she'd swapped dresses with one of the women in her ward who'd lost a good deal of weight from the terrible diet. The new dress draped around her with plenty of room to spare. Natalia had given her a pointed look as they went into breakfast but hadn't asked any questions.

During the weekly bath, she used a towel to cover herself as she dipped in and out of the dirty water left by the other women. No one changed the water in between inmates, so if a woman got stuck at the end of the line, it was a brown soup. But Sara deliberately hung back so the previous occupants of the tub would be busy dressing and she could do her ablutions without an audience.

One bright morning, she and Natalia waited with the others to get their daily work assignments.

"Mrs. Smythe and Mrs. Fabiano." The nurse checked their names off on her clipboard. "Report to the mat factory."

Natalia and Sara shared a look of wonder. The factory was a move up, for the more docile and well-behaved patients. Sara stifled a squeal until they were outside, walking with the other women to the building that housed the workplaces: scrub brush making, mat making, and the laundry. The orderly pointed to a large, sunny room at the back, where rags had been piled on top of wooden tables. "The others will show you how."

"At least we won't have to work with lye anymore," murmured Natalia.

Sara's hands were raw from the soap, and she imagined the jar of hand cream that once stood on her bureau at the Dakota. She could picture it perfectly in her mind, the pretty label covered with faded roses. Hopefully, Daisy had been able to take it so it hadn't been wasted. The thought made her sad. What had happened to her meager possessions? Had the spoils been divided up among the housemaids? Or had they been summarily tossed out or burned in the furnace?

"You all right?" asked Natalia.

When Sara's thoughts ran away like this, the darkness in her head would begin to grow, like a tumor. She pointed in the direction of the worktables. "Imagine, we even get our own stools to sit on."

"Like a queen's throne."

They sat at a table near the window, and one of the women guided them through the process of ripping the rags into long shreds, coiling them up before stitching them around and around to create an oval. Sara reveled in holding a thread and needle in her hand. The only sign that this was an asylum versus a true factory was the quiet gibberish that occasionally erupted from a few of the women.

"I'm beginning to understand what they're saying," said Natalia, after they'd been at it for an hour.

"The way I see it, we're all sane and the rest of the staff and doctors and superintendent are the lunatics." Sara pointed at the head nurse, who was asleep at her desk. "Completely daft."

"I like looking at it that way." Natalia glanced over at Sara, who instinctively pulled in her stomach. "You won't be able to hide it very soon."

Sara put a hand over her belly in a protective motion. "What do you mean?"

"You are with child."

The simple statement brought pricks of tears to Sara's eyes. "Yes." The past couple of nights, in the depths of the bitter darkness, she'd imagined another world, one where she hadn't ventured to the States. Where she'd stayed as head housekeeper at the Langham and never faced the corrosive effect of her own shame, her downfall. But she could no longer deny the truth, even to herself.

"What are you going to do?" Natalia leaned in, her frown deepening the furrow between her eyebrows.

"I'm not sure what I can do. I'm amazed it survived Nurse Garelick's attack. But it's moving, growing."

"He or she, not an it."

"I can't think about it that way." Her chest seized up and she fought to breathe. "What will I do? What will they do with me once they find out?"

Natalia placed her hand on Sara's, giving it a reassuring squeeze. "I believe there's a place at the Charity Hospital for unwed mothers on the island. Maybe you can go there to have the baby?"

"I heard the nurses talking about it. For 'husbandless women and fatherless children,' they said. Always defined by a man, as if it weren't enough to be simply a woman or a child."

"Who is the father?"

She shuddered, unable to say his name. "He doesn't know about it, or that I'm here. And he's not free."

"You will need help, when the time comes."

"What do they do with the babies that are born at the hospital? Do you know?"

Natalia shook her head. "I'm sure they don't want the baby on their hands, another mouth to feed. This could be your key to getting out of here."

"Or it could be an excuse for them to lock me up for good and take the child away. As a way of further punishment."

A couple of the women sitting at the adjacent table glanced in their direction. Sara was certain they were foreign and didn't understand English, but she lowered her voice. "I don't know what to do. What should I do?"

Natalia reached up and patted her cheek, her touch a cool salve. "Don't worry, we'll figure it out. Do you know when the baby will be coming?"

In spite of her determination not to think ahead, she'd done the calculation over and over. "Middle of August, I believe."

"I'll ask around, try to find out if this has happened before. Nurse Alden is the kind one; I'll bring it up with her."

"Would you?" It took everything Sara had to not fall into Natalia's arms and burst into tears.

"Yes. We've made it this far; let's see if we can make your situation work to your advantage."

A week later, during their walk, Natalia pulled Sara around the corner of the asylum, out of view of the nurses and other inmates.

"What is it? Is something wrong?"

Natalia's eyes sparkled. "No, not wrong at all. Yesterday, I found Nurse Alden sitting in one of the offices working. Alone."

"Tell me what you learned."

"She said that any inmate with child—and they have a few each year—is indeed sent to the Charity Hospital on the island, to the ward for unwed mothers."

"The hospital is for the people in the workhouse, right?"

"Yes. It's going to be rough. But less rough than here, I would guess."

"How do we know, though? What if it's worse? The orderlies there are used to vagrants and drunkards and the like."

Natalia lifted her chin and laughed. "We are madwomen, don't you remember? Do you think they are below us?"

"What are you ladies doing here?" Superintendent Dent strode over, pipe in hand. "You're not supposed to be off on your own."

"Sorry, Superintendent Dent." Natalia did a combination head bow and curtsy, which seemed to mollify him slightly.

He waved a hand. "Off you go. Breathe in the fresh air; it will help clear the mind."

"Yes, sir."

The next week, as they were at the beginning of their shift in the mat-making factory, the head nurse called out from the doorway and motioned for Natalia and Sara to grab one of the baskets of completed mats.

"These need to go to the penitentiary. Leave them by the front gate. Don't go inside. Here's a note in case anyone asks what you're doing."

"Yes, ma'am."

Sara could hardly believe her good luck. They each took a basket handle and followed the road south. The walk provided a long-forgotten taste of freedom.

A fresh breeze blew in from the west as they trod down the dusty road. The prison resembled a castle, with tiny square windows and turreted roofs. A rough wooden fence extended around the front entrance, with an iron gate in the center. Together they peered in.

Men in black-and-white-striped uniforms marched by in tight formation, each man pressed into the back of the one in front of him, while guards with rifles and sticks watched. One of the men noticed the women and whistled, and the guard lifted his stick and beat him soundly across the shoulders.

Unwilling to draw any further attention to themselves, Sara and Natalia crept away. Natalia pointed to the building next door. "The hospital."

Indeed, women in nurse uniforms stood outside the front entrance, enjoying the warm summer sun.

"Come with me." Natalia led Sara up to the side of the building. "Nurse Alden said the place for the women and babies is on the first floor."

They peered in one window. The room had clean floors, white-washed walls, and a bare bulb that hung from the ceiling. Plain linens and pillows adorned the beds, the blankets tucked in neatly around the corners. A couple of women sat in chairs, holding their babies as a nurse fussed around them.

Tears came to Sara's eyes. "It's so civilized."

"Wish I could get a pillow. Almost forgot what it was like to sleep with one until now."

"This will do, won't it?" Sara looked to Natalia for confirmation that she wasn't imagining things.

"It will do very well. Tomorrow you go to Nurse Alden and tell her the truth. Ask her if she can arrange for you to have the baby at the Charity Hospital."

"But we don't know what will happen after I've had the baby."

"Women without husbands are put out on the street after two weeks. You'd be on your own after that, and with a child. No one will take you in or have you, but you can leave the baby with the Foundling Asylum on Lexington and Sixty-Eighth."

"I couldn't do that, put my own child in an asylum."

"You could until you found work, a place to stay at least."

Natalia was right. Sara would be unemployable with a baby. But she didn't want to consider that right now. "One step at a time. First, I have to get Nurse Alden on my side and get placed here when it's time." She gave Natalia a hug. "Thank you for taking such good care of me."

"Of course."

"If I do get out, I'll come back for you, I promise."

"I know you'll try." Natalia's chin gave a wobble, the first time Sara had seen her friend break down. "Maybe I can get with child as well, and follow your lead."

"With Superintendent Dent, you mean?"

Natalia laughed in spite of herself, and Sara put one arm about her friend as they headed back to the asylum. When the baby kicked, Sara gave it a reassuring caress.

Deep in the night, she dreamed that Nurse Garelick was punching her in the stomach. She woke up in a sweat, rolled tightly into a ball, but the pain wasn't imaginary. Every muscle in her body contracted as a wave of agony rolled through her. She willed herself to go back to sleep; maybe she could go back into the dream and make it stop. But as her cries grew louder, the other women woke and shouted for her to be quiet. Doing so only made the pain worse. It was as though the baby was trying to claw its way out. With sweat pouring down her forehead, Sara managed to call out for Natalia in a weak voice before falling away, down a deep, dark hole, into nothingness.

Chapter Twenty-One

New York City, September 1985

The morning after her AA meeting, Bailey woke early and lay in bed staring up at the ceiling. In the past, the first few hours of the day were devoted to recovering from the evening before, the remainder to the business of figuring out where the best party was that night. She never drank alone. Instead, drinking and doing drugs were how she connected with others. After a couple of lines of cocaine, her life turned into one of those 1940s comedies starring Katharine Hepburn, with zingers flying back and forth, the world in sharp focus.

Now the world was no longer quite as zippy, and she had yet to figure out how to fill that void. Or at the very least, how to sit with it for a while and see what transpired. Digging around the basement helped, as did her quest to discover more about Theodore Camden and Sara Smythe.

Bailey showered and was finishing up a bowl of granola when the workers showed up at the service entrance. She ran Melinda's latest whim by Steve and asked the crew to finish stripping the ornamentation from the library. Even the foreman shook his head before yelling instructions to his men in Spanish.

She couldn't watch. Instead, she walked out into the bright late-summer day and jumped on the subway. The public library at Forty-Second Street was daunting: a giant block of carved marble guarded by two fierce lions. But she ventured inside and went up to a librarian with frizzy hair and round glasses, hoping the woman would be sympathetic instead of judgmental about Bailey's general lack of knowledge. Bailey's father had been upset that she hadn't applied to a "real" college, and made it abundantly clear that he considered her choice of career frivolous.

"Um, I'm looking for information on an architect from the last century, named Theodore Camden."

The librarian didn't laugh or look annoyed. "Follow me." She stood and led Bailey to a cabinet full of small drawers and pulled one out. Together, they scribbled down the call numbers of several books of architecture, and the librarian showed Bailey where to find them. The librarian even offered to do research into the name Sara J. Smythe while Bailey read up on Camden.

She spent a good hour poring through books on late-nineteenth-century architecture, filled with drawings and sketches and biographies. Theodore Camden's mentions were few, since he'd died so young, but she made note of the pertinent points, as if she were going to be tested later. By the end of two hours, her head was spinning from so much information. She stopped by the librarian's desk on her way out.

The woman handed her a slip of paper. "The microfiche department will have a number of newspapers that Sara J. Smythe was mentioned in, and I've written down the names and dates."

"Microfiche? How does that work?"

"You give them the information, then they'll get the film and show you how to use the machines. It'll take about forty-five minutes for them to round up what you need."

She checked her watch. "I'll have to come back."

Bailey thanked the librarian and headed uptown, where she supervised the workers until they broke for lunch. Bailey grabbed a sandwich from the deli and sat on a bench on Central Park West. When her mother had quit smoking, she'd taken up knitting, and Bailey figured keeping her own hands busy might help with her sobriety. On top of that, finding the cottage drawing from Theodore Camden had rekindled her need to create. She hadn't done much drawing since Parsons, but now, with extra time on her hands and such a grand subject at her disposal, she couldn't resist. Using a graphite pencil, she blocked in the lines of the Dakota's upper gables before filling in the ornamentation with a rapidograph pen and then finishing with a watercolor wash. Pleased with the results, she moved to a different bench and started all over again, this time focusing on a turret on the south facade. The work calmed her, focused her. The quickness of the lines lent the building a kind of animation, as if it were breathing, alive.

"You taking some time off from decimating the building?"

Kenneth stood over her, leaning on his cane and staring down at her sketch with a big smile on his face.

Bailey patted the bench next to her. "I thought I'd wait for the dynamite to take effect out here. Please, join me."

"Thank you, my dear." He lowered himself down. "That's quite lovely, I must say."

"I'm more than rusty. It's been a long time. But I love the building, and it's a challenge to capture it on paper." She put down her pen. "I remember seeing an article in Renzo's dad's scrapbook, written when the Dakota first opened, predicting it would be a landmark. I think they called it '"The Address" of New York's West Side' or something like that."

"She's instantly recognizable even a hundred years later, our Dakota."

"I've been doing some research into an architect who lived here, Theodore Camden. When he died, he was on the verge of being really famous, because he was against all the crazy, show-off architecture of the Gilded Age."

Kenneth nodded. "You know, I never really thought about the fact that it was called the Gilded Age, as opposed to, say, the Golden Age. That the era was all about money and the illusion of success, as opposed to offering anything truly valuable. Reminds me of New York City these days, to be honest with you."

He had a good point. Rolex watches flashed on the wrists of bankers, consumption was king, and everyone she knew partied like there was no tomorrow. "But if the Dakota is an example of the Gilded Age, with all that crazy ornamentation, why do we care about saving it?"

Kenneth's eyes lit up. "Smart girl. By your logic, the Dakota's chaotic array of dormers and finials are the late-nineteenth-century equivalent of Melinda's mauve pedestal sinks and mirrored walls."

"Exactly. But to me, the Dakota represents a moment in time, one that still resonates. I can't imagine mauve sinks holding up that long. Do you think, in thirty or forty years, people will mock what we're doing today?"

"More like five to ten, I would venture."

She burst out laughing. "You're probably right."

A busload of tourists disembarked on the corner of Seventy-Second Street. The guide pointed to the Dakota's front gate, the scene of Lennon's death, as they snapped photo after photo. Kenneth let out a low growl of disapproval.

Bailey didn't want to be reminded of the recent notoriety; she preferred to stay in the past. "Theodore Camden had a vision of what the city of the future should look like, and it wasn't all dolled up the way they liked it back then, but streamlined, sleek." She turned to him. "Did you ever hear anything about him having an affair with the woman who eventually killed him?"

He turned to her in mock horror. "How old do you think I am?"

"No, not personally. But maybe there were rumors that were passed down? It must have been a major event at the Dakota."

"What makes you ask?"

She explained to him about the drawing of the cottage and the photograph she'd found, and her possible connection.

"Let me ask around the old folks in the place and see what I can come up with for you," he offered. "Even though I know a lot about the history of the place, much has probably been lost to time."

"I'm not sure if I want to be related to either Sara Smythe or Theodore Camden, to tell the truth."

"Architects do have a reputation for being maniacs. Sara Smythe seemed to be one already. But from what I can tell, all your marbles are intact."

If he only knew. One drink, and her marbles had a tendency to ricochet about like pinballs. "That's very kind of you to say, but I'm not so sure. I don't know which is worse: to know your family tree, warts and all, or remain blissfully ignorant. Growing up, my family was always such a mystery. My grandfather was clearly unhappy about being thrown out of the Camden fold at the age of fifteen, and my father kept up the grudge. I guess I do, too, to be perfectly honest." She considered her terrible behavior of the past year, her lack of connection with pretty much anyone. About as far from blissful ignorance as one could get. "We're three generations of loners."

Kenneth stared at her with sad eyes, as if he knew what she was thinking. "Deep down, you want to be part of something, I understand that. That's why I cling hold of my apartment so tightly. It's something that's mine, and holds all my memories."

"I wonder if that's why Theodore Camden did that drawing for

Sara Smythe? So she could have her own home full of memories as well."

"We are a couple of romantics, aren't we?"

"I suppose."

"But enough dreaming." He banged his cane on the ground. "Let's get down to business. I want that sketch of the Dakota you just did. And I'll pay you for it."

"Don't be silly. You can have it. The least I can do for all the aggravation Melinda's caused."

"Nope. This has nothing to do with Melinda. You're an artist and I won't have it any other way."

Kenneth insisted she come up to his apartment so he could "finalize the transaction." He disappeared into his bedroom and she wandered over to the mantel, where a photo of Kenneth and a young boy of about twelve sat in a silver frame. Kenneth returned counting out ten-dollar bills.

She pointed to the photograph. "This is Manvel."

Kenneth beamed. "Dear boy. He'd often come up here to hide out from whatever world war was raging in Sophia's apartment. Melinda and Sophia were hardheaded, and Manvel is not, sweet child. Couldn't have been more different from his twin, interested in paintings, music. Oscar was an art dealer and Manvel learned from him, eventually decided to devote himself to art history and criticism. We were so proud."

In the photo, they were seated on a couch, laughing at something. She hadn't seen Manvel in years, but his thick mane of hair and skinny limbs were instantly recognizable, as if he had the head of a lion and the legs of a foal.

"Melinda said he's working in outsider art. What's that all about?"

"Work done by untrained artists, ranges from paintings to sculpture. It's an interesting niche, especially down South."

"I'm sure he was dying to get as far away from New York as possible. Melinda used to torture him."

He sighed. "There's something about this building that seems to tear families apart. Maybe I'm being dramatic, but even the builder of the place, Edward Clark, left the building in his will to his fourteen-year-old grandson instead of his son."

"Why?"

"Because his son preferred to hang out with the more artistic types, shall we say. Chorus boys and the like. And consider the Camdens. Sophia left the apartment to Melinda and Manvel equally, but I doubt Manvel knows that she's ripping it to pieces. Not that he'd care, to be honest. The trappings of civilization were never important to that boy."

"Kind of a free spirit, huh?"

"Exactly right."

"What about you and Oscar? You were a happy family, it seems."

He sighed. "We were. But even Oscar, my beloved, was cruel to me at the very end."

"In what way?" She'd imagined the affair as passionate, the two of them gleefully living together in this luxurious apartment in the sky, with Nureyev and Lauren Bacall popping in to say hello.

"Oscar became angry and paranoid as his mind went. He'd accuse me of stealing from him. Told me that he'd take me out of his will, then the next day forget everything and be loving and kind. After he died, I figured I was safely ensconced here, but Sophia had the nerve to challenge my right to the apartment. I'm sure she imagined joining the two together with a spiral staircase." Kenneth looked up, as if a drill might break through at any moment, before giving a half shrug. "The building is chock-full of misfits and betrayal, wealthy people using their assets to control their loved ones. That's true anywhere, of course, but at the Dakota it's amplified a thousand times."

"Why is that?"

"Imagine the building back in the day, this vast fortress looming over Central Park. No one in their right mind would move so far uptown. It was a risk. The tenants at the very get-go had a lot to prove, is my guess. They had cash, but no cachet. Speaking of." He handed her ten crisp ten-dollar bills.

"That's far too much."

"I simply must have this, and you deserve every penny."

His kindness made her ache inside, but in a sweet way. He'd been through so much. Bailey raced to the bodega and bought a dozen donuts for the workers, to share her unexpected bounty. Upstairs in Melinda's apartment, most of the mahogany was off the walls. Bailey grabbed the key to the storage room that Renzo had given her and led the way down the service elevator to the basement. The guys heaved the wood on their shoulders, maneuvering with care as they turned the corners.

Renzo's office door was wide open, the light on.

She poked her head in and dropped off one of the donuts, wrapped in a paper napkin, on his desk. Pathetic, really, the way Renzo's kindness last night had turned her into a puppy, eager for attention. Awareness was key, they'd said in rehab. In the past, she would have been blind to her tendency to glom on to anyone who showed her attention. Sure, she was glomming. But she was aware she was glomming. Progress, perhaps. In any case, the cardinal rule of AA—no relationships until one year clean—was one she was more than happy to obey. Life was confusing enough in the harsh light of sobriety.

"In return for feeding me last night."

Renzo looked up and smiled. "Fantastic. I was just thinking I needed to eat."

She stood there, awkward as a teenager at a dance. "Okay if the guys start loading in some of the treasures?"

"Go right ahead. Let me know if you need any help."

She watched as they stacked up the wood before covering it with packing blankets. Not much else could be done, unfortunately. If there was a flood or fire, it would all be ruined. But at least it hadn't been tossed into the back of a garbage truck and dumped in a landfill.

After the guys went back upstairs, she turned to the trunks. The bottom one's lock was tricky, even though she'd brought down a paper clip that she figured might finagle it. Renzo walked past as she struggled, trying to find the point of release.

"You need help?"

"You know how to break and enter?"

He studied the lock, retrieved his toolbox from his office, and knelt down with a small screwdriver in hand. "Let's see if this works. Is this another Sara Smythe trunk?"

"No. I think it's Theodore Camden's." Bailey watched as he fiddled with the lock. "I've been doing some research at the library into his life. He was way ahead of his time."

"Too bad he died so young, then." Renzo sprayed some WD-40 into the lock.

"Right. Like Lennon." She paused, unsure how to continue and unable to read his face. "Melinda said your dad was here when he was shot."

"He was. It tore him up that he didn't prevent it from happening. After John and Yoko moved in, there were so many fans trying to get access to him. Leaving letters, trying to call upstairs, sneaking in. He wished he'd hired more security, done something more."

"Why do you think Yoko stayed on?"

"A way of keeping his memory alive, I guess. Lauren Bacall's still here, even though Bogie died in the late fifties. It's a tough place to leave. I guess I'm a prime example."

"I'm sorry your dad felt responsible. I mean, think of all the celebrities who live in Manhattan. There's no way to protect them all the time, especially when people are so crazy. Like, really crazy."

"True. In any event, before then, my old man and I had fallen out of touch. We didn't have much contact and then he died."

"I'm sorry."

She knew all about how a loved one's sudden death could eat away at you, with so much left unsaid. As a form of penance, maybe, Renzo had taken over as super, fighting a losing battle against pipes and fixtures that were falling to pieces. His way of keeping his dad's building or, more likely, his memory, intact.

The lock clicked open.

Inside, dozens of leather tubes lay stacked one on top of another. She lifted one out and carefully pulled off the top. A roll of cream-colored linen slid out easily.

Renzo laid it out. "Architectural plans."

The drawings were gorgeous, a feast for the eyes, the elevations exquisitely rendered and detailed. At the bottom of each page was written *Theo. Camden, Architect.* The exact signature that she'd seen on the cottage drawing.

"Beautiful," Bailey said. "Maybe I'll frame them and have them line the gallery upstairs. What a find."

Together, they looked through each one. The tubes had preserved the linen and ink, so they looked like they'd been drawn a week ago, the lines sharp and dark.

Bailey pulled out another. "This one isn't in the best condition. Looks like something messed it up."

The drawings were stained with what looked like Rorschach blots. Underneath them was the design for a twenty-story building that stuck to strict neoclassical proportions with a solid base, each floor of windows bordered by fluted columns. But the ornate details so popular in the late eighteen hundreds had been replaced with a cleaner, more stripped-down facade. It announced a new, modern century on the horizon.

Renzo pointed to the description at the bottom right. "American Insurance Company, Albany, New York. It's dated November 1885."

"What is this stuff on it?" She ran her finger lightly over several dark and crusty stains. "Guess these can't be framed. Too bad. I like how it's different from the others."

She picked up the tube and heard a rattle. When she turned it over, a piece of metal dropped out, along with some kind of stick.

"What on earth?"

Bailey picked up the metal and held it to the light. About five inches in length, it was covered partly in the same dark substance the drawings were. But the clean half glinted in the light. A dragon's face or maybe an alligator had been shaped in gold and silver with a delicate crosshatching.

She offered it to Renzo.

His eyes grew wide. "Wait here. Holy shit. Put it down really carefully and don't touch it and I'll be right back."

She placed it on the top of the trunk and leaned down to get a better look. She was tempted to scratch away the yucky crust and see what was beneath, but Renzo was back a moment later, holding a newspaper.

"I saw this a couple of days ago. Look at this."

An old black-and-white photo showed a knife with a carved metal handle partially pulled out of a sheath.

The sheath that was right in front of them.

"What is this?" She began reading as Renzo explained.

"Some construction workers found the knife a week ago in Central Park, when they were excavating for Strawberry Fields. It's really old, from Tibet, and disappeared from the collection of a wealthy family named Rutherford in the 1880s."

"And it was only just discovered?"

"Yes. They're trying to figure out how it got there. Right now it's at the Met, being examined, as there are no descendants of the Rutherford family left to claim it. It says here that the sheath hasn't been recovered."

She stared at the object. "It was in Theodore Camden's trunk, who was stabbed to death in November 1885. The same month as on the drawings."

"What about this?" Renzo reached over and picked up the stick that had fallen out of the same tube. "Some kind of drawing tool?"

It reminded her of a rook piece from a chess set, one that had been worn smooth over time. "That's not a pencil." Bailey turned to Renzo in horror. "You're holding Theodore Camden's missing finger."

"What?" Renzo croaked.

"The bone from his finger! It was cut off during his murder and never found. They thought it might have been taken as some kind of grisly souvenir."

To his credit, he didn't drop the bone to the floor. Instead, he waited until Bailey had grabbed two tissues from his office and laid the bone on one and the sheath on the other, before carefully folding them up, like a pair of newborns being swaddled.

"The sheath must be worth a ton of money," said Bailey. "The Met is going to flip out when they see that we've found this."

"The paper says the knife is worth around half a million dollars. It's from the sixteenth century."

"To think the knife and sheath have been not three hundred yards from each other all this time."

"I wonder how they got separated."

A draft ran over the back of her neck and she shivered. "I wonder how his finger ended up down here."

Together, they went back through all the trunks, but more carefully. Bailey checked inside the pockets of the dresses, in the very corners of each trunk, looking for clues. In Minnie Camden's trunk she took out a small red silk purse edged with metallic gold lace.

Inside was a piece of paper, as delicate as the crust of a crème brûlée.

> *My dear Christopher,*
>
> *I have been promised that you will receive this letter on your twenty-first birthday. I know it may be a shock, but I am proud to call you my son, even if you may be ashamed to see me as your mother. Indeed, I am, and everything I have done, I have done for you. To give you a better life. When you were a boy, I loved you and held you and perhaps the fragile memories of that time still remain. No child should be denied what is true. Your father is Theodore Camden. I hope now you are twenty-one you are able to understand the circumstances that prevented you from knowing the truth. And to forgive.*

The name below was illegible, but Bailey was certain it began with an *S*.

She showed Renzo the letter, shaking with exhilaration. "The plot thickens."

"Christopher wasn't a random ward." He studied it closely. "You were right. He was Theodore Camden's son."

"And Sara's." Her cheeks burned with pleasure at the acknowledgment. She was a Camden, as was her father and her grandfather. This proved it. "I knew it. Doesn't this look like the letter *S*?"

He squinted. "Not sure of that. But maybe. Where did you find it?"

"In Minnie Camden's purse. Or at least the purse was in Minnie Camden's trunk."

"Then maybe he was Minnie's child."

"Why would she keep that a secret, though? Makes no sense. In any event, that's definitely not the word *Minnie* at the bottom." The more she thought about the implications of the letter, the faster her heart beat. Excitement sizzled through her body.

She handed him the sheath and the bone. "Take these and put them in a safe place. First thing tomorrow, I'll go back to the library and find out more about Sara Smythe and the murder."

"Shouldn't we contact the Met, tell them what you've discovered?"

"We will, just not yet. You know what this means, don't you?"

Renzo eyed her warily.

"It means that I am a descendant of Theodore Camden. I'm sure of it."

"Be careful what you wish for."

She gave him a quick peck on the cheek. The touch was electric. She hadn't meant it that way, just as a friendly, celebratory gesture, but he felt it, too, and pulled back.

"Sorry, didn't mean to do that." Her face got hot.

"It's okay. Take it slow, though. Don't rush to conclusions."

Was he talking about their friendship or their findings?

Either way, caution had never been her strong point.

CHAPTER TWENTY-TWO

New York City, July 1885

Sara opened her eyes. It was dark outside, and while the pain had subsided briefly, she knew it would be back. During the lull, she tried to take in where she was. The room wasn't in the Charity Hospital, she was sure of that. The bed was hard and the blanket rough and she didn't see any other women in the throes of childbirth. The only other woman in the room, an old lady with a vacant stare and no teeth, got up and turned her back to squat over a waste pail, singing an off-key dirge about the devil. She was still in the asylum.

The evening turned to day and back into evening, and Sara fought for breath and life and pushed. The nurses for the most part ignored her. When one loomed over her with a grim mouth, Sara grabbed her wrist.

"I need to be taken to the Charity Hospital to have the baby. To the ward with unwed mothers."

"What do you know about that?" The nurse pulled out of her grip. "In any event, they don't take crazies there. You'd disturb the rest of them."

"I wouldn't, I know that's where I belong. Ask Nurse Alden."

"You've been saying that the entire time you've been here. Enough, luv. You checked in here as a Mrs. Smythe. That place is for unwed mothers."

She would have laughed if her situation weren't so dire. "It's too early to have the baby, isn't it?"

"I don't know anything about that. You'll have to ask the doctor."

Just then a wave of pain swept over her and she forgot about everything except the muscles and nerves in her body, straining in a way that seemed physically impossible.

Finally, the doctor arrived. Two nurses flanked him. The man was young, with bright blue eyes that darted around the room, taking everything in. He was from the outside and practically smelled of fear.

A nurse pointed at Sara. "She started up last night; we didn't know she was with child."

"How could you not know?" The doctor sat on the edge of her bed and took out a stethoscope, which he placed against her belly. A rush of embarrassment was replaced by a sense of hope. Perhaps he could help.

"She didn't tell us nothing. We can't keep track of everyone in here, all sixteen hundred."

"Can she speak?" He glanced up at the nurses.

Thankfully, she was in between contractions. "I can speak, Doctor."

He looked down at her, startled. "You're English?"

He had a familiar accent of his own. "And you're Welsh."

"Indeed. Now, why didn't you tell anyone about your predicament?"

Another cramp threatened and she winced in pain.

"Get her some water, please." The nurses moved on his command.

"I didn't know what they'd do to me."

"Rather a ghastly place here, no?"

"Yes. I was hoping I could be taken to the Charity Hospital on the island, the ward for unwed mothers."

"You don't have a husband?"

"No." Her cheeks grew warm from shame. How far she'd fallen.

"Why were you put here in the asylum?"

"I'm not sure. They said I was acting funny, that I stole something. But I don't remember doing it. I was with child at the time; maybe my mind wasn't right from that."

She should never have mentioned the theft. He straightened his spine. "I'm sorry to hear that. But I'm afraid it's too late to go to the hospital. You'll have to have the baby here."

"It's so early. I didn't think it would come until August."

The cramp increased until she couldn't think or speak. "Please don't go yet," she whispered. Tears of self-pity poured down her cheeks. "What will happen to the baby after?"

"I don't know. This is my first week and I'm not sure how it all works just yet. But don't worry about any of that right now. You need to keep your strength up so that you can deliver the baby." He stood.

"Where are you from in Wales?" She didn't want him to go just yet.

"Swansea."

"Is it lovely? It sounds lovely."

"It's by the sea."

"Do you miss it?" She clenched her teeth, trying to keep them from chattering.

"That's enough talk. I'll check on that water for you."

"Please don't go. Please. Please help me."

He nodded. "I'll do everything I can."

After he strode away, she burst into sobs. She'd been doing so well for herself, in charge of her own life, running a giant building and its staff, and now she was helpless, trapped in a terrible place with no way out, nothing but pain and anguish pulsating around her. The kind manner of the doctor only served to remind her of all that she'd lost.

"Stop wailing." The nurses had returned. One lifted up her head and poured water into her mouth from a dirty tin cup, not caring that it spilled around the sides and dribbled down her chin and neck.

The water tasted metallic, like something medicinal had been added to it. She tried to ask them what they'd given her, but her tongue became heavy and thick. A sea of sensations followed, but she couldn't figure out where the noises came from or where she ended and the rest of the world began. She dreamed of the baby and of her mother, the two curled up in bed together. In her vision, she drew closer, wanting to pick up the baby and hold her, but she drew back in horror when she realized they were both made of ice. Cold to the touch, not human at all.

She opened her eyes to the harsh summer sun streaming through the window. The room was empty; the humid air reeked of mold and rotting vegetables. Her entire body ached, as if she'd been trampled on by a horse, and her breasts were sore and heavy. She looked to either side of the bed for a crib, for some sign of her child.

"There you are, then." The doctor stepped into the room. His eyes had shadows under them. "How do you feel?"

She tried to sit up, but her muscles refused.

"Don't move. You'll need to rest."

"The baby?"

He didn't answer her question. "The nurses said that you'll need to rejoin the other patients in a day or two. I tried to get them to give you a week to recover, but I'm afraid Superintendent Dent would have none of it."

She didn't care about that. "But where's the baby?"

"I'm sorry, Mrs. Smythe. The baby died."

Sara blinked through her tears. She hadn't admitted to herself how eager she had been to meet this creature, even if she was bringing it into a world of pain and misery. "How? I felt it inside me. Was it too early?"

He frowned. "It was deformed. Horribly deformed. To be honest, it's best it died, for otherwise it would be brought up in a place like this, and you wouldn't want that, would you?"

She didn't answer. "Can I see it?"

"It will be buried on the island. A boy was what you had. They bury them here. It was better you didn't see him. Something had gone terribly wrong."

Nurse Garelick's beating had damaged the baby, just as she'd feared.

He reached out and patted her hand. "In any event, you'll need to try to get stronger quickly. Don't let this bother you. Better this way, I assure you."

She turned away and covered her eyes with her hand. The baby had died and the only thing ahead of her was more pain, more sitting, more cruelty. The child she'd carried, Theo's child, was now under the dirt somewhere on the island, in one of the unmarked graves she and Natalia had seen behind the Charity Hospital. No markers, just mounds of dirt that settled down as the bodies and flesh and bones melted down to nothing.

She retched and the doctor jumped up. "I'll have the nurse bring you a bucket."

Sara listened as his footsteps grew faint, replaced by the sounds of her own grief.

Sara had lasted two days back in her block, not talking, even to Natalia, not eating, and, more important, refusing to make mats, before she was dragged away and placed in a cell on the top floor, the same one she'd been taken to after Nurse Garelick's beating.

Poor Natalia had tried to comfort her, and urged her to pull back from the dark place she'd been driven to by the baby's death, but Sara would have none of it. She had been carved open by the pain and confusion of the birth, and there was no solace to be found. Not on Blackwell's Island.

She lay curled up on the cot most of the day, lifting her head to watch the mice skitter across the floor and devour the tray that had been shoved through the opening under the door. How lovely to exist on instinct alone, to not know anything of the outside world and its delights and scandals. If she could have killed herself, she would have. One of the nurses had threatened to send her to the Lodge if she didn't start obeying orders. "They'll toss you around like a rag doll, and you'll be screaming to be let back to your mates in no time," she'd said, sneering. Sara had turned over to face the wall, and since then, the food had stopped.

She'd lost track of time. Maybe a week had gone by since the baby had died, maybe five days. Maybe five months. None of it mattered anymore.

The door latch clicked.

"You'll stay in here until we know where to put you. Don't mind the dead body over there. She won't bother you."

"Thank you, Nurse Cotter. I have your name right, don't I?"

There was a long pause, long enough to make Sara open her eyes. "That's right."

"Very well. Thank you, Nurse Cotter."

The nurse made a clucking noise and slammed the door shut.

"Well, she's a delight."

Sara turned over and examined her new cellmate. The woman had survived the bathing process fairly unscathed. Her bangs were still curly and damp and her neck and cheeks red.

The woman thrust her hand out. "Well, hello there. I'm Nellie Brown."

Sara closed her eyes. Poor child. She was yet to be broken.

"You all right?"

Sara hoped she'd get the hint and move to her side of the room. But no luck. Instead, she moved closer, studying Sara like a work of art in a museum. Which, in a way, was apt. All hard marble and stone, weighed down with no separation between her and the cot, her pedestal.

"You don't look well. Is there anything I can do for you?"

Sara couldn't help it. She laughed.

"Was that funny?"

Sara remembered the energy she'd brought with her to this place, trying to sort it all out and determine where she stood, how to get out. "You oughtn't bother." Her voice was weak.

"Oughtn't bother to do what?"

"Much of anything." Sara sighed. The girl was not going to be ignored. "There's no point."

The girl walked to the window and looked out. "I can see the city from here."

"Seems so close, doesn't it?"

Nellie moved to her cot and sat down, tucking the calico dress under her legs. "Do they not give you anything more than this to wear?"

Sara shook her head.

"Even in winter?"

"We get coats to wear outside on the mandatory walks."

"Why are you here?"

She certainly got right to the point.

"I got into trouble at my work and ended up here. I'm not sure how."

"Are you crazy?"

Sara shook her head. If anything, the agony of childbirth had strengthened her confidence in her own mental acuity. She had lost a child. And she was here against her will. "No. Not at all." She sat up and crossed her arms in front of her. "Are you?"

"No."

There was no explanation, no accusation of others, and no excuses. "Then why are you here?"

"That's a very good question." But Nellie didn't answer it. "How long have you been here?"

"I came in January of this year."

"How many madwomen would you say are in the asylum?"

"Patients."

"Sorry? Oh, right. Patients. How many are there?"

"Sixteen hundred or so."

As the afternoon sun made its way up the wall, Sara found herself opening up more than she ever had, even to Natalia. Partly, she wanted to give this girl a better chance at navigating the dangerous channels of Blackwell's Island Insane Asylum. But she also wanted to be heard. One last time.

She told her of the beatings, the mistreatment and torture of Marianne. Nellie asked questions but didn't seem overly shocked by any of it. Sometimes she repeated what Sara had said. Maybe she wasn't very bright.

The food came. The woman picked up both trays and brought Sara one, laid it on her lap.

"I don't want to eat."

"I do, and I don't like to eat alone, so you'll have to indulge me."

Sara bit off a crust of bread, shocked to discover her stomach growling for more.

"Where did you used to work, before you were sent here?" asked Nellie.

"I worked at the Dakota Apartment House."

The woman put down her spoon. "I read all about that building during the construction. In what capacity?"

"I was the managerette."

"You were in charge?"

"Under the managing agent, yes."

Part of Sara was pleased to be able to shock this woman. Part of her wanted to sober her up, make her see that the outlook wasn't good for either of them. You could be going along, living your life, and then see everything you've carefully built tumble down. She'd been worried about being with child, of how Theo would react. At the time, the problem seemed insurmountable. Until something else came along, a trip on a ferry into hell, that made her earlier troubles almost trite in comparison.

"What happened?"

"I was accused of stealing a necklace from one of the tenants."

"Did you do that?"

"No. I don't know who did, but it wasn't me."

"For that you were tossed in the madhouse?"

What was the point of playing games anymore? "I had an affair with the husband of the woman who accused me. I think she may have found out."

"And had you committed, set you up, you mean?"

Sara had been turning the idea over in her head since her incarceration, trying to remember what had happened the days before the necklace had been found. If Mrs. Camden had found out about Theo and Sara and decided to get rid of her with a false accusation. "Perhaps."

"Why are you up here and not with the rest of the ladies?"

"I stopped working, stopped doing much of anything. They don't like that much."

"What made you do that?"

Tears began falling down Sara's face. No one had really cared much to ask why. "I had a baby, and it died, and there was no point after that."

The woman took her hand. "The baby of your lover?"

Sara nodded. "He doesn't even know I'm here. They've locked me away and I don't know what he thinks or what happened. I'm done for."

"I'm so sorry about the baby. You certainly don't deserve to be tossed in an asylum for something you didn't do. You didn't do it, right?"

"No. I did not."

The girl was spending far too much energy on Sara. She had to be warned.

"You need to take care of yourself going forward. Don't question the other inmates like this, not in front of the nurses. You'll get in trouble. The main thing is to not attract attention. Do as they ask, eat as much as you can, and in the sitting room, sit on the side opposite the windows, so you have something to look at."

"The sitting room?"

"You'll find out. Don't try to help anyone, it doesn't end well. But there's a woman, Natalia, who's lovely. If you can, find her."

"What about you?"

"I don't know if they'll ever let me out of this room."

"Please don't say that." She walked over and sat beside Sara, swallowing hard. "You are obviously quite sane; I can see that myself. You must promise to keep going for me, and do what they say. Take your own advice, at least for a few weeks?"

A few weeks, a few days. None of it mattered.

Sara didn't reply. The sun had set and the room grew chilly. It was time for bed. They crawled under their thin blankets and spoke no more.

"Who are you looking for?" Natalia tapped her spoon on her plate and gave Sara a crooked smile. "Prince Charming?"

Sara glanced over at her friend. For the past two weeks, ever since she'd been released back to hall 6, she'd looked around in vain for Nellie, hoping to see how her cellmate was faring. Nellie had been taken out of the room the day after her arrival, while Sara had lingered on for ten or twelve days longer, she wasn't sure which. Time had become unreliable.

"The girl, Nellie, the one I told you about."

"Right. She was here for a while but then must have gone to another building."

"But still, then we'd see her outside. It's as if she vanished into thin air."

Natalia sighed. "Wouldn't that be nice."

"I hope she wasn't taken to the Lodge. She was far from violent; there would be no reason for that."

"You see it all the time, women who are calm and then turn into savages. You never know. I'm just glad you're back here with me. Are you glad?"

Underneath the words was concern. Natalia treated Sara differently ever since the baby. Like she was fragile, frail. Maybe she was, deep down. But the emotional and physical crisis, along with the long days and nights in a cell, had hardened her exterior into a tough shell. She did as she was told and didn't ask questions or cause trouble. She knew her place. The asylum had beaten it into her. The baby's death was something to be pushed down, deep, and never thought of again.

"I am very happy to be back with you, Natalia. Of course."

"I'm sorry our plan didn't work out."

"It is better this way. Imagine the alternative. If it had survived." She refused to use a gender pronoun to describe the child.

"I guess." Natalia studied her plate. "We got fish and potatoes again. A feast."

"Don't question it, enjoy it. Who knows when they'll go back to spoiled beef?"

"What about the new bedsheets? Why do you think they did that?"

Indeed, every inmate had been given a pillow and a warm blanket for their bed, unheard-of luxuries.

"Mrs. Smythe."

Sara looked up to see Nurse Alden coming toward her at a brisk clip. "You must come with me at once."

Sara looked over at Natalia, whose face had gone gray. "It's all right. I'll be fine." But what did they want with her? She hadn't done anything to attract attention. Nothing she could think of.

Nurse Alden's eyes were shining. "Just come along."

Superintendent Dent stood with Dr. Fields in the middle of the octagon's floor. A woman in a well-cut brown wool dress stepped forward.

Nellie.

"My dear Sara, I'm so glad to see you."

Sara looked over at Superintendent Dent. Was this a trick?

"You're being released, Mrs. Smythe." He didn't look pleased, and refused to meet her gaze. "The papers have been signed. Off you go, as the boat is leaving soon."

"I'm going?"

"Yes. You're free."

CHAPTER TWENTY-THREE

New York City, July 1885

"I must see Natalia." Sara turned back to the dining hall, but Nellie caught her.

"No, there's no time. We'll figure it out. Not now, though."

"Why am I being released?"

Superintendent Dent cleared his throat. "Miss Bly is a reporter and has cleared your name for you."

"But you were an inmate here just a couple weeks ago."

"I was, as an undercover journalist. Luckily, the press has the power to expose injustice in an unfair, unsafe institution." She stared hard at Superintendent Dent while she spoke.

Sara wasn't sure what that meant, what had happened. Before she could ask another question, she was taken to a room to sign some papers. Then Nellie took her by the arm and they walked outside, where the other inmates milled about.

"Sara!"

Natalia ran over, her face a cloud of concern. "Where are you going?"

Sara hugged her friend. The one person who had kept her alive the past many months. "I'm leaving, I've been freed. I'm not sure what happened." She began to cry. "I can't leave you."

"We'll be back, I promise," said Nellie. She put a hand on Natalia's arm. "This is the best I can do for now, but there will be more visits, and if Sara knows your full name and story, we'll see if we can clear you as well."

"Her name is Natalia Fabiano, and I can't leave her."

Natalia took Sara's face in her hands. "Of course you can. You go now." They hugged.

The horn of the boat blew and Sara and Nellie made their way to the dock, to the cheers of the inmates. The nurses tried to shush them but in vain, and Natalia's voice soared above them all.

"Sara Smythe! Don't forget us!"

It wasn't until the boat pulled away and the sailor in front tossed the thick rope onto the dock that Sara fully understood the sudden change in the course of her life. Nellie shoved a newspaper into her hands. Sara pored over the front-page article where the sordid details of Blackwell's Island Insane Asylum were laid out, one after another: the cold baths, the beatings, the sadistic staff, and the hours and hours of torturous sitting, word after terrible word, for the entire city to read. The byline read MISS NELLIE BLY.

"You're a hero." Sara grabbed Nellie's hand. "You pretended to be mad? What were you thinking?"

"To be honest, I was thinking that it would make a good story. But once I was there, I realized how truly awful it was, and how no one in the city proper knew what was going on. I was certain that if they knew, they'd care, and I was right. This is only the first step. A commission has been set up and they've committed one million dollars to straighten the place out."

A million dollars. The sum was unimaginable.

"But why have I alone been pardoned? What about the others? Many of the women at Blackwell's are there only because they don't speak enough English to defend themselves."

"Believe me, I understand the injustices perpetrated against the women imprisoned on Blackwell's. I'll explain later, at dinner, the reason you are free and they're not. First, we have to get you settled and cleaned up. Don't be offended, but you're rather ripe."

In another time, Sara would have been horrified at the thought. But she couldn't find it in herself to feel embarrassed. She was free.

After taking a carriage that was waiting for them on the other side of the river, they pulled up in front of the marble-clad Fifth Avenue Hotel on Twenty-Third Street.

"Courtesy of the *World*, you are getting a well-deserved pampering," announced Nellie. "And me, too, which I am looking forward to enormously."

A crowd was gathered outside, what looked like newspapermen gathered in a pack. Nellie took her hand. "Ignore them, follow me, just walk right through."

"Why are they here? Do they know who I am?"

"Everyone knows who you are, darling."

A bellboy whisked them up the elevator to a suite on the top floor. The room was lavishly appointed, with a red silk bedspread and matching chaise, purple heart marquetry and Turkish rugs.

"This is for me?" Sara's heart beat fast. The sudden change in her fortune overwhelmed her. What she truly wanted to do was to find Theo, but she'd never be able to leave without stirring up the reporters gathered outside.

"All for you. I'll call the maid to run you a bath, and there are several dresses and underclothes to choose from in the armoire. Take your time and then we'll go down for supper and I'll explain everything."

The warm, welcome buoyancy of the bath nearly did Sara in. Her hands were chafed and raw, and her limbs seemed like they belonged to someone else. Although she didn't want to see her reflection, the looking glass was too tempting to avoid. The loss of weight made her eyes seem bigger, her skull a massive weight on a scrawny neck. She looked like a creature from a nightmare.

A maid helped her into silk underclothes and a fawn-colored gown. After the rough wool and calico of her Blackwell's uniform, it was like having butterfly wings next to her skin. She sat before the mirror and let the woman put up her hair in a chignon.

When her soft touch threatened to send Sara into an emotional tailspin, she remembered sitting at the asylum and concentrated on her breathing. Air in, air out.

Nellie knocked at the door and smiled when she saw her. "Well, don't you look a treat."

"Can we have supper in here?" Sara asked. "I'm not sure if I can be out in public. I don't feel like myself."

Nellie shook her head. "You'll do fine. I've booked a table in the corner, just for the two of us. This is a posh hotel; no one will bother you."

Downstairs, Nellie led the way across the parquet floor to their table, and Sara sat with her back to the room so as not to attract any more attention than she possibly could. Nellie ordered their dinner and then dove into the details.

"After I got out, I did some digging into your story. Did you know that just a few months after you'd been taken off, another worker at the Dakota had been sent to jail for stealing from tenants?"

"Who was that?"

"A Miss Daisy Cavanaugh."

Sara inhaled sharply. "Not Daisy. That couldn't be."

"Apparently, she'd been filching things for some time. They found a stash of timepieces, hair clips, rings, in her room. Like a raccoon, drawn to shiny things."

"But they found the necklace I was supposed to have stolen in my desk drawer." Daisy had been Sara's one friend and confidante since coming to America, and they had grown even closer since the loss of the girl's mother. "What if she was set up as well? I knew Daisy; she was a good girl; she wouldn't have done such a thing."

"She admitted it and is now in prison."

Daisy had been upset when Mr. Douglas had not increased her wages after her mother's death. But would she really resort to stealing from the tenants? And even worse, let Sara take the blame for her misdeeds? Unimaginable. But something else nagged at Sara. Their food arrived. Sara waited until the servers were out of earshot. "If Daisy did admit to the crimes, why didn't anyone come for me, set me free?"

"The agent at the Dakota, Mr. Douglas, told everyone you'd gone back to England. The last thing he wanted was to set you free and have you make a fuss." She took a bite of roast beef and moaned. "Delicious! In any event, he's no longer the agent at the Dakota. Not after it got out in the papers."

"What exactly got out?" Sara's stomach hurt. She couldn't imagine eating anything right now.

"It wasn't enough for my own experience to be told. I also wanted to get you free, to right an injustice, and to do so, I had to write about what had happened to you."

"What did you write about me?" Sara's mind reeled. The affair, the baby. Nellie was an intrepid journalist, and she already knew so much. Sara had been brutally honest when they spoke in that dank cell.

"I'll show you the story when we get back upstairs." She caught Sara's eye. "Don't worry, I wrote that you were a good lady, a proper one, who had been tossed away and that when the real thief was exposed, no one bothered to release you from what was a cruel, terrible institution."

"I see."

"What's even better, as a show of remorse, the new agent of the Dakota is offering you your job back. They need to get on the right side of the public, you see. So you'll be reinstated as lady manager-ette as soon as you're ready."

Nellie's face glowed with pleasure.

Sara began to shake. "I couldn't go back. I couldn't."

Nellie reached over and covered her hand with her own. "No need to make any decisions right how. I imagine the reentry into regular life is going to be a difficult one, after you've spent the past seven months thinking all was lost. I was there for ten days and I'm still not sure which end is up. Sleep and rest and we have a couple of days of hiding out here until you decide what you want to do next."

"I don't belong here. I'm not of this ilk. It's all too much."

"Trust me, you'll get used to it fast enough. Tomorrow there's someone who wants to see you, if you're up to it."

"Who?"

"A man who contacted me the day your story was published. He said you'd want to see him. A Mr. Theodore Camden."

Sleep came fast that evening. Sara collapsed into the down bedding and gave in to the warmth of the room, sensations that she'd only dreamed of at Blackwell's. She startled awake at dawn, the image of Natalia crying driving her out of a deep slumber. How could she have left her behind? And so many others?

Nellie arrived an hour later, followed by waitstaff carrying trays of breakfast food for them, more than either would be able to eat. Potato omelettes, egg toast, biscuits. Sara's eyes welled up at the gluttony laid out on the table.

"Don't cry, please don't cry." Nellie sat back. "I need you to toughen up. We'll take advantage of your fame and this will all be behind you before you know it."

"I can't imagine I'll ever forget Blackwell's. What I saw there." For the first time, it dawned on her what a risk Nellie had taken by being voluntarily admitted. "Why did you do it? Did you know what you were getting into?"

Nellie spooned some jam onto a triangle of toast. "Not really. I'd heard rumors. But I'm not one to report on tea parties or the latest gowns from Paris. My editors know that, and I knew they would protect me."

"Still. What if you'd been lost, like I was?"

"I was more valuable to my editors on the outside, exposing what was going on. They wouldn't have dared leave me behind."

"I envy you, in control of your own life." Sara shook her head. "I thought I was doing the same, but look what happened."

"It wasn't your fault. Remember that and stay strong. You have a lot of decisions to make." Nellie poured her some coffee and insisted she eat a hard-boiled egg. Sara did as she was told, luxuriating in the slipperiness of the egg white in contrast to the chalky yolk on her tongue. As good as caviar.

She knew what she wanted to do first off. "I'll need to speak with Mr. Camden."

"Right. He wants you to come to his offices."

"Hardenbergh's office?"

"He gave me the address. I'll bring you there."

Nellie expertly extracted them from the hotel out the back door, avoiding the wolf pack of journalists, and into a waiting hack. They pulled up in front of a building on Madison Avenue in the Forties. "He said it's on the second floor. I'll stay in the carriage."

Sara welcomed the darkness of the stairway and didn't pass an-

other soul before arriving at the door marked THEO. CAMDEN, ARCHI-
TECT.

He'd gone into business for himself.

She turned the doorknob and found herself standing in a large
room that contained an empty desk and a leather armchair. An open
door on the far wall led to a smaller office. Theo came flying toward
her before she could even register who he was.

"Sara, you're free."

If she had any qualms about how they ought to greet each other
after so long apart, she had no time to question what to do, as he
pulled her to him and held her close.

Her entire body erupted in convulsive sobs. He stroked her hair
and spoke words that soothed, but it was no good. She'd dreamed of
this moment for so long. All of the pain and anguish poured out of
her. But even more, she cried because he hadn't forgotten her after all.

He reached into his pocket and handed her his handkerchief.

"Come into my office." He led her to a settee opposite a large desk
covered with drawings, never letting go of her hands. "My God,
what you've been through. If I'd only known. When I spoke with
Mr. Douglas, he said he'd offered you the opportunity to return
home, and you left on the next ship back to England. I hoped you
might send me a letter, but when none came, I figured you were
done with New York. Done with me."

"Mr. Douglas lied. He locked me away so that the scandal wouldn't
taint the Dakota."

"You've suffered so much. I read the papers, what you went
through."

She looked away. No one on the outside could truly understand. "I
have friends there who need help. Like me, they were locked away
for no reason at all."

"The mayor and the commission are looking into it; there's been a huge outcry. That reporter has single-handedly changed the course of events."

"Nellie. She saved me."

Theo shook his head. "It should have been me. I should have been the one who saved you."

"No. You couldn't have known."

"Are you all right? Now, I mean? Did they hurt you?"

She thought of the baby. To have felt it grow in her womb and then have nothing left, nothing in her arms, was the worst pain she'd ever experienced. Her body shook.

"Are you cold?"

"No. I'm fine. Better now."

She'd never tell him about the child.

Theo's face darkened. "Mrs. Camden is terribly sorry that you were falsely accused. She wanted to apologize in person, but I'm afraid she's taken ill. The doctor says it's bilious fever, and recommended she go upstate to recover and rest. Away from the city. The children are with her."

"I see." Sara couldn't shake the idea that she'd been behind the scheme, in some way.

"As soon as I saw the article, I knew I had to find you."

"It consoles me to think that you cared enough to think about me while I was away, to wonder."

"Of course. I'd go up on the roof of the Dakota and stare across the park, hoping to see someone with your gait, your coloring, that you might return one day."

"To think I was on Blackwell's Island the whole time, staring into the distance at the outline of the Dakota. You can see it from there, did you know?"

"We were looking at each other but didn't know it."

How she'd missed him. She looked away, intoxicated at being so near to him after all this time, but embarrassed, too. "Sadly, yes." She forced a laugh. "But I'm out. Now I have to figure out what to do. I don't like being the center of attention."

"It will work in your favor, you know. The new agent at the Dakota is intent on hiring you back, to show the rest of the city that you have been absolved."

"Who is in charge now?"

"Mrs. Haines."

"Best to keep it that way. I'm sure she's doing a lovely job."

"She doesn't have many friends, if that's what you mean."

Daisy's jolly "hello" each morning, her way of making the most arduous tasks seem enjoyable, came to mind. They had made a good team. "What about Daisy?"

Theo frowned. "She's been put away for good. At Blackwell's Island women's prison, strangely enough."

"How do we know Daisy wasn't set up by Mr. Douglas, too? She wasn't one to steal anything. I knew her well."

"Are you sure?" His expression was guarded. There was something he wasn't telling her.

"What do you mean?"

"Mrs. Haines told us that a couple of months after Daisy's run-in with the intruder, she saw her walking with the same man in Central Park."

Sara thought about it. The night that Daisy had been attacked, something *had* seemed off. The man's lack of urgency when he was discovered, to begin with. The way Daisy avoided Sara's gaze. She knew him, had invited him to her room, then pretended to have been attacked when he'd got caught. Sara and Mrs. Haines had come running to her defense as if she were a damsel in distress. Sara wondered what else she'd gotten wrong, what else Daisy had been up to.

"Why didn't Mrs. Haines tell anyone?"

"Daisy's mother died soon after, so she decided to put off confronting her until after the holidays. And then"—he paused—"well."

Right. Then everything had come tumbling down. "Daisy had to support a large family; maybe that's why she stole. Shouldn't that be taken into account?"

Theo rubbed his brow. "After everything you've been through, you're worried about Daisy?"

He was right. If it were true, and everyone seemed to be convinced of it, then Daisy had taken advantage of Sara's trust and vulnerability.

She stood and looked about the room. "You've done well for yourself."

"I thought it was time for me to stand on my own two feet. More importantly, Hardenbergh finally came through."

"When did you set up shop?"

"A few months ago. I'm afraid clients aren't exactly breaking down my door." He shook his head. "But I refuse to do more of the same. I want to create buildings for the coming century, not this one. Here, look at my ideas."

He grabbed a sketchbook from his desk and handed it to her. She leafed through the pages, unsettled by the feel of him standing so close beside her.

"This one is quite lovely."

"A library." He drew his finger along the roofline. "Any ornamentation is also structural. Like these pillars." Another turn of the page. "Here is an office building for the city. Made out of concrete. The smooth surface draws the eye upward, into the sky."

"It is breathtaking."

"The city would be transformed. It's a completely different way of looking at the world." He looked down at her. "I knew you'd understand. I imagine block after block of these, each with their own personality but not fighting each other the way the big mansions do now along Fifth Avenue."

He sat beside her, no longer looking down at the pages. "If you won't go back to the Dakota to work, would you work for me? As my office manager? Or managerette? Whatever you want to call it. Granted, there's not a lot to do right now, but together we'll make it all work out. I need you beside me, you see."

A lump lodged in her chest. "I couldn't do that. It would attract too much attention."

"I don't care about that. In fact, I could use the attention."

"It wouldn't be right. What about Mrs. Camden?"

"She felt terrible when the truth came out. She has a larger perspective on what is important. To her, it's the children. To me, it's my work. You see, we have never been very happy together. We've reached an understanding, you might say."

"She doesn't know about me, about us?"

"No. Of course not."

Sara considered her choices. She could take over Mrs. Haines's job at the Dakota, but that would be a step backward. Working with Theo on his new projects would be fulfilling. And dangerous.

"We couldn't ever do what we did that one night." Her boldness made her turn red, and the heat crawled up the back of her neck.

He looked away. "Of course not. I understand that. But we'd work together well, don't you think?"

She didn't respond.

"What about this? What if I got you an apartment at the Dakota? There's one on the sixth floor that's vacant, as the tenants both passed away last month."

"The Rembrandts?" Sara remembered them. A much older couple, devoted to each other, who had taken the adventurous step to move uptown. She was sorry to hear they had died.

"Yes. Once the press gets used to the idea that you are free and taken care of, living in the Dakota and working for me, we'd be able to go on with our lives. It's an opportunity seized from a tragedy."

"I can't imagine living in the Dakota again. It would feel so strange."

"But you must. They'll let you live there for a year rent-free. I will insist."

"You would?"

"Of course. It is the right thing to do. Please say yes, Sara."

She'd come to America to do better, to improve her lot, and she had been betrayed and abused. But instead of giving in, she'd figured out how to survive under the most atrocious circumstances. Now she would get to work alongside the man she adored, live in a beautiful building befitting an earl's daughter, and no longer be in service.

An opportunity seized from a tragedy.

His words echoed in her ears.

CHAPTER TWENTY-FOUR

New York City, September 1985

Theodore Camden's murder, not surprisingly, had made big news back in 1885. The most sensational articles Bailey found were in the *New York World*. One stated that Sara Smythe had been incarcerated earlier that year at Blackwell's Island Insane Asylum and released due to the intervention of a female journalist, Nellie Bly. After Sara got out, she'd been hired as an assistant to Theodore Camden before savagely turning on him and stabbing him in the library of his Dakota apartment.

Bailey spent hours at the public library, reading through Nellie Bly's accounts of her time at the asylum, which was located right across the East River on what was now known as Roosevelt Island. The graphic descriptions turned her stomach. As did the fact that alcoholics were often locked away in the workhouse on the island. How lucky she'd been to be born a hundred years later.

Sara Smythe, who might very well be her great-grandmother, had been through a terrible ordeal. After all that, Christopher had never received the letter from her confirming that she was indeed his mother. Minnie had hidden it away from him. The injustice of it all left a sour taste in Bailey's mouth.

But Renzo's warning stayed with Bailey. Maybe the letter was from Minnie. After all, it was found in her purse. The whole thing made Bailey's head buzz with confusion. Still, no matter who his mother was, Christopher's father was Theodore Camden. The letter was proof, proof that Melinda wouldn't be able to deny.

Melinda had always been vague about the amount of money in her trust fund. But surely, there would be enough for both lines of the family to split the principal and still live well. Bailey would be able to put a security deposit down on a rental apartment and maybe even pay back Tristan for the cost of Silver Hill. The luxury of a financial cushion to break her fall.

Her cousin's brittle voice rang out as soon as she entered the Dakota apartment. "Where the hell have you been?"

Melinda stood against the library windowpane, smoking a cigarette.

"You really shouldn't smoke in here." Bailey had spent longer than she'd meant to at the library, and the doorman had warned her Melinda was upstairs. "It's a fire hazard, with all the work going on."

Melinda inhaled again, her mouth forming a perfect pout. "It's fine. Why aren't the bamboo poles up yet?"

"Because I have to order them. It's not like you can go into the bamboo store and just buy them. These things take time." She studied Melinda closely. "What's going on with you?"

"I'm hungry and I've been waiting for you when I'm supposed to meet Tony for lunch."

"Okay." Bailey spoke as if Melinda were a two-year-old on the cusp of a major meltdown. "What can I do for you, then?"

"I'm not sure about the koi pond anymore."

Thank God, she'd seen the light. "That's fine. I think we can find a way to incorporate a really cool aquarium, if you need fish."

A drilling noise threatened to bring down the walls. Melinda shouted above it. "But I don't want anything that looks like it belongs in the room of a disgruntled teenager. I want something that's grown up."

Bailey shouted back. "Of course. Let me work on it." This was ridiculous. "Hey, I found something out that is amazing. I want to tell you about it. Can we talk outside?"

"I'm late. You can come to lunch with me, though."

They met Tony at a bistro on Columbus. He was already seated and halfway through a martini. Once they'd ordered, Bailey dove in.

"I found something down in the basement of the Dakota. Something valuable."

Tony swiveled his head back from watching their young French waitress sashay to the kitchen. "What might that be, a diamond tiara of Melinda's mum's?"

"I wish." Melinda turned to Tony. "No, she's found some silly photo. Bailey's been digging around in the family business, trying to stir up trouble."

She had expected Melinda's resistance, and pressed on. "Down in the basement, there are three trunks. One belongs to Theodore Camden, one to his wife, Minnie, and one to the person who brutally stabbed him to death, Sara Smythe."

Tony perked up. She hadn't meant to be so dramatic, but she hated the way he had dismissed her. Melinda, on the other hand, rolled her eyes.

Bailey ignored her. "In one of the trunks, I found a letter, most likely from Sara Smythe, that was written to the ward of Theodore and Minnie. It says that the ward, who was my grandfather, was her son. Hers and Theodore's."

She waited a moment, to let Tony wrap his head around the various branches of the family tree.

Tony squinted. "Back up. Who's who? How many generations are you going back?"

"Four, if you can believe it. Theodore Camden had Luther Camden, who had Melinda and Manvel's father. So Theodore Camden is Melinda and Manvel's great-grandfather. What I'm suggesting is that Theodore Camden and this woman, Sara Smythe, had Christopher Camden, who's my grandfather."

"That means . . ." Tony trailed off.

"That I might also be Theodore's great-granddaughter."

"Jesus, you've got to stop this; you can't tell anything by old letters. Let it go, already." Melinda lit another cigarette. "Tony, I was thinking it'd be fun to go up to Saranac, see the leaves changing. Don't you think? We could do a weekend, just the two of us."

"Hold on, I want to hear more." Tony held up his hand. "Do you have the letter?"

Bailey took an envelope from her handbag and opened it up. She pulled out the letter and laid it on the table, smoothing it out with care.

Tony studied it and looked at Bailey. "It's hard to tell what the signature is. It's all blurry. Where was it found?"

"In a purse in Minnie's trunk. But it's obviously the word *Sara*. Look, here's the *S*.

"Huh." He didn't seem convinced. "If it was written by her, how can you believe it? She obviously was a nutjob."

He had a point.

Melinda balanced her cigarette in the ashtray, perilously close to the letter. "You said you found something valuable. This is a piece of paper. I don't get it."

Bailey folded it back up and put it in the envelope. "There's something else. Did you see the article in the paper about how they had to stop the work at Strawberry Fields because they found an antique knife?"

Tony nodded, and Melinda, who probably had never read a paper in her life, stared blankly.

"Well, we found the sheath that goes to it. In Theodore's trunk. As well as what we believe was Theodore Camden's finger. Or what's left of it."

Melinda put her finger down her throat and pretended to gag. "Gross."

Tony blinked. "What's the deal with the sheath?"

"They had a photo of the knife in the paper, and we're certain we have the sheath part of it."

"Who's 'we'?" asked Melinda, suspicious.

"Renzo Duffy."

"The super? Jesus Christ, Bailey. I told you to avoid him."

"How can I avoid him? I'm supervising construction in his building."

"It's not his building. The tenants, meaning me, own the building. The super is my employee."

"As a matter of fact, the tenants of a co-op own shares in a building, not the actual building," said Tony, always the expert.

Bailey held her impatience at bay. "Renzo was there when I opened the trunk and he's been very helpful."

"I don't want him in my business, Bailey. I told you that."

Tony interrupted again, thankfully. "Enough about the super. That knife is really valuable. Which means the sheath is really valuable."

Melinda leaned forward. "How valuable?"

Bailey spoke up, relieved that Melinda had been redirected from Renzo. "The paper says the knife is worth half a million dollars. Right now it's at the Met, being studied and cleaned."

"They'll want the sheath, right, to go with it?" Melinda's voice went up in pitch. "If it was found in my stuff, then it's mine, right?"

She should have known this was the road the conversation would take. Melinda wanted nothing to do with their possible blood bond.

"I thought you'd be interested in the idea that we might be truly related. Don't you think that's amazing? That maybe we're second cousins or something like that."

Melinda put her hand on Bailey's. "Your mother desperately wanted you to be part of the Camden family, and after she died, I get why you feel compelled to carry on her wishes. We don't know if we're really cousins, and we may never know. But I will always think of you as my sister, no matter what."

Talk about a brush-off.

"Where's the sheath now?" Tony finished his drink in one gulp.

"At the Dakota, with Renzo."

"What? You left it with the super?" Melinda dug her nails into Bailey's hand.

"Ouch. Yes, it's fine. He's trustworthy. He has a safe in his office. That's where it is."

Tony tossed his napkin on the table. "Let's go check it out before he sells it on the underground market."

Renzo gave Bailey a huge smile when she walked into his office, but it faded fast when he spotted Melinda and Tony behind her.

"Where's the knife sheath thing?" Melinda spoke to him like he was a servant and she the lady of the manor.

Bailey offered Renzo a halfhearted smile of apology. "I told them about the knife and they'd like to see what we found."

"Okay." He blocked the safe from their view as he fiddled with the combination. After he yanked it open, Tony crowded forward, eager.

They were like vultures, he and Melinda. Tony practically licked his lips as Renzo placed the two tissue-wrapped packages on the desk. He unfolded the larger one.

The sheath, a battered remnant of a long-ago era, gleamed in the light.

"It doesn't look that great," said Melinda. She pointed to it. "What's that? Mud?"

Bailey shook her head. "I think it might be blood. Theodore Camden's blood. There's a set of plans in the same trunk, covered with splotches that look like blood."

Melinda pulled back her hand, as if the stain might leap out at her. "Ick."

Renzo picked up the newspaper on his desk, the same one he'd shown Bailey, and pointed to the photo. "It's a perfect match."

"Totally." Melinda put her hands on her hips. "What do we do now?"

Tony wrapped one arm around Melinda's shoulders. "Anything you want to do; it's yours. Finders keepers, right?"

She grinned up at him. "If it was in my storage unit, it belongs to me."

"Don't you think it should end up with the knife, at the Met?" Bailey looked over at Renzo for backup, but he stayed silent. "Ultimately, I mean?"

"If they want it, they should pay for it," answered Tony.

No question that Bailey had seen dollar signs when she'd first realized how much the thing was worth, but Tony and Melinda's crassness made her think twice. Someone made the weapon with their own hands, before it traveled around the world and ended up in New York City. "Think of the history of this piece of metal. Imagine where it's been and who's owned it."

"Who cares?" Melinda lifted it up with her finger and thumb, avoiding the cracked blood on it. "It's all rusty and dented and filthy."

Bailey cringed at her carelessness, holding her breath until Melinda returned it to the tissue. Of course the sheath would be what interested Tony and Melinda, not that Bailey might be a relation.

"There's a problem, though." Renzo finally spoke, his voice quiet and deep. "With the sheath."

"Oh yes, what's that?" Tony looked bemused, as if Renzo was a stammering idiot.

"It wasn't found in your storage unit."

Melinda put one hand on her hip. "It was in my great-grandfather's trunk; that's what Bailey said."

"But the trunk was in the building's storage area. Not yours."

Bailey couldn't believe he was challenging them. The trunks were obviously part of the Camden household. Then again, it was found in the room where people stored things they no longer wanted, that were no longer considered valuable. "He's right. It wasn't in the unit."

"Then who does it belong to, if not to me?" demanded Melinda.

"The co-op, I would assume."

Melinda looked like she was about to spit in his face. "Show me where you found it."

Renzo led the way to the room with the trunks. They opened up each one and Melinda tore through them, tossing ball gowns and shoes and leather tubes on the ground.

Bailey rescued the silk purse from being snatched up by Melinda. "Be careful, these are all antiques."

"Don't tell me what's valuable and what's not. You show me this stuff and now he's telling me it's not mine? Give me a break. All this is mine."

"No. It's not. I'm sorry, but we'll have to go through the management company on this." Renzo held his palms up and shrugged. "That's the way it works."

Unexpectedly, Renzo turned on his heels and walked out of the room. Tony sprinted behind him but had a late start. When Bailey got to the office, Renzo was standing in front of the closed safe, no sheath in sight.

"You can't do that," Melinda sputtered, thrown by his sudden maneuvering. "You're holding it hostage!"

"Until we hear from the management company, that's where it stays."

At first, Bailey couldn't figure out where Renzo was coming from. He hated Melinda, so it must have given him some satisfaction to take something away from her. But it was obvious, even to Bailey, that the sheath came from a Camden trunk. Why make such a fuss?

Maybe, like Bailey, he didn't want to see Melinda separate the knife and the sheath. He was holding it hostage so she wouldn't. She had to hand it to him, he had nerve, challenging a tenant like Melinda.

Tony studied Renzo with a renewed interest. "You say we have to prove that it's the Camdens' knife?"

Renzo shrugged. "You'll have to ask the co-op about that. Mr. Rogers is the board president. I would assume you should take it up with him."

"How do we know you won't make off with it in the meantime?" demanded Melinda.

"Wait a minute." Tony held a finger to his cleft chin. "What if we could prove beyond a doubt that this was Theodore Camden's?"

"How are we going to do that?" Melinda turned to Bailey. "Did you find anything that might be proof, a photo of him holding it or anything like that?"

"No. There's nothing like that."

"What about in my storage unit?"

"That's empty."

"Just my luck." Melinda stared hard at Renzo. "Then we go to the management company. I'll fight for this; no one is going to take it away from me."

"You won't have to fight for it," said Tony. "As I was trying to say, we can prove that it is yours."

"How?"

"My cousin can test the finger bone and blood for DNA and compare it to yours, Melinda." Tony smiled as though he'd solved the famine crisis in Ethiopia.

"Where do you get my DNA from?"

"Your blood." Melinda gave a dramatic shiver, but Tony continued on. "It's called DNA fingerprinting."

"Will that be considered proof, though?" asked Bailey.

Tony nodded. "You bet. It's already been used in an immigration case in England to reunite some kid with his mother."

Everything was moving too fast. Blood, bones, DNA.

But Tony was all business. "I'll ring my cousin and find out how this all works. Melinda, in the meantime, check with the management company. And your family advisor."

"Fred?"

"Yes. You'll want to make sure this is all on the up-and-up."

This was Bailey's chance.

"I have a request."

Melinda looked at Bailey like she was a bother, an irritant. Which wasn't fair. Bailey had been the one who'd found everything, who set all this in motion. If it weren't for her curiosity, the trunks would have stood in the corner for another hundred years, untouched.

"What's that, dear?" The coldness in Melinda's voice stung.

"I'd like my DNA to be compared as well. That way we'll know whether or not I'm a Camden."

Melinda laughed. "You've got to be kidding. No."

"Just 'no'? No discussion?"

Tony moved closer. "This is a very new test, and it's quite expensive. If you have the money to pay for it, go right ahead, but if I'm paying for it, then I don't want to add to the expense any more than I need to. You understand, surely?"

"But it's your cousin who's doing it. Don't you get a family discount?"

"My cousin invented the process, but it will be his lab that will be doing the testing. Someone has to pay for all that work." His voice dripped with condescension.

Bailey had no way of knowing if he was speaking the truth. But it made sense that this kind of scientific process would be expensive.

The possibility of an inheritance appealed to Bailey's practical side, sure. But that wasn't the only reason for her brashness. The hunger of discovering the truth about her birthright gnawed at her, in a way that put her other addictions to shame. Although from the outside it probably looked like she was replacing one obsession with another, this wasn't about sublimating harsh truths with intoxicants. The loss of her mother had put her on a dangerous path, and Bailey was certain that if she figured out who she really was, the future might be less treacherous.

"But if it turns out I am a Camden, I'll be able to pay you back." She was practically begging, and hated Renzo to see her this way. She avoided looking at him.

"No, darling," cooed Melinda. "I can't do that, you must understand. You have no proof, not really. Other than a letter from God knows who. You're clutching at straws and I can understand why. You've been dealt a tough hand lately. But I know you'll do fine. You always do."

She stood no chance, no chance at all.

When she finally glanced over at Renzo, he looked angry.

She'd never wanted a drink more in her life.

CHAPTER TWENTY-FIVE

New York City, August 1885

The new agent at the Dakota made good on the promise of a year of free rent. Sara had moved into the sixth-floor apartment, still furnished with the yellow velvet French settees and matching club chairs of the Rembrandts. The place offered a glorious view north, and she appreciated the cool shade during the hot August afternoons.

Sara had received a jubilant letter from Natalia a week earlier, saying that she'd been released and was living in Boston with her children, where she'd found work as a housekeeper for a kind widow. For that, Sara gave a silent thanks.

Mrs. Haines and Sara had talked in the office when she'd first arrived, right after Mrs. Haines had dashed around the desk and hugged her. A tear even dropped down Mrs. Haines's cheek, an unexpected show of emotion after her previously cold visage. They didn't discuss Daisy at all, or what had happened, but Mrs. Haines had gone out of her way to make sure Sara was well taken care of, sending up a maid with breakfast in bed for her each morning, her plate heaped with hot cross buns and baked eggs. Sara's hair was thickening as she grew stronger, as was her waist, and her skin began to glow again. Every so often she'd still wake in the middle of the night, terrified and breathless, thinking she was trapped on the island again. But that seemed to be the only lasting vestige of her incarceration.

She enjoyed having a proper job, with her own desk and chair waiting for her each day. Unfortunately, for the past month, the only people to visit Theo's office came under the ruse of needing an architect but in fact actually wanted to get a look at the woman who'd survived Blackwell's Island Insane Asylum. They never returned.

"Perhaps we should rethink our arrangement."

Sara had been longing to say the words out loud for the past week now, and when Theo suggested they not go into the office but instead work from his apartment in the Dakota, she decided it was time. Even he couldn't face the effort of pretending to work anymore. There was absolutely nothing to do. Theo had bills to pay, for the grand apartment and his wife's medical care. She'd seen a letter to the Old Chatham Sanatorium that he'd inadvertently left out on his desk, asking for more time for the coming month's fee.

Theo looked up at her and smiled. "Rethink the arrangement, in what way?"

"There's no use in you having an employee when business is . . ."

She trailed off, reluctant to state the obvious.

"Bad? Disastrous?"

"I'm sorry, Theo." She sat down across the table from him, where he'd been working on a speech to the West End Association. "But there's no reason for you to pay me when I don't do much of anything. I can find another job."

Theo leaned back. "No one knows me; I'm just a lackey of Hardenbergh's. I have to find a way to make a name for myself."

"What can I do to help?"

"Not a thing, I'm afraid."

She hated feeling so useless and out of step with him. They hadn't touched since she'd collapsed in his arms upon reuniting. Even when she handed him a paper or letter, she made sure to place it on his desk first, so their fingers wouldn't accidentally brush.

Theo got up and stood at the window, looking out. "Imagine what it will be like here in one hundred years, what this view will entail."

"I can't imagine. Flying bicycles, perhaps?"

"Now, that would be a sight. But the buildings, one after another, lined up block upon block. If we're not careful, the city will fall into madness. A mishmash of styles, from Florentine Renaissance to Transitional Goth to Hispano-Moorish. What a mess. Here we have an opportunity to plan ahead, to decide the aesthetic fate of the city. Yet no one is leading the charge."

"Why don't you?"

He turned around and leaned back on the windowsill. "Who would listen to me? What have I accomplished?"

"Your speech." She pointed to the half-full piece of paper on his desk. "Why don't you make it about exactly that? The city of the future."

"Unfortunately, tonight's audience doesn't care much about that. They all want to know how to make the most money snatching up land on the West Side."

"Then make them care. You speak so passionately about it." She pulled the paper and inkwell to her. "Go on, you talk and I'll write."

"It's no use."

She disliked this version of Theo. He seemed determined to fail. In the past, she might have agreed with him, assumed that he knew better on most things. But after Blackwell's, she no longer accepted another's authority so easily. "First off, what are today's architects doing wrong?"

He paced up the room, and back down. His long legs took only ten strides each way, his footsteps sure and even. "The center of the island is currently located at the southern tip. The courts, the post office, the Exchange. Even with elevated railways, the congestion is terrible, everyone struggling south in the morning and back north at the end of the workday. The business district should be moved up to the Forties, near Broadway."

"Very forward thinking. What else?"

His shoulders straightened and he looked up at the ceiling, lost in thought. "There's no point in having each plot of land owned by a separate person. Instead, we should continue in the mold of the apartment house and create large buildings, vertical ones, that house dozens of businesses. We need to add an entirely new dimension to our thinking, and that's upward. Imagine a city of buildings that soar into the sky, with fast elevators that take workers up to their offices."

Sara scribbled as fast as he was speaking. She loved this side of him, the dashing, daring man with strong opinions. How she wished she could be part of him again. The thought made her feel slightly dizzy. Mrs. Camden would be back soon enough with the children, and they might never be this close again. If this was what life offered her, she wanted to drink it all in, even if there were proprieties to obey. She would respect them but take her fill of her intellectual partnership with Theo while she could. She added her own line, and spoke what she had written out loud, to see if he approved. "We're on an island, there's no way north, south, east, or west. Instead, we rise."

He snapped his fingers. "Perfectly put."

She thought of Daisy's family, in their miserable tenement building. "If you're going to think in such a grand way, what about addressing the issue of class? How do we help the poor, since we must live side by side on this cramped island?"

He clapped his hands together. "Yes. Of course. This is where the economics work in everyone's favor. The model dwelling should take up an entire block, with every room providing air and light. We did it in the Dakota, with cross ventilation. Because we're discussing large numbers of tenants within one building, it can be as cheap, if not cheaper, than the miserable tenements we have now, which are dark and dingy and prone to spreading disease."

"We marry economics with a grand structure that's solid and permanent."

"Yes!" Theo made a fist. "Write that down. Brilliant."

Sara did, beaming with pride.

Theo put a hand on her shoulder and squeezed it. "Here is a speech that I was dreading, and now I can't wait to deliver it. Will you go with me? I want you to be there to see it."

"I'd love to."

She wore a polonaise dress in an olive green that Nellie had given her and felt like a proper lady alighting from the brougham with Theo. There were a number of women in the audience, either accompanying their husbands or present as concerned citizens. Everyone had an opinion on what the West Side of Manhattan should look like, and this was sure to be a lively forum.

Theo took a seat up on the stage with four other architects, all of whom had at least twenty years on him, with wizened features and gray beards. In comparison, he looked like a schoolboy. The fact that he had been invited up there at all was astonishing.

On the hour, the speeches began. Most hailed the status quo, pointing to the grand design of the millionaires' houses along Fifth Avenue as a way of showcasing the affluence of New York City. One insisted that Riverside Drive would be the next grand avenue for the city, due to its prime location on the river and wide plots of land. Many listening nodded their heads.

Then Theo rose. He began by comparing the current state of New York architecture to a masquerade, with architects ransacking all eras and countries and turning buildings into caricatures. The audience members sat a little straighter in their chairs, attentive. "We are like children in a toy shop, dazed with the multitude of opportunities and incapable of fixing our choice."

The man sitting next to Sara grunted out loud at this and murmured something disagreeable to the man on his other side.

But as Theo began speaking of the city of the future, the mood slowly changed. Their argument was sound and succinct, and as he spoke of the coming era, where rich and poor would have the same opportunities to live in a clean, healthy environment, someone near the front called out a resounding "Yes!"

After he finished, the audience burst into applause, several people standing up to do so. Theo's eyes searched the room until he met Sara's gaze, and a thrill of longing and pride ran through her. They'd done it.

Sara had to wait for thirty minutes until the crowd around him dissipated enough for her to reach him, and he held in his hands dozens of business cards. "I believe our day at work tomorrow will be very different than the ones previous. All thanks to you and your brilliant idea."

The evening was warm and they walked back to the Dakota together, chattering on about the reactions and the other speakers. "You were terrific, Theo."

"I love you."

Sara stopped. "No. We said that wouldn't be proper. Mrs. Camden will be back, eventually."

"I know. That can't be helped. But I do love you, and it has to be said out loud every so often or I'll go mad."

"I love you, too, Theo."

"You won't leave me, will you? I can't let you go, now that I finally have you back."

"Of course not."

Theo needed her, and she needed him. If she'd learned anything at all the past year, it was to seize the small moments and enjoy them to the fullest. If that meant being in love with a married man, so be it. Theo was hers.

Chapter Twenty-Six

New York City, September 1885

Theo swore under his breath. "I've forgotten the elevation plans."

Sara rummaged through the leather satchel full of notes and drawings. "Are you sure? I know I put them in here last night."

They were on their way to a meeting with what was their biggest client to date, who wanted to create a handsome office building on Sixth Avenue. In the month since Theo's speech to the West End Association, they'd been inundated with prospective clients and he'd even hired three draftsmen to keep up with the demand.

Theo shook his head. "I took them out this morning at breakfast, to check on the measurements. I left them there. I'm sure of it."

She hated to see him so agitated, but then again, she loved seeing his real self, not the mask that he showed to everyone else. They had fallen back into bed with each other the evening of his speech, but with his family still away, it felt natural, an extension of their work life. Sara was his partner in all respects, and for now she preferred to ignore the fact that he had a wife and children upstate.

She leaned forward. "Let me out here. I'll walk back and catch a hansom cab and meet you at the site."

He gave her a tight smile. "Are you sure?"

"Of course. It's a lovely morning and we've only just set out. I'll be right behind you."

"Have I told you how crucial you are to my success?"

"Every day."

He called for the driver to stop. She stepped down and started north on Eighth Avenue, thinking through the elevations in her head. The pressed-brick building, trimmed in terra-cotta, utilized a new type of steel column so it could soar tall on a proportionally narrow lot.

But without the elevations, the grandeur of the place would be impossible to convey to the client. She hurried into the Dakota and up to Theo's apartment, where Mrs. Haines was exiting the front door.

The woman formed a smile that didn't reach her eyes. Their touching reunion after Sara's release had been tempered by Sara's close alliance with Theo. Even though Sara and Theo were as circumspect as possible, the servants talked. They always did.

But Sara's stint in a madhouse and the resulting notoriety had offered up a freedom that she'd never imagined. It no longer mattered what other people said or thought. Her pain and suffering absolved her from gossip, or perhaps it was more that she was inured to it at this point. Which meant she could do as she liked, and at the moment, she liked being partners with Theo, in more ways than one.

Yet Sara hated to think that she was causing any problems for the woman, who certainly had enough on her hands. "Mrs. Haines, is there something I can help you with?"

"No, just overseeing a delivery to the children's room. It's been taken care of."

"I see."

She didn't, though. The children's room had been closed up since

Mrs. Camden and the children had left. Sara had popped her head in once when she'd awoken early to climb the back stairs to her own room. The room had an air of neglect about it, as if the only occupants had ever been the dolls lined up on the neatly made beds. Her heart tugged, very slightly, at the thought of the children having to suffer the fright of their mother's illness, but she had pushed it aside, too caught up in the charismatic pull of Theo. They had ventured beyond the rubric and the expectations of society.

Mrs. Haines disappeared without another word. Sara found the drawings on Theo's drafting desk in the library and placed them in a rucksack. There was no time to waste, but a loud bang pulled her down the hall to the bedchambers. One of the porters, a new one, she couldn't remember his name, stood in the middle of the children's room, unwrapping a large piece of furniture that had been bound in burlap for protection.

"Sorry, I didn't mean to disturb you." The young man smiled at her.

"Not at all. Is this the delivery Mrs. Haines mentioned?" She didn't want him to think she didn't know what was going on. Even if she didn't.

"Yes, ma'am. A crib."

Her heart leaped to her throat. A crib for a baby.

Could Mrs. Camden have had another child and Theo hadn't told her? Would he have kept that information from her, knowing it would drive a wedge between them?

Maybe that was why Mrs. Camden had been trundled upstate. Not because of illness, but so Sara didn't find out right off. So he could woo her and pull her close to him again before breaking the news.

She made it to the meeting quickly, after urging the hansom driver to pick up the pace. The horse seemed to sense her nervousness and stomped his feet as she paid the fare. In the distance, Theo stood in the center of the lot, which had previously held a blacksmith and a saloon. The owners had vacated months ago and the buildings had been razed. As she approached, he greeted her, and the men all nodded. She handed over the drawings and stepped back, knowing that her role right now was to be the dutiful assistant. Theo was never dismissive of her in front of clients, but the one time she'd made a suggestion, he'd cut her off with a curt "No, that won't do."

Later, he'd apologized and incorporated her idea, but she knew he was right. The outside world wouldn't understand how they worked together, nor approve.

The meeting seemed to go on forever, and even once they were back at the office, there was still no way to speak privately. The last draftsman peeled off at seven o'clock, offering a cheery "Good night" as he put on his hat and coat.

By then, the knot in Sara's stomach seemed to have tripled in size.

She got right to the point. One of the things Theo said he liked about her.

"When I was at the Dakota getting the plans, Mrs. Haines said that your wife and family are returning."

Theo sat back in his chair and rubbed his eyes. "Yes. I'm sorry. I meant to tell you. We've been so busy."

"When are they due back?"

"Next week."

She crossed her arms. "When were you planning on mentioning it? When I bumped into Mrs. Camden in the courtyard?"

"No, no. Of course not. I was going to tell you tonight over dinner. But you see, it won't make any difference, not to our work, our lives."

"How can you say that? Do you really think she'll put up with you running about town and being seen with me?"

She hated the way she sounded, like a scolding shrew.

Theo hung his head. "I don't want her to come back. I know that makes me a terrible human being, but that's the way I feel. I love you. We talked just the other day about how we don't care what other people think. But now you do?"

No. Her pain was deeper than that. She drew a deep breath. "Did you and Mrs. Camden have another child?"

"What? No."

How he could deny such a thing shocked her. "A crib is being set up in the children's room."

"Yes, right." He came around to the front of the desk and sat on the edge of it, hands out. "This is why I wanted to tell you over dinner, where we could sit and I could explain things."

She stood firm. "Please do."

"While Minnie was upstate, she befriended a woman who was also ill, who had a small child. The woman passed away and Minnie said that she'd promised to look after it for her. I was aghast; I don't want another child."

"It will be your ward?"

"Yes."

"Is it a boy or a girl?" She held her breath, praying it not be a boy.

"A boy. They named him Christopher."

A chill went up her spine. When Sara didn't speak, Theo continued on. "I wasn't happy about it, but it gives her something to focus on, something that's not the two of us. Don't you see? It was my barter. I keep you and she can keep the child. It's an agreement."

"You spoke to her of us?"

"Not in an obvious, crass way. But she'd heard rumors. To be honest, I doubt she's surprised or angry. We never really got on. It was all for the families' sakes, hers and mine. She loves the children; that is her passion. I love you. You are mine."

"You will live together, and we will carry on, and she'll take care of this boy?"

"Christopher. Yes. You'll see. It's a splendid arrangement."

"For you, perhaps. You get the attentions of the devoted wife, while the mistress stays close at hand."

He stood, indignant. "You are not my mistress. That's a useless word when it comes to describing who we are and what we do. We are business partners, lovers, all sorts of things. You are an indispensable part of my happiness. I hope I am to yours."

"But the boy."

"What is one more child running around? I will take care of it because by doing so, I get you." He drew close to her and put one hand around the back of her neck, the other over her heart. A wave of claustrophobia washed over her.

Was he heartless or practical? Or both? What he was proposing was outrageous. But she couldn't imagine going anywhere else. "How will your wife and I manage? Won't that be terribly awkward?"

"You'll see, it won't be that bad. We'll have to be careful in the early stages, as they settle in."

"Theo. You're mad."

"I am. But I know what I want: you by my side. Always. I'll do anything I can to make that happen. Now that I'm making money hand over fist, I can take care of you and take care of my family. I want to do right by you."

He touched his lips lightly to her forehead. "Will you try it? If it's awful, I will write you a glowing recommendation, and you can do work for another architect in the city."

"No one would hire a woman to do what I do."

"I will do everything I can to make you happy, always. I promise you, Sara. Will you trust in me?"

"It's a horrible idea. I can't put myself in that position. I wouldn't be able to hold my head up and walk around the streets."

"My marriage, like so many others in our social circle, is solely an arrangement. Times are changing quite quickly. The old guard that monitored what you did and who you did it with is falling. It's the age of enjoyment and money and indulgence."

He took her face in his hands.

"Please. Indulge me."

❧

She never overtly agreed to the new arrangement, but they went on as they had before, and she braced herself for the arrival of his family. Yet after two weeks, she and Mrs. Camden still hadn't crossed paths, although she'd seen her stepping off a carriage one day and quickly walked around the block instead of entering at the same time. Sara gave a quiet thanks to Mr. Hardenbergh for the layout of the Dakota. Once she got through the main portal and crossed the courtyard, she was out of danger of running into Mrs. Camden or the new baby, safe making small talk with the elevator operator who served only her corner of the building. Work, luckily, kept her busy throughout the days and well into the evenings, so that before she knew it, a new pattern had emerged. Theo never spoke of his family, and she never inquired. They had far more important things to discuss.

Theo had gotten another commission, this time for an insurance company in Albany run by a wealthy financier. It was enormous, twenty stories high, and would bring in a decent sum of money. The steady work and creative freedom exhilarated him, and often when they came home late, he'd stay with her for a couple of hours, then take her to her bed and make love to her. He constantly surprised her in that regard, being tender and kind one minute, gently kissing the instep of her foot after removing her stockings, before falling on her in a frenzy of longing. She hadn't been to his apartment at all since the family's return. Which was fine. She loved her own flat, and she spent far more hours a day in Theo's company than his family did. But she hated it when he had to get up and leave, returning to his own bed, leaving her cold and alone.

One Friday afternoon, she accompanied him to the Grand Central Depot, where he was off to spend the weekend in Albany.

"Enjoy your time away," she said. "I'll see you on Monday."

His eyes twinkled at her, full of mischief. "Even better, I'll stop in Sunday evening. My train gets in late, but I'll pop up to you before . . ."

Before heading home. There was no need to finish the sentence.

Sunday evening, Sara made herself a simple dinner of beans on toast and sat down to read, hoping the book would keep her mind off the sound of his knock on the door. His train was due to arrive at nine thirty. By eleven o'clock she began pacing. She was silly to think that he'd remember to stop by. He'd surely be there in the morning, apologizing and carrying sketches for her to look over.

Mrs. Camden and the children and that baby, the new one, kept coming to mind. What were their lives like? Did they miss Theo, feel the absence of his interest? Or did he turn into another person entirely when he stepped over the threshold of their door, one who made up for the long hours away with smiles and hugs and presents?

She couldn't bear it. The hour was late enough that the children would have been put to bed by now. All she wanted was to walk past their door. The one he went through and became an unknown presence to her. The pain of being apart, of not knowing every inch of him, drove her out of the quiet safety of her rooms.

She tiptoed down the stairway to the west side of the building.

When she turned the corner to their hall, she froze. A ghost of a small child stood in the middle of the hallway about twenty feet away. Sara stifled a scream and the ghost did as well, the two of them terrified by each other.

Peering through the dim light, Sara recognized one of the twins, Lula. She wore only her nightdress, and gave a small hiccup.

Sara wasn't seeing things, this was indeed an actual human being. As she drew near, she noticed that the girl's face was red and streaked with tears.

"Lula? What are you doing out here?" She knelt down and took the girl's hands in her own.

The girl shook her head, unable to speak, and fell sobbing into Sara's arms.

"What's wrong, where's your mother?"

"Inside. She's sick. She told me to get help, but I don't know where to go."

"Why didn't you fetch a servant or ring downstairs?"

"They're all gone out tonight. And after Mother caught me playing with the electric bell, she told me never to use it again."

"Poor girl. There now, I'm here."

Sara held Lula's hand as they entered the front door. Only a few lamps were lit, and the place was full of gloom and shadows. From the far rooms came the sound of a baby crying.

"Show me where your mother is."

An eerie tableau greeted Sara when she opened the door to the main bedchamber. Mrs. Camden lay on the bed, her skin as pale as the pillow. Emily and Luther stood around her silently, patting her arms. They barely moved as Sara drew closer.

"Mrs. Camden?"

The woman opened her eyes and tried to speak, but her breath caught in her throat.

"Don't talk, I'll call for the doctor."

"Thank you." Her lips were chapped and her eyelids fluttered and then closed.

Sara went to the kitchen, Lula trailing behind her like a dutiful sheepdog. Why was there no one home? And where was Theo? She rang the bell for the night porter and met him out in the hallway to tell him to call for a doctor right away. The baby's wailing had grown louder by the time she returned.

Lula shrugged. "He won't stop crying. He wants Mother."

A lump caught in Sara's throat. She didn't want to see or make any kind of contact with Theo's new ward. This boy that was now part of his family, when the boy she should have had was gone, buried in an unmarked grave on that hellish island. But she couldn't stand the desperation that grew with each cry.

The child had thrown off all his bedclothes and was circling his arms and legs, such chubby limbs, like he was trying to swim to the surface of a pond. His peony-pink mouth was open in a big O, while his eyes were closed tight. She leaned over and picked him up. He weighed more than she'd expected. She sat on the rocking chair next to the crib and tucked him into her, bouncing him softly in her arms.

Lula spoke with a reverent hush. "He's hardly ever quiet."

"He's hungry, perhaps."

Lula just shrugged.

"Where is your nanny?"

"Not here this week. Traveling to some place or other."

"Your mother is alone with you?"

"Yes."

"Has she been ill long?"

The girl sighed. "Forever, it seems."

Theo should have been back, taking care of his family, who obviously needed him. Needed someone to take charge.

Sara rose, the baby still in her arms, and walked back to the bed-chamber. Mrs. Camden opened her eyes and looked up at the ceiling, as if she were trying to remember where she was. Her head slowly turned in Sara's direction and she stared for several moments without blinking. Her expression was neither grateful nor hateful. But she knew everything, of that Sara was certain.

When the doctor arrived, followed by a nurse as well as Mrs. Haines, Sara reluctantly put the boy back down in his crib. He was fast asleep and didn't stir, although she waited a few moments in case the lack of human contact brought him out of his slumber. Part of her wished it might.

Unnoticed, she slipped out of the Camden apartment and back up the stairs to her own.

CHAPTER TWENTY-SEVEN

New York City, September 1985

The work on Melinda's apartment reached a feverish pitch over the next week, swarmed by painters who transformed the dark walls and columns into swaths of faux marble and stucco. Melinda had insisted they paint a long trompe l'oeil "crack" in the living room wall, so that it resembled a Parisian apartment she'd seen in a French movie, the kind that were once grand but had gone to elegant seed.

In the meantime, Bailey successfully distracted herself from beginning each day with a shot of vodka by going to an AA meeting in Midtown before hitting furniture showrooms. She'd even found a sponsor, a retired theater publicist named Lydia who had a deep-throated laugh and a wicked intuition. Bailey hadn't been back to the Sixty-Ninth Street meeting, and on the few occasions she ran into Renzo, she tried to be polite but not too forthcoming. Melinda had warned her to stay away from him until the lawyers came to an agreement.

They were deep in negotiations with the co-op board and the Met to determine who owned the rights to the sheath, all dependent on the completion of the DNA testing.

While Melinda had warned her away from Renzo, she hadn't said anything about the Camdens' family advisor.

Bailey had located him using the Yellow Pages and gotten an appointment two days later. The offices, as expected, were formidable for a firm that handled generations of clients' money: mahogany walls, a mid-century sofa in the waiting room, and a receptionist who looked as if she sucked on lemons in between phone calls.

"Miss Camden?"

An older man in a well-cut suit beckoned her into his office. He had a long face and chin that reminded her of Dick Van Dyke, whom she'd developed a mad crush on as a young girl. "I'm Fred Osborn; very nice to meet you."

"Yes, thank you for seeing me." She took a chair opposite his desk and looked about. Behind him, on the window ledge, were dozens of trophies, the kind that children receive for signing up for a soccer league. He caught her looking at them.

"My grandchildren's. Their rooms were overrun with the things and they insisted I display them here."

She liked him already. "Mr. Osborn, I won't take up too much of your time, but I want to be tested to find out if I am a true Camden. Not only in name but in blood."

He studied her, no reaction on his face. "First off, please call me Fred. Now, what makes you think you might be? I know about the ward, your grandfather. But you think you're related to Theodore and Minnie Camden?"

"Not exactly. Theodore Camden, yes. I believe he had an affair with the woman who killed him, Sara Smythe, and that Christopher Camden was the result." She explained what she had discovered, and dug into her handbag to show him the cottage drawing, the letter, and the photo. "You see, I discovered the sheath and bone. I think it's only fair that I be included in the DNA testing."

"What do Melinda and Manvel think of this idea?"

"I don't know about Manvel, but I know Melinda isn't too pleased."

"I can imagine." His eyes were guarded, but she got a hint of impatience in his face at the mention of Melinda's name. "I have to warn you, at this point the provenance of the sheath is hazy. You would think the government of Tibet might be interested, but they're being bullied by China, who are trying to destroy Tibetan culture. The Rutherford family, who owned it in the 1880s, when it was stolen, has died out and there are no descendants. At this point, it may indeed end up in the hands of either the co-op for the Dakota or Melinda and Manvel."

"I don't understand why the co-op is trying to stake a claim. I mean, it was found in the man's trunk, along with his finger bone."

"Mainly for the sake of precedence. Not to mention the finances of the co-op are consistently in the red." He shrugged. "And my guess is that Melinda Camden isn't high on the list of their favorite shareholders."

"I know Melinda is concerned about the sheath, but as far as I'm concerned, it belongs in the Met with the knife. I'm more interested in the DNA sampling. When is the package being sent out?" she asked. "Or has it already?"

"It goes out Monday. They'll be sending along the bone you discovered and the blood samples from the plans and the sheath. Turns out the bone is the key to the testing. Without that, Melinda would have had little chance of getting back any results either way." He rubbed his chin. "I've learned more about the science behind this testing than I'd have thought possible, this past week. Fascinating stuff."

"I'd like to know if I'm a Camden for real or not. I hope you can understand my position."

"I do, Miss Camden. The evidence you've assembled, if we may call it that, is quite interesting. The trust was set up, as common in that era, for the 'descendants by blood' of the trustor, Theodore Camden. Today, with all these scientific breakthroughs, we can take that quite literally. My duty as trustee requires that I distribute equal portions of the funds held in trust to all living heirs of Theodore Camden on their thirtieth birthdays. I could make the argument that, in my capacity as trustee, I'm honor bound to test you, to determine, once and for all, if you are entitled to be brought into the trust. But even if I were so inclined, I'm afraid it wouldn't be possible."

Her heart dropped. "Why's that?"

"The testing has to be done via the male line. For example, we can connect Theodore Camden to Melinda's twin, Manvel, by way of Luther Camden and their father. In which case, along with all the newspaper accounts of the murder and such, we should be able to prove that the sheath was part of the family's items. But you can't be matched, being a female, I'm sorry to say. Unless you have a brother."

So close. "No luck there. But what about my father? What if he agreed to be tested? His father was Christopher Camden, so that would be a direct line, if Christopher is indeed Theodore Camden's son."

"That would work. He's still living?"

She nodded.

"In that case, we'd test him, and if it's a match, he would be added as a beneficiary of the trust. You would inherit what is left, and so on, down through your descendants. Would your father agree to be tested?"

"I'll ask him." Maybe, if she explained it the right way, he'd agree and take part in her crazy plan. He had to see that it was for her future, and for their family name, their rights.

"Luckily for the heirs, the architect Henry Hardenbergh took over the firm after Theodore Camden's death, and a significant portion of the profits went into the Camden trust each year. My family's company has handled the estate since the very beginning, and been strategic in our investment strategy, which has paid off nicely over the past century."

"And way back when, they set it up so my grandfather, Christopher, couldn't inherit anything?"

"I'm afraid not, as he wasn't a blood relative, and they didn't make any other accommodation for him."

"I wonder if Theodore might have set aside something for him, if he'd lived?"

"We'll never know, I'm afraid. Such a tragic death, and quite early in his career."

She rose to go, eager to get Jack on the phone. But Fred raised a hand to stop her.

"One more thing. If you do get your father to agree to be tested, I won't be allowed to use any of the Camden family money to cover the expenses, as you can understand."

"Right. Of course. How much would it cost?"

He did the figures on a notebook on his desk, using an old fountain pen. "Somewhere around a thousand dollars."

A thousand dollars. She didn't have anything close to that on her. Even if she did get Jack to agree, she had no chance of raising that much money so fast.

She closed the door behind her before slinking away.

The phone at the house in New Jersey rang and rang, so Bailey tried the repair shop. Her dad had stepped out but she left a message with Scotty, asking him to call her back right away.

"He's out fishing, probably back in a few hours."

Great. Right when time was of the essence, her dad was out on a boat fishing.

To keep herself occupied, she headed down to Kenneth's apartment, where he was holding what he called a "high tea." Inside, a dozen or so men and a few women were chatting away in groups, nibbling on cucumber sandwiches and macaroons. Kenneth gave her a quick kiss on the cheek before heading back to the kitchen to refill the trays.

Bailey curled up in a nook in one of the large window seats facing Central Park, with a cup of tea and a scone, and let her mind wander. She was so close to finding out the truth. But although she had yet to speak with her dad, there wasn't much point of getting her hopes up. Even if he agreed, there was no way she could afford a thousand-dollar test.

A familiar, deep growl broke her out of her reverie. Renzo stood near the fireplace, listening intently as Mrs. Stellenbach, who lived in a studio apartment up on eight, explained some kind of repair job in great detail, barely pausing for breath.

He caught her eye and she smiled quickly, then looked away, pretending to be absorbed by a young man plucking away at "You Are My Lucky Star" on the piano. After a few minutes, Renzo put his hand on the woman's shoulder and made his excuses, then joined Bailey on the window seat. It was the first time they'd been face-to-face since the debacle in the basement with Melinda and Tony.

"I assume you can't go to a tea party without being monopolized about a clogged sink."

"Clanging radiator, in this case. Hazard of the job. I try not to socialize too much with the tenants, but I couldn't pass up Kenneth's scones." He leaned back against the wall and studied her.

She blushed. To distract him, she asked the question she'd been wondering for weeks. "How did you get your unique name?"

"Is Lorenzo Duffy unique?"

She laughed.

"My father was Irish and my mother Italian. Deadly combination, as the probability of turning into a boisterous drunk increases two-fold. At least that's my theory."

"You seem to be doing all right."

"I'm hanging on. How about you?"

"Meetings every day."

"I haven't seen you."

He'd been looking for her. Her heart skipped over a couple of times. "Melinda warned me, well, to steer clear. Until things have been decided one way or another."

"Steer clear of me?"

She nodded. "Although you were right to stash away the sheath in the safe the way you did. Melinda and Tony were ready to sell the thing on the black market. The fact that it's an artifact, an impor-tant one, means nothing to them."

"To you it does?"

"Of course." She looked out the window, the view a sea of spar-kling leaves. "Okay, I did think about the value. How could I not? But to me, the most important items from those trunks were the letter and the photo. And, in a weird way, the finger."

"What's the latest from the battle of the basement?"

"The co-op agreed to allow the results of the DNA test to deter-mine who it belongs to. If the DNA from the finger bone and blood match that of Manvel Camden, it's his and Melinda's."

"How are they certain that what's in the tube belonged to Theo-dore Camden?"

"The plans are dated the month he died, and there are newspaper accounts about how his finger was never recovered, grisly details like that."

"It all sounds kind of hocus-pocus-y."

She couldn't agree more. "I know. It's a crazy mix of old evidence and cutting-edge science. The results will be in by the end of the month. But I don't think I'll even get a chance to get my DNA tested, although not for lack of trying."

"Why not?"

She didn't want to go into it. The money, the fact that she wasn't a male. "Long story. It's probably not going to happen." She paused. "Look, I'm sorry if I've kept my distance. I wasn't sure where you stood."

"I don't stand with Melinda and Tony, I'll tell you that much. I hear the apartment is a disaster."

She frowned. "God, it's getting worse every day. It sucks that I have to do her bidding."

"You don't, actually." Something dark brewed behind his slate-gray eyes.

"Until I get paid next month, I'm stuck. At that point, I'll have enough to get me through."

"Seems to me that you're making excuses, staying in a poisonous relationship because you don't have the courage to break out of it."

She hadn't asked him for his advice, and the implication infuriated her. As did his audacity to analyze her decisions and motives. She'd put herself out there by approaching Fred Osborn, and now having to ask Jack for a favor that she was sure he would deny. "You have no idea what I've been trying to accomplish the past couple of days. It's taken every ounce of courage I have."

"That's great. Because I couldn't stand the way Melinda and Tony treated you down in my office, like you were beneath them."

He might as well have thrown a bucket of cold water over her. She felt attacked, exposed. He'd seen her prostrate herself before the two of them, and was calling her out. "What exactly was I supposed to do? Tell them to include me in the testing or I'll quit? Melinda would have laughed in my face. The power is all theirs; I'm working with reality here."

"You don't see in yourself what I see. You have more power than you think."

He was wrong. "I'm barely hanging on, here. What if it all comes crashing down? You may make fun of Melinda, but she's stood by me and given me a chance when no one else would. I can't forget that. If I push to get tested and it turns out I'm not a true Camden, I'll not only lose one of my only friends, I'll be totally banished from the New York design community."

"So you would back down in order to placate Melinda? Do you think she would do the same if the roles were reversed?" He touched her shoulder gently, and she bristled in response. "Sometimes I worry that you're using this wild-goose chase to avoid dealing with who you really are. In the end, who cares if you're a real Camden or not? You're a healthy, smart woman with a bright future ahead of you. Which means it doesn't matter if Melinda causes trouble. You'll get a job doing something else; you'll figure it out. What's most important is that you move beyond the tragedy of the past, start fresh."

She wondered which tragedy he was referring to, Theo Camden's or her mother's. The shock of her mother's death, as if it had happened twelve hours ago, not twelve years, hit Bailey in the gut, and she struggled to catch a breath. This usually happened in the middle of the night, when she woke up, heart pounding, certain that the world was disintegrating beneath her. Not in the middle of a crowded party.

Renzo continued on, taking her silence for encouragement. "I understand what it's like to be barely sober, barely hanging on. But I want to see you stand up for yourself and be counted, not get pushed around by a prick like Tony or a princess like Melinda."

"I'm confused here. Are you telling me to demand to get tested, or to give it up?"

"Not my decision. Whatever you do, don't go into it blindly, for the wrong reasons. Or expect it to solve all your problems. That's all I'm saying."

Before she could reply, Kenneth came over, pulling two of his friends.

"How many more of those sketches do you have, my dear?" He pointed to the one that was now hanging above his fireplace in a handsome frame.

"Far too many." She'd gone crazy the last couple of days, trying to capture the building from every angle, as if it might disappear when she no longer lived there. She knew it was silly, but her obsession blunted the pain of having to move on.

"Rory, John, and Edward all want one. I spoke with my neighbors and have already sold six here in the building. I won't charge you a commission. Yet."

She did the math. That would do it. She'd have enough to pay for the DNA testing. "You're amazing, Kenneth. You have no idea." She gave him a huge hug before he was swooped up by another guest.

Renzo stood and began to congratulate her, but she stopped him. "I know what you're trying to say, and I appreciate it. I realize I have to figure this out on my own."

The confusion in his face crushed her. He fixed her with a serious look, all shadow and gravity. "In meetings they say to stay on your own side of the street. For some reason, this has me all stirred up. I guess because all this—the building, the tenants, the history inside these walls—it means something to me. I know it affects you the same way." He lifted both hands, then let them fall to his sides. "As a matter of fact, you mean something to me."

Her breath caught in her throat and she looked away, overcome.

The pianist's last note quivered in the air before dissipating. Renzo took a couple of steps back. "I'm sorry I veered into your lane there. I'm normally a much better driver."

"Thanks." If she had had the courage, she'd have let him know how much his concern meant to her, but he'd caught her off guard. And she had to get to Jack; there was no time to smooth things over. "I appreciate it, I really do. But I gotta go."

"You're kidding, right?"

Bailey's father sounded tired when she finally reached him at eight o'clock that night. Apparently, the fishing had been fruitless, or rather, fishless. Which, from past experience, meant his mood would be impatient and surly.

So she'd botched the explanation of her meeting with Fred Osborn and the DNA testing, all logic lost in a nervous dribble of words. Jack had been confused at first, and then wary, before she'd finally gotten around to the urgency of his taking a blood test to prove that they were, indeed, real Camdens.

"I'm not kidding, Dad. I hope you'll consider doing this for me. For us."

She'd learned to use *consider* from Tristan, which was employed when they wanted to push a client beyond their budgetary comfort zone. It softened the request, and almost everyone took the bait, believing they'd made a conscious choice, when in fact the decision had already been made for them.

"How much did you say this testing costs?"

"I didn't. Because I am paying for it myself."

"How much, though?" he insisted.

She told him.

"You're going to blow a grand on the hopes that you land a bigger fish? Why on earth would you want to do that?"

She didn't bother making a joke about the fish metaphor. "I have the money, and I don't mind spending it on this. I know I'm right. I'm absolutely sure of it. There's research and documentation to back it up."

Of course, if the test came back negative, not only would she be out a grand, but there'd be no chance of getting any payment for all her work for Melinda, who'd be livid at Bailey's workaround. She'd be right back at square one.

Through the receiver came labored breathing. "My father wanted nothing to do with that family, and for good reason. I regret the day I allowed your mother to get us back under their influence. I don't see why neither of you are able to settle for what you already have."

He spoke as if her mother were still alive. Which broke Bailey's heart and pissed her off at the same time.

"We have two different perspectives." She kept her voice even, trying to persuade him, not put him on the defensive any more than he already was. "The way I see it, and the way Mom saw it, was that it's a big world out there. You and Granddad hid from it, and Mom and I didn't."

"It's not a matter of hiding. You've been trying to run from me ever since you were in high school. Like you're ashamed of me, who I am."

She couldn't deny that it wasn't true, because it was. "I want more out of my life. What's so wrong with that?"

"So go ahead and go after it."

"That's exactly what I'm doing. But I need you. The blood sample has to come from the male line: from Theodore Camden to Granddad to you."

"Here's what I don't get: You disappear for months at a time, then call demanding me to prove I'm related to a family my father despised."

The words stuck in her throat. "I was in rehab, Dad. I should have told you earlier, but I wasn't sure how. I'm sorry."

"When did you get out?"

"Last month."

Silence. She pictured him shaking his head, his shoulders caving in under the weight of disappointment.

"You're battling the same demons as my father. I saw what it cost him."

He was skidding the conversation off topic, and she refused to be deterred. "Maybe there are some long-lost family members who deserve to be brought into the light, ones that your father never even knew about. I've been reading about the madhouse where Sara Smythe was sent to. It's horrifying, the suffering she most likely endured. The woman who might very well be your grandmother."

"What you're doing here, trying to unravel the past, is no good." His irritation radiated through the phone line. "Whatever happened back then, in madhouses or fancy apartment houses, has nothing to do with us, with you. I know who I am. I run an auto repair shop and when I have free time, I go out on the ocean and fish. That's it, but it's real. You, meanwhile, are chasing ghosts. Stop muddying your life up with all this crap."

How dare he tell her what to do? First Renzo, now this. She might have made bad decisions in the past, but she was trying to make amends. In the meantime, there was a good chance she shared a bloodline with a woman who'd fought her own demons and lost. Bailey refused to let that happen to her, and Sara Smythe was the key to figuring out how. Certainly not through any of the men in her life, who had let her down when she'd needed them most. Jack was the one who'd retreated into a shell since his wife's death, letting his daughter run amok in the city with no guidance, no refuge.

Her voice cracked, as it always did when she was livid. "I've admitted I'm an alcoholic. I'm going to meetings; I've been trying to stay sober. You may not have the same drinking problems, but I learned all about dry drunks in rehab. They're withholding, negative, defensive. That's you. So don't think that you're any better than me or Granddad. Or that you've escaped the past."

For a few seconds, she couldn't hear anything other than the blood pounding in her ears. Until it was replaced by the faint *click* of Jack hanging up and the dull murmur of a dead phone line.

CHAPTER TWENTY-EIGHT

New York City, October 1885

"**W**here were you?"

Sara didn't waste any time when Theo came in to work the next morning. She followed him into his office and closed the door. The air behind him smelled of sweat and alcohol, although he looked fine. Fresh, almost.

"Good morning to you, too."

"Your wife was ill last night and there was no one there to take care of her. Your daughter was out in the hallway, the boy crying in his crib."

With a deep sigh, Theo hung up his coat and hat on the coatrack. He didn't bother answering right away, instead leafed through the stack of correspondence she'd put on the corner of his desk. "Has the check from Mr. Smith-Roberts arrived?"

The audacity of the question, and lack of response to her own, stunned.

"You are trying to change the subject?"

He rubbed his eyes, and for a brief moment a look of utter exhaustion crossed his features. "No, I am not trying to change the subject.

Minnie needs to be sent back upstate, the doctor is insisting on it, and that sum will cover part of the funds to do so."

"I see." She sat down in the chair opposite him, still unwilling to offer any comfort. "Yes, it did come and I'll deposit it today."

He smiled and stared at her as if for the first time. "You are a goddess, Sara. I am sorry to put you through what you went through last night. I have tried so hard to keep you and my family separate, as I promised to do."

"Where were you?"

"I ran into a couple of potential clients on the train back. They invited me to the Murray Hill Hotel for a drink, and as they are planning on building on a plot they own on Broadway, I thought it was a good idea to go. For the business. For us."

She had worked herself up into a lather over nothing. The Dakota had the ability to do that, to make you feel like you were the only person within its walls, causing you to become desperate for human contact, particularly at night. The loneliness would dissipate upon awakening the next day, as it had on other nights.

He picked up on her uncertainty. "I know I seem ungrateful, but I am very, very pleased you were there. Minnie had sent the maid home, then fell into a fever. It was all a terrible mess." His eyes grew teary, his face red. "I should have been home. I had no idea."

She stood so she blocked the draftsmen's view through the glass window and lowered her voice. "You couldn't have known. I'm sorry I was so hard on you. It was a frightening scene."

He took out his handkerchief and dabbed at his eyes. "Once again, you've saved the day. Minnie said to say thank you as well."

"Will she be all right?"

"The doctor seems to think so. Says it's common for patients to have recurrences. She was looking brighter this morning, before she left."

"What about the children?"

"The governess is on her way back. The maids are taking care of them. Such is the privilege of living in an apartment house where the building's housemaids can take charge in an emergency."

She thought of the children in that cavernous apartment without their mother. "When is the governess due back?"

"In two days. After all that you've done for me, can I ask yet another favor, Sara?"

"Yes, I suppose." She held her breath, not knowing what to expect from him.

"This morning, Lula asked for you. Would it be a bother if you could stop by the apartment and say hello? I have that blasted dinner with the Builders' Society. Would that be all right?"

The sweet scent of the baby, the way his fingers curled around hers, invaded her senses. She should say no, but there was no way to explain why not without seeming heartless. "Of course."

"I wouldn't be able to manage without you."

"Thank you, Theo. I'm sorry I was so angry."

Later that afternoon, he stopped by her desk and placed a piece of paper facedown on it. When she turned it over, it contained an address on Thirty-Ninth Street.

She looked up at him. "Yes?"

"Why don't you leave early and stop by there. Ask for a Mr. Carmichael."

"Then what?"

"You'll see. I don't want to give away the secret."

She tucked the address into her satchel and walked along the streets, feeling ever so much lighter. Mrs. Camden being gone again had nothing to do with it, she told herself. Having Theo all to herself again had nothing to do with it.

She couldn't help but smile when she came to the address. SINGER SEWING MACHINES SOLD HERE. The storefront window overflowed with ribbons and fabrics, needles and thread, and in the middle of it all sat a beautiful black machine, just like the kind the tailor in the Dakota had.

Mr. Carmichael smiled when she said that Mr. Camden had sent her. "Yes, of course, it's right here. I'll have one of the boys help you bring it to your carriage."

She explained that she didn't have a carriage.

"That's fine, we'll get you a hansom cab. There's no way you'll be able to carry this yourself."

The enormous box was wrapped in brown paper and string, with no sign of what was inside. She couldn't wait to get it home; it was like being a little girl again on Christmas Day. Even if the gifts her mother ultimately gave her were a disappointment—a pincushion or a dreary pinafore—the unwrapping was always a delight.

Two porters carried it up, opened the box, and extricated a brand-new Singer sewing machine. The jet-black body was decorated with apple blossom and cornflower decals, the wrought-iron legs connected with an intricate, weblike pattern. Walnut inserts in the front of the oak cover lent it the air of a valuable piece of furniture, not a practical machine.

Her sewing basket had been stored away in a closet, taken out only for emergency repairs. But now she took it out and spooled black thread on the machine, then laid a scrap of fabric under the needle. Pumping with her feet, she watched as the thread crawled its way up the center of the fabric in perfect even stitches. She could do anything with this machine. Make a runner to cover the scratches on the dining room table, or a new dressing gown.

The Rembrandts' grandfather clock chimed seven. Sara remembered her promise to check in on the children, and reluctantly packed up her sewing basket and placed the cover over the machine. Downstairs, the Camden flat was in chaos. Emily and the twins were screaming at one another in their room, while the baby cried fat, frustrated tears in the maid's arms. Sara had hired the maid before she'd been sent away to Blackwell's, an Irish girl named Siobhan who seemed overwhelmed by the noise and commotion.

"Let me take him." Sara lifted the boy up and put him over her shoulder, patting his back.

"I'm so sorry, ma'am. I'm not quite sure what the children are going on about, but I can't get them to stop fighting."

The girl looked worn and miserable.

"Have you had your supper yet, Siobhan?"

"No, miss, there's been no time."

"Then down you go to the servants' dining room. Get yourself something to eat. I'll handle the children until then."

"Thank you, ma'am. I won't be long." Siobhan bobbed her head and hightailed it out of the flat.

As soon as the door closed behind her, Christopher let out a loud burp followed by a sigh.

"You were unhappy then, my boy. But now you're all right." She kissed him on the head, covered with fine black swirls of hair. A beautiful boy, in such a sad position. An orphan child.

In the twins' room, Emily had hoarded all of the dolls, which were piled up on her bed. She sat in front of them, arms crossed, her mouth an angry line. The twins ran to Sara as she entered the room.

"Emily won't share!" Both faces featured upturned noses and bow lips, like beautiful dolls themselves.

"I won't because they keep on breaking them. Look." As proof, Emily thrust a porcelain doll at Sara.

Indeed, the doll's head had a crack that ran down one side of the forehead.

"I didn't mean to step on her," wailed Luther.

"You did; I saw you stomp her on purpose."

Sara fixed her gaze on each child, one at a time. "Now then, let's stop fighting, shall we? And you'll have to share the dolls, Emily. Perhaps we can divide them up so that every child has the same amount. That way you will each be responsible for the care of your doll, and if something happens, it won't affect the others."

Emily looked up at her, dubious. "Where is Siobhan?"

"She went downstairs to have something to eat. Your father asked me to look in on you. Now, I know it's difficult with your mother away, but Miss Honeycutt will be here in the next couple of days and then everything will return to normal."

"What if Mother dies?" Emily spoke with a quiet candor.

"Yes, what if Mother dies?" the twins echoed.

"I have no doubt the doctor will take very good care of her." Sara should stop speaking. She didn't know anything about the situation and was possibly giving them a false hope. But her job was to comfort them, and this was the best she could do, under the circumstances. "For now, shall we divide up the dolls, then I'll ring up for some sweets?" Today was Thursday, when the downstairs chef made pineapple pudding.

"Yes, please." Luther twirled about with excitement. "I'll take the doll with the cracked head. I don't mind."

Sara smiled. She put Christopher down in his crib and he settled in nicely, staring through the slats as they went through dolls of all shapes and sizes, and divided them up. The last one, made of rags, had seen better days, and all the children agreed that it should live in Christopher's crib and be his first doll.

When she laid the doll down beside him, he gave her a silly, drunken smile.

She rang for the pudding and the four of them had a tea party in the bedchamber, full of giggles and gentle teasing. When Siobhan's footsteps were heard trudging down the hall, Sara reluctantly gave her good-byes, promising to return soon.

By then, Christopher was fast asleep.

Even after Miss Honeycutt's return, Sara stopped in daily to visit with the children either before or after she returned from work. When Miss Honeycutt needed a break, Sara'd take them up to the roof promenade and let them run around, while she held Christopher in her arms.

Although Mrs. Camden had been gone less than a week, something about having her away, winning this temporary reprieve from the very fact of her in their lives, had made her and Theo even bolder. He slept in her bed most evenings, and she welcomed his presence, even if she couldn't sleep through the night with him there. She would lie awake, wondering how much longer they had. He didn't seem to mind that she was getting closer to his children.

For the past two nights, instead of lying awake in bed, listening to Theo's snores, Sara crawled out and slipped on her dressing gown before sitting down at the sewing machine. Its whir made her heart sing. Deep into the night, she would work on her fancy new machine with fabric she bought at Stewart's Department Store. First up were sashes for the girls and a necktie for Luther, all in different shades of blue, from cyan to a deep azure. For Christopher, she had already made a sailor outfit with a navy collar and matching tie.

In the back of her mind, she knew she was trying to make up for the baby she'd lost. Trying to prove to Theo that she was a perfect mother, much better than his wife. This morning, in the depths before dawn, she had wished the woman would die. She'd almost run her own finger under the needle and barely missed getting an awful prick, as if the machine had understood her selfish sentiment and decided to punish her.

On Friday evening, when Sara went downstairs to tuck the children into bed, Theo announced that he had a surprise for them all for the next day. The kids pressed him for information, and he held off for a couple of minutes, telling them that he couldn't possibly let on about the secret or they'd never be able to get to sleep.

Which, of course, only served to rouse them more.

"Please, tell us!" Emily was now standing on her bed, jumping up and down.

"You might as well; they will never sleep as it is now," said Sara.

"All right, then. Tomorrow we're all going to see the ship carrying the Statue of Liberty."

Sara had read about it in the papers, that the enormous sculpture, packed up in pieces on a French ship, had finally arrived in New York Harbor. Great festivities were planned for Saturday, including a parade of yachts.

The children erupted into cheers but crawled back into bed after promising to be ready to go at precisely seven o'clock the next morning.

In the brougham going downtown on Saturday, Sara sat next to Theo, with Christopher on her lap and Emily and the twins lined up on the other side, chattering away to one another. Christopher wore his pretty sailor outfit, the girls had insisted on their sashes, and Luther wore his necktie.

They looked like the perfect family. Which they were not.

Sara couldn't shake a feeling of unease. "Theo, are you sure I should be in attendance with you?"

"Who else? Miss Honeycutt's a bore."

"I mean, people will talk."

"Let me worry about them. You enjoy yourself. You deserve some fun, after how hard I've been making you work, Miss Smythe."

She'd gone back to using *Miss* after returning from Blackwell's, and it made her feel ridiculously dainty and young to hear it on his lips.

Theo climbed out of the carriage first, then turned to help out Sara and the baby. Emily came next, with Lula leaping out behind her.

Theo turned to Luther, irritated. When the child pulled back from his hand, planning on jumping down as his sister had done, Theo reached out and grabbed his arm, hard. "Act like a gentleman."

"Yes, Papa."

The boy rubbed his arm and went to stand beside his twin, grumbling softly.

Maybe Theo wasn't as unconcerned about their appearance together as he let on. She didn't like the way he took it out on the children, though.

Theo led them to a landing beside an enormous yacht. Before getting on board, a photographer asked to take their picture. Theo declined, but the children insisted Sara stand with them, holding the baby. The man scribbled down their address and promised to put it in the post after Theo had given him twenty-five cents.

The ship filled up with passengers, and Sara and the children found a spot to sit at the rear, while Theo wandered about and hobnobbed with the dignitaries and businessmen on board. As the yacht headed out into the harbor, Emily, Lula, and Luther squealed with delight and Christopher slept in Sara's arms, lulled by the rocking of the waves.

How different this journey through the harbor was from the last. When Sara had arrived a little over a year ago, she was a lowly housekeeper. Now she was an assistant to an architect and lived in a flat in one of the newest and most splendid buildings in New York City. How far she'd come.

"There it is!"

The captain cried out from behind the helm and pointed at a great ship with a white hull out near the Narrows. Sara pointed out the French flags, and their vessel joined a parade of similar ones, all lined up behind the French frigate. A band on a neighboring ship played "La Marseillaise," but the music was soon drowned out by the horns of the steamships and the deafening roar of cannon fire from Fort Wadsworth and Fort Hamilton.

The noise was too much for Christopher, who began to fuss.

Finally, Theo returned. "What a day. Are the young ones enjoying themselves?"

"They certainly are. It's too much for him, though."

A couple who lived on the Dakota's third floor wandered by. Sara smiled up at them, but the man stared and his wife made a point of turning away.

Her face reddened. "I feel we are making an embarrassment of ourselves. It could hurt your business."

"You know what I wish?" Theo placed his hand on hers. She wanted to pull it away, stop anyone from seeing their intimacy, but he held it firm. "I wish Minnie wouldn't come back at all."

Christopher began to cry. She rocked him gently. "He's overwhelmed by the noise. You shouldn't say things like that."

"Why not? We're both thinking it. I know that makes me a terrible person. But then I could marry you and you could move in with me where you belong. I hate what I'm doing to your life."

"I love my life. I love the children. I love you."

"My dear. We will figure this out, I assure you. To think that I almost lost you. What a mistake that would have been. Please have faith in me."

It was the most he'd spoken of his feelings in a while. They'd both been under such stress.

As if on cue, Christopher began to wail. The ship was close to shore and Sara offered to take him back to the apartment house so Theo and the other children could carry on to the speeches in front of City Hall. How she wished she could keep speaking with him, but the moment was too raw, too exposed.

Back in the dim light of the Dakota, the air was heavy and thick and there was no sign of Miss Honeycutt. Christopher had calmed down in the carriage, but now his fussiness resurfaced. She undressed him, lifting his outfit up over his head. He gave a deep sigh and promptly fell asleep. His skin was as pale and smooth as an eggshell, the blue veins beneath it like a map of crisscrossing rivers. He was no one's child, really, so he might as well be hers.

The front door opened and shut. The governess returning from gossiping about Theo and Sara's "arrangement" with the other staff, most likely. Sara didn't care. Theo loved her. That was what mattered.

The air changed imperceptibly. The scent of rosewater. Sara twirled around.

Mrs. Camden had returned.

CHAPTER TWENTY-NINE

New York City, October 1885

The woman who stared back at Sara was a completely different person from the sickly patient who'd been carted off a week ago. Mrs. Camden looked almost regal, wearing a handsome black-and-cream silk afternoon dress. The only giveaway of her illness were the creases under her eyes and gray shadows that emerged even under a coating of powder.

"Miss Smythe."

"Mrs. Camden." Sara took her hand off the side of the crib and stood limply, trapped.

Mrs. Camden walked over to the crib and Sara moved out of the way, allowing her by. But Mrs. Camden didn't reach down, smooth the blanket, nothing at all maternal. Just stared at the boy as if she'd never really seen him before. The sailor outfit hung over the rails at the head of the crib.

"What's this?" Mrs. Camden fingered the material.

"A sailor dress I sewed. While you were away, Miss Honeycutt asked me to help out with the children in a pinch, and I thought this might suit him."

"You made him this?"

"As well as small things for the others." She had meant the statement as a way of showing that her attentions had been equally parsed among the children, but judging from Mrs. Camden's pinched lips, it had come off as possessive. "I didn't mean to intrude."

Mrs. Camden appraised Sara from her feet to the top of her head, assessing every inch. She must know. Of course she knew. The servants talked; the other neighbors must have seen Theo coming back from her rooms in the morning. Sara was no better than her mother, who had succumbed to the advances of the Earl of Chichester with devastating results. The point of coming to America was to escape the old habits, the patterns of destruction. She'd wandered right into the thick of it.

"I overstepped. I'm sorry." Sara hoped Mrs. Camden would understand the multiple layers of meaning that swirled around the four words. She'd wrought havoc in the home of a sick woman. Like her mother, she'd lose everything. She would take the sashes, necktie, and sailor suit away, store them in her trunk, out of view. "I must go." Sara turned to leave.

"No, wait." Mrs. Camden's voice was no less than a command. But suddenly her head dipped forward. A trembling hand went to her forehead.

"You're ill; let me help." Sara put her arm around the woman, who leaned into her.

"I feel faint."

No wonder, returning home to find your husband's lover hanging about in the children's nursery.

"Please, let me make you a cup of tea."

Sara led her to the kitchen. They didn't speak for a while, as Sara boiled water, steeped the tea, and then poured it. Being back in the kitchen, instead of one of the formal rooms, made the idea of the two of them having tea together somehow palatable, weirdly cozy.

Mrs. Camden took a sip, then placed the cup carefully back on the saucer. "Where are the others?"

"They are out with Theo, I mean Mr. Camden, at the Statue of Liberty celebrations."

"Emily sent me letters every day that I was away, filled with what you were doing. Together."

"I wanted to help. Mr. Camden seemed out of his element, and Miss Honeycutt . . ." She paused.

"Miss Honeycutt is far too concerned with the attentions of the new porter, Davin, these days."

Davin was a strapping boy with dark eyes. Mrs. Camden's acuity surprised Sara. "I believe you are right."

Mrs. Camden laughed. "He's a handsome lad."

"The children missed you. They are quite lovely. As is Christopher."

"Yes. My ward." An odd way to refer to the boy. Or maybe it was the tone of her voice, like she'd bitten into a fruit and found it to be unripe. "I never formally gave you my apology for accusing you of stealing the necklace. I am sorry about that. I wasn't sure how to broach the subject. But I should have."

How long ago that time seemed now.

Mrs. Camden continued on. "I'm still recovering, and I want you to take care of the children the way you have been."

"Are you sure? I don't want to intrude." Maybe she hadn't heard her correctly. Or maybe Mrs. Camden was only saying this for effect, to appear generous.

"You should continue taking care of Theo as well."

At this, Sara's heart pounded. The woman was staring at her, not with malice or judgment. Her face was clear.

"Mr. Camden is a difficult man. I don't have the energy right now to handle him in the way he wishes."

Could she be saying what Sara thought she was? The conversation was tipping over into dangerous territory. "I am happy to work as Mr. Camden's assistant in whatever way necessary."

"No. I want you to take care of him beyond that." Mrs. Camden put a hand out on the table, as if she were going to cover Sara's, but stopped short. Instead, she drummed her fingers on the wood. "Arrangements like this happen all the time." She looked out the window before adding, "It's quite simple, really."

"I don't know what you mean."

She fixed her gaze on Sara. The twins' eyes had the same hazel coloring, the same gold flecks near the iris. "Of course you do. Don't be shocked. It's for the best. Theo responds to you in a way he doesn't to me."

The woman was feverish, maybe.

"You're not feeling well; you must lie down and rest."

Mrs. Camden sat up straight. "No, the weakness has passed. I am recovered, according to my doctor. The illness was unrelated to my prior one. I am weak, yes, but it's from the realization that this is what I wanted all along.

"It's better for you to be with Theo. He's all yours."

A month after Sara's conversation with Mrs. Camden, the arrangement had settled into a routine: Theo slept up in Sara's flat each night and had dinner there with her when he didn't have a business event to attend. Sara visited the children on Saturdays when Mrs. Camden was out making calls, and if they passed in the courtyard, they nodded at each other and continued walking.

Theo, meanwhile, was a madman at the office, juggling multiple commissions, overwhelmed. There were no more outings after the harbor cruise, neither with the children nor just the two of them. She'd suggested they bicycle in the park one Saturday, but he either didn't hear her or pretended not to.

She comforted herself with the thought that it was only until the business was on its feet. By next year, Theo would be able to slow down and enjoy himself. She couldn't help but wonder if Mrs. Camden knew exactly what she was doing when she abdicated her role to Sara.

One night, when she knew Mrs. Camden had taken the train to the country for the weekend to visit friends, Sara slipped down to read the children a good-night story. To them, Sara was a special friend, not a rival, and she appreciated that Mrs. Camden had done nothing to taint that relationship.

Theo sat in a club-back chair in the study, smoking a pipe and reading the newspaper.

"Well, aren't you the very picture of a successful, satisfied man?"

He grunted. "That damn Albany project will be the death of me. They want more revisions on the drawings. On top of it, McKim, Mead have been asked to design the Goelet Building. We won't have any success if they keep on yanking out projects from right under our nose."

"You yourself said it was a long shot. They have over ten years' start on us." She walked over to him and leaned down to give him a quick kiss.

He clasped her hand. "I do realize I brought all this on myself."

"Is there anything I can do to help?"

He kissed the inside of her wrist before guiding her onto his lap. But she tripped over the chair leg, almost falling to the floor, before he grabbed her arm and caught her.

"Ouch. Be gentle, kind sir." She rubbed her arm, which was already turning red.

"Sorry, my love." He lifted up her arm and kissed the spot. "I'm turning into a beast these days. There I was complaining about not getting enough work, and now there's too much."

"Once we hire the new draftsmen and another junior architect, you'll have less to worry about."

"You're right, as usual. Off you go, say good night to the children, and then join me in a sherry."

The children were sleepy already. Christopher gave her a bubbly smile when she leaned over his crib. Luther cuddled close when Sara sat on the side of his bed.

"You have an ouch here." The boy pointed to the inside of Sara's elbow, at what was going to be a bruise tomorrow.

"I certainly do."

"Now we match."

Luther rolled up the sleeve of his nightdress to show a purple circle on his upper arm.

The boy's arm was no bigger in circumference than a cucumber, and as fragile. "Did Miss Honeycutt do this?"

"No." Luther looked over at Emily, as if for permission to speak.

"He's fine," said his older sister. "He was playing in the library, among Papa's things. Papa doesn't like that."

"Your father grabbed you?"

A flash from the day of the boat parade crossed her mind. When they'd descended from the brougham, Luther had flinched when Theo had held out his hand to help him down. It had only been a moment, a second.

Emily rolled her eyes and gave an exasperated sigh. "Lula and Luther are always getting into trouble."

Although she was tempted to bring up the subject over sherry with Theo, she didn't. But later, upstairs in her sitting room, Sara mulled over Emily's statement. The sewing machine sat in one corner. She hadn't had the energy or time to make anything new since the children's outfits. The outing in New York Harbor seemed like years ago.

That day, the day of the boat parade, Theo had said something strange. Like the boy's flinch, she'd not examined it closely.

A mistake.

On the yacht, Theo had said, "What a mistake that would have been" if he'd lost her. An odd choice of words. Whose mistake?

She had been mistakenly sent away. Then Daisy had been found guilty of a similar crime. Daisy, with her romantic aspirations and helpful nature.

What if Daisy had been railroaded, just as Sara had, and was now sitting in prison for a crime she did not commit?

Sara sighed. She was overtired, overthinking things. Theo had lost his temper, as many men do, and taken it out on his child. It was a bruise, nothing else, and he probably regretted it the moment after.

But that night she dreamed of Daisy calling to her. Showing her the bruises on her pale arm.

And crying out for help.

CHAPTER THIRTY

New York City, September 1985

Bailey's work at Melinda's apartment was wrapping up. Luckily, most of the major design decisions had already been made, as Melinda was now distracted by plans for her blowout birthday party, to be held at the Palladium's Michael Todd Room in two days' time. Renzo had stopped by the apartment with the building architect a few days earlier for an inspection—the first time they'd seen each other since the high tea at Kenneth's—and they'd been polite at first. But his laughter had gotten louder and crazier with each room he entered. Which had made Bailey laugh. It'd been a relief to make fun of the renovation, instead of feeling guilty for having given a grand old lady the face-lift from hell.

They'd met for coffee the next day, but kept the conversation light. Renzo was politely sympathetic about her father's refusal to be tested and didn't push further, but the disappointment in his eyes made her want to burst into tears. He knew the truth about her. Her weaknesses, her struggles. Which was reason enough for Bailey to keep her distance. She'd had plenty of time to think the past few days, and she'd come to the conclusion that her dad and Renzo had been right to question her motives. This crazy goose chase to figure out her lineage was in fact a way to avoid dealing with who she really was, and the misguided effort had left her drained and lost.

She hadn't spoken to Jack since the disastrous conversation about the DNA testing, but she planned on heading down to the shore next weekend, to make peace and apologize. Better to do so in person.

"Where did you go? I need help with this."

Melinda's voice cut through Bailey's fog of thoughts. Right. The drawer pulls for the kitchen cabinets still needed to be picked out. They'd headed to Simon's Hardware on Third Avenue early so that Melinda could make it to Fred's office by eleven. Bailey pointed to a couple of options that she thought might work, but didn't push back when Melinda chose lime-green plastic ones instead.

"And I forgot to tell you, Fred wants you in the room at the meeting today."

A shard of guilt-induced panic sliced through Bailey. "Why?"

"No idea. Maybe he wants you as a witness, since you were there when we found everything. Tony will be there as well."

When *Bailey* found everything. She didn't bother to correct her.

Great. One more humiliation to suffer through. Then again, in the past couple of weeks, Melinda had been more than kind. Probably felt sorry for her dirt-poor, messed-up cousin, and she even suggested Bailey stay on for a couple of months in the guest room. But Bailey knew where that road lay: mornings of waking up to wineglasses piled up in the sink and a coating of white powder on the Lucite coffee table. Bailey's life had been artificially propped up post-rehab, as the Dakota had become her refuge from the storms that raged outside its thick walls. It was time to move on with her life and start over again.

And for the first time in years, she had a plan, instead of blowing wherever the wind took her. She'd found a fifth-floor walk-up apartment in the West Eighties that would be available next month, and sweet-talked the landlord into giving her first dibs. Once Melinda's job was completed, she'd sign up at a temp agency and answer phones or type letters, whatever it took to support herself and pay off her debt to Tristan while she cultivated clients for her new business, Bailey Camden Design.

The waiting room of Fred's office offered a floor-to-ceiling view north. Bailey stood close to the glass, taking in the expanse of the landscape, from New Jersey to the Bronx to Long Island, while Tony and Melinda gabbed on about the upcoming party, their voices too loud for the hushed environment.

The elevator opened and a man stepped out, looking completely out of place. He wore a ratty denim jacket, and the lower half of his face was covered in a bushy ginger beard.

But the eyes were the same celestial blue as Melinda's.

"Manvel!"

Bailey went and gave him a big hug. He smelled of leather and peppermint. She'd always enjoyed spending time with Melinda's twin, even though most often his sister would insist they play hide-and-seek and then run off to the roof of the Dakota, leaving him behind. But now that Bailey knew she and Manvel shared a connection with Kenneth, and that Manvel had found refuge in his downstairs apartment, she felt closer to him than to Melinda. "How are you?"

"I'm fine." He scratched at his beard. "Can't wait to get out of here and head south again, though."

Melinda gave him a cursory hug and introduced him to Tony. "Sorry to drag you back to the big, bad city, my shaggy brother, but we had some excitement and I figured you'd want a piece of the action."

Manvel shook his head. "Action's not my thing. This is all for you, sis."

Melinda purred with delight. "Well, thank you for that."

"No thanks necessary. I knew you would've showed up in Montgomery and drawn my blood yourself if I didn't do your bidding."

"You know me so well. Now here we are, together again. About to get the results that tell us if we're rich, or really rich."

The receptionist spoke, her voice a whispered rebuke. "He'll see you now."

The group awkwardly maneuvered through the door of Fred's office in order of rank: Melinda, Tony, Manvel, then Bailey.

"Uncle Jack?"

Bailey's father sat in the same chair Bailey had been in a few weeks ago. He was dressed in the suit he'd worn at her mother's funeral, including the tie that Bailey had chosen for him in tears, trying to avoid looking at her mother's clothes in her parents' walk-in closet.

Melinda looked over at Fred. "What's going on?"

Bailey gnawed at her thumbnail, a childish habit she'd thought she'd shaken. Her father was here, so he must've done what she'd asked. But why? This made no sense.

"Please, take a seat, everyone," directed Fred.

Bailey hunkered down into a love seat against the wall, feeling like an impostor, while Melinda took the chair next to Bailey's father. Tony perched on the arm of the sofa, arms crossed, and Manvel stood near the door, as if eager to escape as soon as he possibly could.

"Why is Uncle Jack here?" demanded Melinda.

Fred cleared his throat before answering. "I wanted to make sure all parties were present."

"'All parties'?"

"I hope everyone will keep in mind that while we have some answers, this matter is far from settled, as the provenance of the sheath is murky, to say the least. Others may come forward and try to claim it, as well as the knife."

"What others?" asked Melinda.

"The Tibetan government, descendants of anyone who might have owned it before it came into the Rutherfords' possession, for example."

Tony waved his hand. "That was hundreds of years ago. Never mind about that. What are the test results?"

Fred opened up a file on his desk and then peered at them over his reading glasses. "The lab in England did extensive testing on the finger bone and what they could of the blood residue. The genetic line was then traced using yDNA technology, meaning along the male line. If there was no match, the sheath would not be considered part of the Camden family estate and would become property of the Dakota cooperative."

"Right, and what did you find out?" Melinda spoke to him as if he were twelve.

Fred looked up from his notes. "The co-op has no claim to the sheath."

Melinda yelped. "Fantastic. I knew Renzo was talking bullshit. Now we can have him fired." She turned around to Bailey. "I know you like him, but he should never have meddled. He's toast."

"Not so fast." Fred held up one hand and swallowed, his Adam's apple bobbing above his silk tie. "It's not your property either, Melinda."

"What the hell does that mean? Whose is it, then?"

Fred looked straight at Bailey. "It's Jack Camden's."

Melinda swiveled around and regarded Bailey and Jack the way a python might a mouse. "They weren't part of the testing process."

"As a matter of fact, Jack was." Fred turned the paper on his desk around so she could see the results. "And Jack Camden is a match to both the blood evidence and the bone."

Bailey felt like she was sinking into quicksand, and not just because the couch seemed to be swallowing her whole.

"That was not part of the deal," Melinda screeched. She turned to Jack, eyes bulging. "How the hell did your blood get added to the test results?"

"What did you do?" Tony glared at Bailey.

Bailey squirmed forward and tried to sit upright, but the cushion on the love seat was too soft. She sank back and tried to find her voice. "I told Fred what I'd found. He said that it had to be done through the male line, so I asked my dad. But he said no."

Fred jumped in. "As a matter of fact, this was not entirely Bailey's doing. I was intrigued by the evidence she presented, and it led me to review the old files. As we've represented the family for over a hundred years, the archived documents were still in existence. I discovered a letter in the files, dated from 1900, from Minnie Camden, stating that she wished to set up an annuity for Christopher Camden when he turned twenty-one. But she died before it was established."

Christopher had been considered part of the family. He hadn't been intentionally cast out. Bailey let out a deep exhale, not realizing she'd been holding her breath.

Fred continued on. "That, along with the evidence presented by Bailey, convinced me to request a DNA sample from her father for testing."

She stared at the back of Jack's head. He'd done it after all. She wished he'd turn around and look at her so she could get a sense of what he was thinking. Was he still furious with her for foisting the truth on him?

Melinda's nostrils flared. "We did not agree to pay for that. You were not allowed to pay for this scavenger hunt with money from the trust."

"I paid for it myself." Jack's deep baritone rumbled around the room like thunder. Bailey remembered that voice, the one he used when neighbors stopped by to give their condolences after her mother had died. He'd sent them away, casseroles in hand, while Bailey hid up in her room.

Yet Fred's announcement couldn't be right. If Melinda and Bailey were related, both sides of the family would match. If Bailey wasn't related to Theodore Camden, Melinda would match and Jack would not. Those were the only outcomes Bailey had considered.

"You bitch." Melinda looked like she was about to swallow Bailey whole.

"That's enough, now." Fred jabbed a finger at the papers on his desk. "You signed a document to abide by the results. There was nothing amiss."

Melinda's oversized hoop earrings swung with each turn of her head: to Bailey, then back to Fred. "So now Bailey and her father get the sheath?"

Bailey didn't care about the sheath. She'd wanted to be part of a legacy, to feel some connection with her past.

Still, it was worth it to see the look on Tony and Melinda's faces. Take that for desecrating the family apartment.

Tony went white. "This isn't only about the sheath, though, is it?"

The earrings swung again, in Tony's direction. "What do you mean?"

"This means that Bailey and her father get the trust. Not you or Manvel."

Melinda leaped up, towering over them all in her four-inch heels. "That's not true. I'm the great-granddaughter of Theodore Camden. Manvel and I are due our trust in two days, when we turn thirty. That's the way it's always been. This doesn't change anything."

Fred spoke succinctly, clearly. "This changes everything. The trust states that it's solely for descendants of Theodore Camden *by blood.* Neither you nor Manvel are. Therefore, it's no longer your rightful property, Miss Camden."

Bailey looked over at Manvel, who had a wide grin on his face. He seemed amused by the turn of events. Or at least at his sister's indignation.

"Who am I, then?" Melinda looked blindly around the room. "If Theodore Camden isn't my great-grandfather, who the hell is?"

Fred refused to rise to her level of aggression. "Sometimes we don't know the answers. It was a long time ago."

Melinda squawked a few times before finding her voice. "We will fight this. Won't we, Tony? We'll hire a lawyer and fight this. I don't care what I signed or what the DNA says. I know who I am."

Tony's eyes shifted back between Fred and Melinda. Never one to hide his feelings well, Bailey could tell he was adding up the cost of the renovations he'd paid for as well as all the other loans he'd probably extended Melinda this past year.

"We will fight it," Melinda repeated, less emphatically this time. "After all, it was your stupid idea to get the DNA testing in the first place, Tony. You owe me that, at the very least."

Fred cleared his throat. "There is good news, however."

"What's that?" snapped Melinda.

"The Dakota apartment remains yours and Manvel's. It's outside the trust, so you both own a considerable asset."

"Great. A stinky apartment in the shitty part of town. Thanks a lot."

Melinda grabbed her purse and stomped out. Before she left the room, she leaned over Bailey, who was still wedged in the couch. "You'll be sorry for this, for meddling. After everything I've done for you? I will take you down so fast you'll end up in the streets, begging for handouts."

Tony followed her, calling for her to wait for him.

Bailey took another deep breath, letting the air clear from all the arguing and harsh words. Melinda, even with all her faults, had been a friend and the only one who'd stuck by her after rehab, and the injustice of the revelation stung. She'd have to find a way to make this right. She heaved herself to the edge of the couch and sat there, numb. "So my dad and I are the heirs?"

Fred smiled. "Yes. The way the trust works, the money goes to your father, and then, upon his death, to you."

Manvel sat beside her and patted her on the back. "Congratulations, Bailey. Nice detective work."

"I didn't mean for you and Melinda to lose everything. Your trust, your identity."

"You kidding? I'm happy to take off the mantle of being a Camden. Never meant much to me to begin with. Maybe I'll invent a new name, like Bowie did."

Jack rose, extending his hand. "We really should make up for it. Include you in some way."

"We can donate to your outsider artists," offered Bailey.

Manvel stood and shook Jack's hand, covering it with his own. "It's not about money, what they do, and I've learned a lot from that. These artists want to create art because they've got an image or idea in their head and it just has to get out. They paint it or turn it into a giant mobile of scrap metal, but it comes from in here." He tapped his head. "They don't care about furthering their careers or making a ton of cash."

A wave of tenderness swept over Bailey. "Kenneth is so proud of you, everything you've accomplished."

"You've met Kenneth? I'm stopping by to say hello before I head out. Can I tell him the news?"

"Sure. Will you be staying at the apartment while you're in town?"

"Nah, it's not my home anymore. Never really was. I prefer a life on the road."

"I like that," said Jack. "Hey, I consider myself an outsider artist, working on cars all day. It's its own kind of art."

Manvel poked him in the chest, giddy. "That's it exactly, man."

He thanked Fred for his time before hitching his backpack over one shoulder and sauntering out. After he'd left, Bailey and Jack took the seats across from Fred's desk.

Manvel was right; the news of actually being a Camden was bittersweet, considering the awful legacy of the family. She addressed Fred, avoiding her father's eyes. "How are Melinda and Manvel not part of the family? I figured if I was related, we'd all be able to share the trust. Who are they, then?" The photo of Sara and the children took on new significance with these revelations.

"As I said to her, it's one of those mysteries we may never solve."

It pained Bailey to think that they might never know the full story. What exactly had happened between Theodore Camden and Sara Smythe? Bailey imagined the woman had been sent over the edge by her love to a married man, and that after her release from Blackwell's, she'd bided her time before killing the man she considered responsible. But no doubt, there was more to the story.

"I think the Met should have the sheath," she said. Jack nodded in agreement but didn't say anything. Learning the truth seemed to have alienated the one family member she had left. What had she done?

Fred made a note on his desk. "Very well. I'll let them know."

"I'm sorry I lashed out at you, Dad." Bailey's eyes welled up with tears and she was glad Melinda was gone, so as not to see her so vulnerable. "I know I forced you into this, that you don't want to be a part of this family, what's left of it. But I swear I don't care if the trust is worth two thousand or twenty thousand dollars. That's not why I did it. I had to know the truth."

Jack spoke slowly, carefully. "After I heard from Fred, I spent a long time sitting out on the docks, thinking. I figured I'd held you and your mom back, nursing the same grudge that had driven my father mad all those years. Watching as it affected you, too, like a poisonous birthright, passed down from generation to generation. I'm sorry I closed myself off and did nothing to help you. I didn't know what to do, or what to say, to make it right." He tilted his head, one eyebrow raised. "And, of course, Scotty told me I was out of my mind to pass up a potential windfall."

She took his hand in her own. "Thanks for covering the cost of the testing. Let's just hope the trust has enough to reimburse you."

Fred laughed. "Oh, I don't think you'll find that a problem. How happy I am to spread some good news today." His features relaxed for the first time since the meeting had begun. "You are now in charge of three million dollars."

Bailey yelped. "Three million!"

Jack blinked a couple of times. "I'm not sure I'm capable of handling that much money."

"Don't worry, we're here to help," offered Fred. "You'll get all the guidance and advice necessary."

Jack turned to Bailey. "First off, I want you to consider it *our* money. Yours and mine. We'll make decisions together, promise?"

She promised. "And second?"

"Let's take care of each other better." The words came out a hoarse whisper. "Your mother would've wanted that."

Bailey buried her face in his chest and wept.

CHAPTER THIRTY-ONE

New York City, November 1885

Blackwell's Island. The one place to which Sara vowed she'd never return. But it was the only way of reclaiming her own past. Of finding out the truth. All the strange dreams and ruminations of the past few weeks had gnawed away at her, and it was time to close out that chapter in her life for once and for all. If Daisy had been wrongly accused, Sara would make things right. Only by seeing the girl's face would she know.

She almost didn't recognize the asylum, if it weren't for the familiar octagon. The land to the right of the walkway had been transformed into a garden, where dozens of women in serviceable dresses and aprons weeded and chattered away in the unexpected November warmth, clearing the flower garden for the winter to come and picking large gourds that they put onto a wheelbarrow.

Sara walked past the building, to the south end of the island, clutching the piece of paper that Nellie had sent her. Her friend had responded quickly to Sara's request, and for that, she was grateful. Sara had informed her of her trip today, so someone knew where she was. Part of her regretted not accepting Nellie's invitation to accompany her, as she had a not-so-irrational fear that she might once again disappear into the madhouse.

But Nellie was a journalist. Sara didn't want to let on too much. Not yet.

In the penitentiary, Sara waited in a dingy room with scuff marks on the walls, Nellie's referral having created an immediate response to her request. The door opened and Daisy shuffled in behind a woman guard wearing a stony expression. "You have ten minutes," the guard said before walking out.

Daisy scowled at Sara. Her hair, once shiny with curls, was a matted, dirty nest. Two of her teeth were missing and it made her seem even younger than she was, like a seven-year-old, albeit one who was chained by hands and feet. She sat down, hard, in the chair opposite Sara.

"Daisy." Sara leaned forward, near tears.

Daisy considered her for a moment. Then she sneered and spit on the ground.

Sara drew back, repulsed. She'd imagined the girl pouring out her heart, telling her that she was innocent, pleading for help. Anything but this cold grimace.

She didn't know how to begin, what to say. In spite of the curl in Daisy's lip, she recognized in her eyes a desperation to make contact. Sara had felt the same way in the asylum, the animal need to communicate with someone else, about anything. To find a measure of humanity in the rigid structure of each day.

She began again. "Daisy, what happened to your teeth?"

"Got knocked out. That's the least of my worries. Trust me."

"Are your brothers and sisters all right?"

"Dunno." She kicked the leg of the chair with her heel.

"I think you know why I'm here. I want to find out what exactly happened last year."

"Why should I tell you?"

"Because we were friends once. I want to understand. I need to understand."

Daisy's tone softened. "You sure about that?"

Sara remained quiet, letting the silence between them grow. For what seemed like ages, the only sound was the wind.

Finally, Daisy sighed, her body caving in on itself. "Mr. Douglas should have come through with what you asked for after my mum died."

"I'm sorry he didn't."

"Then I wouldn't have been so desperate."

Sara leaned forward. "You never let on that something was wrong."

"Because there was nothing you could've done about it, obviously. You'd tried and failed. Stupid Seamus. Christmas Eve, he got himself put in jail for pickpocketing and I had to get him out, to take care of the wee ones. I borrowed a large sum and then had to figure out how to pay it back. There was no choice in the matter."

"No choice about what?"

She stuck out her chin, defiant. "I told Mr. Camden you were with child, and said that if he didn't pay me, I'd tell his wife."

No. Daisy was lying. Theo couldn't have known about Sara's pregnancy all along. That couldn't be correct. Poor Daisy. All her talk of marrying a wealthy man, her infatuation with rising above her station, had turned her into an ugly, wretched person.

"Don't look at me like that." Daisy's voice was a menacing growl. "You have no idea what it's like to feed that many mouths."

She'd test her. "In that case, what did Mr. Camden do when you told him?"

"He grew silent, for a while. Said that he was in a bind. That there was nothing he could do, but something had to be done. He paced about and grew upset and then I had an idea. I offered to take care of it and then he would pay me for my trouble. Solve both our problems."

Theo had been waiting on Hardenbergh's approval at that time. Any scandal of a mistress or a baby would have ruined his chances of starting his own business.

Dread brewed in her gut. "What did you do?"

"I thought it'd be as easy as taking you to see the doctor. But you kept on putting it off. So then I took a bottle of something that the doctor gave my mother when she was in your situation. I added it to that tonic you drank."

She remembered those weeks before she was taken away. The lack of focus, not being able to remember what she was doing one day to the next. "What did you give me?"

Daisy shrugged. "Dunno. I felt bad, watching you reel about, get sick, and the first installment of Seamus's debt was due. So I nicked the necklace from Mrs. Camden. It's easy, in a big apartment house, where lots of people are always coming and going. Figured I'd sell it and be done with it all. But no one would take it." A flash of irritation crossed her face. "Seamus said I was a dolt, stealing something so fancy. So I put it in your drawer, the day that Mr. Douglas was due to stop by."

Sara closed her eyes for a moment, picturing that dismal day, how distracted she'd been by her illness, giving Daisy the perfect opportunity to frame her.

Daisy was telling the truth.

Theo had known everything.

She wished she could go back in time, to when she didn't know any of this, didn't suspect a thing. Go back to before the truth emerged.

Theo had manipulated them both for his own purposes, treating

Sara like a marionette who was allowed out of her box as long as she was of use. He'd played her for his own purposes and she'd joyfully accepted whatever nonsense he'd thrown her way, taking it for love. Fury rose in her chest like a thick, polluted fog.

The clanging of a prison door brought her back to the present. "Daisy, how could you have done this to me? I was your friend."

"I had made a promise to my mother we'd stay in the tenement. What were the little ones going to do when we were thrown out into the streets into the cold? If you'd gone to the doctor with me at the beginning, it would have been finished up right off. You should have done as I said."

"You're horrible."

A sharp laugh erupted from Daisy. "Don't pretend you were better than I was, having an affair, getting with child. We're the same."

"No, that's not true." She was about to say that she'd been in love, but Theo didn't deserve that. "Why did you keep on stealing after you'd had me sent away?"

"They said you'd gone back to England. I figured I'd held up my end of the deal, but Mr. Camden strung me along, promising a payment but never coming through, and I didn't have anything left to hold over him. I began pilfering small things here and there, enough to stave off the thugs."

For all her hard edges, Sara couldn't shake the ghost of the girl that Daisy had been. Eager to please, kind. Not this dirty, bitter urchin. Yet there was a time, near the end of her days in the asylum, when Sara had been equally heartless. To herself, to others. Behind Daisy's vicious posturing was a profound sadness and loss.

"Where is your family now?"

The girl lowered her chin to hide it from wobbling. "Don't know. Scattered. Lost."

"Daisy, you've done terrible things. But I am sorry that you ended up here. On this island. It's an awful place. I'm sorry you lost your family."

The girl recovered fast, blasting Sara with a garish smile, the gap in her teeth black between cracked, dry lips. "I hear the asylum is a fancy hotel compared to what we criminals put up with. You don't know anything. Never did. Don't you pity me. I can take care of myself."

The guard came in. "Time's up."

She grabbed Daisy by the back of the neck and shoved her out of the room in front of her. Daisy's cackling reverberated down the hallway after her.

Sara tore back to the ferry pier, breathing hard. Daisy. Theo. She was never to trust a soul again. Anyone might turn on you, at any time. She might as well check back into the asylum for all life offered her. Let the nurses tell her when to eat, when to sleep. She didn't want to have to face each day. The loss of everything she'd held dear.

Her mother's suffering should have been warning enough, but Sara had convinced herself that her own story would have a different ending.

No such luck. Men betrayed, women endured.

She had forty minutes before the ferry departed. Lifting her skirts, she moved at a fast clip to the building where she and Natalia had peered in the window. She showed them Nellie's golden pass and a nurse took down the relevant information.

"But he was born in the asylum, does that make a difference?" she asked.

"No. We have all records of every *bairn* here. Dead or alive." The woman's Scottish brogue spoke the awful words with a melodic spin.

Sara waited, checking her timepiece, for twenty minutes. She couldn't leave without visiting the grave of her child. Of saying a prayer over the mound of dirt that pressed upon his tiny bones.

Finally, the nurse reappeared, holding a clipboard. "A stillborn, you say?"

"Yes. Born in July of this year. To Sara Smythe."

"No stillborn. The boy was alive."

"Well then, he was alive but then he died." Arguing over the semantics cut her to the core.

"No. He was taken away. To the Foundling Asylum on Lexington and Sixty-Eighth."

The room spun and Sara held hard to the wooden countertop to keep herself upright. "He was alive? Why was I not told the truth?"

"They never do, as a rule. No point in driving the nutters madder than they already are. Easier this way, I guess."

During the ride across the river, Sara keened on the hard bench, wishing the ferry would speed faster. So much time had already passed. Would he still be there? Was he still alive? She didn't know what she'd do once she found him, how to prove that the child was hers. Would they just give him to her, hand him over? She moaned and the other passengers stared. The boy must have suffered so, without his mother. Her baby was alive. Her thoughts wound around each other like a dust storm.

More waiting, more sitting. The nurse in the Foundling Asylum was no kinder than the one on Blackwell's Island. They must turn brittle fast, in order to stay inured to the cries of the babies and children that echoed down the stairwell.

A form was thrust at her on a clipboard. The words swum for a moment before she focused, reading them softly out loud. The boy had been taken in by a family, just as Sara was released from Blackwell's.

She recognized the signature on the document. The same that she'd seen scrawled on countless letters and contracts.

Theo had known all along.

Christopher was her son.

"Where is he?"

Sara tore down the long gallery of Theo's apartment. Her first priority was Christopher, getting him out of Theo's hands, taking him somewhere safe. She'd had plenty of time to figure out a plan on the ferry and cab ride back to the Dakota. First off, she'd head with Christopher to the offices of the *New York World* and tell Nellie everything. Nellie would protect them and provide them with safe shelter until Sara could arrange to sail back to England. Only an ocean between herself and Theo would do to put her mind at ease.

She'd planned on appearing calm, offering to take Christopher for a walk in the park, then absconding with him, but as she grew closer to the Dakota, panic gripped her. Once inside the apartment, the memories of everything Theo had said and done to her flooded back. The evening after the ball, the picnic. The betrayal.

Mrs. Camden stepped out of the children's room, the three children scampering behind her. She saw the look on Sara's face and turned around. "Off you go, children. Play in the parlor, please."

The children trotted away quietly, no doubt tuned into the strange vibrations that Sara was giving off.

Sara barged into the nursery, Mrs. Camden close behind. Christopher was in his crib, asleep.

"Where is Theo?" Sara said.

"He's due back any minute. You seem upset. Let's sit down and have a cup of tea."

Sara wanted to throttle her. "You knew. You were raising my son and you knew it, didn't you? How did he get you to agree?"

Mrs. Camden didn't answer, but a tremble went through her body.

"Why would you do such a thing? Don't you have any shame?"

"He said I owed it to him."

"'Owed it to him'? You're as mad as he. He took my child. I want him back."

"He'll never let you do that."

A child's wail pierced the standoff.

"Luther?"

Mrs. Camden ran to the library and this time Sara followed. Luther sat at Theo's desk, staring down at his open palm.

"My God, what's happened?" cried Mrs. Camden.

Sara took the boy's hand in her own. It was unblemished, other than a small pinprick.

Mrs. Camden knelt down. "There, there."

As the child's cries died down to a dull whimper, Sara looked around to find what had caused the injury. She reached down to pick up a letter opener that had fallen from the desk, and gasped.

It was a knife, a sharp one with a curved blade. She'd seen it before.

In the Rutherfords' library.

"Where did you get this?" she asked Luther.

He pointed to an open drawer.

"Father usually keeps that locked," said Mrs. Camden. "How did you get into it?"

"I found the key in the top drawer," he mumbled. "I wanted to see if it fit. Then I saw the toy."

"My dear boy, you could have cut yourself terribly." Mrs. Camden took the knife from Sara and examined it. "This is no toy. What on earth was it doing in Theo's desk?"

Sara imagined Theo slipping it into his pocket at the ball, while he distracted her with his touch. Taking whatever shiny object he wanted. Just because he could. Angry at the men's dismissive insults about poor street children, wanting to strike back. Feeling that everyone else owed him something.

The front door opened.

Theo.

He stopped and surveyed the scene before him. "What on earth is going on?" He spoke cheerily, in a good mood.

Sara straightened. With the knowledge of the knife, she had leverage. She could threaten to turn him in if he didn't let her leave with Christopher.

"Luther almost cut himself playing with this knife from your desk." Mrs. Camden spoke with a harshness that Sara had never heard before.

"I told the boy not to play in here. Is he all right?"

"Luther, take your sisters and go to the nursery," ordered Mrs. Camden. "Shut the door."

The child scrambled away, calling out to Emily and Lula as he did.

Theo patted Luther on the head as he ran by. "He seems fine. I'm sure there's no harm done."

Sara pointed to the knife in Mrs. Camden's hand. "What was that doing in your desk?"

For the first time since he'd arrived, Theo seemed off balance. "Right. It's a keepsake, from an important night that I wanted to remember." He gave her a pointed look.

"It's the Rutherfords' knife." Sara stood tall, firm, even though inside she was terrified. His audacity astonished her. "You stole it."

Mrs. Camden looked like she was about to pull her own hair out. She turned to Sara. "What are you talking about?"

"We went to a ball. Together, the night before you arrived from England. I saw this knife there. It's part of the Rutherfords' collection."

"Don't be ridiculous." Theo dismissed her with a wave of his hand. "It's not that at all."

She ignored his lies. "That's not the least you've done, is it?"

"What do you mean?"

"I spoke with Daisy. She told me she tried to blackmail you. Got me sent away. Then you took my child." Her breath came haltingly. She couldn't speak any more than a few words at a time, and her emotions threatened to overpower her.

"You saw Daisy? In prison?" Theo took a step forward, then stopped. "I don't know what to say. The girl's a crook."

"She told me everything."

His shoulders sagged and he seemed more like a boy about to be reprimanded than a grown man. All bluster was gone. "I made a terrible mistake."

"Yes, I remember you saying that. The day on the harbor. I didn't understand at the time. How could you do such a thing?"

He avoided his wife's gaze, directing his words at Sara. "When Daisy told me that you were with child, I knew that everything might come crashing down. My business, my reputation. She said she would take care of it, and I thought that meant she'd bring you to a doctor."

"She tried," said Sara. "You were a coward, trying to protect yourself."

He pressed on. "But then there was that business with the necklace. I didn't know what to think, until Mr. Douglas informed me that you'd decided to go back to England voluntarily. At the time, I thought that was best, for all of us."

Sara shook her head. "Why would he lie to you?"

"Probably because, like me, he wanted everything tied up neatly, swept away. No hint of scandal. But after I read that terrible article in the paper, I realized that you were not in England. You'd been holed up in the madhouse all that time. The thought made me wretched. I realized what I'd set in motion, that it was my fault. Right away, I tracked down the reporter, to find you."

"You not only found me, but Christopher as well. I saw your signature, where you took him out of the Foundling Asylum." Sara turned to Mrs. Camden. "Did you know you've been raising my son?"

"I suspected." She glowered at Theo. "But I had no choice. He told me to take him in, and never speak of the circumstances."

"How could you agree to such a thing?" Sara spun back to Theo. "After trying to get rid of the child, why bother?"

Mrs. Camden's voice was bitter. "Because he was a boy. Theo wanted a son."

"You already have Luther."

A terrible silence fell over the room, the only sound the metallic ticking of the grandfather clock in the corner.

"Tell her," Theo instructed Mrs. Camden. "Go on, tell her the truth."

Mrs. Camden flushed. "The twins were born when we were apart for a period of time. They are not Theo's."

The memories tumbled over in Sara's mind. How Theo was less affectionate toward the twins than to Emily. The bruise on Luther's arm. The way Theo's own stepfather had mistreated him. And that day in the Langham hotel room, when the nanny had insisted Theo was supposed to be watching the twins. She'd been telling the truth. He'd gone out and left them alone in a room with an open window.

Theo paced the room, the words pouring out, like an actor practicing a soliloquy. "I'm not a terrible person. I made one mistake, and it threatened to bring everything tumbling down. I was panicked. You see what my work means to me; you've been by my side the entire time. Half of it's yours, Sara. You've earned it."

"Money won't solve this problem, Theo."

"It's not about the money. I'm creating something phenomenal, we're creating something phenomenal, and I want a son, a true son, to carry on my vision." He looked up, tears in his eyes. "I figure I'll teach him everything I know, so he can carry on after I'm gone. I vow to take good care of him, and you, to set things right. If I'd know that was where Douglas was sending you, I would have swum across the East River to rescue you. Don't you see? I had a moment of terrible weakness, of panic. But then I tried to rectify it, to save both you and the boy."

"Who is Luther and Lula's father, then?"

Theo glanced at Mrs. Camden, who stood unblinking, furious. "She fell for some romantic poet who professed his love and then left her with child. Twins, no less."

Mrs. Camden began to shake, her shoulders trembling. "You're a beast. An unforgiving beast." She appealed to Sara. "I tried to get away with the children as much as possible. I didn't want to stay, the situation made me physically ill, but my choices were limited."

Before she'd known the truth, Sara would have given anything to be Theo's wife, to be beside him day and night. Her toxic envy had made her blind to the truth.

Mrs. Camden was still holding the knife, her grip fierce. "I was never bright enough for him. He brought me books and newspaper articles and insisted I read them. Quizzed me on politics and Tolstoy, and I tried at first but it was never enough." When Sara stayed mute, unsure of what to say, Mrs. Camden swiveled back to Theo, her fury at full pitch. "I could never please you. You never loved me, then punished me when I sought comfort elsewhere."

"Calm down, Minnie." Theo eyed her right hand. "Look at what I've done." He gestured at the room around him. "I've taken care of you and your children. We live in this grand palace, where you can get anything you like with a ring of a bell. We were both weak at times, but I've finally succeeded. I kept both of our scandals out of the limelight. I have everything I want. Now both of you do, too. It's a relief, in a way."

"Everything I want?" Mrs. Camden erupted. "I live with a tyrant, across the sea from my country. My family is fractured, broken, and I can't even retreat to the safety of a private home. Instead, we live in this monstrosity, where your lover lives down the hall and every tenant and servant knows that I am not enough. Done in by the man who swore to love and protect me."

At first, Sara thought that Mrs. Camden was running out of the room, away from his venomous tone. But she was headed right for Theo, knife raised. He lifted up his hand as she approached, and for a second they looked as if they were about to begin some kind of macabre quadrille. Until she slashed at him hard, wildly.

Sara screamed for Mrs. Camden to stop, but at the sound of the knife cutting through flesh, she instinctively turned her head, sickened. Theo cried out, clutching one hand with the other, as blood seeped between his fingers and onto his white shirt, staining his waistcoat within seconds. Mrs. Camden pulled her arm back and lunged at him again, this time aiming for his chest.

"Mrs. Camden, stop!"

Sara ran to her and wrenched the knife out of her hand.

Theo fell sideways, onto the drafting table. The entire structure crashed to the floor below him, pens scattered across the room as he landed on his stomach with a *thud*, his face turned to the side, mouth partly open.

He blinked once. And then went still.

CHAPTER THIRTY-TWO

New York City, July 1886

Still waiting. Biding time.

But this was a different kind of waiting because there was no hope. And that was freeing, in so many ways. In the past eight months, Sara had mastered the art of doing nothing, of letting her mind wander while her body sat still. Her mind could go anywhere it liked. Down the dark hallways of the Dakota, into the children's nursery, along the walkways of Central Park. She'd close her eyes and see the world outside, the one that she would never see again, only in her mind.

Mind's eye. It was better than reality. If she tried hard enough, she could remember the scent of Christopher's baby breath, the sound of his cooing. The way he'd wiggled around inside her belly when they were one person.

A bell rang. The door to her cell clanked open. Then she was walking down the cellblock, to the jeers and yells that she usually could shut out. The cacophony of the incarcerated.

She hadn't been sent back to Blackwell's after her trial. Instead, she'd been put on a wagon, shackled hand and foot, and carted a hundred miles north of the city, to a prison in the woods.

Sometimes, Sara revisited the day Mrs. Camden killed Theo, in her mind's eye. Where she'd gone wrong. If she could have made it right. But she'd been caught off guard by Mrs. Camden's attack. Then she'd made mistakes.

After Theo had fallen, Sara and Mrs. Camden had stared at each other for what seemed like ages, before Mrs. Camden began to shake, trembling as if she was about to fly off into the air and out the window. So Sara took over. She told her to go to the children, close the door to the nursery while she figured out what to do, what to say.

There was no way to make it look as if Theo had accidentally fallen on the knife. But the night with Daisy and the intruder came to mind. Yes, that would work. An intruder had broken in. They'd found him here, dead. She left the library, closing the doors behind her, and directed Mrs. Camden and the children to go up to the roof promenade. Take the stairs, stay there. Don't come back down until I say so.

Back in the library, the stolen knife lay in the very center of the rug, where Mrs. Camden had dropped it. That wouldn't do; it would raise too many questions. She slipped it into the pocket of her dress and walked downstairs, through the courtyard, and into the park, where she buried it beneath a thicket of bushes. No one must find it.

Back inside, past the porters who gaped at her and asked if she were all right. She caught her reflection in the apartment's foyer mirror, noticing for the first time that her skirt and her cheek were stained red, as if she'd been out picking raspberries. Theo lay in a pool of blood, his mouth open, face white. A glint of metal caught her eye, lying on a litter of linen drawings splattered with blood. The knife's sheath. In her haste, she'd missed it.

And next to it, a ghastly stump of a finger, covered in blood.

She picked up the sheath and dropped it into one of the leather tubes that held drawings. Drawings that would no longer come to fruition. All of Theo's ideas, buildings. Lost.

The finger was soft, still warm. He'd drawn masterpieces with it, the sure, even lines issuing from the nub of the pen in its clasp. She had an irrational desire to put it back on his hand, to try to make him whole again. At a loss, she placed it in the tube as well, closing the lid tightly. The tube went back under his desk. She'd tell Mrs. Camden to dispose of it later.

Voices in the hallway. Men's voices.

The door to the apartment opened. She'd locked it behind her, but Fitzroy had the master key. He and two policemen stepped inside. Carefully, politely, like they didn't want to make a fuss, didn't want to muss up the silk rug and shiny floorboards. Not expecting to see blood and mess and a body. A woman in a dress with red stains on it, red stains on her hands and face.

Fitzroy spoke for her when she didn't answer any of their questions. Her name, who she was, who Theo was. That he didn't know where the rest of the family was. One policeman had rushed off to search the other rooms, fearful at what he might find.

No, she wanted to say. Everyone else is safe. It's just Theo who's dead.

And Sara who was red. Red with blood.

"Sara."

She was in the visitors' room of the prison. Not sure how she'd gotten here, not remembering the walk from her cell to here.

Mrs. Camden stood before her. She looked pale and thin. Not good. She had to stay healthy for the children. For Christopher. She'd promised.

"I'm sorry it took so long to come. I didn't want the newspapers to know. I had to wait."

"Of course."

They sat down on either side of a small wooden table. Once, Daisy had been the one in shackles and Sara had been free. Theo had brought everyone down with him that he possibly could.

But not Mrs. Camden. Nor the children. Sara had made sure they were all right.

"How is Christopher?" Her voice creaked from disuse.

Mrs. Camden smiled. "He's lovely. We celebrated his first birthday two weeks ago. Growing fast, healthy. A good boy. You have a good boy."

Sara nodded. She rarely spoke these days. Figuring out which words to say took too much effort.

"Sara, I should have confessed." Mrs. Camden looked about the room, her eyes red and wet. "I should be here, not you. I should have taken the blame. You did nothing, nothing at all."

"No. We agreed when you came to see me before the trial. It's better that Christopher is raised by you. I wouldn't have been able to give him everything you have. Such a chance at a grand life."

"I will, I promise." She trailed off.

Blinded by love. The phrase had always seemed silly to Sara, something poets invented. Yet nothing could have prepared her for the devotion she'd felt for Theo. He'd enveloped her in his intellect and his charm, making her feel she was an indispensable part of his life. And maybe she had been, for a time. He had needed her around, as a reflection of all the good qualities of himself, because his wife, by that time, reflected the worst. His irritability, his spite, and his thirst for success. Sara had refused to see the shadows in his temperament or question why his relationship with Mrs. Camden was so strained. Most likely, he'd lavished similar attention on Mrs. Camden early in their relationship, before turning on her when she failed to live up to his high standards.

But these regrets were no longer of consequence. The boy was what mattered most, and she was determined he be given every chance in the world to succeed, independent of the sordid story of his parentage.

"Did you find the drawing in my room?"

Mrs. Camden took out a handkerchief and dabbed at her eyes. "I've hung it over his crib as you asked. It's the first thing he sees when he wakes and before he goes to sleep each night."

Her dream cottage, so her child might also dream of lovely things. For all of Theo's betrayals, he'd left behind many beautiful creations. Including the drawing. And their son. "What about my letter, you have my letter?"

"It's in a safe place and I promise to give it to Christopher when he turns twenty-one. Then he'll know everything, and he can come and visit you."

Sara smiled. That was twenty years from now. She wouldn't be around. She could feel it in her bones. Something inside her was eating away at her. Guilt, maybe. Anger at having been so misused. Anger at herself. Her insides were a stewy, nasty mess and would kill her eventually.

Nothing more needed to be said on the subject. They had an agreement. Mrs. Camden spoke of Christopher and Luther and the girls, telling her what they'd said and did, the words he spoke, the way he wobbled about on his fat little legs. Sara drank in every word, every image, to fill her library of thoughts for later use.

She would feed on them until the next visit. Until her energy faded and her soul dissipated into the night air. Her last remembrance was that of holding her boy, in his sailor suit, on top of the roof promenade of the Dakota, the city gleaming below her.

CHAPTER THIRTY-THREE

New York City, September 1986

A year after Strawberry Fields was officially dedicated, the hilltop had become a hive of activity most hours of the day, the gray-and-white "Imagine" mosaic strewn with flowers and candles.

To be honest, Bailey avoided the area if she could. It wasn't a place she felt comfortable striding through, veering around the tourists wielding cameras. Doing so was like galloping through the Sistine Chapel to get to St. Peter's. Covered in a canopy of American elm tree branches and lined with hollies and mountain laurel, the site demanded an air of reverence and respect.

She found a spot on an open bench vacated by a couple of college students in torn jeans, carrying backpacks. Red roses had been arranged in a peace symbol, and three guitarists sat together on a bench opposite, strumming out tunes to a receptive crowd. She watched as a little girl danced about, jumping and swinging her arms to the beat, unaware of the tragedy behind the music.

One year sober. She'd made it. Not only had she made it, she'd risen to the challenge, supporting others at meetings, newcomers who came in weeping and scared, or those who'd relapsed and walked in amid a cloud of self-hatred. Each time she'd helped someone else, she couldn't help but reanalyze her own journey and mark her own progress, remember what it was like. And vow to stay healthy and strong.

Soon after the insanity in Fred's office, Bailey had reached out to Melinda. She'd hated the way things had ended, and could only imagine what it felt like for Melinda to have lost everything, to be cast out from her own family history. To make Melinda suffer had not been her goal.

So Bailey and Jack had offered to buy the Dakota apartment from Melinda and Manvel. Melinda had demanded a princely sum, which they'd gladly paid, hoping it would bring Melinda some peace and help Manvel's outsider artists. From what Bailey had heard, Melinda was on a rampage these days, partying hard in her white-brick condo on the East Side. Bailey had called several times, trying to make amends and explain her actions, but Melinda refused to return her calls. With time, Bailey hoped, they might be able to renew their friendship, but on more equal footing. But if not, at least Bailey had tried.

She checked her watch. It wasn't like Renzo to be late. Then again, it wasn't like Renzo to ask to meet in the most touristy spot on the Upper West Side. Usually, they wandered around the park's reservoir, comparing demanding clients and tenants. His advice was invaluable and he'd even stopped by her latest project a few times to offer a second opinion when the electrician or plumber came in with a bid that seemed high.

Together, Renzo and Bailey had restored the Dakota apartment to its original grandeur: Gone were the bamboo poles and sponge-painted walls, and in their place stood the original architectural details, down to the cast-iron washbasins and solid brass hardware. She'd held an open house for the other tenants once the work was done, spurring requests for her expertise. In a year, she'd become the go-to interior designer for the restoration of town houses, penthouses, and prewar apartments around Manhattan, a niche that separated her from the pack of postmodernists like Tristan. The fact that she'd repaid Tristan in full for her time at Silver Hill had helped ease her reentry in the design community considerably.

Theodore Camden would have been pleased, she hoped. Sara Smythe as well. Fred had dug further into the family's records and discovered that Minnie died suddenly of the flu in 1900. Which explained why Christopher never got the letter or the annuity.

Sara, meanwhile, had passed away in prison from some kind of cancer, a few years after being sentenced. Bailey was glad she and Jack finally knew some concrete details about their family's past, no matter how lurid. Knowing that Minnie Camden had attempted to take care of Christopher financially had gone a long way to ease her father's mind. Once the trust money was transferred over, Jack scooped up the lot next door and doubled the size of his auto repair shop, and bought a boat of his own. "Simple pleasures," he'd said one day, after taking her and Renzo out for a cruise.

So many unknowns, though. But, as Fred had said, some things were simply lost to history.

Renzo appeared on the far side of the plaza. He smiled at her and gave a little wave. She waved back, then her mouth dropped open. By his side was a puppy with a fluffy apricot-colored coat and big brown eyes. It mouthed the leash as it walked along beside Renzo, before a rose lying in the mosaic caught the dog's eye and it scooped it up, holding it in its jaws like a Spanish tango dancer. The dog trotted up to Bailey with the relaxed, happy expression of an animal to whom everything was either a plaything or a treat.

She reached down and gently extricated the rose.

"This is the surprise?" She patted its head and laughed as the puppy tried to gum her hand.

"Yes. I'd like to introduce you to my new best friend, Eleanor Rigby. Who will go by Rigby, as Eleanor is a little too nineteenth century for my taste."

"I wholeheartedly agree." Bailey reached down and scooped her up and placed her on her lap. "She's adorable."

"Hopefully, she'll settle down and won't chew up the baseboards."

"You have your work cut out for you. How fitting that this is where I learn that I'll be displaced as your best buddy. Very kind of you to break it to me in this peaceful environment."

"Right." He sat on the bench beside her. Rigby stopped squirming and lay down on Bailey's knees, entranced by a group applauding the musicians. "I was thinking about that."

"You were?"

"I figured that maybe you were due a promotion from best friend. After all, it's been a year since you've been sober, hasn't it?"

Renzo knew well and good that it had been a year. He'd been at the meeting last night, beaming with pride, when she'd shared her story. In fact, the last few months had been a sublime agony, the two of them not even holding hands in a concerted effort to wait the year out in its entirety.

"It certainly has. What kind of promotion were you thinking? Bestest friend, perhaps?"

She couldn't help but tease. Because she knew what was coming as well as he did. They'd been friends and confidants for longer than each had believed possible, and the time had come. Thank God, because she didn't think she'd be able to wait much longer.

He leaned in and kissed her softly on the mouth.

It felt right, perfect, and sweet.

Until another tongue broke in. Rigby attempting to join in the action.

They broke apart, laughing, wiping their mouths, as the guitarists broke into the chorus of "In My Life."

As if hypnotized by the music, the puppy settled down and Renzo sang along quietly, softly, in Bailey's ear to the very end.

Author's Note

The Address is a blend of historical fact and fiction, and I took a couple of liberties that Gilded Age enthusiasts will surely catch. The Statue of Liberty arrived in New York in the summer of 1885, not the fall, and Nellie Bly went undercover at Blackwell's Island Insane Asylum in 1887. The Rutherfords' mansion is loosely based on William and Alva Vanderbilt's, and Theo's speech is drawn from Edward Clark's 1879 speech to the West End Association.

Several books provided inspiration, including Stephen Birmingham's *Life at the Dakota*; Andrew Alpern's *The Dakota: A History of the World's Best-Known Apartment Building*; Elizabeth Hawes's *New York, New York: How the Apartment House Transformed the Life of the City (1869–1930)*; Nellie Bly's *Ten Days in a Mad-House*; and Tessa Boase's *The Housekeeper's Tale: The Women Who Really Ran the English Country House.*

Thanks to all the experts who helped flesh out my research; any errors are my own.

Acknowledgments

I'm grateful to everyone who helped bring this book to life, including my agent, Stefanie Lieberman; my editor, Stephanie Kelly; and the incredible team at Dutton, including Liza Cassity, Becky Odell, Elina Vaysbeyn, Christine Ball, Amanda Walker, Ben Sevier, and Alice Dalrymple. Thanks also to Kathleen Zrelak and Molly Steinblatt.

In terms of research, I'm indebted to Coco Arnesen, Tony Converse, Andrew Alpern, Jennifer D. Port, Jeffrey I. D. Lewis, Dr. Angelique Corthals, and Dr. Mechthild Prinz. Lisa Nicholas, Madeline Rispoli, Jess Russell, Dilys Davis, Julie Miesionczek, and Hope Tarr read early drafts and provided me with their brilliant insights. Tom O'Brien offered his architectural expertise, talked through the plot on long hikes, and encouraged me every step of the way. Angelise Sambula made me laugh; and my parents, as always, inspired me with their love and compassion.

The ADDRESS

FIONA DAVIS

Reading Group Guide

An Excerpt from The Masterpiece

BOOK
ENDS

DUTTON

Reading Group Guide

1) Sara's mother projects many of her hopes and dreams onto Sara, expressing great disappointment when Sara ends up working as a maid and following in her footsteps. Ironically, Sara and her mother wind up in similar stations in life for almost identical reasons. Why do you think they choose to avoid sharing their experiences with each other? What does their silence say about women's lives at that time? How does it speak to the relationship between mother and daughter? If this scene were set in contemporary times, would they have been more likely to relate to and open up to each other? Why or why not?

2) Part of Theo's charm is his ability to provide Sara with access to experiences that someone of her social class normally would never have access to. Was there anything inappropriate about their first encounter in her office, when Theo came to thank Sara for saving his daughter's life? Why or why not? As Theo's advances toward Sara grew bolder, how did the uneven power dynamic show itself in their relationship? Did you feel that it was fair to Sara? Why or why not?

3) Bailey, Renzo, and the other tenants of the Dakota view Melinda's renovations as disrespectful to the history of the building. How do you feel about renovating historic buildings? What value, if any, do you think there is in preserving the original architecture and design of historic buildings? What value is there in updating and modernizing facilities, amenities, and possibly even aesthetics?

4) Kenneth's stories reflect another facet of the Dakota's history: when "they began letting in the artistic types" who were known to throw wild parties that offended "the snooty old guard" of the building. He is the Dakota's unofficial historian, yet he continues to be looked down upon by the other residents because he originally worked as a butler in the building. Why do you think Kenneth stays at the Dakota? Have cultural attitudes toward certain custodial professions shifted over the past century? Do you know anyone that works at a job that others might consider beneath them? Have you spoken to them about their experience of the job? If so, how do they feel about it?

5) Fiona Davis based Sara's experience at Blackwell's Island Insane Asylum on historical accounts of conditions at inpatient mental health institutions in the 1800s. Were you surprised that patients were treated so poorly at the asylum? What practices or treatments were most affecting? In what ways has society changed (or stayed the same) in its understanding and treatment of mental illness? Do you have any personal experiences from your own life, anyone you know, or even from the media, that inform your views of mental illness?

6) Nellie Bly appears in *The Address* as a fictionalized portrayal of the real journalist who went undercover to expose the brutality and neglect at the women's lunatic asylum on Blackwell's Island, which she described in a series of articles for the *New York World* and later in her book, *Ten Days in a Mad-House*. Were you aware of Bly's work prior to reading this novel? What impression of her were you left with after reading *The Address*? What role does her character play in the development of the story? Is she a major or a minor character, and why?

7) Sara decides to keep her pregnancy secret during her time on Blackwell's Island, despite the additional health risks for her and her child. Why do you think she makes that decision? What would you have done? Is there a moral or ethical element at play?

8) Bailey has a complicated relationship with her father. In what ways are they similar or alike? Why does Jack resent the Camdens? Why do you think he is so hesitant to look more closely into their family's past?

Put yourself in his shoes. How would you feel about this situation? Does your opinion of Jack change or stay the same as the story unfolds?

9) Both Sara and Bailey are drawn to situations that have the potential to damage their reputation and future. Though both suffer to some degree as a result of their choices, Bailey is able to turn her life around, while Sara is not. What might this indicate about the differences in class fluidity, cultural morality standards, and gender norms in their respective time periods?

10) What do you think about Mrs. Camden and her relationship with Theo? Do you truly believe she was relieved that Sara and Theo had an intimate relationship, as she implied? Why or why not? Why do you think she agreed to raise Christopher as her ward? Do you think she, Theo, or both of them are to blame for their unhappy marriage? Did your opinion of her change throughout the novel? Why or why not?

11) Finally, why do you think Sara decides to take the blame for what happens to Theo? Did she have another choice? Why or why not? What would you have done?

TURN THE PAGE FOR AN EXCERPT

In her latest captivating novel, nationally bestselling author Fiona Davis takes readers into the glamorous lost art school within Grand Central Terminal, where two very different women, fifty years apart, strive to make their mark on a world set against them.

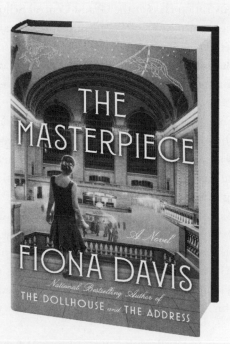

CHAPTER ONE

New York City, April 1928

C lara Darden's illustration class at the Grand Central School of Art, tucked under the copper eaves of the terminal, was unaffected by the trains that rumbled through ancient layers of Manhattan schist hundreds of feet below. But somehow, a surprise visit from Mr. Lorette, the school's director, had the disruptive power of a locomotive weighing in at thousands of tons.

Even before Mr. Lorette was a factor, Clara had been anxious about the annual faculty exhibition set to open at six o'clock that evening. Her first show in New York City, and everyone important in the art and editorial worlds would be there. She'd been working on her illustrations for months now, knowing this might be her only chance.

She asked her class to begin work on an alternate cover design for Virginia Woolf's latest book, and the four ladies dove in eagerly, while Wilbur, the only male and something of a rake to boot, sighed loudly and rolled his eyes. Gertrude, the most studious of the five members, was so offended by Wilbur's lack of respect that she threatened to toss a jar of turpentine at him. They were still arguing vociferously when Mr. Lorette waltzed in.

Never mind that these were all adults, not children. Whenever Wilbur made a ruckus, it had the unfortunate effect of lowering the entire class's maturity level by a decade. More often than not, Clara was strong enough to restore order before things went too far. But Mr. Lorette seemed possessed of a miraculous talent for sensing the rare occasions during which Clara lost control of the room, and he could usually be counted upon to choose such times to wander by and assess her skills as an educator.

"Miss Darden, do you need additional supervision again?" Mr. Lorette's bald pate shone as if it had been buffed by one of the shoeshine boys in the terminal's main concourse. The corners of his mouth curled down, even when he was pleased, while his eyebrows moved independently of each other, like two furry caterpillars trying to scurry away. Even though he was only in his early thirties, he exuded the snippety nature of a judgmental great-aunt.

He'd been appointed director three years earlier, after one of the school's illustrious founders, John Singer Sargent, passed away. The school had increased in reputation and enrollment with each new term, and Mr. Lorette had given himself full credit for its smashing success when he'd interviewed Clara. She'd been promoted from student monitor to interim teacher after Mr. Lorette's chosen instructor dropped out at the last minute, putting her on uneven footing from the beginning. It hadn't helped that the class had shriveled to five from an initial January enrollment of fifteen. Ten of those early enrollees had walked out on the first day, miffed at having a woman in charge.

Mr. Lorette's dissatisfaction, and the likelihood that she'd not be asked back next term, mounted each week, which meant tonight's faculty show would probably be her last opportunity to get her illustrations in front of the city's top magazine editors.

Since coming to New York the year before, Clara had dutifully dropped off samples of her work at the offices of *Vogue* and *McCall's* every few months, to no avail. The responses ranged from the soul-crushing— "Unoriginal/No"—to the encouraging—"Try again later." All that would change, tonight. She hoped. By seeing her work in the hallowed setting of the Grand Central Art Galleries, alongside the well-known names of other faculty members, the editors would finally appreciate what she had to offer. Even better, as the only illustrator on the faculty, she was sure to stand out.

Mr. Lorette cleared his throat.

"No, sir. We don't need any assistance. Thank you for checking in." She maneuvered around to the front of the table where she'd been working, in an attempt to block his view of her own sketches.

No luck. He circled around and stood behind it, his nose twitching. "What is this?"

"Some figures I was working on, to demonstrate the use of compass points to achieve the correct proportions."

"I thought you'd covered that already."

"You can never go back to the basics enough."

He offered a suspicious nod before winding his way through the tables, his eyes darting from drawing board to drawing board. Her students stood back, hoping for a kind word.

"Why is it each student seems to be drawing something completely different from the other?"

She nodded at the novel she'd left out on the still-life table. "The assignment was to create a cover for a book. I encouraged them to use their imaginations."

"Their examples of lighthouses and beaches are apropos. Yet you are drawing undergarments?"

Even if he had been a more sympathetic man, there was no way to explain how the hours stretched painfully long with her having so few students. How the skylights diffused the light in a way that made each day, whether sunny or overcast, feel exactly like every other. She routinely made the rounds, suggesting that a drybrush would work best to create texture or offering encouragement when Gertrude became frustrated, but at some point, the students had to be left alone to get to their work. Which is why today she'd pulled a chair up to a drawing table and sketched out the figures for her latest commission from Wanamaker Department Store: three pages of chemises for the summer catalog. The work paid a pittance, but at least it was something.

"This is for tomorrow's class," she lied. "As we do not have a live model to work from, I was planning on using a work of my own to guide them."

As she hoped, the mention of her standing request for a model redirected his attention.

His voice rose in pitch to that of a schoolgirl. "The students are free to take a life class at any time. This is an illustration class, and right now our models are reserved for the fine arts classes. As you said, they can use their imaginations, no?"

"But it is not ideal. If we can have a model to understand the anatomy underneath the fashions, to have the model begin nude and then add layers of clothing, we could build upon what we've learned already."

She never meant to be ornery, but somehow Mr. Lorette brought out a stubbornness in her every time.

"As yours is a class of mixed genders, taught by a woman, having a nude model would be most inappropriate. I'm sorry you find our school so deficient, Miss Darden." He clucked his tongue, which made her want to reach into his mouth and pull it out. "The other instructors, who have vastly more experience than you do, seem to manage just fine."

The other instructors—all men—had their every whim met by Mr. Lorette. She'd seen it in action, the director encouraging them to stop by his office for a smoke, the group laughing at some private joke, the director's feet propped up on his desk in an attempt to convey casual masculinity. Clara didn't fit the mold, which made her vulnerable.

"I'm sure we can manage, sir."

He shuffled off, closing the door behind him.

She directed the class to continue. Gertrude's work had only three rips from her overuse of the razor for corrections, a record low for her.

"Your stormy clouds are exquisite, but where would the lettering of the title and author go?" Clara asked.

Gertrude rubbed her nose with her wrist, leaving a gray streak at the tip. "Right. I got so caught up, I forgot."

Clara pointed to the top edge. "Try a damp sponge on the wet areas to lift out some color."

The girl was always eager, even if her strong hand was better suited to clay or oils than to the careful placement of watercolor, where mistakes were difficult to correct. Use too much water, and a brilliant cauliflower pattern would bloom where a smooth line ought to have been. Too dry, and the saturated color would stick to the page, resisting softening. But Clara loved watercolor in spite of, or perhaps because of, its difficult temperament. The way the paper shone after a wash of cool orange to convey a sunset, how the colors blended together in the tray to form new ones that probably didn't even have a name.

Finally, five o'clock came around. The students stored their artwork in the wooden racks, and once the room was empty, Clara hid her own sketches up on the very top of the storage cabinet, away from Mr. Lorette's prying eyes.

Starving, she headed downstairs to the main concourse, where cocoa-pink walls trimmed in Botticino marble soared into the air. Electrically lit stars and painted constellations twinkled along the turquoise vaulted ceiling, although the poor artist had inadvertently painted the sky backward, a mistake the art students loved to remark upon.

The first time she'd entered the hallowed space, stepping off the train from Arizona last September, she'd stopped and stared, her mouth open, until a man brushed past her, swearing under his breath at her inertia. The vastness of the main concourse, where sunshine beamed through the giant windows and bronze chandeliers glowed, left her gobsmacked. With its exhilarating mix of light, air, and movement, the terminal was the perfect location for a school of art.

Since then, she'd been sure to glance up quickly before joining in what seemed like an elaborate square dance of men and maids, of red-capped porters and well-dressed society ladies, all gliding by one another at various angles, yet never colliding. She liked best to lean over the banister on the West Balcony and watch the patterns of people flowing around the circular information booth, which sat in the middle of the floor, its four-faced clock tipped with a gleaming gold acorn.

Her stomach growled. She followed a group of smartly dressed men down the ramp to the suburban concourse and into the Grand Central Terminal Restaurant, where she secured a seat at the counter.

"Miss Darden?"

A young woman wearing a black velvet coat trimmed with fur hovered behind Clara, offering an inquisitive smile. "Yes, I thought that might be you. I'm Nadine Stevenson. I take painting classes at the school. You're having a bite before the show?"

"I am, Miss Stevenson."

"Oh now, call me Nadine."

Nadine's nose was large, her eyes close together and deep-set. Her right eye was slightly larger than the left, and the asymmetry was unsettling but powerful. Clara couldn't help but imagine how Picasso might approach her, all mismatched cubes and colors. Next to her stood an Adonis of a man whose symmetrical beauty offered a fascinating counterpoint. Shining blue-gray eyes under arched brows, hair the color of wheat.

"And this is Mr. Oliver Smith, a friend and poet."

Even though Clara had hoped to eat dinner in peace, she didn't have much of a choice. "Lovely to meet you both; please join me."

They took the stools next to her as the waiter stopped in front of them, pen in hand. Clara ordered the oyster stew, as did Oliver. Nadine requested peeled Muscat grapes, followed by a lobster cocktail.

Many of the young girls at the Grand Central School of Art had enrolled only so they could list it in their wedding announcements someday—a creative outlet that wouldn't threaten future in-laws. Nadine seemed to fall into that category, with her airs and pearls.

"Miss Darden is the only lady teacher at the Grand Central School of Art," said Nadine to Oliver. "She teaches illustration." She turned to Clara with a bright smile. "Now tell us about what you'll be showing tonight."

"Four illustrations that depict four seasons of high fashion." Clara couldn't help but elaborate. She'd put so much thought into the drawings. "For example, the one for winter depicts three women draped in fur coats, walking poodles sporting matching pelts."

"Well, that sounds pleasant."

Was Nadine making fun of her? Clara couldn't tell. She'd hardly had time to socialize, other than occasionally trading a few words with some of the other women artists who lived in her Greenwich Village apartment house. She'd been far too busy trying to make a living.

Nadine placed one hand on the counter and leaned in closely. The citrus scent of Emeraude perfume drifted Clara's way. "Did you know that Georgia O'Keeffe—she does those astonishing flowers—was a commercial artist at first? There's no need to be ashamed of it, not at all. Illustration is a common stepping-stone into the true arts."

"I'm not ashamed in the least." The audacity. Clara didn't enjoy being talked down to by a student. "I don't intend to do the 'true arts,' Nadine, as you put it. I enjoy illustration; it's what I do best."

"Well, I adore my life drawing and painting class. I'm learning so much from my instructor, Mr. Zakarian. He made me class monitor, and he's magnificent."

Jealousy pinged. None of Clara's students would describe her in such superlative terms, of that she was quite certain. "Class monitor, that's quite an honor. Do you plan on becoming an artist, then?"

Nadine gave out a squeak of a laugh. "Oh dear, no. I'm only taking classes for personal enrichment."

The waiter dropped off their bowls, and for a moment nothing was said. If Clara were alone, she would have surreptitiously folded a dozen or so oyster crackers into her handkerchief, to have something to snack on before bed.

The poet, who'd been silent the entire time, finally spoke. "My mother was an artist, although my father insisted she give it up after they married. She's been sick lately, but she very much misses going to museums and exhibits."

"I'm sorry to hear that," offered Clara. "Nadine mentioned that you're a poet?"

"Nadine is too kind in her description of me. Struggling poet, you might say. I suppose I take after my mother in that regard, having an innate love of the arts. My father is hoping I'll give it up eventually and go into banking."

Nadine placed a protective hand on his arm. "Oliver was accepted to Harvard and refused to go. Can you imagine? Instead, he's slumming it with us bohemians."

By all accounts, Nadine was hardly slumming it. But Clara understood firsthand what it was like to disappoint your family. "When I told my father I was moving to New York, he told me to not bother coming back. It's not an easy decision, but I'm glad I made it."

Oliver's blue eyes danced. "So there's hope for us miscreants?"

"Never."

They shared a look, a quick knowing smile, that sent Clara's pulse racing.

Usually, men didn't give her a second glance. Her father generously described her as "ethereal" for her blond hair, pale skin, and towering, skinny figure. Her mother said she looked washed out and encouraged her to wear clothes that added color to her complexion, but Clara preferred blacks and grays. Her ghostly pallor and height had always been sore points, embarrassing, and she preferred to avoid drawing attention to herself.

Oliver tucked into his stew. She did the same, embarrassed. She must have imagined the exchange.

Nadine took over the reins of the conversation. "Now, where are you from, Miss Darden?"

"Arizona." She waited for the inevitable intake of breath. The American West might as well have been Australia, for how shocked most East Coast natives were at her having come all this way.

"You've come all this way! Gosh. What does your father do? Is he a cowboy?"

"He sells metals."

Clara deliberately used the present tense instead of the past when speaking of her family's fortunes—now their misfortunes. Her father's fraudulent scheming was no longer any of Clara's concern, nor of anyone else's. Luckily, Nadine went on and on about her own father's real estate business, more for Oliver's benefit than Clara's, as Clara quickly finished her meal.

She looked up at the clock. "I must go; the doors will be opening soon."

But there was no slipping away. Nadine locked arms with Clara as they walked out of the restaurant, as if they'd been friends for years. To the left and right, ramps sloped back up to the concourse, framed by glorious marble arches, and a vaulted ceiling rose above their heads in a herringbone pattern. Clara had tried to duplicate the earth-and-sable tones of the tiles in one of her illustrations to be shown tonight.

"Wait, before we go, stand over there." Oliver pointed to a spot where two of the arches met. "Face right into the corner and listen carefully."

Clara had no time for games but watched as Nadine did as she was told. Oliver took up a spot at the opposite corner and mouthed something Clara couldn't hear. Nadine giggled.

"What's so funny?" Clara asked.

"You've got to try it. We're in the Whispering Gallery."

Begrudgingly, Clara took up Nadine's position.

"Clara, Clara."

The words drifted over her like a ghost. Oliver might as well have been standing close by, speaking right into her ear. She looked up, trying to figure out how the shape of the ceiling transmitted sound waves so effortlessly. She faced the corner again. "Recite a poem to me."

For a moment, she wasn't sure if he would. Then the disembodied voice returned.

> *That whisper takes the voice*
> *Of a Spirit, speaking to me,*
> *Close, but invisible,*
> *And throws me under a spell.*

She swore she could feel the heat of Oliver's breath. They locked eyes as they met once again in the center of the space.

"Thomas Hardy. The poem's called 'In a Whispering Gallery,'" Oliver volunteered.

Nadine crossed her arms, indignant. "You didn't recite verse to me."

"I'll regale you next time, I promise. For now, I must head to a poetry reading downtown and amass further inspiration."

Clara shook hands and they took their leave, the poem still echoing in her head.

❧

The mob of nattily dressed art lovers trying to squeeze their way through the gallery's doorway had already backed up to the elevator by the time Clara and Nadine arrived. They toddled through, taking small steps so as not to get their toes crushed, until they were safely inside.

The Grand Central Art Galleries predated the school by two years, when a businessman-turned-artist named Walter Clark had enlisted the help of John Singer Sargent to convert part of the sixth floor into a massive exhibition space, a kind of artists' cooperative where commissions were kept to a minimum. Clara stopped by at least once a week to see the latest works, and she encouraged her students to do the same. The rooms were rarely empty, as visitors to New York and everyday commuters continually drifted through.

Tonight, the room buzzed with energy. The faculty's work would stay up for a week, before being replaced with the students' work, a celebration of the school's spring term and its growing prestige. Clara's illustrations would be on the same walls that once displayed Sargent's portraits. The thought made her giddy.

Located on the south side of the terminal, the Grand Central Art Galleries were four times as long as they were wide, a warren of rooms and hallways, twenty in all, that encouraged visitors to circulate in a counterclockwise manner without ever having to double back. Clara scanned the walls of the first gallery for her work, with no luck. In the middle of the space, the sculpture teacher stood beside a table featuring two nymphs, both nude, one standing on a turtle.

"Now, that's unremarkable," said Nadine.

Clara agreed but kept her mouth shut. They continued on, to where a group of students surveyed an oil of an ungainly horse. Towering above them all was the artist, an instructor for the life drawing and painting class.

Clara had seen him a few times before. A foreigner, he was known to sing loudly during his classes and even dance about at times. This evening, he stood to the side, listening with intensity as his acolytes buttered him up, every so often tossing his head in a futile effort to flick a thatch of hair out of his eyes. Indeed, he was more horselike than the horse in his painting.

"That's my teacher. Mr. Zakarian." Nadine sidled up next to him. Clara had seen women like her before, flinging themselves into the orbits of handsome or powerful men to fend off their own insecurities. Clara had no time for such nonsense.

Back to the task at hand. The air had become stifling as more people crammed in. She ventured into room after room before circling back and still she didn't see her illustrations.

A flash of panic seized her. Her job with Wanamaker was ending soon. They'd recently announced that they'd be using only in-house artists going forward. Her salary of seventy-five dollars a month from teaching covered her expenses, but not much more. And she could not count on the next term.

She wormed her way back one more time through the mazelike space. Nothing. Down one hallway, off to the right, was a door marked SALES OFFICE. She'd passed by it in her first go-round, assuming it to be a place for clerks to write up invoices. The door stood halfway open, the lights on. She peered inside.

It was more a closet than a room, with a scratched-up desk against one wall and a wooden file cabinet wedged into a corner.

There, above the desk, equally spaced apart and centered on the wall with great care, were her illustrations.

By the time she found Mr. Lorette, Clara's limbs shook with rage. He was in an animated conversation with Mr. Zakarian while Mrs. Lorette looked on. Clara had met her in passing at one of the faculty get-togethers, awed by the puffy, out-of-date pompadour that perched on the woman's head like a long-haired cat.

She inserted herself into the group. "Mr. Lorette, my illustrations have been hung in a back office. A back office!"

While Mr. Lorette sputtered at her rudeness, she continued on. "I am a faculty member of the School of Art, and yet my work has been placed in a cave where no one would think to go."

"I am sorry, Miss Darden. We were in a tight spot, you see." He paused. "Quite literally."

As Mr. Lorette laughed at his own joke, Clara noticed the editor of *Vogue* headed for the exit. For certain, he'd never even seen her work.

Mr. Zakarian spoke up. "Where was her art hung?"

"Just off a main gallery," said Mr. Lorette. "They are illustrations. We concluded they were more suited to an intimate environment."

"Perhaps you could guarantee her a spot here in the first room next year, to make it up to her?" Mr. Zakarian held out his hand to Clara. "I don't think we've met. I'm Mr. Levon Zakarian, one of your fellow teachers."

She shook it without looking at him, her glare fixed on Mr. Lorette. "Next year it'll be too late. It's already too late."

Unlike students such as Nadine, for whom the Grand Central School of Art was just a pit stop on the way to marital bliss, Clara had sunk every ounce of energy into her career as an artist. Against her parents' wishes, she'd arrived in New York, knowing no one, and done everything she could to make it as an illustrator. What made it worse was knowing she'd been given a shot that other artists would have been envious of—to teach at the Grand Central School of Art, to show her work at the galleries—only to see it vaporize.

Mr. Lorette shrugged. "I can't seem to please anyone tonight. We will make it up to you; my deepest apologies, Miss Darden." He turned to Mr. Zakarian. "Have you seen Edmund's latest work? Come with me. I assure you it'll give you something to think about."

"I believe Miss Darden may give you something to think about, if you try to shake her off." Mr. Zakarian wore a crooked smile. "I have an idea. Let's take down one of mine, and we'll replace it with her work. Get it right out there in the center."

She didn't need one of the faculty stars to swoop down and protect her. The very thought made her sick with embarrassment.

Unwilling to give Mr. Lorette any further satisfaction at her distress, Clara stormed out without uttering a reply.

FIONA DAVIS

"The master of the unputdownable novel."

—*Redbook*

For a complete list of titles,
please visit prh.com/FionaDavis